THE COMING OF THE HAWKLINGS

The ship that foundered on Threeclaw Rock brought two strangers to live among the People: The Woman Silken and her son Brightspear, heir to the crown of their ancient enemies the Suns.

As Brightspear, heir of the Suns, grew to learn the ways of war and reclaim his title, Eyas, heir of the People, gifted with a rapport with all living things, traveled widely, befriending all the creatures of this strange world: the centaurs, fierce warriors and forgers of metal, the windwalkers on their floating islands, even the catlike lotors, the walkingtrees, the brooding forest giants.

At last came the day of reckoning, when Brightspear brought his Sunnish troops to sack and destroy the People. In a desperate quest for vengeance, Eyas forged a mighty army out of a half-dozen warring races, and battled his kinsman for the future of the Earth.

EYAS
by Crawford Kilian
Author of *Icequake* and *The Empire of Time*

EYAS

Crawford Kilian

BANTAM BOOKS
TORONTO · NEW YORK · LONDON · SYDNEY

EYAS

A Bantam Book / August 1982

ISBN 0-553-20930-2

Published simultaneously in the United States and Canada

Bantam Books are published by Bantam Books, Inc. Its trademark, consisting of the words ''Bantam Books'' and the por-
trayal of a rooster, is Registered in U.S. Patent and Trademark
Office and in other countries. Marca Registrada. Bantam
Books, Inc., 666 Fifth Avenue, New York, New York 10103.

PRINTED IN CANADA

U   0 9 8 7 6 5 4 3 2 1

To Mike and Vic and Harold

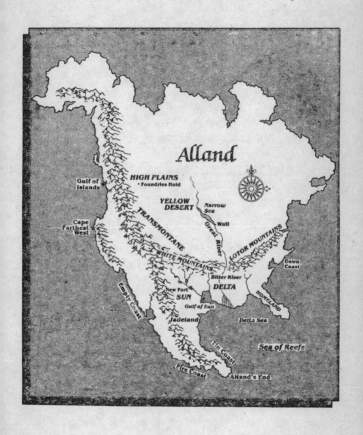

I

Longstrand

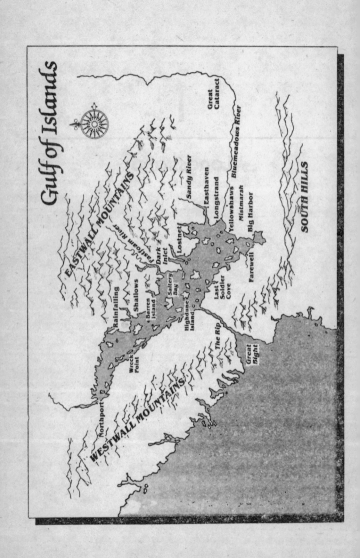

1

Out of darkness came dawn.

Darkhair Fisher lay warm in the arms of his wife Quiet. Under them was the smooth deck of *Waveskimmer*; above them, the sky was turning from black to deep blue.

He slipped from beneath the blanket and stood up. His husband Netweaver and his other wife Firewing slept nestled together near the mast; between the four adults were their three daughters, asleep in a tangle of sleek arms and legs. The only sounds were familiar ones: Netweaver's snores, the slap of water against the hull, the distant barking of a flock of dabblers.

Darkhair was a man of medium height, with the powerful shoulders and arms of one who had spent his life pulling oars and lifting nets heavy with fish. Like most men of the People, his hips and legs seemed almost spindly in proportion to his torso. He wore no clothes. His skin was a deep brown, adorned only by a white tattoo that ran down his right forearm from his elbow, branching at the wrist into five lines ending at his fingernails. His hair was straight and black, and beginning to streak with gray. He had more beard than most men, and kept it trimmed as short as the hair on his head.

No doubt the same Sunnish ancestor who had bequeathed him his hair and beard had also given him eyes almost black, unlike the blue or green of most of the People. Those eyes were keen and restless, with a sadness sometimes in their depths. Darkhair's wives liked to tease him when they saw it, calling him Bad Weather or Rocks Ahead. His husband Netweaver, a man of stolid good humor, took no notice of Darkhair's grim moods.

Standing on the stern of the narrow little boat, Darkhair looked about him at the waters of Gathering Cove and the shore of Highdune Island, which embraced the cove to the south, east, and north. The sun was up, but still behind the island, so that all of its western side—including Gathering Cove and its waiting boats—lay still in shadow. The sky was blue-brightening now, and across the calm waters of Deep Passage, just to the west, the forests of the Westwall Mountains honored the morning with a hundred colors. Darkhair could trace the steep mountain streams by the crimson blooms of water-loving bloodwoods. Tall groves of flowing club dappled the slopes with white and yellow, purple and blue. The light green of new skyseed pods was vivid against the darker green of cedar and hemlock. The pinnacles of the Westwall, still heavy with snow, gleamed against the sky.

It was the first day of spring, the first day of the Year of Freedom 242, which by the old Long Calendar was the year 2703 since the Concord. Above the southern horizon, reaching like a thin cloud from east to west, was the Bridge of Heaven. Today the sun would stand upon the Bridge, and then through all the lengthening days of spring, rise above it until Firstsummer Day. The Bridge seemed pale now, and no more substantial than a mist, but last night the Fishers had seen it blazing and glittering in the empty darkness of the sky. Free at last of the earth's winter shadow, it had been an unbroken curve of light, brighter than the moon.

Now across the Bridge a dark speck soared sunward: a hawk. Though he was not a superstitious man, Darkhair felt disturbed by such a sight on New Year's Morning. Hawks were rare and strange. Their beaks, their feathers, their egg-hatched young all set them apart from proper flying creatures like waveskimmers, firewings, and summersongs. Yet they held the air with the ease of ancient mastery, fearing nothing, caring nothing for the terror they struck in the leather-winged creatures they preyed upon.

He watched the hark for a long time, unable to make out which kind it was. When it vanished at last in the sun's glare, Darkhair turned to look at his immediate surroundings.

Within the long arc of Gathering Cove, dozens of other boats rode at anchor, their village pennants unmoving in the windless air. Darkhair smiled to see that a boat from Lostnet, the *Spray*, was aground on a sand bar. Redspark Carpenter, its skipper, would be furious and embarrassed when she woke. Well, she was young and inexperienced, and it was easy to misjudge the tides at this time of year.

He let himself down into the water and stood only waist-

4

deep in it. Yes, the tide was going out; *Waveskimmer* itself would be aground in an hour if they stayed at anchor. Soon he would rouse the rest of the family, but for now he rejoiced in the clean cold of the water on his naked skin, the living movement of the sea. He tasted it, sharp and salt: it told him of the clams and threeclaws beneath the tidal sands, of the minnows and of the kelp they darted through. Despite the nearness of the fresh streams of the Westwall, there was little taste of them. At home, at Longstrand, the sea tasted of ferns and rotting logs, of the flowers on the banks of the Bluemeadows River, and of the muddy river itself.

In a day or two, Darkhair thought, the water here in Gathering Cove would taste very different. Even now, hundreds of boats were on their way here, following the fishing fleet. Soon those boats would fill the cove, and thousands of the People would wade out to Gathering Bar to offer yeargifts to the Seagoddess. Then the water would taste of babies' urine, women's loins, and men's sweat, of the fish to be offered, and at last of the Goddess herself—

He pulled himself back on board, dripping and glad.

"Wake up!" He laughed, pulling the blankets from his sleeping family. "Happy New Year, and let's get going before we end up grounded like poor Redspark."

They woke, yawning and stretching. The adults embraced in New Year's greeting, then took up each of their children: Moonhorn, at thirteen the oldest, then ten-year-old Harper, and then Goldarms, who at four was not quite ready to give up being the baby of the family, and fretfully demanded her breakfast.

While Netweaver gave the children bread and smoked salmon wrapped in paperbark, Darkhair raised anchor; then he and the women paddled the boat out of the cove. The crews of the other boats were stirring as well, but *Waveskimmer* was first to clear the bar and reach Deep Passage. They raised sail and took the wind; the green-and-gold pennant of Longstrand lifted from the mast. Darkhair felt the tiller come alive in his hand, and the morning sun was warm on his body.

"Father, I see Skyland!" Moonhorn said, pointing toward the Westwall. Darkhair turned on his bench and saw a tiny, pale-green disc just above the peaks. In daylight it always seemed wan and insubstantial, like a spot before one's eyes; only at night did it reveal its true magnificence.

"Skyland green, Skyland bright, grant the wish I wish tonight," Harper chanted.

"It's *not* night, stupid," Moonhorn objected. "It's morning. So you can't make a wish."

"Yes, I can too, Moonhorn. Can't I, Mother?"

"Wish if you like," smiled Firewing, not really listening as she fastened the great nets to their circular frames.

"All right. I wish we get a special yeargift for the Goddess."

"That's a good wish," Netweaver said.

"I like it when She gets a gift She likes," Harper went on. "Like a big fat redfin. It makes me feel all happy. I want to jump straight out of the water, just like She does."

"What a sight you would be," Firewing said, catching Darkhair's eye and winking at him.

They rounded Sandy Point and stood out to the southwest. Other boats followed, but none could move as swiftly between wind and water as *Waveskimmer*. As the morning passed, they came closer to the steep, unpeopled western shores of the Gulf of Islands. Every little cove had its flocks of dabblers and whitebacks, but the only sign of man here was a shattered boat, cast up on a rocky beach with the rest of the driftwood.

Near noon, the sun stood at last upon the Bridge of Heaven, and cast a diffuse and glaring light while the Bridge itself glowed with evanescent rainbow colors. Then the boat skirted Blackrock Island, and the Fishers saw Ripmouth.

Only here did the Gulf of Islands connect with the outer sea. Here the Westwall parted to form a dark and narrow channel, below cliffs so steep only moss could cling to them. This was the Rip. At its western end, where it opened into the Great Bight, the Rip was more than an hourmarch wide, but as it ran northeast through the Westwall it narrowed and shallowed until, at Ripmouth itself, it was little more than thirty spans from cliff to cliff. At low tide one might walk dry-footed deep into the canyon, but at high tide the smooth-scoured bottom was ten or twelve spans below the waves. At spring tides, such as on this day, the tidal bore was like an avalanche of water, crashing and foaming in a wall higher than *Waveskimmer*'s pennant.

Only a sailor skilled or desperate would venture into the Rip; to travel its tortuous, treacherous length between tides was a feat accomplished few times in a generation. Darkhair's grandparents had done it, in their great boat *Strongsail*, but they had been killed on the return when the tide threw them against Threeclaw Rock.

They had not been the first to perish there, or the last. Many came to Ripmouth seeking the great schools of redfin and salmon, finnet and candlefish, that swept in on the tides. Before they scattered to spawn in the clean gravel beds of their home streams, the fish crowded Ripmouth in countless multitudes; a single dip of a butterfly net might then take enough to feed a family for a month. And there was the fun as well as the danger, of matching wit and windskill and muscle against the blind force of the tide. The Fishers knew that pleasure, and grinned at one another as their boat neared Ripmouth.

A long tentacle of fog reached out of the Rip and far into the Gulf. *Waveskimmer* sailed slowly alongside the northern edge of the fogbank, picking its way daintily among weedshoals and reefs. Darkhair looked over his shoulder and saw other boats taking up positions at a more respectful distance. He smiled wryly, anticipating the clucking criticism other skippers would offer him at the Gathering, chiding him for his recklessness. Just to give them something to talk about, he steered *Waveskimmer* to within a couple of spans of the cliff, knowing it was safer than it looked: the bottom was deep here. Wavelets slapped against the black, barnacle-crusted cliff; water dripped musically from springs higher up.

Darkhair put the boat about. A few tendrils of fog coiled about the sail.

"I want to be lookout," Harper announced.

"No, I'm lookout!" Moonhorn protested.

"Me, too—Mothers, Fathers, I want to be lookout," wailed Goldarms.

"Be still, and take turns!" snapped Firewing as she checked the nets. "You're all behaving terribly. Quiet can't farhear if you make so much racket."

The girls subsided, glaring at each other, while Quiet came aft. She sat on the deck, leaning against Darkhair's legs. He stroked her long brown hair for a moment; then she closed herself in.

Though Darkhair had seen her do it many times, it still made him slightly uncomfortable. Few of the People had the gift of farhearing; it usually ran in families. Quiet had been born one of the Windinvokers, an Easthaven family famous for such powers, and Harper, her blood-daughter, seemed to have the beginnings of farhearing and windinvoking as well.

Without a change of expression, Quiet drew a stillness around herself. The sail banged and the rigging creaked, but

7

the sounds seemed muted. Water still dripped from the cliff, but it fell noiselessly.

Suddenly the sunlight changed on her smooth brown skin, as if the muscles under it had relaxed. Sounds grew sharp again; everyone looked at her.

"The tide is coming around Little Bend." Her voice was flat and tired. Darkhair calculated: about a quarter of an hour, then, until the tidal bore reached Ripmouth. Almost automatically he began to think out the best course available to him, and when Quiet went on speaking her words took a moment to sink in.

"There are boats on the tide."

"—What?"

"Two boats. Large ones, I think. There are women and children in the first one." Her voice began to show feeling, a feeling that chilled Darkhair. He looked sharply at Netweaver and Firewing, whose faces reflected his own alarm. Even the girls had caught Quiet's fear.

"They're screaming, Darkhair. The children, even the women and men. The boat is out of control."

"What about the other one?" he asked, wondering: Who— outcoasters? Voyagers from north or south?

"I heard them dimly. Their boat is farther back on the tide, and I heard no screams. But a voice—a man's voice, cold and strong." She gripped his hand; her eyes pierced into his. "If they get through the Rip, they'll strike Threeclaw Rock in the fog."

Darkhair looked astern at the other fishing boats. Even if he ran up a distress streamer, the others were too far to help in the little time remaining. And if they saw *Waveskimmer* sail into the fog, the other skippers would think the Fishers had gone mad.

He shook his head grimly and called everyone to the stern.

"You all heard what Quiet said. We must go into the fog and try to rescue the people in the boats. Girls, stack the butterfly nets out of the way."

"What about the yeargifts?" Moonhorn asked.

"We'll worry about yeargifts later," Firewing said. She turned to watch the fog pouring out between the cliffs. "We'll need a stiff breeze to carry us across the tide to Threeclaw Rock," she added.

"Not at first," Quiet answered. "The tide itself will do that. As the boats hit the rock we will have to swing in close, and pick up as many survivors as we can. We'll need the wind then, to clear the fog and then to carry us away before we strike the rock ourselves."

"Can't we reach them before they strike, Mother, and warn them away?"

"No, Moonhorn; we are too far from Ripmouth."

"Invoke a wind, then, and blow away *all* the fog, so the boats can see to steer," said Goldarms with a four-year-old's common sense.

Quiet smiled at her daughters. "Not even your grandmothers could invoke such a wind. Only the Goddess has such power, and She rarely uses it for the help of men."

"Here comes the tide," said Darkhair. "Netweaver—girls— keep a lookout in the bow. We'll be sailing nearly blind until Quiet windinvokes."

The tide came in, unseen within the fog until it was well into the Gulf and beginning to spread out after its long and violent confinement. It was a line of boiling white that thickened and rose, at an angle to the edge of the fog, until it was higher than a man, higher than a longhouse. It spouted and plumed as it struck rocks and islets, and its thunder echoed from the steep cliffs of the Westwall.

Darkhair turned the boat stern-on to the tide, and his body quickened with joy and fear as the tide took hold, lifted them, and swept them swiftly eastward. He leaned all his weight on the tiller, steering *Waveskimmer* at an angle across the tide.

The sea was as chaotically alive as the upper rapids of the River Fastfoam; here and there a fish broke the surface, leaping silver in the sun. A small redfin, no longer than a man's arm, fell suddenly into the boat just at Darkhair's feet. It thrashed violently for a moment before he could hook his foot under one of its handlike pectoral fins, and flip it over the side.

"Seek us on next year's tide, little brother." Darkhair laughed. "We fish for men today."

Now, with tiller and sail, he edged the boat southward, into the central stream of the tide. They slipped quickly into the fog; at once, the green and gold, blue and white world of the Gulf was abolished, and a world of roaring grayness took its place. Darkhair could not even see his husband and daughters in the bow; he watched Quiet, who had shut herself in again. Soon even his own dulled ears could distinguish the crash of the tide against the high cliffs of Threeclaw Rock. The rock was very near.

"Hard a-left! Hard a-left, or we'll hit 'em!" screamed Netweaver.

Darkhair saw a high, dark shape looming out of the fog, and heaved on the tiller with all his strength. As the boat grudgingly responded the dark shape grew nearer. "Goddess, look under us," he whispered.

It was no boat; it was a great three-masted craft, bigger than any the People had ever built. Windwalkers sometimes told dubious tales of craft this big—ships, they called them— but who believed all that a windwalker said?

The ship, if that it was, was painted black and gold; when it yawed, its fouled bottom told of a long voyage. Its decks were high above that of *Waveskimmer*; along the tall sides of the ship, blunt tubes jutted out. The sails and rigging were in disarray; Darkhair saw no sign of a tiller, nor could he imagine one that might reach from the high stern deck to the water. When that stern swept by, only three spans from the Fishers' rightboard, Darkhair gaped up at the windows of the stern cabins: he had never seen glass before, except in windwalkers' tools and weapons. Below the windows, in letters strange but readable, was painted the name of the ship: *Deliverer*.

"We've missed the other boat," Quiet called out above the roar of the tide. "No—that terrible voice again—well astern of us. They've steered to the south; they'll miss the cliffs."

Deliverer, however, could not. At the mercy of the current, it moved faster than *Waveskimmer* and vanished again into the fog as Darkhair managed to slow his craft a little.

Quiet invoked the wind. Her hands were clasped, her face upturned to the blank gray of the fog. Her invocation was a high, keening wail that seemed at times to soar beyond the range of human hearing. Darkhair felt his skin prickle and tighten as the power of the invocation gathered around the boat. And then the wind was there, filling the sail, just as the ship crashed headlong into the cliffs of Threeclaw Rock.

"Netweaver, ready the ropes." The fog was thinning, brightening. Sunlight broke through, blazing down on the dying ship. It was already sinking by its shattered bow, but the tide was swinging it around faster than Darkhair had expected. Within a few breaths, its leftboard side would be crushed against the cliffs, and then the tide would pull it under.

Quiet's wind swept the ship, lifting from the mainmast a long black pennant emblazoned with a twelve-pointed sunburst. It had been two and a half centuries since such a pennant had waved over the Gulf of Islands, but Darkhair knew it well from remembrance.

"Mock me for a fool," he muttered. "Of course they're Sunnish."

Now he could see frightened faces, pale and black-bearded, along the ship's side. The foremast had snapped and fallen like a tree across the deck, preventing the lowering of boats. Two women in loose gray robes leaped screaming into the water, too far away to be reached, and disappeared.

Still the tide and wind carried *Waveskimmer* in. The Fishers were under the great stern windows again; the glass was gone from them now. A woman stared wildly down at them, her face pale with shock, and cried out wordlessly.

"Jump! Jump!" Netweaver roared, waving a coiled rope in one big hand.

She was holding a bundle, and seemed ready to leap, but someone pulled her away. Two men leaned out, grim in battered black helmets and cuirasses. If they jump in that armor, thought Darkhair, they'll sink like plummets.

A third man, young, cleanshaven, and hard-faced, appeared in the window. He was armored like the others, but instead of a helmet he wore a yellow hood over his head and shoulders. In his arms he held a boy, a black-haired child of five or six. The boy had the man's proud features and seemed unfrightened.

"This is my son," cried the hooded man. "He is Brightspear, Heir of the Dominance! I beg of you, guard him well!"

Pulling off his hood, he thrust it into the boy's hands; then, after a last, fierce kiss, he threw the boy into the sea. Quiet leaped to the side of the boat, grasping a line with one hand, and clutched at the boy as he hit the water.

"Jump or be drowned!" Darkhair screamed up at the pale faces. The hard-faced man shook his head.

"Better to go down now, than be hunted and slain like vermin. Let Brightspear avenge us."

The woman who had first appeared in the window now leaned out, still clutching her bundle. She held it in an

11

agonized embrace, then wailed and let it fall. It struck the water a span or more from the boat, and the Fishers heard a faint cry. Firewing sprang over the side; the tide nearly swept her under the sinking ship, but she caught the rope Harper hurled to her, and Netweaver drew her safely back.

Another woman, tall and young, climbed onto the ledge of the adjoining window. The man who had worn the yellow hood saw her, and reached out his hand. She took it, and a look passed between them. Then, without a sound, she leaped; her thin red gown fluttered around her.

For an instant she disappeared under the foam. Then she surfaced, swimming strongly, and gripped the gunwale while the tide tried to tear her away. She held on and pulled herself aboard. Before she sprawled face-down on the deck, shuddering, Darkhair glimpsed her beauty and caught his breath. When he looked up at the ship again, there was no one at the windows.

Deliverer listed sharply to left and swung around toward the cliffs. A few people leaped from the main desk, but could not reach the Fishers' ropes and were swept under. Darkhair pulled on the tiller; *Waveskimmer* drew away as the Sunnish ship smashed its full length against the rock, heeled over, and went down.

The Fishers came within a dozen spans of the cliffs before wind and tide carried them away. For what seemed a long time, the boat rode alone in the gray murk; then they were north of the fog, in open water. The Gulf looked just as it had, calm and bright in the noontide.

Darkhair let the current sweep them eastward, through the deep channel between Blackrock Island and the north shore of Ripmouth. Ten or twelve distant sails made bright white triangles against the glittering waters.

"Is the boy all right?" Darkhair asked.

"Yes," said Quiet. She sat against the mast, holding the boy in her arms. He shivered in his soaked gray tunic and trousers, and still clutched his father's yellow hood, but his face was impassive as he looked over Darkhair's shoulder at the receding fogbank.

"We have *two* boys," Firewing said. She walked to the stern, holding an infant in her arms. His swaddlings had been replaced by a warm blanket, and he seemed unhurt. Firewing smiled as she held the infant for Darkhair to see.

12

"Isn't he beautiful? And he's newborn, with his blackbutton still on him."

"He was born two days ago," said the boy. His accent was strange, but understandable. "My mother's maidservant Peacebringer bore him."

"What is his name?" asked Firewing, rocking the baby gently against her breasts.

"I do not know."

"And you are Brightspear?"

"Yes. My father was Steeledge, the Sun." He showed no sign of grief.

Darkhair glowered at him. The boy looked levelly back. "Well, you can't help being who you are, can you? But what are we going to do with you?"

"What about the other ship, Darkhair?" said Netweaver. "They must have gone south, on the other side of the fog. We could find them and hand the children and woman over to them."

"You must not do that," Brightspear said solemnly. "Admiral Thorn is our enemy. He serves my uncle Silvershield, the usurper. He followed us all the way from the Tin Coast."

"Admiral Thorn commands the other ship, eh? Well, I don't care who slaughters whom among the Suns," Darkhair snapped.

"But you can't give the boy to the others if they mean to harm him," Firewing said. "And the baby's no concern of theirs at all."

"I wouldn't give my worst enemy into the power of the man with the terrible voice," said Quiet. "There was evil in that voice, of a kind I've never dreamed before."

"What about—?" Netweaver nodded toward the woman, who was sitting up and looking about her.

"I don't know."

Darkhair studied her. She was very lovely, with such thick yellow hair that she might be taken for a woman of the People if not for her pale skin. The wet red gown, clinging to her body, gave her an allure lacking in the plain nakedness of Quiet and Firewing. When her eyes met his, Darkhair felt himself being assessed by a high and arrogant intelligence that understood his maleness as he himself understood wind and water.

"What's your name?" he barked, trying to conceal his alarm in surliness.

"I am the Woman Silken."

"Ah. And I am the *man* Darkhair."

She ignored his sarcasm. "I am the concubine of the Sun Steeledge. You will address me as Your Womanhood."

Her clipped, unfamiliar accent gave him some needed distance from her. "You're not in the Dominance now." He was tempted to add that her precious Sun was now feeding the threeclaws, but held his tongue. She was in shock, after all, and for all her strangeness she was a young woman alone.

"I'm sorry if we seem rude," he said more gently. "Come and sit beside me. Girls! One of you find another blanket."

Unsteadily, Silken rose and obeyed him. She was shivering from more than cold, but when Moonhorn brought a blanket she ignored it.

"Take off your wet dress; once you're warm and dry, you'll feel better," Darkhair said. She glared at him.

"No man but the Sun may see me naked."

Firewing and Quiet sputtered with laughter. Still carrying the baby, Firewing came aft, grinning.

"Don't be silly, girl. These two see tits and slits all day—there's nothing special about yours."

"That's enough!" Netweaver blurted. "Save your filthy talk for the women's festivals." Like most men of the People, he and Darkhair disliked women's bawdry, especially when it seemed intended to assert their superiority. It was all very well to possess the powers of sex, love, and motherhood; to flaunt those powers was coarse and insulting.

Silken undressed and wrapped herself, shuddering, in the rough blanket. As if for the first time, she saw Brightspear, and held out her arms to the little boy. He left Quiet and walked slowly to Silken, still holding the yellow hood; he allowed himself to be embraced. Though his clothes were wet, he seemed tranquil and relaxed; his eyes swept around the boat and the gleaming waters of the Gulf.

"Where is Admiral Thorn?" he asked.

"Far away, lovely one. Don't worry," Silken said softly.

"Is the other craft as big as yours was?" Quiet asked.

"A little smaller, but better armed. It's a warship of twenty cannon. It nearly sank us at Cape Farthest West, when his fleet overtook ours. We escaped, but our two other ships were lost."

"What do you mean, 'cannon'? How long is a 'cannon'?" asked Netweaver.

14

Silken stared at him. "Cannon are—iron tubes that throw lead or iron balls."

"Ah," grunted Darkhair. "You had some too, sticking out of the sides of your ship? We've heard rumors of something like them from the centaurs. Nasty things."

"Yes," she smiled without amusement. "Nasty indeed, when they're turned against their rightful owner."

Darkhair tugged on the tiller, changing their course a bit to the north of east. *Waveskimmer* approached three other boats whose crews were busily dipping their nets. The tide was little more than a strong swell now, sparkling as fish broke the surface and vanished again. Waves rumbled distantly on the shores of Blackrock Island.

"Where are we going?" Silken asked.

"To the Gathering," Darkhair answered. "The Seagoddess will soon be there; we'll ask Her what to do with you."

She said nothing. But she began to follow Brightspear's gaze, searching for the other ship, and Darkhair realized that the ship would be hunting just such survivors as these. He cursed silently: the tide had brought trouble to the Gulf.

"Hello, *Waveskimmer*!" It was Peter Summerbloom, the fat old skipper of *Reedwhistle* out of Wreck Point. "Filled your nets already?"

"You might say that," Darkhair called back. "See you tonight." He grinned sourly at the Wreck Pointers, who squinted across the water trying to make out who the extra people were aboard the Fishers' boat.

The afternoon grew warm despite the light breeze that carried them back toward Highdune Island. Brightspear's gray tunic soon dried; he sat crosslegged against the mast and ignored the girls' attempts to make friends. Silken put on her gown again and sat near the boy with her feet tucked under her. She said little, and looked constantly astern. They accepted a little bread and salmon, and a basket of winterberries. With his cheeks stained purple by the berries, Brightspear looked more like a child and less like a small, animated idol.

The nameless baby grew hungry and fretful. Firewing gave him a little honey in water and let him suck at her breast. Goldarms, who had weaned herself not very long before, watched in a kind of jealous amusement. The older girls found the baby more interesting than Brightspear, and fussed happily

15

over him; their fathers exchanged a look of mild relief at the respite from sisterly bickering.

When the baby went to sleep, Moonhorn turned to Silken and asked: "What's a concabine?"

"Concubine," Silken corrected her brusquely.

"Well, what is it?"

Silken said nothing. Her mouth trembled for a moment. "I was—I shared the Sun's bed when he desired me."

"So you're his wife?"

"No—what a thought," Silken exclaimed. "His wife was the Woman Emerald; she died in the battle at Cape Farthest West."

"Why aren't you his other wife, then, if he only had one?"

"Not even the Sun has more than one wife, child."

Moonhorn realized she was in romantic but dangerous territory. "So you coupled with him even though you weren't married?"

"Moonhorn," Quiet called. "Leave the poor woman alone."

The girl came aft to whisper excitedly to her mother: "Isn't it *awful*? Coupling with somebody you can't marry?"

"The Suns are different from us, as you should know perfectly well," Quiet reproved her. "No need to squawk like a dabbler about it. Now go and help your sister put the nets away."

As they neared Deep Passage the Fishers saw many sails gleaming on the Gulf: the Gathering of the People was under way. Netweaver came aft to spell his husband at the tiller.

"This is a strange business," Netweaver muttered. "I look at those three and I can't believe what happened today."

Darkhair grunted. "It was like a dream, wasn't it? To go into the fog and see that great ship breaking up—and then come out again, as if nothing had happened."

Netweaver rubbed a hand along his leg—a sign of worry. "Everything's changed. Everything. I used to think the future was as sure as the past, a song waiting to be sung. Now—" He shrugged. "Perhaps the Goddess will know what we must do."

Perhaps? thought Darkhair. Netweaver must be alarmed indeed.

The sun was low above the Westwall when the Fishers reached Gathering Cove. The long, narrow beach was already thick with tents, and the smoke of cooking fires rose hazily

16

against the sandy cliffs of Highdune. Boats were moored so thickly on the water that in places one might step easily from one to the next. Their pennants glowed in the golden afternoon: the colors of Lostnet and Wreck Point, of Longstrand and Big Harbor, of Last Soldier Cove and Easthaven, of Dark Inlet, Farewell, 'Shallows, Northport, Rainfalling, and a dozen other villages. Thousands of the People mingled on the beach and the boats; children shrieked gaily in the shallow water. In earlier years the sight of the Gathering had always filled Darkhair with joy, but today he felt only a dull worry.

Longstrand's boats were moored in their usual spot, just inside Sandy Point. Darkhair steered in alongside *Whiteback*, his mothers' boat, and Netweaver dropped anchor while the wives lowered the sail.

Darkhair's fathers were dead, lost in a squall off the Mistmarsh three years before, but his mothers still fished the Gulf better than most families. He waved to his mother Hemlock, who smiled and waved back as she fried daggerfish over a little stove on the deck of her boat. His blood-mother, Griptiller, stepped lightly as a girl to her son's deck. She was lean and dark, with short-cropped hair gone very white, and as Speaker of Longstrand she wore the clamshell pendant. Her eyes, black as her son's, sparkled with pleasure.

"You're back very early," she said, but as she reached out to embrace him she saw the baby in Firewing's arms, and then the woman and the boy.

"And who are these?"

"Our yeargifts."

"Don't mock with your mother, Darkhair."

He never did. Darkhair was quite as much in awe of his mother as the rest of Longstrand was, and still a little frightened of her as well. She had never been an affectionate woman, even to her husbands, but her approval was worth seeking. She was very wise; centaurs and windwalkers had taken counsel with her.

Briefly, he told her who the strangers were, and how they had come to be on his boat. Griptiller and Silken exchanged disapproving glares, and Darkhair for a moment saw his mother as Silken must: a skinny, wrinkled old woman with withered breasts and a sagging belly, wearing only a clamshell on a thong and the scars of a long life. And Silken, in Griptiller's eyes, was a sullen young she-prowl affecting a gaudy gown and an insolent air that ill became a foreigner who owed her life to the family. That much he understood, but he sensed that more passed between the two women than a man would notice.

"A fine yeargift indeed," the old woman grunted. "The Seagoddess won't like this."

"Nobody will. If we'd known what ships they were, we'd have left them to the rocks."

"Not you."

"Well—in any case, they're here. The Goddess can decide what to do next."

Griptiller squatted on the deck, looking out across the crowded cove. "Some of us want the Goddess to tell us when to blow our noses. And some of us think we know the Goddess's mind better than She does. I'll bring this up when the Speakers meet tonight. Some will vote to kill the Suns at once, and others to throw them on Her mercy. As if we didn't have enough to quarrel about already."

"It can't be concealed from the Goddess," her son remarked. "She'll know."

"Tell that to those idiots from Big Harbor and Dark Inlet." Griptiller grinned. "At least it'll be a more interesting fight than the usual squabbles over fishing rights and coppersmiths' prices."

"Especially if the other Sunnish ship arrives while we're all here."

His mother looked grim. The sun sank below the Westwall, and the Bridge of Heaven burned brighter in the darkening sky.

"We'll worry about the ship when we need to. The Suns were no sailors in the old days, and a great hulk won't fare well against us in our own waters. Now bring your family and your guests over for supper."

The Fishers did not sleep well that night. The baby cried. Griptiller returned late from her meeting ashore with the other Speakers, and made a lot of noise before she finally settled down on *Whiteback*'s deck. Darkhair lay under a blanket beside Firewing, listening to the baby's wails and to the murmur of the People on their boats. He wished he knew where Admiral Thorn was.

2

The next morning seemed as endless as the night had. At breakfast Griptiller said little about the Speakers' meeting, except that they had agreed to let the Suns be judged by the Goddess. Silken seemed contemptuous of the news, and of everything else. She ignored the dozens of the People who found excuses to sail round the Longstranders' moorage, gawking for a glimpse of the three Sunnish prisoners. The tide ebbed and turned; the sun moved up through the Bridge of Heaven.

At last the tide was rising. The People slipped off their boats or walked off the beach into the placid waters, wading out onto the shallows of Gathering Bar. Children sat on their fathers' shoulders, or paddled about excitedly. The adults stood waist-deep in the water, impatiently tasting it for a hint of the Goddess's arrival. Each family pulled a floating reed mat, shaped like a boat and bearing yeargifts of fish, threeclaws, and clams.

The Fishers usually parceled out their catch to the other Longstrand families, but this year they had only the woman, the boy, and the baby. Some grumbled about that, but the novelty of human yeargifts was compensation for most.

As the girls jumped into the water and began swimming toward Gathering Bar, Silken looked at Darkhair. "Are we to do this also?"

"Yes."

"I refuse."

"You've caused us enough trouble," Darkhair said coldly. He picked her up, feeling surprise at the soft smoothness of her skin, and dropped her over the side. "Stay with our family," he ordered her as she gasped and spluttered. He turned to Brightspear. "Can you swim?"

"A little."

"Then you'll ride on my back." Without complaint, the boy put his arms around Darkhair's neck, and the two of them went into the water. Quiet followed, then Firewing with the baby. The water, even this soon after high tide, was only half a span deep, and the bottom was firm and level. The Fishers waded slowly out to the Bar to join the thousands of others.

At the edge of the Bar, where the bottom dropped steeply away, the Speakers stood in a silent line. The air smelled of fish; the only noises were the squallings of babies and the excited giggles of older children. The sun glared down out of a cloudless sky; a breeze rippled the surface of the water.

The Goddess's arrival was imminent. A few farhearers whispered that Her breathing was in their ears. Some people claimed they could taste Her in the water; Darkhair could not, and doubted that anyone else could. But at length all the People could feel Her presence in the water, and then Her thoughts were in their minds:

I greet you, my children. It was not in language, but it was as understandable as an embrace.

"We greet You, Mother," the People murmured. Darkhair saw from Silken's face that she could not sense the presence of the Goddess or hear Her thoughts, and he felt pity for her. Nor did Brightspear, heavy on his back, seem aware of anything but the People's voices. The baby lay still in Firewing's arms. "We bring you yeargifts, for remembrance."

I accept them gladly.

Families at the back of the crowd began hastily passing their little reed boats ahead, up to the line of the Speakers. The Speakers emptied each boat in an order set by ancient precedence, saying, "The families of Lostnet give thanks." "The families of Big Harbor give thanks." "The families of Northport give thanks..." Soon the water was covered with hundreds of dead fish and threeclaws; their bodies attracted live fish that leaped and struck in growing numbers.

The Goddess rose from the sea, less than ten spans from the Speakers. For a breath or two She seemed to hang in midair, a pillar of gray and white; the sea foamed down Her smooth flanks. Her small eyes glinted; Her great mouth gaped. She was fifteen spans long, from Her great blunt head to Her broad tail; each of Her flukes was bigger than *Waveskimmer*'s sail.

When She sank again in a crash of spray, Darkhair felt the old joy return. Whatever might happen, the Goddess would always be there, as sure as the tides themselves.

She began to feed, and little could be seen of Her except

Her vast back. But the People sensed Her pleasure in their gifts, and they relaxed to chatter together.

I thank you all. Your gifts are in remembrance, and I give you remembrance in return.

To the People standing in the cold water, the Gulf of Islands became thin, vaporous, unseen. With the Goddess's gift of remembrance, they saw the outcoast as it had once been, thousands of years before. Mountains were mantled in glaciers that flowed down into deep valleys and out across the surface of the sea itself. The glaciers melted, retreating up the Westwall peaks. The People saw tides flow at last through the Rip, saw a great white plain become the Gulf, blue and cold with the gifts of a thousand torrents. Seedlings struggled to survive on the bare mountain slopes, and grew into forests. Winged creatures nested in the new beds of reeds around the islands' shores, feeding on finnet and salmon; little splithoofs slipped silently through ferns and salal thickets.

The People glimpsed some of the firstcomers, tall men and women in furs, taking fish with bone-tipped spears; others followed, with spears and axes of stone. They remembered war and fire and starvation; they remembered fierce battles in hunters' camps when the windwalkers glided from their flying islands with glass-pointed darts in their long-fingered hands. They saw again the Concord made between the woman Greenreed and the windwalker Manyscars, and the planting of the first skyseed forests on the heights above the River Fastfoam. They saw again the arrival of the first centaurs, new wars, and the Second Concord. They saw the Goddess Herself, and the bond She made with the People of the Gulf.

And they remembered too the arrival of the first Suns, a ragged army that came to the Gulf through the unpeopled South Hills. They were tall men who rode the lesser centaurs called sixfeet; they wore shirts of chain mail and curved swords in beautiful scabbards. Their eyes were black, unreadable, and their dark hair streamed behind them as they rode into the Bluemeadows. Their leader was a silent man called Fletcher of the Whisperers, and of the five hundred warriors he had started with, far to the south, only a hundred had survived.

A hundred men; most of the People's villages could put more men into battle than that. But the Suns brought disease and iron-barbed lances as well. The lances took Yellowshaws and the other Valley settlements; bleeding fever took all the Gulf. The Suns had come in high summer, and when the Goddess returned in spring She found only twenty of the People awaiting Her in Gathering Cove. When She approached them, Sunnish warriors in ambush tried to slay Her with lances. She sank their boat and drowned them all, and went away.

The villages of the People were deserted or destroyed; the bones of the People were blackened with the ashes of their longhouses. Those who survived were enslaved. They toiled to build the Suns' castles and towers; they cast their nets to load the Suns' tables; with Sunnish lances at their backs, they put torches to the skyseed forests and watched them burn. More of the conquerors came, arrogant warriors and implacable priests with the brand of the Sun burned into their pale foreheads. The windwalkers came no more; when the centaurs came to trade, they were driven away by arrows and swords.

Those were the dark years, when the children of the People were born into slavery. The family posts were overthrown, and rotted on the beaches. Bitter smoke rose from the new Temples of the Sun, and the chants of the priests carried far across the water. The old language was lost and forgotten, and the People spoke only the harsh, barking tongue of their masters. No man was allowed a husband, no woman a wife; a thousand simple acts were now sins against the Sun, expiable only by death.

Those deaths the People now remembered, and they cried out in sorrow and wrath. To them, as to their ancestors, it seemed as if smoke and blood would rule the Gulf and the People forever.

Then they remembered how the Goddess had returned to the Gulf and risen in Her beauty beside the little canoe of Quickhand Fisher as he paddled across Deep Passage. They heard in their minds what he had heard in his: that the rule of the Suns was coming to an end, and that he must go among all the People to prepare them to rise against their masters.

Quickhand obeyed; he gathered five followers, then fifty, then five hundred. But when he came to Easthaven the Suns captured him, tortured him, and carried him home to Longstrand. From the top of the tower they had built on the cliffs behind the village, they hung Quickhand by his feet in chains of iron. For three days and nights he lived, and on the fourth day he died.

On that same day, news reached the Gulf that the Sun in faraway New Fort had died, and that his sons were at war for the Iron Throne. The garrisons of the Gulf villages fell upon one another as their soldiers took sides.

Then the People rose: first in Longstrand and Yellowshaws, then on all the shores and islands. The garrisons fell to fire and the bitter edges of centaurs' iron, hidden for long years. The Temples burned, and their priests with them. Perhaps a few survivors escaped over the South Hills, but after that summer of cruelty and slaughter no Sun ever ventured back to the Gulf of Islands.

Now the People remembered the Years of Freedom. They were years of peace, of turning seasons and strong children growing into proud and fearless men and women, of old people dying gently and going into the sea and the songs. The People remembered themselves, and were glad.

Remembrance ended, and again the People stood on Gathering Bar. The Speakers rose their arms in thanks and appeal, calling in unison:

"Now we ask Your guidance, Mother, Your kindness and Your wisdom."

The surface curled and formed as the Goddess rose to breathe.

Ask.

Each Speaker in turn sought guidance in resolving a quarrel or judging a claim. Dark Inlet asked for fishing rights north of Point Deception; Saltery Bay wanted to exile a murderer to Barren Island. Wreck Point sought the Goddess's blessing for a new boat, and Three Springs Her approval for an increase in their prices for copper tools. Usually the People stood in patience through the judgments, but this time they muttered and complained to one another, glancing often at the Longstranders.

Griptiller spoke last.

You had no yeargifts, my daughter.

"My yeargift is also my asking, Mother." Her voice carried far across the cove. "On the first tide of the year, our boat saved three people out of a great Sunnish ship that sank at Ripmouth. They are here with us: a woman, a boy, and a baby. We offer them to You, and give their fates into Your keeping."

Bring them closer.

Darkhair gripped Silken's arm and led her through the water to the very edge of the Bar. The boy on his back said nothing, but his arms tightened around Darkhair's neck. Firewing waded behind them, the baby squalling in her arms.

For what seemed a long time, they stood unmoving. When the baby stopped crying, the silence was deep. The Goddess floated nearby, so close that the smell of Her was strong on the air. Her breath was an occasional puff of whiteness above Her gray back. Darkhair felt Her power through the water, and trembled. She rolled, and one bright eye regarded the little group.

Yes, they are Suns. But I bid you to spare them. Their deaths would serve no purpose.

"The boy is the Heir of the Sun," Griptiller said quietly.

I know.

"He is sought by another Sunnish ship here in the Gulf," the old woman went on. "They want to kill him."

I know. The searchers shall not find him, nor anything but their own deaths at your hands.

"As You bid us," said Griptiller, looking relieved.

The newborn one hungers. Bring him to me, Firewing.

Firewing looked at Darkhair, astounded. Someone passed over one of the little reed boats, and she put the baby in it. Then, guiding it with one hand, she swam out toward the gray bulk of the waiting Goddess. An anxious murmur rose from the People.

With heavy grace, the Goddess turned onto Her back. Firewing reached an outstretched flipper, climbed upon it, and took the baby in her arms again. Then she stepped carefully onto the belly of the Goddess, white and smooth and broader than the deck of any boat.

She walked a little way toward the Goddess's tail, then stopped and knelt. To Darkhair she seemed very small and fragile, for all the strength he knew she had. He loved and feared for her more than he ever had before, and gripped Brightspear's arms so tightly that the boy grunted in protest.

Only those close behind the Speakers could see, but all could feel the sudden warmth of the Goddess's love, and mixed with it a deep and unexplainable sadness. The baby lay upon Her, gently held by Firewing's hands, for a hundred breaths. He cried at first, but only for a moment. When Firewing rose again with the baby, he slept against her breast.

The Goddess moved closer to the Bar, so that Firewing could step from Her flipper into shallow water. Griptiller stood aside for her; the old woman's face was unreadable.

I name him Eyas, the Goddess said without words, and the People whispered the name uncertainly.

The nestling of the hawk, Darkhair thought, remembering the flight of the hawk he had seen in the new year's dawn. Never had any of the People named a child for such a creature of danger and swift cruelty, and he wondered if he had misunderstood. As if in answer to his thoughts, the Goddess sent them all another image, more vivid even than those of the remembrance: a young hawk, wings outstretched, hovering against the blinding glare of the noon sun.

He is Eyas. I give him understanding of the brutes, and my love. Guard him well, Fishers of Longstrand.

She rose again, Her majesty greater than that of a winter storm, and vanished beneath the sea. The waves of Her going passed across Gathering Bar, and the water was still once more.

Slowly the People waded back to their boats or their camps on the beach, chattering and laughing as if this had been just another Gathering. But the Fishers said nothing until they were back on *Waveskimmer*. They squatted on the deck, looking at the baby sleeping in Firewing's embrace. Griptiller and Hemlock were with them.

"She nursed him," Firewing said softly. "She told me where to put him down, by a—a little bump. And it was a nipple, hardly any bigger than my own." She looked into their faces, to let the wonder in her eyes speak to each of them. Even Silken and Brightspear seemed to feel something of it. "I never thought She would have breasts—though we call Her Mother. And Her breast gave milk—thick and white, and strange-smelling. He got a taste, and began to suck.

"As hard as I did?" asked Goldarms loudly.

"Yes, love, as hard as that," she smiled. Darkhair and Netweaver winced a little at such women's talk, but knew that this was too important a matter for mere politeness. "And when he was full, I felt something from the Goddess. Maybe you felt it too—it was like what I felt when Goldarms first

25

took my breast. A sweetness, and sadness. As if She loved him and gave Herself to him, but knew he'd grow into someone who wouldn't need Her."

"This is close to impiety," Griptiller muttered.

"No," Quiet said. "It is what every mother feels. You felt it for Darkhair, and I for Moonhorn and Harper."

"Fathers feel it too," Netweaver said boldly. Such a remark would ordinarily have been laughed at, but the women only nodded.

"Well," said Hemlock with a nervous smile, "who says there are no wonders left in the world? Suckled by the Goddess! There'll be clapstick songs about it before nightfall."

Her wife gave her a sour look. "We won't wait to hear them. I've got to call another Speakers' meeting at once; then we sail for home."

"Why a meeting?" Darkhair asked, and got a sour stare for himself.

"To plan for the other ship, of course. We don't want them poking around, and the Goddess has guided us on that matter. It'll be a nasty business. Especially for you men."

Darkhair looked at Quiet and knew she was remembering the farheard voice of Admiral Thorn. With the Goddess gone, and the People on their own for another year, he felt fearful. Something was loose in the Gulf of Islands, something untouchable by men's guile or centaurs' iron. He reached out and took comfort in Quiet's smooth, soft skin. They smiled at each other, than at their children.

Silken, sitting cross-legged by the mast, caught his eye: she too was smiling, but whether in gladness or contempt he could not tell.

3

The Old Stories went back before the Goddess had first taken notice of the People. In them it was told how Two Bows, living in an empty canyon of the eastern mountains, saw the Gulf of Islands in a dream. Waking, he called his family to follow him, and set off across the snow in the middle of the night, following Redspark's path down the western sky.

He met with many adventures. The centaurs barred his way, and took his left eye as payment. Old Snow Woman imprisoned him in a glacier until he deceived her into giving him flints whose fire melted her into a puddle. He wrestled a giant for three days and three nights, and escaped when the giant tired and fell asleep. A walkingtree challenged him to a mockery duel; Two Bows won with an insult so great it could not be repeated, and the walkingtree in revenge lashed him with its stinging vines until he was striped like a splithoof.

Two Bows' family followed him, sometimes close enough to hear him breathing, sometimes far behind. At last they came to the Great Cataract of the Bluemeadows River, and in a cedar tree found one of his arrows. They cut down the tree and hollowed it out with fire; then, in the first boat, they went on down the river, over the Cataract, until they came to the Bluemeadows Valley and the Gulf beyond it. Near the mouth of the river, the land rose up in cliffs on the right and sank down in the Mistmarsh on the left. Under the cliffs, broad white beaches sloped to the sea. Here they found Two Bows, grown old and blind, building the first longhouse.

"What is this place?" his wife Anger asked.

"Longstrand," Two Bows replied.

"Are there woodsrunners to hunt here?"

"No."

"Are there browsers?"

"No."

"Then what shall we eat?"

"The fish in the sea," Two Bows said.

"Then go and get them, foolish old man!" Anger cried and threw him into the water. He was turned into a rock, and the river, in sorrow, buried him in sand and so made the spit that ever after sheltered the boats of Longstrand.

The four sons and four daughters of Two Bows and Anger were outraged at their mother's crime, and beat her with their stone clubs until she turned to stone herself; then they set her in the sandy beach as the first family post. They paddled out into the Gulf, naming its shores and straits, and returned to finish their father's longhouse.

If the Old Story was true—and few but children believe in Old Stories now—Two Bows' longhouse must now lie deep beneath the soil. Longstrand stood on a steep, narrow hill between beach and cliffs: a hill made of shell middens, potsherds, and the rotted logs of ancient halls. Each time a new house was dedicated and a family post set up, those who dug the postpit always found fishhooks of barbed bone, stone arrowheads, and incense burners of fire-hardened gray clay.

Over a hundred longhouses stood above the harbor, straggling in four uneven rows with muddy streets between them. Near the center of the village was the Speaker's Hall, one of the greatest in the Gulf. Its porch was three spans high and ten wide, splendid carvings covered its bloodwood columns, and the high doors were inlaid with spiral designs of copper and jade. Within were long benches arrayed in a square about the fire pit and the Speaker's Stool, and the murals on the walls were still bright though a century old.

Steps of granite ran down from the Hall to Traders' Beach; here, at most times of the year, merchants from all the islands pitched their tents. They haggled over bolts of spidersilk, jars of cider, copper adzes, and iron nails; they argued politics and passed on the latest rumors; they staged wrestling matches, heard the latest clapstick songs, and bet heavily on mockery duels. Longstranders, who loved bargaining, politics, and games, spent half their time on the sand of Traders' Beach.

Behind the village, the hill dropped into dense thickets of salal and blackberry, giving way to the sheer rock cliff mottled with yellow-gray lichens and clumps of ferns. Paths ran through the bushes, made by generations of berry-picking children and by shy nocturnal splithoofs.

One half-eroded trail, steep enough in places to be a stairway, rose fifty spans to the old Sunnish tower. It was a roofless ruin, its thick walls crumbled by the frosts of six hundred winters, its outerworks overwhelmed by the slow assaults of moss and fern and wild grape. The wooden floors within the tower had long since been burned and rotted out; salal grew thickly over the Suns' long-buried dungeons. Firewings nested in the cracks of the walls; the only people who came here were adventurous and disobedient children.

On the plateau beyond the tower, alder and maple struggled under the spreading shadows of cedar and fir and hemlock in a forest that stretched north to the shores of Easthaven Inlet, west to Beacon Point, and eastward along the northern slopes of the Bluemeadows Valley. Here and there, in the gloom of the forest, bloodwoods stood crimson along a stream bed. On south-facing slopes, skyseed groves lifted their swelling, pale-green pods high above the ground.

Over the land that Two Bows had found, a long silence hung in the misty air.

Waveskimmer anchored in Longstrand harbor at noon of the day after the Gathering. Darkhair saw *Whiteback* already moored, and felt rueful admiration for his mother's sailing skill. The old woman must be a windinvoker herself, he thought. Others her age would be content with their family-standing; Griptiller must have deed-standing as well.

A breeze from shore brought the familiar smoky stink of Longstrand, and Darkhair saw Silken's face turn pale, like drying sand. Truculently, he said:

"Over the side with you, now—it's not deep." When she hesitated, he shoved her; she stepped awkwardly into the water and looked up at him, her face a mask of distaste.

The girls tumbled merrily into the water beside her, and Brightspear chuckled as he jumped into Silken's arms. The adults followed, Firewing holding Eyas in his blanket above the water, and they waded ashore.

Only a few Longstranders had stayed home from the Gathering, but every one of them seemed to be on the beach, gawking at the strange woman and boy. Evidently Griptiller and Hemlock had told them what had happened at Ripmouth and Gathering Cove. Several people clustered around Firewing to examine Eyas; they looked disappointed to find him a perfectly ordinary baby, a bit paler than most but just as fretful. The rest of the onlookers stood at a wary distance from Silken and Brightspear, staring at the woman's ragged, dirty dress and the boy's yellow hood, which hung on him like a cloak.

"I'd've thought Sunnish children were bigger," someone observed. "This one looks pretty spindly."

"The boy's sturdy enough," said a woman. "But the woman must have been starved, or she's a freak. Look at her—big tits and a waist like a little girl's."

"That'll do," Darkhair growled. "There are men present. And they understand you."

The woman looked astounded. Silken muttered; "Get us away from them, Darkhair."

"All right, everybody, let us through. The baby's tired and we all want a meal."

They walked up the beach, past the family boatshed, and up the steps of their longhouse. Like all the others, it was a narrow rectangular box, walled with cedar planks and roofed with shakes. Small windows, hung with spidersilk, interrupted the walls; the door was a span wide, hung on hinges of centaur iron. Beside the door was the family post, as austere as the door was ornate: a single trunk of bloodwood, with the radius, ulna, and phalanges of Quickhand himself set into the wood. Atop the family post was a roundstone, a fist-sized black sphere of some material no metal could scratch. Such stones were sometimes found floating in the Gulf, or even embedded in trees, and some claimed to have seen them fall from the sky. Pretty but useless, roundstones were common as decorations; the Speaker's Hall had a dozen or more set into the walls.

Around the doorway grew an old grape arbor, half-dead but still sending out a few new leaves. Something large, black, and furry leaped from the arbor onto Moonhorn's chest and began scuttling up onto her head. Silken saw what it was—a spider, with a body as big as a man's head, and long shaggy legs—and drew back with a gasp, her hand involuntarily reaching out to grip Darkhair's arm.

"Chirp, get down!" Moonhorn said crossly. The spider clicked and chittered and leaped from Moonhorn's shoulder to Firewing's.

"Hello, Chirp," Firewing smiled. With her free hand, she stroked the spider's body behind the gleaming eyes. "Did you miss us? Were you a good girl? Yes, of course you were." Chirp reached out a foreleg and curiously tapped Eyas's face. The baby stopped squalling and tried to focus his eyes on the spider. "It's a baby, Chirp. His name is Eyas. Isn't he nice? Remember when Goldarms was this little?"

"Does it—does it understand you?" Silken asked. The Fishers looked at her and laughed.

"She's just a spider, you know," Moonhorn said patronizingly. "Don't you have them where you come from?"

"Yes, but not this big. Our spiders are vermin, something to get rid of."

The children looked scandalized. "Well, Chirp's a nuisance sometimes, but we love her," Moonhorn said as she pushed open the door. "She catches mice, and she makes really nice silk. Grandmothers! We're home!"

The house was a single large room, with broad benches along the walls and a stone fireplace in the wall opposite the door. The narrow windows let in little light, and the fire was too small to dispel the gloom. The house smelled of smoke and the fish stew Hemlock was cooking in an iron kettle over the fire.

Griptiller sat cross-legged in her accustomed place, a blanket-covered bench on the far wall beside the fire. "About time," she said. "Somebody—you, Harper—get that spider out of here; she knows she's not allowed inside at mealtimes. Boy—Brightspear—sit there, on the men's side of the fire. Girl, you're on our side."

"I am the Woman Silken, and my place is beside the Sun."

"Your place is where I say it is. Sit here, or stand hungry."

Grimly, Silken obeyed. Darkhair suppressed a smile: the old woman was as peremptory with a Sunnish concubine as she was with everyone else. Brightspear, obviously pleased to be classed with the men, grinned impudently at Silken until she narrowed her eyes at him.

The girls settled at once into routine, bringing out shallow stoneware bowls which Hemlock filled with stew, and then taking them to the adults. Everyone waited in silence until the children were also served and seated.

"Thanks to the Goddess," Griptiller said.

"Thanks to the Goddess," the Fishers murmured, and began to scoop out their stew with their fingers. Silken looked revolted, but at length began to eat, as daintily as possible.

"We'll have to find a place for the girl and boy to live," Griptiller remarked. "Perhaps down the beach toward Beacon Point, or up the river near Yellowshaws. Some place quiet and out of the way."

"We will require a house at least the size of this one," Silken said, "with ten guards and as many servants."

Hemlock guffawed. Her wife snorted. "You'll have a very small house indeed, girl. And no servants at all."

"Your Goddess said—"

"To spare you, not to pamper you. If you don't like what we offer, take the Eastway up the river and see what hospitality the centaurs will offer you."

Silken set her jaw.

"She could marry," Hemlock said slyly. "The Merchants could do with another wife; so could the Gardeners."

"I'd sooner die!"

"So would they," Firewing spat. "Hemlock, you silly old woman, be still. Griptiller's right," she said to the whole family. "These two have to be put away somewhere, out of sight. The village will decide where, when everyone is back from the Gathering. Meanwhile," she told Silken, "keep your mouth shut and do what you're told. Or, by the Goddess, we'll hand you back to your Sunnish friends and bid you farewell."

". . . I beg your pardon," Silken mumbled. "I shall try not to offend anyone again."

"Good," nodded Griptiller. "Now let me tell you what the Speakers decided to do about the other Sunnish ship: nothing."

"What?" said Darkhair.

"They couldn't make up their minds. Some thought we ought to hunt them down; others said we should hide if they turn up, and wait for 'em to go away. Figured that if the Goddess said the Suns would find death at our hands, it could be by leaving poisoned food in our houses." She hawked and spat into the fire. "They must have been smoking resin."

"What do *you* think we should do, Mother?" asked Darkhair.

"Warfare is a man's skill, not a woman's."

Darkhair bit back a growl. "A man's skill, perhaps, but there's been no war in the Gulf since Quickhand. A couple of feuds, but nothing serious. We have remembrance from the Goddess to guide us, but we'd be facing real soldiers, fighters who drove the Sun himself to flee." He gestured at the ancient weapons racked along the wall of the men's side of the house. "We've got bows, slings, axes, and a few old spears. The Suns have those cannon things, and a smaller kind called guns that a single man can carry—so Silken tells us. They may have still other weapons."

"Are you afraid of them?" his mother sneered.

"I am." He gathered all his boldness. "We've seen them in their power; you've seen only these three."

"Very well, then! When these gods arrive, we'll bow before them and give them back everything."

"That's not what I'm saying! But now I see why war is a man's skill—you women turn it all into a mockery duel."

"Now, now—you are too harsh to an old woman. No doubt you're right, dear son. I'll leave the matter to you and Netweaver and the other men. Perhaps by the time we meet in the Hall tonight, you'll have a plan to suggest. I leave it in your hands."

"Very well." Mollified, he still felt the sly old browser had maneuvered him into a position he didn't want to take.

* * *

All that long afternoon, boats returned from the Gathering. Traders' Beach was thick with gossiping women and excited children, and few noticed how the men tended to drift off past Anger's Rock to the Fishers' boatshed. It was more interesting to loiter near Speaker's Hall, waiting for another glimpse of the Sunnish captives, who waited inside the Hall for the meeting that night.

Near sundown, as Darkhair impatiently prowled up and down the beach, he looked south across the estuary to the low green line marking the edge of the Mistmarsh. Something glinted out on the water: a paddle, flashing orange in the lowering sunlight. A few breaths later, he could make out a canoe, of the sort used in the tangled channels of the marsh. It was a dangerous craft for a trip across the mouth of the river, where wind, current, and drifting logs were unpredictable hazards.

Netweaver emerged from the boatshed with three other men, said farewell to them, and walked down to the water's edge to join his husband.

"Someone's coming from the Mistmarsh in a great hurry," Darkhair said. "It must be news."

"Ah—" Netweaver's unexpressive face tightened.

The canoe reached Two Bows' Spit as the last of the sunset guttered out of the sky and torches began to flare on the porch of the Hall. Darkhair and Netweaver were on the spit to meet the newcomers; everyone else in the village was crowding into the Hall.

"It's young Snowfall Wright," Netweaver exclaimed. "And his brother Sedge."

The peddlers ran their canoe onto the sand and stepped out, falling to their knees with exhaustion.

"What brings you boys all the way from Big Harbor?" Netweaver asked. They were panting too hard to be understood at first, but soon caught their breath.

"Oh, cousins," Snowfall said, "the Sunnish are back in the Gulf!"

"We know, but how do you?" Darkhair replied. "You weren't at the Gathering."

"No—but last night a great boat came into Big Harbor. There weren't many of us there. They came ashore—said they were looking for somebody called Steeledge. We didn't know what they were talking about—"

"And then they took our mother Summersong, and they cut

33

off her fingers!" Sedge interrupted shrilly. "We hid beneath the house, and they kept asking her, 'Where's the Man in the yellow hood?' and then they'd cut off another finger, and another, and now she's d-dead. Dead."

Darkhair gripped the sobbing boy's shoulders, and with an effort kept his voice calm and level. "How did you get away?"

"They w-went to the Tanners'; we slipped out and ran for the trees, and th-then got on the trail to the Mistmarsh."

"Did the Suns stay in Big Harbor?"

"For a while," said Snowfall. "Just before we got over Spring Ridge, we looked back and saw them setting sail."

Darkhair thought for a moment. Big Harbor was the southernmost village in the Gulf. If the Sunnish ship had come down the southwest shores of the Gulf, it must already have touched at Last Soldier Cove and Farewell—and it would now work its way north and east along the edge of the Mistmarsh to Longstrand. The few tiny settlements in between might hold their attention for an hour or two, but the Suns were almost sure to reach Longstrand sometime tomorrow. Too little time.

"Come with us, boys," he said. "The whole village is in Speaker's Hall. All will hear your news."

The sun was far below the horizon now, and the moon had not yet risen. The soft light of the Bridge of Heaven, and the westering twinkle of Evenspark, were almost lost in the Darkness of the sky. Darkhair took both boys by the hand and led them toward the distant torches of the Hall. He felt very frightened.

Not many of the People lived in the Mistmarsh, and those few were solitary and secretive. It was a waste of tall reeds; ponds and sloughs laced it, fed by the Bluemeadows River to the north and the Gulf to the west. Fish and flying creatures— insects, dabblers, even hawks and spoonbills—thrived in the marsh, but men often fell sick there, shaking with fevers when they drank its brackish water.

Like most Longstranders, Darkhair knew the edges of the Mistmarsh very well, but its interior hardly at all. The channels and muddy islets were rich with game, and he had often hunted in the marsh's shoreward channels. The day after the meeting, he was paddling a small canoe south through Mud Bay, taking whiteback with slingstones. By noon he had three fat ones in the bottom of his craft; but he felt no pleasure in killing what he did not expect to eat.

An overcast had moved in from the west at dawn, and the waters were an oily gray. A damp breeze, smelling of rain, chilled Darkhair's naked skin. It was quiet: he heard the rustle of wind in the reeds, the slap of wavelets against muddy shores. The distant bark of a dabbler was answered by the squeak of a wild spider in its nest. Pursing his lips, Darkhair mimicked the spider's call as he turned the canoe down a narrow channel leading to the open waters of the Gulf. Far to the south, another dabbler barked, three times. That was the signal: the Sunnish ship had been sighted.

The channel was little more than a span wide, and on its banks the reeds grew thick and high—too high to permit Darkhair to see the ship. He halted the canoe with a twist of his paddle, and listened.

Calls of dabbler and whiteback, waveskimmer and greentail came to his ears, answering one another across the narrow channel. Then came the sound of a man's voice, singing out a leadsman's phrases:

". . . four stands and a third . . . four stands . . . four stands and a half . . ."

The Suns were picking their way close inshore, as Netweaver had predicted they would; the westward stretch of Saltspring Point, on the north side of Mud Bay, would conceal them until they were less than half an hour away from Longstrand across the estuary. But their progress was slow across this unknown shallows.

Darkhair murmured, "Goddess, look under me now, and bear me up." Then he paddled smoothly out of the channel.

The ship was closer than he had expected, and his startled gape was unfeigned. The ship's long bowsprit seemed almost over his head, and its big square sails loomed high against the gray sky. Along the bow, in white letters on the black hull, he read its name: *Liberator*. It was smaller than the first ship, yet seemed far more dangerous: it was, after all, intact. No banner identified it.

Lying on the bowsprit, a round-faced man in blue shirt and trousers held a weighted rope: the leadsman. He stared down in surprise at Darkhair, then called, "Hi! You, there. You talk Sunnish?"

Slowly, Darkhair nodded. The leadsman looked over his

shoulder. "Your Manhood, sir! There's a Naked here."

A row of flat, bearded faces appeared almost instantly along *Liberator*'s side. One man, wearing a dull silver helmet, stood near the bowsprit. He smiled down at Darkhair.

"Greetings, O friend! Will you come up and let us give you fine gifts?"

Stupid as a browser, Darkhair thought. He smiled back and nodded again. "And I will give you these, O friend!" he called, holding up one of the whitebacks.

Someone threw down a line to secure the canoe. Darkhair slung the whitebacks around his neck, along with his sling and pouch of stones, and climbed up the line to the deck of the ship. The man in the silver helmet graciously accepted the whitebacks and gave in return a small sack of many-colored glass beads.

"My name is Captain Huntwell," the man said. "I am a trader from Jadeland, far to the south."

"And I am Darkhair Fisher; I have heard of Jadeland, but never did I expect to meet their people. This is a great day for me."

"And for me as well, friend Darkhair. Come with me." He took Darkhair by the arm and led him away from the crowd of blue-clad sailors, up a flight of steps to the afterdeck. The only other man here stood gripping a large wheel; Darkhair saw no sign of a tiller, and asked about it.

"We steer with a rudder under the stern," Huntwell said, speaking slowly and clearly. "The wheel here pulls ropes that move the rudder and enable us to steer."

"Truly, this must be a boat of marvels," Darkhair said, and meant it. How had landlubbers like the Suns come up with the skill to build such a craft? "What a shame that the other one was lost."

"You know of—our friends?" Huntwell said, a little too quickly.

"A little only. I have been hunting here in the Mistmarsh for many days, but yesterday some friends passed by and told me that a ship like this one had been wrecked at Ripmouth, and almost all aboard were lost. I grieve to be the one to tell you this."

Huntwell seemed undisturbed, but his eyes narrowed. "*Almost* all, you say?"

"A boat from my village was nearby, my friends told me,

and its crew rescued a woman and a boy. The woman is said to be very beautiful, and her name is Silken."

"Silken, yes. I know her. And the boy?"

Darkhair shrugged. "He's just a little boy. They say he wears a yellow thing on his head and shoulders. I don't know—"

"Where are they now, friend Darkhair?"

"Why, in my village, I suppose. In Longstrand."

"And is it near here?"

"You could be there this afternoon. I'm sure your friends will be glad to see you. As will our people."

"No doubt, no doubt. Friend, will you guide us there? We do not know these waters, and as you see we must make our way slowly. I will reward you well."

"I will be glad to guide you, friend Huntwell."

"Good. But you heard of no other survivors?"

"My friends said all the others were lost. The ship hit Threeclaw Rock and went straight under. A great sadness. My grandfathers met their deaths in the same place, so I share your sorrow."

"I see. Well, perhaps those who rescued the woman and the boy will be able to tell us more. I must go and tell Admiral Thorn, our leader, of your news. Meanwhile, stay here, good friend, and guide our steersman, if you will."

"With great gladness, friend Huntwell."

The captain clattered down the steps (how could he stand having his feet encased in those great boxes of leather?) and vanished into the cabin beneath the deck. Darkhair scanned the ship; the crew, in return, studied him with expressions of disgust and amusement. He grinned moronically at anyone who caught his eye. A Naked, they'd called him—little better than the brutes they so foolishly despised. Let them think so.

With great politeness he suggested a course to the steersman that would take them offshore and then between Weedshoal Island and the end of Saltspring Point.

"Why not go around the island?" the steersman asked.

"Very shallow and rocky out there, and bad currents. But the passage is good—very deep and safe."

The steersman grunted and obeyed. Over the voices of the crew and the creaking of the ship, Darkhair could hear the calls of wild animals deep in the marsh and felt heartened.

Huntwell returned and beckoned him to the steps. "The

admiral wishes to meet you, friend Darkhair. Will you please come below and have something to eat and drink with him?"

"I am honored." To the steersman he said, "Keep the course as I said, and all will be well."

The cabin was at the end of a short, dark passageway. Huntwell opened the door and ushered Darkhair into a wide, low-ceilinged room whose far wall was lined with glass windows. The floor was carpeted and soft beneath his bare feet; the walls were paneled in some unfamiliar wood, and a long table of the same wood stood in the center of the cabin. Behind the table, a dark outline against the gray light from the windows, sat a man.

"Your Manhood, this is Darkhair Fisher, a native of these parts. Darkhair, this is Admiral the Man Thorn of Brokencliff."

"I greet you, uh, Your Manhood?" He made it tentative, as if unsure of his manners but trying to please.

"I greet you, Darkhair. Please sit down." A pale hand gestured to a chair across the table. Darkhair sat, smiling uncertainly. The admiral's voice was deep and powerful, but it had nothing frightening or evil in it.

The dark figure was a little easier to see now: a very tall man, dressed in a richly embroidered blue-and-gold robe. His face was craggy and lined above a grizzled black beard. His eyes were hard to make out, set deep as they were under a heavy brow.

"There is food here, and good wine. I beg you, refresh yourself while you tell me what you told Captain Huntwell."

The captain handed Darkhair a square wooden tray, glossy with yellow lacquer, and from a cabinet in the wall he brought bowls of strange grains, vegetables, and meats, hot and steaming. Darkhair wondered for a moment how the Suns contrived to cook without a fire; then he heard the clatter of pots below the floor and guessed that some sort of kitchen connected with the admiral's cabin. Tentatively, he tried the grains and vegetables, finding them odd but tasty. The meat he left alone: it might well be centaur's flesh.

While he ate, he repeated what he had told Huntwell. Admiral Thorn listened in silence, his hands folded on the table.

"Did the woman say anything about herself?" he asked at last.

"I don't know, Your Manhood. Indeed, I was on my way home to see the castaways for myself when I found you."

"Well. She is one of ours, and we shall be glad to take her home, and the boy as well. Your village will be well rewarded for their rescue."

"Your Manhood is very kind." This was something like a mockery duel, Darkhair decided, except that the admiral thought that only he was engaged in it.

"Will you have more to eat? Or drink? No? Then I will keep you no longer. Captain Huntwell will escort you back on deck. You are kind to help pilot us to Longstrand."

"It is my pleasure, Your Manhood."

Bowing and grinning, Darkhair let himself be taken out of the cabin. In the passageway he relaxed a little, and realized how tense he had been. If Admiral Thorn had seen through him—if his attempt at deception had been as naive as he had tried to appear—he would have been dead in moments, and Longstrand might be in flames before nightfall. *Goddess, look under me now. . . .*

Liberator sailed slowly north across Mud Bay. Darkhair stood between Huntwell and the steersman, exclaiming about the ship's marvelous size and complexity while offering occasional advice on its course. Meanwhile he scrutinized the crew, who seemed to have little to do but gawk at the shoreline. No one seemed interested in the cannons, ten to either side, lined up along the main deck. Silken had told him that they required careful loading, and must be cleaned before firing again. If his plan worked, they would not fire at all. He saw nothing that resembled a handheld gun.

The overcast was thickening, and the horizon to the north and west was obscured by distant squalls. As the ship neared the passage between Saltspring Spit and Weedshoal Island, Darkhair said, "Now steer a little to the left. And a little more." He glanced to his right. The dense reeds of the point were less than a bowshot away.

"It looks as if it's shallowing," the steersman mumbled, but he obeyed.

"The waters here are deceptive, friend," Darkhair said.

It seemed now as if time had slowed. The breeze slackened; the great sails banged softly. Near the bowsprit, the round-faced leadsman uncertainly fingered his plummet, casting glances at Huntwell as if expecting to be ordered to sound the water again. Darkhair listened to the bark of a dabbler in the nearby reeds. Affecting casualness, he tapped the pouch slung round his neck, feeling the stones within it; the sling itself was tied loosely around his neck as well. The bag of glass beads lay on the deck by his feet.

With a single brief thud, *Liberator* went aground and heeled over sharply to rightboard. The cannons on that side rumbled down the tilted deck and thumped into the closed gunports. Two or three of the sailors lost their balance and fell. The steersman swore, his hands tight on the wheel. His eyes flaring with anger, Captain Huntwell turned to confront Darkhair, just in time to be struck full in the face with the pouch of slingstones.

"Ah!" he cried, falling back against the steersman. Darkhair swung the pouch again and heard the steersman's skull crack. Both men fell to the deck. Darkhair plucked a curved dagger from the captain's belt, marveling at the intricacy of the decorations on the steel blade, and plunged it into the captain's throat. Bright, hot blood spouted onto Darkhair's hand, across the bone-white tattoo. Huntwell's body shuddered, convulsed, and went limp.

The crew recovered quickly from the shock of the grounding, and when they saw only Darkhair standing by the wheel they ran aft to seize him. Obeying a last-moment thought, Darkhair sawed rapidly at the rope that controlled the rudder: the blade was sharp, and the fibers parted readily. Before the first of the sailors reached the afterdeck, the ship was hamstrung. A sword glinted dully; Darkhair ducked, turned, sprang to the railing, and dived into the shallow water.

It was like home after the strangeness of the ship, and he rejoiced in its cold cleanness. Even if a stone or spear or arrow found him now, at least he would die in his own place. Swimming hard, he stayed beneath the surface until his lungs ached; breaching, he gave himself one gasp of air before he dived again.

When he came up the second time, the shouts of the Sunnish sailors seemed far away, and the reeds were close ahead. Something splashed behind him. A few strokes carried him into the reeds, where his feet found bottom and he began groping his way forward. The reeds hissed and rattled against each other, masking the shouts from behind.

Abruptly, he came into a reed-walled stretch of open water. Six canoes floated in line; in each, an archer sat aiming a long arrow at him. The men slackened their bowstrings when they recognized Darkhair. Netweaver, alone in one canoe, smiled and paddled close to his husband.

Darkhair rolled into the canoe, sat up, and caught his breath. The others approached, their questions soft and anxious. Darkhair, panting, said nothing. He pointed to one of the paddlers, then to the far end of the little inlet.

The canoe slipped away, rounded the reedbed, and returned almost at once. Summerbloom Merchant, the archer in the canoe, was wide-eyed with excitement.

"They're coming, Darkhair! Two long boats, ten men in each, pulling on oars. I didn't see any bows—just spears and clubs. They're nearing the edge of the reeds."

"Did they see you?"

"No."

"Go back and show yourselves. We don't want them blundering south toward the other group. The rest of us will be right behind you."

Darkhair strung his bow and pulled a quiver of arrows around in front of him. Summerbloom's canoe retraced its course, with the five others following. The channel narrowed between banks of reeds, then opened wide. Summerbloom's paddler, a lanky young man named Sandy Brewer, sent the canoe out into open water. Darkhair and the others heard a distant shout and the splashing of oars.

"Now back in again, quickly," Darkhair called. Sandy paddled strongly until he and Summerbloom were back with the others. The canoes slipped into the reeds, waiting for the Sunnish longboats to come round. The wait was short.

Eight rowers were in each boat, as well as an armed lookout and a tillerman, but only four were still at their oars; the others gripped spears and oddly shaped clubs. They wore armor like that of the men on *Deliverer*—armor that had seen much use. Their eyes were bright under the rims of their ridged helmets.

Darkhair let the first boat get a little past them, then whistled. From the canoes in the reeds, arrows sang out. Good—the first volley had been aimed at the tillermen, though Darkhair hadn't thought to give the order. The men screamed; one leaped up, a shaft pierced through both cheeks, and fell into the water. The other, with arrows in his arm and neck, struggled to keep hold of his tiller.

The second volley was more ragged and had little effect. All the Suns had abandoned their oars now, and one or two hurled spears into the reeds. The boats collided and drifted apart. One of the men in the leading boat raised his club and

41

whirled it around his head; the spiked knob of the club flew off and arced into one of the canoes, narrowly missing the paddler. The man quickly attached another knob, but fell dead before he could hurl it.

Order vanished on both sides. The archers shot at will, but the reeds that concealed them also impeded their arrows. The Suns, startled by the ambush, cast spears and clubs almost at random. In a moment, Darkhair realized, the men would gather their wits and retreat to open water. There they would see the second group of canoes making for *Liberator*, and perhaps intercept them. At the very least, the men in the boats would reinforce their mates on the ship, and People's lives would be needlessly lost. He must act at once.

"Attack!" he screamed, and shot an arrow into the second boat. Netweaver dropped his bow and dug his paddle into the water. The canoe slid out of the reeds, closing with the second boat. From the corner of his eye, Darkhair saw the other canoes move forward.

A barbed spear struck out at him; Darkhair gripped it and pulled the spearman into the water. Reversing the spear, he threw it full in the face of another man—the round-faced leadsman. A clubhead whirred past him. Darkhair nocked an arrow and let fly at a pale-faced sailor, who cried out in pain and fear: the arrow had struck under the armpit, and struck deep.

Then the battle was over. Three men survived in the first boat and five in the second; their empty hands rose above their helmets. The canoemen turned to Darkhair, who did not hesitate:

"Kill them all."

Arrows struck from point-blank range; the defeated men made no resistance. One of them began a strange chant:

> "Sun our life, Sun our death,
> Giver of our every breath,
> What you give is yours to take,
> Yours to shatter, yours to make—"

The last word was a cry, a shriek, as an arrow went into the man's eye. The water in the little channel turned pink; curious finnet darted just under the surface, tasting the strangeness.

Weighted by the armor, the corpses sank at once. The men

rowed the boats into shallow water and ran them onto a mudbank; then they paddled out toward the grounded ship.

The twelve canoes of the other group were approaching *Liberator* from the south. Darkhair saw that the ship was listing still more steeply to rightward, so that the cannons on that side pointed uselessly down and those on the other aimed at the overcast. The sailors seemed to be trying to haul some of the cannon inboard; from what Silken had said about them, the weapons could be tilted and might still be dangerous. Darkhair did not intend to give the Suns time to defend themselves.

"Now, paddle for the ship and don't stop for anything!" he shouted.

The canoes closed in. Some of the sailors stood along its stern rail and rightboard side, gripping heavy tubes with flaring mouths like horns. Those must be the guns Silken had mentioned; they were a hazard that would have to be faced and endured. He wished the boat crews had brought some guns with them; his own men could not have used them, but their loss would have reduced the odds against the attackers.

While Netweaver paddled, Darkhair unwrapped a bulky package in the bottom of the canoe. It contained a flint and steel, a clay bowl, dry grass and sticks, and six fat cylinders of bloodwood resin wrapped in paperbark. The canoes worked their way around the ship to its exposed left side, while Darkhair made fire in the bowl. Others were doing the same thing in their canoes.

The Suns had moved to the left side and leveled their guns. Darkhair heard a bang; something kissed the water less than a span from his canoe. Bad! The cursed things had too much range. Working fast, he slid the cylinders over the points of six arrows and down onto their shafts. The arrows would not fly far or true, but it wouldn't matter at close range. Another gun went off, and something like a flock of hornets zipped overhead. With the third shot, Sandy Brewer cried out and toppled into the water, blood spraying from his head.

The canoes were now approaching the ship in two curving lines, giving the archer in each canoe a few moments at short range. Darkhair's canoe led his group; as he reached the closest point to the ship he saw someone in the leading canoe of the second group fire his first arrow. It rose in a wobbly

43

trajectory, smoking and flaring, and fell just short of the barnacled hull.

Nocking his first arrow, Darkhair held it over the firebowl. The bloodwood resin sputtered into flame, giving off pungent smoke. Despite the excitement of battle, Darkhair felt a pang of resentment at having to throw away a quantity of resin the centaurs would have paid handsomely for. He turned, aimed, and shot. The arrow struck the hull and embedded itself. Another arrow—and another.

Something hit the canoe right beside him, but Darkhair kept shooting. Four of his arrows hit and stuck. Toward the ship's stern, five more arrows were burning with fierce, pinkish-orange flames.

"Turn!" he commanded. Netweaver obeyed. Looking back, Darkhair saw Admiral Thorn standing on the afterdeck, shouting orders. Now there was indeed something terrible in his voice, a coldness and power that made Darkhair catch his breath: as if, where only silence should be, a voice should call out from the dark.

The guns went on banging away, and two of the canoes in the second group lost their men. A clubhead splashed futilely, spans away from the nearest attacker. But now the burning arrows were doing their work. More than forty had hit, including a few into the admiral's cabin, and the ship was beginning to catch fire. The sailors dropped their guns and began pouring buckets of water down the ship's side; one even lowered himself on a rope and tried to beat out the flames with a sodden garment.

"Darkhair—you've been hurt." Now that they were out of range, Netweaver put down his paddle and hurried to his husband. Darkhair looked at himself and found four small punctures in his right leg, halfway between knee and hip. A fifth, just above the hipbone, oozed a trickle of blood. Darkhair felt only a numbness around the wounds. He hoped the pain would hold off a little longer.

"I'll be all right. Get back to your paddle."

He waved his bow above his head; the canoes circled out from the burning ship, surrounding it. Smoke rose and thickened. An orange flame ran up into the rigging. The sailors worked frantically; they must have known they were doomed, but none tried to abandon ship. Darkhair saw the blue-and-gold robe of Admiral Thorn again on the afterdeck.

"Darkhair! Darkhair Fisher! We will remember you and all

44

your people, and we will feed upon you in Hell." Faint and clear, the admiral's voice ran across the water like the first freezing wind of winter. Darkhair raised his fist, little finger extended in obscene reply. But he felt something cold settle upon him, something more than the first pain of his wounds, and was silent.

For perhaps half an hour, the ship burned. For most of that time the sailors tried to control the fire; then they gave up. The attackers saw them standing on the tilted deck of their ship, and again the strange chant rose to the gray sky. Then, with a red-black flash, the ship exploded. The masts fell, and the hull broke in two. Burning chunks of wood flew up and fell back into the seething water. With a cracking of timbers, the burning ship turned over. Another explosion, smaller than the first, burst through the exposed keel; smoke wrapped itself around the hulk, and then blew away. Flocks of whiteback and dabblers rose from the reeds, barking and squawking in alarm.

Shaking, Darkhair forced himself to wait. Silken had told him of the reserves of gunpowder the ship would have below decks, and what might happen if they caught fire, but he had not expected such violence. At last, when the shattered hull had sunk almost completely beneath the surface, he raised his hand in a tired gesture and the canoes ventured in close to the wreck. Three wounded survivors, clinging to wreckage and moaning horribly, were swiftly killed, and left to float with the other bodies. Those of the People who had died in the attack were retrieved from the water; then the men turned north and paddled slowly homeward.

4

"Metal that touches flesh to heal must be purified in fire," Silken said. Griptiller, seated cross-legged in her usual place, looked impassive, though her family saw the glint of contempt in her eyes. But Silken knew something of gun wounds, and the People did not; Sunnish superstition would be tolerated if not respected.

Darkhair lay on his left side near the fireplace, drawing each breath with care. His right leg was stiff with pain, and the hole in his side felt large enough to hold a roundstone. He watched impassively as Silken held a pair of iron tweezers over the fire.

"It will hurt," she warned. With her left hand she touched the wound in his side, pressing gently but firmly until her fingers found the little lump of lead. The tweezers went into the wound, and Darkhair gasped despite himself. He was remotely aware of the smell of his own scorched flesh, and of metal grating on metal in his side.

"Ah!" His field of vision contracted to a narrow tunnel. Silken's hand appeared in it, pale and slim. The blood-streaked tweezers held a red-and-black lump.

"You were lucky," she said. "It wasn't too deep." She put a small square of spidersilk over the wound; impregnated with bloodwood resin, it would both stick to his skin and dull the pain.

"Get on with it," Firewing said thickly. Silken gave her a cool smile and held the tweezers once more over the fire.

At last it was over. Quiet gave Darkhair a mug of wine with a drop of resin dissolved in it, and drew blankets over him. He felt the pain subside a little, and grew drowsy in the warmth of the fire. Everything seemed to retreat to a comfortable distance, and the others' voices were remote.

"I'm no healer," Silken was saying. "His wounds may grow poisoned despite the fire. But I think he will be all right."

"My son has saved your life; if you have saved his, the debt is paid," Griptiller said.

"I am grateful for what he has done for the Heir and for me. It will be remembered."

Griptiller spat into the fire. "The debt is paid. You owe us nothing more, and we want no Sunnish gratitude. Now we must find a place for you and the boy, somewhere close but out of the way."

"What about the cabin on the Easthaven trail?" Hemlock suggested. "No one's used it since old Singleton Coppersmith died. It can't be seen from the trail, but it's not too far from here. Very snug, too," she added to Silken. "Perhaps a bit cold in winter, but it could be fixed up—"

"Whatever you find suitable will be acceptable to me." Little remained of her original arrogance; she was adjusting quickly, Darkhair thought.

"Good." Darkhair heard Griptiller sigh. "This has indeed been a nasty business, and it's not over yet. Sometimes I almost wish we were not the Fishers. Our standing can be a heavy burden. . . . Well, enough of this. Hemlock and I will see to supper. Netweaver, go outside and make sure the children have put away the war gear properly in the boatshed. Firewing, can you nurse the baby when he wakes?"

"Not yet, but soon. The Merchants have given me some milk from their browser; it'll do until my own milk comes in."

Darkhair heard Netweaver scramble to his feet and hurry outside. The way their wives talked in front of men really was scandalous, and Griptiller was just as bad.

"Darkhair must rest," Silken said. "Is there somewhere we can put him, where he can be alone and undisturbed?"

He did not open his eyes, but he could imagine Griptiller's expression from the tone of her voice. "Alone? Why should he be alone? His eyes are closed; he doesn't speak. That's alone enough."

After a pause, Silken said, "I see. I have much still to learn about your ways."

"That you say with truth."

Darkhair thought: Yes. I am alone. Alone I struck Huntwell and the steersman, and alone they died. Alone died the others, Suns and People alike. Alone I feel my pain, alone I hear the voices of the strangers around me, and I remain alone. Then why do I feel the presence of Admiral Thorn so close?

He heard the baby wail, sounding like a distant hawk, and thought: He is well named. But I am still alone.

Spring hastened across the Gulf of Islands and up the slopes of the mountains. The People of Longstrand were busy with a thousand tasks, yet the battle of Mud Bay stayed fresh in their minds. The young men who had taken part in it were stuffed with pride and deed-standing, and walked Traders' Beach with a gravity that would have seemed pompous even in centaurs. Those who had stayed at home regretted their missed glory; visitors from other villages clicked their tongues and murmured dryly to one another that Longstrand could always outdo itself in vanity.

The three Sunnish guests—as they were ironically called—were almost forgotten in the buzz of gossip and the chatter of clapsticks. The baby was so often seen on Firewing's hip that

47

no one gave him a second glance. In the warm spring sun he soon darkened until few could tell him from the dozen other babies his age. And, apart from the stories about him, there was nothing unusual about Eyas. He nursed greedily at Firewing's newly full breasts, fattened like a browser calf, howled with colic, and filled his family with the delight and exasperation that go with any new baby.

Silken and Brightspear soon dropped out of Longstrand's sight. They were settled in the old Coppersmith cabin, as Hemlock had suggested. It was less than an hourmarch north of the village and on the edge of the Forester family's land; old political allies of the Fishers, they kept discreet watch on their new neighbors. The cabin was a hundred spans east of the trail, at the end of a stony path that was half-brook. In the midst of a clearing, the cabin was small but snug, with the brook nearby and enough room for a sizable kitchen garden. Beyond the clearing, the path ran on to the Foresters' longhouse; if Sunnish agents ever did penetrate this far, the woman and boy at least had a bolt-hole.

Darkhair recovered slowly. Each day he went out to sit by the family post, warming himself in the sun. He spoke politely to all who came to see him, but such a reserve enfolded him that conversations were brief. Soon his only visitors were the men of the war party, and even they came mostly out of loyalty. Darkhair's wives, accustomed to his moods, saw that his needs were met and then found work elsewhere. The girls sometimes kept him company, but their chores—and the excitement of Traders' Beach—soon drew them away.

Neither the pleasure of sunlight on his skin, nor the gradual ebbing of the pain in his wounds, could ease his depression. Spring was even lovelier than usual this year, and he mourned for Sandy Brewer and the others who had died without seeing it. For all the deed-standing he had won at Mud Bay, he felt inadequate and shamed by those deaths: he tortured himself devising different strategies that might have destroyed the ship without losing any of the People's lives.

One night, as he lay sleeping beside Quiet, he seemed to wake. A shadowed figure leaned over him, and he knew its face: it was Admiral Thorn, staring at him with a terrible yearning smile, looking down into the faces of the sleeping children, smirking at Quiet and Firewing and the old women.

We will feed on you in Hell, he whispered. *Oh Darkhair, we will feed on your wives and mothers and daughters, and on your nestling, and then we will feed on you, you, you . . .*

He sat up, gasping for breath, and the vision was gone. The room was dark and still; the only sound was the distant splash of waves on the beach. Darkhair began to tremble. The world outside the longhouse seemed to coil itself menacingly around the old walls: they were all in peril and he could think of nothing to protect them.

The dreams came often after that. At last he began to befuddle himself every afternoon with resin in wine; it offered a dull forgetfulness of Mud Bay, and gave protection against the dreams. Now, when Thorn leaned hissing over him, Darkhair stared blankly back until the dream faded away and he slipped back into the shallows of sleep. What he dreamed he did not share, though there were times when Quiet slept restlessly, and Darkhair could sense the presence of the dead admiral. Yet she woke lightly in the morning, while Darkhair lay abed thinking bleak thoughts.

The People preferred superstition to religion. The yearly Gathering was as much traffic with divinity as most of them cared for, and even She gave them love, not theology. Her presence answered few questions; it made the questions seem foolish. Who had made Alland and the seas around it? Why? Did humans, brutes, and animals have purpose in their lives? Or in their deaths? The Suns worshipped their namesake, and other gods that could not even be seen. Were these truly gods, or mere delusions, like children's imaginary companions?

Darkhair watched many dawns while such questions asked themselves in his mind, and the Goddess seemed very far away. In memory he sailed again to Ripmouth, to Northport and Three Springs and the heads of a dozen other inlets; in memory he walked again, as he had in his wanderyear, to the Great Cataract. Those were the boundaries of the People's world, and they seemed very narrow. Beyond them was Alland, vast and unknown. Two Bows had turned away from it; when the Suns had brought Alland to the Gulf, and children of Two Bows had risen at last to turn away from Alland yet again. Now Alland returned a third time, and the People still struck out ignorantly against a world they neither

49

knew nor cared to know. But that world curled around the Gulf as the night coiled around the longhouse, close and inexorable.

Finally a day came when Darkhair woke from his grim dreams, took a half-loaf from the bread jar, and walked stiffly out the door, past the family post, and onto the beach.

Ah, the Gulf was beautiful in a spring morning's first light! The waves glittered in the sun as if no other waves had ever broken on smooth sand. The clouds, cooling now from fiery red to white, were as new in the sky as words in a baby's mouth, and as wonderful. The cliffs behind Longstrand could have been no greener in Two Bows' time; even the broken tooth of the tower seemed gentled by the light. Thick and rich in his nostrils were the smokes of a hundred chimneys, the stinks of a hundred privies.

If the Gulf was beautiful, it was vulnerable as well. Without his willing it, he had somehow become the protector of the Gulf and the People against the world outside; he must learn more about that world before it struck again at them.

He walked along the water's edge, chewing on the crusty bread and tossing crumbs to waveskimmers as they swept squeaking around him. When the bread was gone he walked back to the longhouse without pausing to touch the post.

The family was up. "Netweaver, I'm going up to the cabin to talk with Silken."

His husband blinked at him, surprised. "If you wish."

Silken had asked for a number of items; these Darkhair found around the house and put into a large pouch, which he slung over his shoulder.

"Are you sure you can walk that far?" Firewing asked. Darkhair nodded. "Good," his wife said. "I'm glad to see you getting off your backside at last. But don't push yourself too hard."

"A wife who doesn't fuss and a fish that doesn't swim," Darkhair growled, hugging her.

The trail up the cliff and past the tower was the worst part; after that, the going was easy. Darkhair carried a staff to ease his hip, but used it more for the pleasure of thumping its end into the rust-orange gravel of the trail. The woods were thin, mostly young second growth; sunlight fell brightly on his shoulders and on the new ferns uncurling among the trees. The Bridge of Heaven stood out clearly above the treetops, giving the sky an almost dizzying height.

At the edge of the clearing, Darkhair paused to watch Brightspear. The boy was playing at war with a stick: he swung it like a two-handed sword, then held it like a gun, tracking some imaginary victim. The stick pointed at Darkhair.

"Pah!" shouted Brightspear. "You're dead."

Darkhair felt embarrassed. At Brightspear's age, to be playing at war was unpleasantly precocious. Boys of the People showed little interest in fighting until they were inducted at thirteen into their village brotherhood, and taught the warlore all men must know. A five-year-old was too young to treat warfare as the sacred and terrible duty it was.

Looking steadily into Brightspear's eyes, Darkhair was relieved to see the boy glance away. The child unnerved him; even in the silly tunic that flapped about his knees, Brightspear looked like a warrior. Darkhair suspected that the boy's father had not been half the man this one would be. The father, after all, had given up; the son would not.

Silken appeared in the doorway of the cabin and smiled in greeting. She looked more like a proper woman these days, Darkhair thought. Her yellow hair was brushed back and tied at the nape of her neck so that it fell in a golden cascade down her back. The Sunnish gown had been replaced by a tunic and trousers of splithoof hide—what one might wear to venture into dense bush—which somehow she contrived to make attractive rather than merely functional. Silken's skin had browned, and her eyes were a brighter green.

"I wish you good day," she said as he approached the little porch before the door.

"And good day to you. I've brought you some of the things you asked for."

"I am grateful. Please come in."

The cabin was a single narrow room with a hard dirt floor and a sleeping loft under the rafters. A stone fireplace stood in the wall opposite the door. Silken offered him a seat on the bench before the fire—on the men's side, he noted—and stirred a pot hanging above the coals. It smelled like a creditable attempt at fish stew.

Darkhair unloaded his pouch. "I brought some books, and a little paperbark. It's too early for the new crop, and we haven't much left of last year's. And an inkstone and some brushes, and half a span of spidersilk—good stuff, Chirp spun it herself. And a good kitchen knife. An iron skillet." He did

51

not mention that it was centaur iron. "Some seed for the garden. And a ball of string."

"I thank you for your kindness." She reached first for the books. Each was made of square pages about a fifth of a span on a side, tightly stitched and bound in covers of ornately engraved spitfar skin. "They look like old books in the library at Great Camp," she said, surprised.

"The Suns taught us writing and bookbinding," Darkhair said without expression. "We haven't changed much since then."

"Much as you hate the Suns, you kept our language?"

"We had no other. The Suns saw to that. Our own tongue, it's said, was much like Sunnish anyway."

She nodded. "And so like Bandish and Deltan. But if your Goddess gives you visions of the past, can you not remember your own first tongue?"

"The Goddess gives us visions only. In some of them we see our ancestors speak, but we hear nothing. The Goddess Herself speaks to us in—we have no word for it, but we understand Her in our minds."

"I think I understand," she said, but obviously did not. "So when you want to record something in words, you make a book." Darkhair nodded. The books he had brought were ones he had made himself; he was proud of them, and irrationally anxious about her reaction to them.

She opened a book at random and began to read, while Brightspear looked over her shoulder. "Some words here are oddly spelled, and some I do not understand, but I will try to learn. Will you help me?"

"If you like," Darkhair said slowly. "But why are you so interested in the writings of Nakeds?"

She ignored his mockery. "I must live among you; so must Brightspear. It is only right that we learn your ways."

The morning passed pleasantly. Darkhair helped her learn to read the books—histories, mockeries, songs, riddles, and Old Stories—while Brightspear listened and watched, sometimes putting a grimy finger on a letter he recognized. At noon they ate the fish stew. Brightspear was silent, but listened to all that the adults said. When they paused once, he slapped the bench.

"Talk! Talk!" he demanded.

"A willing student," Silken laughed.

"We've talked enough for now about the People," Darkhair said. "Tell me what the Dominance is like."

52

"I don't know where to start."

"Since we drove them out, two and half centuries ago, we've heard little—just rumors from the centaurs and windwalkers."

"Then you've missed the greatest part of our history," she said. Then she began to speak of that history, while Darkhair and Brightspear listened.

When the People had risen against the Suns, the Dominance was weakened and divided by the Inheritors' War. The last Sun, Subjugator, had died in a great plague called the bleeding fever. His death was so sudden that he had had no time to name one of his twin sons as Heir and to put the other to death: he had loved them both, and had put off the hard decision. Now the twins, Courage and Lefthand, were strong young men; they warred for the Iron Throne, and the Dominance fell into confusion. Provinces took one side or the other, or rebelled against both. The Deltans, ancient enemies of the Suns, invaded the Eastmarch and held its meadows and cities.

The war lasted five years, and then Lefthand slew his brother at the Battle of Windridge. He restored the Three Families—the Whisperers, Standings, and Marchwardens—who had once ruled the Dominance, and with their help he drove out the Deltans. The rebel provinces were reconquered. But what had been quickly shattered took long to restore.

"The Divinities Cults had held great power in the old days," Silken said, and Darkhair nodded. He remembered the visions of the Sunnish priests and their grim temples. "It was said that the cults' priests could foretell the future, and bring the vengeance of their gods on anyone who opposed them. In the war they sided with Courage, and promised him the victory. But Lefthand despised the cults, and when he struck off his brother's head, Courage's followers lost their faith, and bowed to the new Sun.

"Lefthand restored the old faith, the Sunteachings. He overthrew the cults, burned their temples, and seized their lands and herds. Some priests hid from him, or fled the Dominance, but most were put to death. The cults were not utterly destroyed, but they were silent and powerless. The Sun in Heaven sent Messengers to guide the Sun on Earth, and their wisdom was proof of divine favor.

"Then began the Age of Glory. Lefthand and his line rebuilt the Dominance, from Eastmarch to the Western Ranges, from Transmontane to the Tin Coast and Alland's End." She looked at Darkhair with a faint smile. "We could have retaken the Gulf of Islands, but it seemed not worth the trouble. Compared to the great lands and cities of the south and east, this is a poor and savage country."

"Long may the Suns think so," Darkhair grunted. Silken's smile broadened.

"Tell me more about the Sunteachings and the cults," he went on, and was surprised to see Silken's smile vanish.

"You—you are not among the Vanquished, and we are not in swordshadow. But I will tell you about the cults, and then perhaps what I can say of the Sunteachings will shine in your heart.

"The cults hold that many gods rule the world and heaven. Each cult honors all, but worships one god above others. One believes that Skyland is both a god and the home of the faithful who die in the service of the cults. Another reveres Redspark as the god of war. There are many others—gods of the seas and forests, storms and crops and herds, even a god of the brutes." Contempt thickened her voice. "The cults once practiced human sacrifice, and perhaps still do, in secret. It is a crude and stupid faith, lost in folly and superstition—a gift from Delta," she added, as if quoting a proverb. "It's said that when we first came down from the White Mountains to the Grasslands and the Lake Country, we met tribes who owed the Deltans much, and from those tribes we first learned of the cults."

She fell silent for a long time. "Talk!" Brightspear shouted again.

"I will tell you this much about the Sunteachings. Lefthand took the faith to all the Dominance, saying that it would vanquish error. All who accepted the Teachings became known as the Vanquished, those who bow to the One God Sun in Heaven and His incarnation on earth." She bowed her head to Brightspear, who nodded almost smugly.

"When the Teachers brought the word to the reconquered peoples, it was given them beneath the raised swords of Lefthand's soldiers, who would slay any who refused to believe. Ever since, none may speak of the Sunteachings unless one man at least stands with raised sword to strike down the impious."

Darkhair's face must have revealed his horror; Silken smiled reassuringly. "It is only a ritual now. No one is actually struck down—at least, not in many years. And we aren't actually vanquished, not when we're born in the Teachings."

"Yet," said Darkhair, "if the Sunnish soldiers ever came again, such things would befall us."

"You need not fear, Darkhair. The Teachings—" Her voice almost broke, and sank to a whisper. "The Teachings are themselves overthrown, and the cults now rule the Dominance again."

"Tell me."

"I will be brief. The last Sun of the Age of Glory was Axmaster. He ruled long and well, but he had a single child—the Heir Greenflag. Greenflag was sickly as a boy, it's said, and full of fears and strange frenzies." Bitterness burned coldly in her eyes. "Though he himself was the vessel of the Sun's incarnation, he fell under the power of secret cultists in his youth, and kept his apostasy secret from all—even from his own wife and children.

"When Axmaster died, fourteen years ago, Greenflag took the Iron Throne. Perhaps we should have known at once that something was wrong, for he named neither of his sons as Heir. The older of them was Steeledge, whom you saw at Ripmouth; the younger was Silvershield. Both were brave and intelligent, and when they saw which way the grass bent in the wind, each began to gather followers, and to prepare for civil war.

"At first, though, all seemed well. The new Sun even put down a revolt in Transmontane, and chastised the Desert Bands, though he had never been much of a soldier before. No one noticed when he changed a few laws, or brought unknown Men into the Eastern Yard to advise his government, or raised squadrons of handpicked soldiers. A year passed, and then he changed his name to Divine Voice. He cast down the Teachings and proclaimed the cults as the only true religion."

More than bitterness was in her eyes now: it was hatred, serene and implacable. Darkhair almost winced at the thought of religions that could inspire such feelings in their believers.

"He knew what would follow, and he was ready for it. The Vanquished rose in protest, still calling him the only God on Earth. But the new squadrons were cultists. All cultists. They fell upon the crowds in the streets, and slaughtered thousands. It's said that the Lake of Reeds, where New Fort stands, was red with blood. It was the same all across the

55

Dominance. I remember well the killings in my own town, Warfield, in Jadeland.

"After that, we Vanquished learned from the cultists to hide our own faith, and to profess what we knew was folly. We were under another kind of swordshadow, from the humblest slave to the highest of the Inner Suns. Even the sons of Greenflag were astonished by their father's madness, but they chose different ways to survive. Steeledge retired to the country, taking his wife, the Woman Emerald, with him. Silvershield took up his father's cause, and pretended to believe in the cults. He suppressed a few revolts in the west and south, and even claimed that the cult gods had sent Messengers to give him his victories. As his reward he was given supreme command over the armies.

"We Vanquished saw in Steeledge our only hope. In secret we appealed to him, begging him to take up arms in the cause of the Teachings. He rejected our pleas, knowing that the cultists' power was growing every day. And he could not bear the thought of rising against his own father."

Darkhair thought Steeledge sounded more like a vacillator than a loyal son, but said nothing.

"For eight years," Silken went on, "the cults ruled through Divine Voice. The Dominance was restless; the Sun knew it, and planned a war against Delta. The cults now said that all the human domains of Alland should be ruled by the Sun—as indeed they should be, but by the true Sun. Then, five years ago, Divine Voice died. The cultists said he had been poisoned, but I believe it was the punishment of the Sun in Heaven. And still he had not named his Heir. Steeledge had always been his favorite, and I think the old man hoped to convert him to the cults and then to send him to conquer Delta.

"Silvershield was in New Fort when his father died, and proclaimed himself the new Sun. But the Vanquished rose in the name of the Teachings, and Steeledge could no longer spurn them. So began the second Inheritors' War.

"My father, the Man Longstaff, had taken his herds from the hand of Axmaster, and now he drove them into Steeledge's lands. My brothers and uncles and cousins enlisted in the cause of the Teachings. I was given to Steeledge, who favored me—it is hard to speak of this."

"You need not speak of yourself and him."

"Well. In a word, we lost. It took five years. Silvershield

56

held the cities, and Transmontane. Guns and cannons were rare when I was a girl, but somehow the cultists learned how to make them in endless numbers. We learned too, but we had little to make them with. To make things worse, the commoners—ordinary males and females—no longer honored the Sunteachings as much as Men and Women did. They supported us when they had to, and the cultists when they could. So we lost.

"By then the Woman Emerald had given Steeledge his own Heir. Steeledge sent an embassy to Delta, asking for asylum for his family if not for himself, but Guardian refused. He is an evil and sly old man; he rejoiced to see us fight among ourselves, but he feared the vengeance of Silvershield. We were in retreat south into Jadeland by then, and Steeledge decided that our only hope was to escape to the far west. At Copper Bay he seized three warships. What was left of the army—five or six thousand men, and half that many mounts—he sent west on foot, telling them to build strongholds and await his commands. His own household went on the ships. I think he hoped to raise an army from the tribes along this coast, to join with the men in the mountains."

Little chance of that, thought Darkhair. The outcoasters were few and simple, without warlore, and he could imagine what sort of welcome Steeledge would have had from the People.

"But the people of Copper Bay sent word to Silvershield, who raised a great fleet to pursue us. Some of them were lost rounding Alland's End, and some sank off the Fire Coast. Still they followed us, and at Cape Farthest West we were nearly taken. The other two ships were sunk, with all aboard them. Only *Deliverer* broke away and escaped."

"And Admiral Thorn still followed us," Brightspear said. Silken nodded.

"And still he followed us. In the battle at the cape, Emerald was slain. I think . . . I think Steeledge gave up after that. He told me he believed the Sun in Heaven wished to punish the Dominance for its sins, and had not reincarnated in Greenflag or himself—only in Brightspear."

The boy snuggled comfortably against her. "I think perhaps he was right," she whispered. "When he is grown, he will redeem his people, and restore the Age of Glory."

The afternoon was still young, but Darkhair stood up and

gripped his staff. "I have taken enough of your time for one day. I thank you for what you have told me. May I come again, to learn more of the Dominance?"

"I am your guest, and I shall always welcome you."

"Until next time, then."

Darkhair walked across the clearing and down the stony path to the Easthaven trail. There he paused, and looked back. Brightspear stood in the path, just a few spans behind him, the stick raised to his shoulder.

"Pah!"

5

Spring turned to summer. The People fished and planted. The bloodwoods gave their sticky, red-black resin; the pods rose and swelled in the skyseed groves. In Longstrand, Speaker's Hall was full of songs and the songs were full of politics and the latest gossip.

Every boat brought news. A walkingtree, doubtless old and sick, blundered out of the mountains into Rainfalling and killed a child before being burned to a stinking lump. Woodsrunners, the wild cousins of the centaurs, were a nuisance in the eastern end of the Valley: they invaded the breadseed fields, trampling and devouring the young stalks. The farmers, cursing, chased them away with drums and clanging bells. A prominent family in Three Springs, the Breakaxes, dissolved in brawls and recriminations; the village Speaker resigned, shamed at his failure to save the marriage. A giant was reported seen gathering clams and threeclaws on a beach near Easthaven.

But Longstrand itself inspired most of the gossip. Everyone in the Gulf heard the clapstick songs about the battle of Mud Bay, and wanted to see the men who had fought it. Lurid rumors flew about the women's benches: the Sunnish girl was pregnant, or coupling with singletons in return for coppers, or threatening to spread bleeding fever if she were not fed on centaurs' flesh. Some said the boy Brightspear was really a mad dwarf. Those who wanted to see the captives were disappointed: Longstranders refused to say where they had been hidden, and old Givenlast Forester kept one or two of his tall sons near the trail to the cabin, to discourage trespassers.

Eyas was almost as disappointing. Apart from the loudness of his bellowings and the darkness of his thickening hair, nothing set him apart from other babies. Once, when Firewing took him down to Traders' Beach, a woman from Wreck Point asked if Eyas's paleness was due to a skin disease; Firewing drenched the silly woman in a flood of obscenities that drove every man in earshot right off the beach.

"You didn't have to do that," Netweaver chided her that night.

"We're Fishers, aren't we? We have standing to keep up."

"So we defend our precious standing with the dirtiest mouths in the Gulf," Darkhair snorted.

"I won't have to do it a second time," Firewing snapped back. "Nobody's going to make insulting remarks about Eyas while *I'm* around."

Darkhair, both saddened and amused, said nothing. She was much like Griptiller, he thought: fiercely proud of her standing and fiercely protective of her children. He recalled the countless times when Griptiller had fought his battles for him, and the price he had paid through a boyhood that had seemed unending. His husband and wives, from other villages and less famous families, had never understood how vulnerable were the children of the powerful.

He looked at Eyas, sleeping near Hemlock with his little backside in the air, and felt abruptly sure that Firewing would fight no battles for the boy: his battles would be too great.

Summer brought the windwalkers, and a little later the centaurs. Longstrand grew more crowded than ever, and Traders' Beach was busy day and night. The windwalkers, as always, kept to their flying islands or to the trading depots near the skyseed groves, and so were little seen, but their glass and wickerwork and gemstones were in every longhouse.

The Fishers at last went sailing, more for peace than for food, and stayed out in the Gulf until the winds of autumn blew everyone home. The windwalkers' islands lifted anchors and vanished eastward into the clouds. Their packs full of resin and fish, the centaurs returned to their holds on the High Plains. And the People's boats scattered to the shelter of their home shores.

Winter came, with women's festivals and snow flurries out of a dull white sky. The spiders slept in their nests, and the People pinned blankets over themselves when they went outdoors. The longhouses' shutters banged in the bitter winds that raged down the Valley; fires burned high on the hearths. The chimney of Longstrand's sweatbath smoked all day, and icicles hung thickly on its eaves. Steaming brown bodies burst out of the sweatbath door, rolling on the snowy beach or plunging into the water. Laughter rippled the quiet air.

The cold deepened. Longstrand harbor froze over, while the boats slept in their sheds. The Bluemeadows were drifted deep in snow tracked by splithoofs and prowls. The River itself was armored in ice, and in good weather the People sledged up and down it, visiting friends in Yellowshaws or Sandybank. On clear nights the Bridge of Heaven burned brighter than the moon: separated by the earth's shadow, two long arcs climbed from east and west, glittering horns against the empty sky. Skyland gleamed like a green gem, sometimes deep as emerald, sometimes pale as jade.

So went the reassuring cycle of the year, the pattern of the People's lives.

That winter, Hemlock died in her sleep with a single cry, like the whimper of a dreaming child. The next day the Fishers carried *Whiteback* from the boatshed and sailed out into the estuary to give Hemlock back to the sea. Her name went into the family song, and they grieved for her.

Quiet, wanting another child, conceived with Netweaver but miscarried. She took it hard, and seemed to find no consolation in her other children; sometimes she would go days without speaking.

The girls grew taller, and Moonhorn's breasts began to swell. Eyas became a sturdy little crawler, curious and lively and always underfoot. His sisters fussed over him and complained about him, and seemed to enjoy doing both. The adults watched him grow, marveling at how like each baby was to all others, and how different. Darkhair and Netweaver thought he was much easier than the girls had been; his mothers thought him much worse, and were always hauling him away from the fire or some sharp tool. Quiet often lost her temper at him, which always provoked Firewing to defend him; at last Quiet simply ignored him. His summer tan faded, and his thick black hair made him seem even paler; his eyes lost their baby blueness and turned gray.

Sometimes, especially after Quiet's miscarriage, Darkhair would watch Eyas and feel a vague anxiety. He was their only son, and so the only child who would stay a Fisher. What kind of family would it become, when a Sunnish-born man carried its name and standing?

After such thoughts, he would mock himself for becoming like the old browsers who despaired of the younger generation, and then he would turn to other concerns: work, food, coupling, books, or wine. And then he would sleep until Admiral Thorn returned to leer down at him, hissing in his ear, and Hemlock called to him from great distances, wailing like a child caught in a nightmare.

The New Year found them once more at Gathering Cove, even Silken and Brightspear. The Goddess came and went, without taking special note of Eyas or the other Suns. But She took memories of Mud Bay and wove them into remembrance; thereafter, all who came to the Gatherings would see Huntwell convulse with his own knife in his throat, see the Sunnish soldiers die in their longboats, and feel the shock of Darkhair's wounds.

For Darkhair and the others who gave their memories of the battle, it now seemed oddly unreal: a vivid vision, like that of Quickhand's death, rather than a private recollection. Darkhair felt somehow cheated, as if he had lost standing through no fault of his own.

Odd, also, was the People's response to sharing memories of the battle. They stopped thinking about the Suns. The veterans found themselves boring others; war-party drills, which had been fashionable for a year, were held less often, and finally abandoned altogether. The gleaming weather of the spring and summer of the year 243 turned everyone's thoughts to fishing, farming, hunting, trade, and wandering. The battle was now as remote as the Goddess's visions of the Gulf under the glaciers.

Yet every month Darkhair walked up the Easthaven trail to Silken's cabin, to bring her new books and to learn all he could about the Dominance and its world. She told him of the Suns' origins as a Desert Band, their migration south through Transmontane into the White Mountains and then into the Grasslands and Lake Country; of the early wars, the rise of the War Kings, their supplanting by the Three Families, and the final triumph of the royal cause in the founding of the Sun Dominance by Topaz Savior. Darkhair learned—or tried to learn—how the Dominance was organized and governed, but could make little sense of it.

When Darkhair asked about the Suns' warlore, she could give little more than descriptions of sack and slaughter: castles wrecked by cannon, pikemen and archers cut down by guns. That had been the fate of Steeledge's armies, once those of Silvershield had been equipped with firearms, but the better-armed cultists had been stalled for years by ambush, speed, and stealth. Darkhair thought of the ancient feuds still alive in remembrance, and brooded over similar strategies that might be used if Silvershield ever sent his forces into the Gulf.

She told him more as well, tales of magnificent cities and vast plains, rivers so wide they seemed like seas, mountains grander and crueller than the Gulf's, and of the countless swarming peoples of the Dominance and Delta. Darkhair's imagination swelled with her stories like a dabbler pup tearing itself from its birth sac and spreading its wings for the first time.

The Fishers listened at first with interest to the stories he brought from Silken's cabin, but eventually they grew bored. Netweaver listened impassively and then laughed that not only windwalkers could tell lies.

"Warlore is men's concern," Griptiller said. "And Sunnish politics are those of fools ruled by murderers. Learn what you can, but don't trouble us about such things."

"You're too tolerant of her," Firewing chided him one night as they lay together. "Lugging all those books back and forth, listening to her brag. There's something sick about her, anyway. A woman shouldn't live alone, without wives or husbands."

"She is sick, you know."

"What with?"

"It's women's business, but the Suns have no shame and she told me once."

"Well, spit it out."

"She can't control her fertility."

"Can't—" Firewing's body tensed against his.

"Sunnish women never know when coupling will make

62

them pregnant. A woman may conceive without wanting to."

"That's—terrible. And they call themselves human! No wonder there are so many of them."

"They breed like spiders. All the People would scarcely fill one of their cities."

"Disgusting. It's just as well, then, that she seeks no family. She'd be dropping a child every year. What do they do after they've had two children?"

"Have more."

"But the Goddess—their own gods must tell them not to have too many."

"Just the reverse. So they keep on spreading out, looking for more land."

"I don't want to hear any more. Are you coupling with her?"

It was his turn to be shocked. Adultery was a serious offense, one of the most serious that the People could judge without recourse to the Goddess. The penalty was a loss of all standing unless the adulterers' spouses chose to give up some of their own standing by forgiveness. Even then, the scandal usually outlived those involved.

"After what I just told you? How could I face the Goddess, or my family?" Realizing at last that she was mocking him, he added, "I contend with enough women in my life."

She rubbed herself against him, warm and sleek, and nipped his ear. "Contend with me," she whispered.

Silken had thought she would be bored and lonely in the cabin; instead, she sometimes yearned for a moment's peace. She had not put pot to fire since girlhood, and now she must cook; clothes tore, and with growing skill she mended them. On a shoulder-yoke she carried water from the brook; on her knees she weeded the garden.

The work had the interest of novelty at first, and before it palled she challenged herself to grow skilled at her chores. But sometimes she wished her father had been one of the old-fashioned Men who made their children do males' and females' work. Instead, new to wealth, he had raised his children in idlenss and gaming. She did not resent his misguided love and indulgence. He had lived to see his sons die at the cultists' hands, his wife raped and burned alive. He himself had died, gratefully, on the last retreat through Jadeland to Copper Bay, knowing his last child's fate was bound with that of the defeated Sun. Whatever his failings, her father had paid for them.

But not even the most gently reared Woman could have survived five years of battles and retreats without gaining useful skills. Silken had grubbed for water root, set snares for longears, and used a bow; in one desperate night skirmish, she had stabbed a young cultist soldier who thought her a helpless girl. She had been good enough at axhand—the deadlist of combat arts—to delight Steeledge and scandalize his lieutenants.

One gift her parents had given her, as she grew into womanhood: "Use your sex, or it will use you," they had told her. When Steeledge had taken her into his household, she had obeyed that advice. She made love with him when he desired her, but did not hunger for him when he slept elsewhere. Now he was gone forever, and she slept alone without regret.

The Woman Emerald had not been a friend to Silken; they had shared the same man but little else, and had kept their distance from each other. Yet now she wished the Sun's Consort were here to watch her son growing.

Brightspear had always been strong and sturdy, and now he flourished like a tree in summer. He grew quickly and was tall for his age. If he had much of his father's grim reserve, his mother's gaiety sometimes glinted in his eyes, and laughed on his beautiful mouth. Before the flight from Copper Bay he had known only a vagabond life in a succession of camps and castles; the pet of the soldiers, he had known tactics better than his letters. Now Silken resolved to educate him so that when he returned to claim his birthright he would be more than a mere bumpkin-warrior.

At first, for lack of anything else, she drilled him from the Fishers' books. He mastered the Gulf dialect readily, and was soon translating short passages into Jadelandic, the Sunnish dialect he had learned on his nurses' laps. Silken taught him High Sunnish as well; the old ceremonial dialect was much like that spoken by the People of the Gulf.

As paperbark became available, she wrote down as much as she could remember of the great books of the Dominance: *The Boast of Twice Vengeance, The Precepts of Topaz Savior, The Fall of Palisade,* and *The Death of NameWoman Whiteflower*. She wrote as well a history of the Dominance, so he would know the extent and value of his inheritance.

Night after night, through their long second summer in the cabin, Brightspear's clear voice lilted through the darkness and rose toward the glowing Bridge, sounding the proud words of warrior poets and his own divinely inspired ancestors. One evening, when the northwestern sky still held a deep blue twilight, he recited a famous passage from *Redsandal's Glories* that ended:

> "While the Bridge shall stand
> The Sun will rule with much might.
> His sword will slay cloudbrutes.
> His lance will fell centaurs.
> He will cast down all rebels.
> Fear and sharp sorrow shall scourge his foes.
> Out of night he will come, startling Alland,
> His squadrons' hoofs heavy, breaking stones.
> The Sun will overthrow all folly and evil.
> The Sun will bring life and joyous light—
> Sun unsetting, pursuer of darkness,
> While the Bridge shall stand."

"So may it be with you as with the Sun Redsandal," Silken said in High Sunnish. Sitting beside her in the doorway of the cabin, Brightspear stroked her arm.

"It will. Someday, when I am grown, I will take back the Dominance."

"Perhaps. With an army of Nakeds at your back," she smiled.

"Do you think they would follow me?"

"When they see what a true Sun is, I think they would. They are savages, but good warriors, or they would never have beaten Admiral Thorn. You could offer them good fighting."

"I will make them wear clothes and drive away the brutes, and obey the Sunteachings."

"I am sure you will."

"I will take them to the armies my father sent into the west, and then we will conquer my uncle and kill him. Then I will raise a big, big army and march on Delta, and then on the Dawn Coast and Homeland. And when all men are under the Dominance, I will conquer the centaurs and lotors and windwalkers."

"Ah, will you indeed!"

"Don't laugh at me. I am the Sun, and I will do what I say I will do."

She studied his grim face in the twilight. This was no boyish boasting. Brightspear was scarcely seven years old, yet majesty was in him. If accident or the usurper's spies did not strike him down first, his manhood would be very great. Future generations would recite his deeds, and yearn for a tenth of his glory. The Sun in Heaven had willed that she must rear and protect him and set him on his path to become the Sun on Earth.

With an urgency that dizzied her, Silken gripped his shoulders.

"Yes. What you say you will do, will be done. It will be done."

Late that summer, Longstrand drowsed in heat. The centaurs slept in their tents far down the shore; across the cloudless sky, a distant flying island drifted like a jellyfish in a tide pool. Darkhair and Netweaver sat cross-legged on the sand in front of the boatshed, repairing nets. Despite his name, Netweaver was bad at the job, and kept clicking his tongue in annoyance at his own clumsiness. Darkhair worked with a baleful concentration. Eyas wobbled about on the sand nearby, trying to catch Chirp; the spider avoided Eyas's clumsy fingers without abandoning him.

"What's bothering you, Darkhair?" The question was gently put.

"It shows, does it?"

"To me, anyway?"

"The women?"

"I don't think so. They know your moods; they think this is nothing special. . . . It's Silken, isn't it?"

Darkhair took his time replying. "In a way. It's mostly myself. I anger myself. A man ought to be more of a man when he nears forty, but I feel like a silly boy."

"What, dreaming of young girls?"

"They're the least of my worries." He squinted across the sand at the calm water. Squeaking like a spider himself, Eyas pursued Chirp down to the water's edge and back again. "I wish I were young and somewhere else, seeing the great cities, having a real wanderyear. Netweaver—I wish for wars."

"It *is* Silken," his husband muttered. Darkhair ignored him.

"Look out there. In four days we could be at the head of North Inlet—the far side of the world. In a day and a half we could be at Ripmouth. Anywhere we went, we'd find relatives and friends, and enemies, who all know us as well as we know them. We'd hear the same gossip, the same songs. Everything the same as here, the same as a century ago." He studied the tattoos on their forearms: Netweaver wore the Fisher tattoo on his left arm and the stylized triangular leaves of his birth family, the Summerblooms, on his right. "The past lies on us like a stone. The dead guide our every step."

"No, the Goddess does."

"By showing us our past, Netweaver. And all it holds is ourselves, over and over again. It—it used to be enough for me, but not anymore."

"Her tales make you want wandering."

"But I'm a happily married man, with children and standing, not some dreamy boy. I feel stupid. Eyas! Quit pestering Chirp."

Eyas came running up from the water, a grin on his round face; the spider was perched on his head. She chittered and tapped nervously on Eyas's hair, but she wasn't seriously upset.

"Funny, funny. I'm funny!" Eyas bellowed.

"You're funny, all right," Netweaver chuckled. He put down the net and took Eyas onto his lap. Chirp jumped to the sand and minced into the shade of the boatshed; then she sat still, her eight eyes gleaming like miniature roundstones.

"Here's someone different," Netweaver remarked, hugging the boy.

"Is he? For all the fuss She made over him, he's just a little boy."

"Who plays tag with spiders."

"He was just chasing her."

"Look at her now. She's waiting for him to chase her again. She's never done that with anyone else. She'll jump on you when she wants some petting, but she won't play."

The boy, ignoring his fathers' conversation, sucked his thumb as he snuggled against Netweaver's brown chest. He giggled at Chirp, who irritably waved her front feet.

"Darkhair, I think he and Chirp understand each other."

"She's not stupid."

"More than that. Chirp—climb on my arm. Come on, good

67

girl, climb on my arm." Netweaver held his hand close to the spider, but she didn't move.

"You'll be talking to walkingtrees next," Darkhair snorted.

"Eyas—tell Chirp to get on Father's arm."

"Geh ah Fah ahm," Eyas said without removing his thumb. Chirp scuttled backward. "Doh wah."

"I know she doesn't want to. Tell her no nonsense."

With a good imitation of Firewing's firmest tone, Eyas said, "Geh ah Fah *ahm!*"

The spider slowly advanced and crawled up Netweaver's arm to his shoulder. She chittered at Eyas, who only laughed and pulled out his thumb.

"Chup wah pway, Fah! Down, down!" And he waddled across the sand while Chirp—abandoning Netweaver in a single leap—went racing after him.

"Goddess look under us," Darkhair said slowly. "If this isn't . . . happenstance, he has a power greater than all the Windinvokers put together. What could stand against a mind that knows a spider's thoughts? Could a windwalker lie to him? Could a centaur best him in trade?"

"We'll see." Netweaver began to shake with laughter. "You sit here, complaining about the dull life we lead, and our son speaks with a spider at our very feet!"

6

Some men look back on their childhood as if it were a dream of another world: the sun was hotter on their shoulders then, and brighter on the water. The bloodwood blooms were a richer red, and springbringers came sooner over the South Hills. The paths to the berry patches were broad and dappled with dusty sunlight, and two blackberries were all that a hand could hold; now the paths are narrow and dark, and the berries seem small and tasteless.

So it had been for Darkhair. But now he seemed to savor again the delight of a boy crushing summer's first ripe blackberry between tongue and palate. For him the sun was hot, the rain hard and clean, and the air sharp with salt. He skippered *Waveskimmer* with his old dash, alarming and delighting his wives and daughters. A life on the water aged some people too quickly; Darkhair seemed not to age at all, though each year went by more rapidly than the last.

Had Moonhorn ever been a little girl? She was a proud young beauty now, away for her wanderyear and then back again with a retinue of suitors; soon she was gone once more, the wife of two tall young fellows from Big Harbor and a plump girl from Wreck Point. Harper's turn came next: as good a farhearer as her mother Quiet, she married into the Summerblooms of Rainfalling and was considered likely to become that village's next Speaker. Goldarms, still the spoiled baby, was a great gawky girl, quick-tempered and bright.

Quiet neared middle age with little more than a few lines about her eyes and a softening of her hard, strong body. Firewing's yellow hair began to darken, and her big breasts sagged, but her tongue was as sharp as ever. Netweaver developed a paunch and a double chin that seemed to suit his cheerful stolidity. The Fishers, thought Darkhair, were aging well.

Silken gained acceptance in Longstrand, if not affection. She was seen more often in the village; she had become a good weaver and seamstress, and her winter cloaks and trousers of spidersilk were in demand. Within two or three years she was independent of the Fishers' generosity and soon after that was actually prosperous. A few families even included her in their children's schooling; the children seemed none the worse for the experience. Physically she changed little. Her hands were hard and calloused, like any woman's; her hips thickened a bit, though it was hard to tell since she persisted in wearing clothes. But even her modesty came to seem just an eccentricity.

Brightspear at eight left the cabin for his schooling, first in the Fishers' household and later in others. He was intelligent, a quick learner, and strong for his age. He was often picked on by other children, but never twice by the same ones. Darkhair, seeing a couple of the fights and hearing of others, was angry to find so many bullies among the People's children but took consolation in seeing them thrashed. Children usually fought each other by wrestling and clumsy kicks; Brightspear used the edges of his hands, and one or two punches were enough to discourage his tormentors.

The last of the fights was in Brightspear's twelfth summer,

when some young men from Northport arrived in Longstrand in the course of their wanderyear. The three of them, meeting the boy on Traders' Beach, began to bait him in front of a crowd, and tried to yank down his trousers. Though Brightspear was a big boy, he was only half the size of his attackers. Yet he bested them all in a strange dance of kicks and edge-handed blows. When it was over, one youth was curled up clutching his groin; the second sat gasping like a redfin on the sand, his breath knocked out; the third had a broken nose and a dislocated kneecap. Brightspear, not even breathing hard, looked calmly at his victims and walked away. By nightfall the clapsticks were rattling about the fight; for years afterward, "Northport odds" was a common phrase for any sure scheme that went wrong.

To the adults' relief, Brightspear attracted no followers. He could have caused real mischief, with a gang to do his bidding, but the other children treated him civilly and left him alone. He did not seem to mind.

The families who schooled him found him apt, but uninterested in choosing a special skill. By the time he was twelve he could make wine and beer, weave spidersilk, sail a boat, and work wood. He was a good athlete, and knew almost all the People's books by heart. He was good with clapsticks (though an indifferent singer), and promising as a mockery duelist.

At thirteen Brightspear was inducted into Longstrand's brotherhood, though several men objected. He was not the quick student of war that many had expected him to be: unable to share in remembrance, he could not easily master the centuries of experience open to other men. Nor was he willing to share his own fighting secrets, which Darkhair wanted to make part of the brotherhood's warlore.

"I know only a little, which Silken has taught me," he explained. "And she, as a woman, knows fighting only from watching warriors like my father." Darkhair suspected that both Brightspear and Silken knew more than they admitted, but he had learned that there was no point in trying to force the boy to do anything he didn't want to.

Apart from his size and his pale skin, Brightspear seemed much like an ordinary boy. But he would not go naked, even on the hottest summer days, and he would have nothing to do with brutes. He avoided the centaurs' camp when they came to trade each summer, and never went up to the skyseed groves when the windwalkers came. He despised centaur iron, saying that the smiths of the Dominance threw away better work than that for which the People paid so much; and he would not even touch a bottle or spearpoint of windwalkers' glass. As he grew older he saw how his hatred of the brutes embarrassed others, and kept his opinions to himself.

Accepted but friendless, Brightspear grew up like Anger's Rock: people saw him until they ceased to notice him, and went around him by force of habit. If he resented such treatment, he gave no sign of it.

Only Eyas seemed to like Brightspear. When the older boy came for his schooling at the Fishers', Eyas was a lively three-year-old; he soon learned Brightspear could not be nagged, but when asked politely would carry him on his shoulders or tell him Old Stories. Gripping Eyas by wrist and ankle, Brightspear would whirl him around and then fling him into the water. Squealing and splashing, Eyas would clamor for more.

Perhaps because Eyas was also Sunnish, or because the younger boy's liking for him was so sincere, Brightspear was patient with him. Even after Brightspear moved on to other families, Eyas followed him around; if only for that, the Fisher women were ready to forgive Brightspear almost anything.

"That boy would madden a family post," Firewing often said, usually after Eyas had come close to burning the house down, or drowning himself. "At least Brightspear knows how to keep him out of trouble." But she tolerated no criticism of Eyas from anyone else.

"Everybody spoils that child," Griptiller complained when Eyas was ten. "He's a great lump, never does a chore if he doesn't feel like it, and he's always playing pranks." She was sitting in her usual place by the fire, wrapped in a blanket though the spring afternoon was warm; age was telling on her at last.

"That's not so!" snapped Firewing. "He's as hardworking as any boy his age; he's just high-spirited."

"Scatterbrained. Just the other day I set him to roasting a dabbler, and he wandered off to watch Netweaver smoke some fish. The dabbler was burned black. Black!"

Firewing sighed and bit back an argument. The dabbler had been burned almost two years before.

"And Goddess look under us when there's a centaur within

71

an hourmarch," the old woman grumbled on. "That boy just vanishes. Comes back smelling like a centaur himself, spouting words they teach him. Don't know why he bothers—they all know our tongue well enough."

"Eyas is the only one I've ever heard of who *could* learn their tongue," Firewing said. "I'm proud of him."

"All that coughing and hacking—he'll ruin his throat, trying to talk like them."

"Perhaps you should ask the Goddess to make him quit," Firewing suggested dryly.

"Oh, the Goddess dotes on him. She wouldn't hear a word against him."

This was as close to impiety as Griptiller had ever come. Firewing looked at her, and saw in her wrinkled face the signs of pain concealed. Griptiller's bowels and joints had been troubling her for a long time; Firewing realized it was pain that made her so testy.

"Perhaps She has Her reasons."

"No doubt. But I wish She wouldn't seem so sad when She greets him each year." Griptiller pulled her blanket more tightly around her, and glanced at the bench where Hemlock had always sat. "She knows more than She tells us. I think some horrible fate will befall the People through him. At least I will not live to see it."

Quiet and Firewing often picked blackberries along the foot of the cliff behind the village. It gave them a respite from the family's squabbles and demands, and from the hectic socializing of the beach; a few scratches were worth it. On one hot afternoon, they filled their bags and sat in a shady clearing to cool off before the walk home.

"I've been having strange dreams," Quiet said.

"You're lucky; I never remember mine."

"Then you're the lucky one. I see Hemlock in them, and others. I think the others are dead too. They speak to me, and I try to understand, but I can't. It's—I remember my father Cedarburl, after he lost his speech. He used to watch us, as if our words almost made sense, and sometimes he tried to say something but nothing came out. That's what the dreams are like."

"Do you think they really mean something?"

". . . I'll tell you a secret, Firewing. In the Windinvokers, there are tales about the dead speaking to the living in dreams. They guide those who understand, and give them great power. I think the tales are true."

Her wife frowned. "I've heard such stories too, from old browsers losing their wits and silly girls who haven't found theirs yet. The Goddess says nothing about such things. Why should we wonder about them?"

Quiet shook her head in irritation. "Don't you ever wonder about anything? *Think*, Firewing. The Goddess guides us in some things, but not in all; perhaps the dead can tell us much."

"They speak to us through remembrance. Isn't that enough for you?"

"No. Not any more.—Do you wonder what happens to us when we die?"

"What a question! We go into the sea with the Goddess, and the songs with the People, and we live in remembrance. If we've been good People, the Goddess sends us to live on the Bridge of Heaven. Everybody knows—"

"Then why does Hemlock call to me? Why do I wake from my dreams as if something marvelous, something precious, had just escaped me?"

Firewing said nothing. Mosquitoes keened around her, and she slapped one; it left a red smear on her arm, blood mixed with berry juice.

"You're smarter than I am," she said at last. "If you want to talk with the dead, you'll find a way to do it. But don't tell me what they say, Quiet."

"If you wish." She seemed flattered by Firewing's respect. "And don't tell the men."

Quiet laughed, a melodious sound in the shimmering air. "Never. How would they understand? Come; it's time to go home."

They walked slowly, lazily out of the clearing, down the sun-dappled path: two women in graceful middle age, their long hair bound up, complaining cheerfully of the heat and mosquitoes. In the deep shade of the berry vines, Bright-spear squatted still and silent, watching the women go.

7

The skyseed grove nearest Longstrand was several hour-marches away, on the south-facing slope of a large hill beyond Easthaven. It was a damp, misty place. The skyseed trunks rose thickly from the ground cover of ankle-deep winterberry and patches of salal. Depending on the tree's age, its trunk might be pale green or mottled yellow, and as narrow as a man's wrist or as thick as his leg. Without a single leaf, each trunk reached ten to fifteen spans above the ground before it swelled into the sphere of the pod, three spans in diameter and taut with the pressure of the gas within in. At the base of the pod was the brown ring of the seedcase.

Crowding each other for light, the pods formed a solid roof overhead. They tugged and swayed in the breeze, hissing as their tough skins rubbed against each other. Untended, the pods would yellow and lose much of their buoyancy before breaking free to fly. But this grove had been carefully tended by Longstrand and Easthaven for over a century.

One day in early summer, Eyas and his sister Goldarms walked up an old path that wound through the grove. Goldarms was fifteen now, tall and a little gangly. Next summer she would go on her wanderyear and—her parents hoped—find a family to marry. With the older girls gone now to Big Harbor and Rainfalling, the adults were looking forward to a few years of peace before Eyas went off and brought home the beginnings of a new Fisher generation.

That time was still far away. At eleven, Eyas was still just a skinny boy, all elbows and knees. Thick, dark-black hair fell low over his gray eyes and onto his shoulders. The white tattoo of the Fishers stood out on his tanned forearm. Like his sister, he carried an iron-headed ax on his shoulder. As he walked he gave each skyseed trunk what he liked to think was a judicious look. Goldarms, behind him, snorted amusedly.

"Can't wait, can you?"

"Sure I can." But this was the first year he'd been allowed

74

to do more than tag along to the harvest, and he had been looking forward to it.

They came to a small clearing, made partly by a rocky outcrop and partly by last year's harvesters. It was ringed by trees struggling to reach the extra sunlight. The rock was steep; when they clambered to the high north side, they could look down across the grove, over the tops of the pods, to the hazy green of the Bluemeadows Valley. The South Hills bristled on the horizon, their sharp peaks snow-crested. The afternoon was hot and still.

A gong sounded from the direction of Easthaven, faint and metallic. "They'll be here soon," Goldarms said. "Now, remember—no cutting till the island's right overhead and they've lowered their anchors. You judge the wind by watching their ropes, and seeing how the windwalkers fly. They get mad if too many pods blow away."

"I know, I know." Eyas fingered his ax.

"And don't cut the light-green ones. Just the dark greens and the ones with a little yellow on the pods."

"Yes, Goldarms." Eyas sighed. He paused, listening. From the west came a familiar blend of sounds: shouts of men and women, mingled with whoops and howls. Then came a low, rhythmic creaking, like that of a boat's rigging, only louder. A flying island was near.

It was not the first of the season; two others had arrived in the past ten days, one mooring near Three Springs and the other at Wreck Point. Seeing those islands over the Gulf, the People of Longstrand and Easthaven had known that Unsheath would soon be overhead; harvesters had headed for this grove, which Unsheath's line had owned for generations. Some of the harvesters grumbled, as usual, about the inconvenience of having the grove so far from any settlement, but most preferred it this way. An island moored over a village would be not only unnerving but dangerous: windwalkers were notoriously careless about what they dumped overboard.

The clearing was partly shaded by the pods overhead, but now a deeper shadow fell. Looking up, Eyas saw the irregular curve of the island's edge slowly block the sky. Within a few breaths, it covered the gap above the clearing.

The island looked, to Eyas, a little like a jellyfish. The main part was a shallow dome of netting, containing thousands of skyseed pods. The dome was hundreds of spans across and perhaps twenty spans thick. At its center, invisible from this

75

angle, rose a tall cone of pods at least fifty spans high. The yellow-green mass of pods looked, from the ground, as a cloud might with its underside lit by the setting sun.

Beneath the dome, suspended by long ropes, hung the cylindrical wicker gondolas that the windwalkers lived in. Other ropes trailed like the tentacles of a jellyfish; some carried great stones, to stabilize the island in flight, and others ended in iron hooks, to anchor it. These anchors were now falling swiftly, burying themselves in the soil of the grove.

The island was almost fifty spans above the clearing. At that height the gondolas, platforms, and rigging looked very small and fragile; the windwalkers themselves were small white dots or pink-and-white triangles, gliding from one rope or gondola to another. Their musical whoops and shouts were sharp and clear, announcing ritually their repossession of the grove below them.

Ax blows sounded among the trees. Skyseeds were rising now, their narrow, pliant trunks dangling below the pods. Windwalkers soared around them, sometimes gripping a trunk with their feet and guiding the pod to a particular part of the dome.

"We'd better get to work," Goldarms said. Choosing a tree, she swung her ax into its soft trunk. A few blows were enough to release it. Turning to Eyas, she saw him drop his ax and start running westward, darting between the trunks. "*Ey*-as!" she bellowed. "What are you—"

Goldarms stopped, hearing frightened wails in the distance. They didn't sound like a child's, but the distress in the cries made her follow her brother. As she ran she realized the cries were coming from above, and getting closer.

In the middle of a stand of immature skyseeds, Eyas stopped and looked up. The wailing rose to a shriek, and then stopped. Something thudded into a pod. A moment later, a small, grayish form fluttered down; Eyas caught it, staggering under the impact. Goldarms steadied him and then gaped at what he held in his arms.

"It's a baby windwalker!"

The little brute seemed scarcely larger than a human child of two. His downy fur was dark, and his limbs were very thin. Pink membranes, thickly laced with veins, hung slackly between his wrists and heels. Huge dark eyes stared fearfully in his squarish face; his protruding lips were parted in a grimace, showing dark gums and four baby teeth. Two slits in the long upper lip were all the nose he had; his large, round ears were flattened to his head.

"He doesn't weigh more than a spider," Eyas murmured. He cuddled the infant until the wails subsided to hiccuping sobs. Then the infant put his thumb in his mouth; Eyas and Goldarms burst out laughing.

"Silly little thing—you really scared yourself, didn't you?" Eyas said, rocking him gently. "He must have fallen from the island and glided down, without anyone noticing." He started back to the clearing, with Goldarms beside him.

"We'll have to get him back," she said. "We can take him to Anchorwood and give him to one of the traders."

"The traders don't come down till all the pods are cut. That won't be for another day and a half. He'll need his mothers before then."

"Mother, stupid. They only have one."

"Never mind." The infant squirmed and whimpered. Eyas smoothed the fine dark-gray fur; a long arm reached up, and fingers gripped the hair on the boy's nape.

"You've made another friend," Goldarms said.

"He's all right now, but he's upset and tired."

Goldarms saw a gleam in her brother's eye. She knew it well, and wondered what it meant this time. He tried to hand the windwalker to her, but the infant squeaked and clung tighter. Eyas sighed and let go; the infant seemed undisturbed, and went on clinging with one hand while sucking the thumb of the other.

With his hands freed, Eyas picked up his ax and chopped at a nearby skyseed, one a little larger than most. When the trunk was almost cut through, he climbed onto it, clinging to it just as the windwalker infant clung to him. With his ax still gripped in one hand, he swung clumsily at the cut below his feet while Goldarms stared in astonishment at him. Three more blows severed the trunk completely, and the pod rose slowly under its burden. Eyas dropped the ax and held tightly to the trunk; his hands and feet found purchase on the rough but flexible surface. The infant yelped when one of his wings was pinched between the boy and the trunk but made no other noise.

At last Goldarms found her voice: "*Eyas, get back down*

here!" It was a scream, and it brought others trotting into the clearing in time to see the skyseed lift above the grove and rise steadily toward the yellow-green mass of the island.

Netweaver watched his son and then turned to Goldarms with fear and something else, something worse, transforming his placid face.

"Father—I didn't know—I never dreamed—the baby fell. Eyas grabbed it—oh, ohh Eyas." She burst into tears. Netweaver held her, but his eyes were on the other men and women who had come into the clearing; he would not look up. Most of the others watched the slow rise of the pod, but one or two met Netweaver's gaze, and knew his thoughts. He spoke them anyway, without willing them:

"It's a breach of the Concord."

Eyas could see the whole forest beneath his feet. He wanted to wave, or to shout to the upturned faces in the clearing, but he didn't want to startle the infant.

He had not expected noises to be so sharp and clear: the *chunk-chunk* of axes, the whoops and howls of the windwalkers, Goldarm's sobs—all were intensely vivid. His sight seemed sharper too. He saw the smokes of Easthaven rising white against the blue of Elbow Inlet and the green mountains on the other side of the water. The pod turned, and he saw the Sunnish tower far away on the cliff above Longstrand. Two days ago he'd been playing People and Suns with other children in the tower; now he saw it as no one ever had before. Beyond its broken-tooth outline, the Gulf sparkled blue and white, and all the shores and islands rejoiced in the greens and golds of summer. Eyas laughed, dizzy with the height, and felt his ears pop.

The pod was rising more slowly than the others, and now no more were being cut loose. Two windwalkers banked and dropped to investigate; when they saw Eyas and the infant, their jutting lips skinned back from their teeth in astonishment, and one of them hooted sharply. They caught an updraft, soared above the pod, and circled down with slender weapons in their long-fingered fists: wooden swords, edged and pointed with glass.

These windwalkers looked much more formidable than the infant nestled under Eyas's chin. As tall as the boy himself, they had arms and legs twice as long as his, and short but massive torsos. Each wore a black leather harness that ran over the shoulders, down either side of a jutting breastbone, and joined at the crotch. White fur covered their pinkish-brown skin over most of their bodies, and their faces were made fierce with ornate scars.

"Hello, brothers," Eyas called to them. "I'm bringing your baby home to you."

They hovered without replying for a moment; then each in turn rose, dived, and kicked out at the pod, deflecting it to the center of the island where most of the gondolas and platforms hung. Eyas almost lost his grip with the first kick, but he was ready for the second one. The pod drifted past one of the furled sails that were used to help steer the island, bounced sluggishly from a rope, and rose to within two or three spans of one of the largest gondolas. A windwalker standing on the roof of the gondola flicked out a weighted rope that wound itself tightly about the trunk, not far above Eyas's head; Eyas whistled, impressed at the accuracy of the throw and aware of what would have happened if the stone on the rope's end had hit him.

The pod halted, bobbing gently. The windwalker pulled until Eyas and the infant were above the gondola.

"Get down," the windwalker commanded. Eyas slid down the trunk and dropped half a span. The gondola's roof scarcely vibrated.

It was much larger than it had seemed from below. Its roof was almost six spans long, and three spans wide before curving down into the walls. The tightly woven wicker had been coated with some clear, shiny substance, perhaps as weatherproofing. At each end of the gondola roof, and in the middle, were closed hatchways. The middle one, almost at Eyas's feet, flipped open; a windwalker's head emerged. The infant yelped and struggled for the first time to free himself from Eyas.

The windwalker shot out of the hatch and swept the infant into her arms; he whimpered fretfully until he found a nipple in her yellowish-white fur. His mother uttered a few sharp cries—"Ah! Ah! Ah!"—and dropped back inside. A confused chatter erupted inside the gondola.

Eyas looked at the male windwalker, who had just released the pod and was coiling his rope without a glance at the boy. The pod was already far overhead, and the ground even farther below.

Another male, large and wearing a red harness, landed on the gondola. Eyas saluted him with an open palm.

"I greet Unsheath the Great Wing," he said formally, as he had heard his fathers speak during the trading at Anchorwood. "I am Eyas Fisher of Longstrand."

"Am I Unsheath?" the windwalker asked in a hoarse, sibilant voice.

"You wear the red harness."

"You are the Goddess boy. The Goddess nursed you."

"She did."

"But you break the Concord, Goddess boy."

"I brought back a baby. Perhaps he is your son."

"Ah!" Unsheath called down through the hatch. Someone replied in a nervous burst of hoots and squawks. The windwalker turned his gaze on Eyas again. "Come inside."

He followed Unsheath down a rope, into a wide, low room about two spans long. It was compactly furnished with wooden boxes and shelves. In a corner stood a big clay pot, with Longstrand's distinctive red glaze. The floor was thickly strewn with a dry, sweet-smelling grass that served as carpet, seat, and blanket. Two round windows, with real glass, admitted a soft, indirect light.

The mother and baby were not the only ones in the room; three other females and four or five children sat crouched in the grass, their wings wrapped around them. All looked down, and seemed afraid to look at Unsheath or Eyas. Unsheath took the rescued infant from his mother, sniffed him, and stroked his gray fur. He spoke briefly to the mother, who replied almost inaudibly. Unsheath sucked in his breath with a hiss, and the mother cowered.

The Great Wing turned and went through a narrow doorway into the next room. Eyas followed. This room was much like the first, except that it had four windows—two of them in the end wall—and its walls were hung with short-shafted, glass-tipped spears. Both of the end windows were swung open on what looked like leather hinges.

Unsheath seated himself between the end-wall windows, and regarded Eyas expressionlessly.

"My son fell from one of these windows. His mother saw nothing. I would have slit her wings and sent her after him if he had died. She would find no place in the endless sky of the deathworld. She would fall forever."

Eyas was alarmed at the casualness in Unsheath's words,

but interested too: he had never heard mention of windwalkers' religion or beliefs. Hoping his tact was not too obvious, he tried to change the subject.

"He is a strong little flier."

"He is my son. But you have broken the Concord. No human may set foot on an island."

Eyas said nothing. He began at last to be truly afraid.

"You are a child. But you know the Concord."

"Yes. My fathers tell me it is for the good of both our peoples."

"Ah, ah. But we both pay prices. We do not raid your villages. You do not attack our islands. To make sure, we never come to land until the harvest is done. You never come to our islands, anytime."

"I know the Concord," Eyas said with a hint of sharpness. "Should I have slain your son when he fell into my arms?"

Unsheath's hands rose to his face in surprise. "He is only an infant."

"And I am only a boy, offering help."

"I obey the Concord."

"Great Wing, you would have taken vengeance if you learned your son had died by the Concord. If I die, will the skyseed groves last another day? My fathers would set fire to them, and the People would honor them for it. What is the good of obeying the Concord if you destroy the Concord?"

The windwalker grinned and rocked a little on his haunches.

"Ah, ah, you are the Goddess boy," he said, as if that explained a great deal. "I owe you my son's life."

"And I owe you mine."

"I am pleased." Eyas knew that meant a satisfactory bargain had been struck. "Sit." Unsheath barked a command in his own language; his wife, the infant clinging to her, appeared in the doorway. She held a strange orange fruit in her hand; shyly, she offered it to Eyas.

"I give you food. You are my guest and my friend."

"I thank you." Eyas took the fruit, peeled it, and ate the tart, pulpy segments. The infant wriggled away from his mother and crawled into Eyas's lap. The boy gave him part of the fruit, and smiled as the infant gobbled it down. Unsheath looked pleased.

"Soarfar he was named, and named well. He has made his own concord with you, and we shall abide by it."

"So shall the People," Eyas replied.

They ate and talked together. As house-proud as any newlywed husband, Unsheath showed off the gondola's furnishings. He boasted of his glassware, saying his glaziers were the finest among all the windwalker lines; he used his sword to split one of Eyas's hairs as proof. He spoke also of raids and warfare.

"When the winds will it, we fly south across the mountains to the big river, where the canal diggers live, and we raid them. Ah, they make good iron, good as centaurs'—and free for the taking. If the winds are very kind, we cross the mountains sooner, to the many lakes where the cannon men live in big cities. They are strong fighters, stronger than the canal diggers, and it is hard to take prizes." Unsheath opened a box and displayed four blackened lumps. "Ears I took from cannon men."

"They are the men we call Suns?" Eyas regarded the trophies with mixed awe and disgust.

"Yes, Suns. Many of them, like trees on the mountains. And the others are many too."

The canal diggers must be the Deltans; Silken had told him about them, an ancient empire that would inevitably fall under the rule of the Dominance.

"I wish I could see them someday."

"You go where you wish, Goddess boy. To the centaur country, the desert men, the river men, the lotors by the Narrow Sea."

"I've heard of lotors—tall brutes, covered with fur."

"Yes, yes. Very strange. Good archers. We do not fight lotors. Their women live in some towns, their men live in others. Very strange. All groundwalkers are strange."

Eyas laughed, and Unsheath laughed with him.

Feet thumped on the roof, and a hoarse voice called out. Unsheath replied tersely. The hatch swung up, and a scarred face peered down at them. The newcomer spoke at some length, but received only a negligent wave for an answer. The hatch closed again.

"Your family wants you back. Are you ready?"

"I wish I could stay longer, but I will go. Perhaps someday I will come back."

"Yes. And journey with us across the far seas to the other lands, to our home cliffs on the other side of the world."

That they came from a place outside Alland was an often-repeated windwalker claim, and one that few People believed.

Alland, after all, was Alland; what more could there be? But Eyas believed. He sensed power and cruelty and pride in Unsheath, but no deception.

"That would be a journey worth taking. May it come soon."

Unsheath stood and reached out an awesomely long arm to a box by the wall; opening it, he drew out a red harness.

"Only the Great Wing among us may wear red," he said. "But this shall be a gift, and a sign of our friendship."

"I accept it gladly."

The harness was almost too small, and it felt odd and constricting in his crotch. Eyas gave Soarfar a last hug and handed him, wailing, to his mother. Then he followed Unsheath out the hatch, which was not far above his head.

The Great Wing's appearance drew a swarm of attendants, all of them males carrying swords in scabbards fixed down their backs. A few orders from Unsheath sent them whooping off in various directions. Some returned with ropes, which they hooked to Eyas's harness and then to their own. He felt a spurt of fear again: he was too heavy to be sustained by four windwalkers; he would pull them all to their deaths. A shout made him look up. Down from the dome came a windwalker, clinging easily to the trunk of a new skyseed. He must have pierced it, for it sank slowly under his weight.

"Hold tight to it, Eyas," Unsheath said. Then the long, powerful arms embraced him, and the wings enfolded him.

Eyas drew in a breath and stepped quickly off the roof. The skyseed pod jerked downward under his weight, and he could hear the hiss of escaping gas. Spreading their wings, his escorts hung almost motionless on either side. Their wings filled like sails, slowing their descent. When Eyas looked up, he saw Unsheath standing on the roof, one hand raised; just beneath the Great Wing, a small pink face peeped through a window.

The air was full of windwalkers and their shouts: dozens circled, curious to see the human boy. Some of the younger ones shot to within a span or two of Eyas's bearers, until a warning bark drove the gawkers to a more respectful distance.

Their course was a tightening spiral that seemed endless until the grove was just below; then Eyas wished they might fly on forever. But the pod to which he clung was almost empty, and the windwalkers' wings beat hard now to slow their descent.

Brown faces looked up from a harvested patch. The boy,

the windwalkers, and the pod came close to the ground and the People scattered to give them room. Eyas's feet crushed winterberry leaves, and he let go of the pod. He unhooked the ropes from his harness and the four windwalkers rose again with powerful wingbeats.

Netweaver and Darkhair walked slowly to their son; Goldarms was sobbing on some other girl's shoulder. Darkhair gripped Eyas's shoulders and looked into his gray eyes.

"Thank the Goddess your mothers weren't here. They'd have—" He shook his head, and then embraced his son in arms as powerful as Unsheath's. "Goddess look under us— what a deed!"

8

On a drizzly morning in early spring, Eyas splashed up the path to Silken's cabin. He wore a spidersilk blanket that shed the rain, but his hair was soaked and lay in black strands down his neck and back. He was just twelve, but walked with a grown man's deliberate stride.

"What is it?" asked Silken as she opened the door. Behind her, Brightspear sat cross-legged on the hearth, a book open on his lap.

"Have you seen Goldarms? She went out hunting yesterday, and didn't come back."

"No—Brightspear, have you seen her?"

He shook his head and stood up. At seventeen he was a full span tall, and still growing; Silken, herself tall for a woman, scarcely reached his shoulder.

"Where was she going?" he asked Eyas.

"Toward Easthaven, she said."

"She usually visits when she comes this way," Silken said. "But we didn't see anyone yesterday. Brightspear was out hunting too—"

"South, toward the Valley," Brightspear said. "But I saw no one. Eyas, we'll have to search for her. She may have hurt herself. Where are your fathers?"

"They're searching already—they've gone up the Easthaven road. And Firewing and Quiet, and some others."

Brightspear pulled on a blanket much like Eyas's, but woven in a Sunnish pattern by Silken. "Let's go. We'll get the Forester boys first."

It was like him to take charge; Eyas had seen Brightspear grow into a leader needing only followers. But he had remained solitary, seeking no friends and only rarely accepting even Eyas's company. For his part, Eyas had lost his early fondness for Brightspear. On a hunting trip once, Brightspear had slain a woodsrunner before Eyas could protest—and then had cut open the shaggy, humanlike torso to eat the brute's heart. It had been done not out of hunger but to show that Brightspear did not feel bound by the ways of the People. Eyas had felt humiliated and guilty just to witness the blood-soaked feast, though he had been only ten at the time and unable to stop the older boy. But Brightspear had reminded Eyas of their common Sunnish origins, and that perhaps had also been part of his purpose—like his contemptuous words about Gulf men's failure to rule their women, and his obscene boasting about his father's twenty concubines.

Eyas had left Brightspear alone lately, but in woodlore the older youth was the best in the Gulf. If anyone could find Goldarms, it was he.

Brightspear took a pouch and filled it with bread, then lifted a spear from its rack on the wall. Its head was a leaf of copper, since Brightspear refused to use centaur iron. The metal glinted redly in the light from the fire.

"Don't expect me before dark," he told Silken brusquely.

With the Forester boys, Eyas spent the rest of the day following Brightspear down a score of trails. Some were mere splithoof runs, invisible beneath the salal, and even the Foresters were strangers to most of them. But Brightspear knew them all, and moved along them as silently as the mist. More than once they surprised game, and even glimpsed the black-and-gold stripes of a prowl. A dozen times they came down to the shores of Easthaven Inlet, and then climbed back into the woods. Once in a while they heard distant voices calling Goldarms, but Brightspear ordered the boys to keep silent: "We'll hear better if we don't deafen ourselves with our own bellowing."

In midafternoon the rain stopped; shafts of sunlight pierced the misty forests. The searchers walked into Easthaven to learn whether Goldarms had been found. It was a much smaller village than Longstrand, facing the north arm of the inlet. Not many people were on the village's single muddy street, but Eyas recognized Sky Dunehouse, a girl of his own age, and greeted her.

"Everyone's off searching for your sister," she told him. "Your father Darkhair was here a while ago, and your mother Quiet. They looked worried. Oh, Eyas, she'll be all right. She's really good in the woods."

"Yes," Eyas nodded. "We just have to make sure."

But he was beginning to fear for his sister. Even Brightspear, good tracker that he was, had found no trace of her.

"Where did my parents go?" he asked.

"Down the Sandybank Road. Your grandmother Salal went with them."

Eyas grunted with surprise. Salal Windinvoker, Quiet's blood-mother, rarely left her longhouse these days; she hadn't even been to a Gathering in two or three years.

"Let's try to catch up with them," Brightspear said. The four searchers said good-bye to the girl and began jogging through the village and out along the road that led eventually to Sandybank, on the north side of the Bluemeadows River. The Forester boys, older than Eyas, commented appreciatively on what a beauty Sky was becoming; Eyas agreed, but saved his breath. Brightspear set an exhausting pace.

The road was steep and rocky, and exposed to the sun. They ran through knee-high mist, their tough feet impervious to stones. A blackbeak croaked from a hemlock as they passed, and then the rest of the flock moaned and yelped. Their cries carried a long way; then, when the searchers were well past the blackbeaks, the cries became suddenly muted.

Brightspear halted, looking puzzled. He spoke to his companions, but the faintness of his own voice made him stop. Eyas recognized what was happening, and leaned close to Brightspear:

"Someone is farhearing nearby."

Brightspear nodded, a little nervously, and they continued down the road. Just around a curve, where four logs bridged a creek, Quiet and her mother squatted together on the road. Darkhair stood beside them, leaning on a spear. He was watching the women and could not hear the four youths approaching until they were almost beside him.

Quiet and Salal paid no attention to the newcomers. They held each other's hands; their foreheads touched. Darkhair nodded to Eyas and the others, and then looked back at the women. His face was calm but weary. Eyas thought for the first time in his life that his father looked old: his beard was almost all white, and his face was deeply lined.

For a long time, nothing happened. Then Eyas felt an odd sensation—a kind of roaring in his ears. It faded. From a long distance, he heard heavy steps, the snap of a branch, the rustle of leaves. He was farhearing.

With startled detachment, Eyas stepped forward and placed his hands on the women's. At once the distant sounds sharpened. Quiet and Salal looked up, as surprised as Eyas. Then all three stood and turned to the east, where the sounds had come from, and at the same moment the sounds around them returned to normal. The creek splashed, the blackbeaks moaned, gravel rasped under Brightspear's feet.

"You heard it too," said Quiet.

"Yes. What was it?" asked Eyas.

"A giant," Salal said. "Only a giant. No human sound this side of Easthaven."

"Maybe the giant could tell us something," said Eyas.

His father shook his head impatiently. "Not many humans can converse with them—even if the giants wish to."

"I'm going to find him."

"No," Quiet said. "They can be dangerous. Perhaps he—"

She left the thought unspoken. Sometimes giants killed humans, seemingly out of curiosity or clumsiness rather than malice. The thought of Goldarms meeting such a death was unendurable.

"Mother, I must." He kissed her cheek and then Salal's, and gave his father a reassuring smile. Then he pulled off his cloak, tossed it to Winterberry Forester, and set off into the trees. He heard Darkhair call after him, and then the rustle of leaves as someone followed him. But he kept on, moving as swiftly as he could through the woods.

A hundred spans from the road he found a splithoof run, and followed it around a low hill; when it veered south, he went into the bushes again, keeping always east. The forest was dense and dark here; the ground was boggy. Only new ferns' bright green relieved the gloom.

Eyas kept on for almost an hour. Deadfalls blocked his way; thorns ripped his arms and legs. At last, on a steep hill, he paused. Which way? He had lost his bearings. The trees were so dense overhead that it was hard to tell whether the sun was still on his right. The woods were silent.

He tried to farhear again, unsure whether he could do it without the power of Quiet and Salal. He could: far behind him he heard squelching footsteps in a bog, and down the slope ahead something snuffled and chewed. Eyas moved down the hill. He put his feet down with care, not wanting to disturb the giant.

Fire had burned through this stretch of forest some years ago, leaving a long, narrow scar up the side of the hill. Blackberry, winterberry, and alder had made it green again, but it still seemed desolate. Coming to the edge of the scar, Eyas looked out from behind a blackened trunk. At the bottom of the slope, a stream ran glittering in the sun. Halfway between Eyas and the stream, waist-high in the young alders, stood the giant.

He was a span and a half tall, and proportionately broad and heavy. His face, with its flattened nose and protruding lips, was something like a windwalker's. But there the resemblance ended. The giant's body was massive, with limbs as thick as Eyas's chest. His face was hairless, with gray-brown skin. Elsewhere his body was covered in dense, glossy black fur.

The giant was facing Eyas, but was upwind and engrossed in eating winterberries. Very slowly, Eyas stepped out into the sunlit clearing. "Hello, giant," he said softly.

The great head lifted; dark eyes met his. Eyas kept walking into the alders, ignoring the occasional stab of a thorn. He followed the track the giant had made into the alder patch, a track of snapped saplings and crushed vines. When the giant shifted his weight, Eyas stopped, perhaps five spans away.

"I'm looking for a girl," he said. "As tall as I am, with long yellow hair. Her arm looks like my arm." He pointed to his tattoo. "Have you seen her?"

The giant watched him impassively. One vast hand, stained blue, carried a mass of berries to the gap-toothed mouth. The giant munched the berries.

Eyas repeated his question. Into his mind, unbidden, came an image of himself—small, hairless, absurdly frail. He realized he was seeing himself through the giant's eyes. The sensation was something like remembrance, and with that thought he suddenly saw the Goddess Herself—not in the

88

waters of the Gulf, but sporting on a strange, empty sea, along a coast of rocky cliffs. On the horizon, the sun was setting under orange clouds; the Goddess gleamed like gold in the water.

Now images tumbled into his mind: wooded valleys where men had never walked, Traders' Beach, Goldarms raising *Waveskimmer*'s sail, two infant giants rolling in play down a scree slope, an ice field high in the Eastwall, a hawk hovering over the Mistmarsh. It was a conversation, but the strangest Eyas had ever known. Dizzy, he tried to concentrate on images of Goldarms and the terrain around Easthaven. The giant replied with simple memories of drizzle in deep woods, a salmon scooped from the stream below, and then Eyas standing again amid the broken alders.

Eyas slumped, tired and disappointed, and angry with himself. Giants, after all, were almost never seen; this one was the first he had ever met. Why had he imagined the giant would know where Goldarms was? He felt like a foolishly impulsive little boy, seeking glory and only disgracing himself.

The giant strode forward. His hands lightly brushed Eyas's shoulders; the black eyes met the boy's. Eyas felt himself in the presence of something unimaginably old, older than the Goddess, than the mountains. The giant was no ordinary brute, and yet not a man. He was a mystery, as strange and free as the Goddess and as simple as a splithoof. Through the hard skin of his hands, a gentleness could be felt, and a strength not even centaurs could match.

Letting himself be consoled, Eyas stood still for a few breaths. Then he reached down and picked a handful of berries. Gravely the giant took them from Eyas's extended palm. Then he turned and walked purposefully across the alder patch and into the cedars on the far side of the clearing. When he was gone, Eyas turned back.

Brightspear stood behind a hemlock on the edge of the clearing. He studied Eyas with a mixture of amazement, respect, and distaste.

"Did you talk to it?"

"In a way. He didn't know anything about Goldarms."

Brightspear sighed and said, "That's no surprise. Come along; we've wasted the afternoon. We'll be lucky to reach Easthaven by nightfall. I wouldn't like to sleep in the woods with something like that lurking about."

Eyas laughed, a little shakily. "If a giant wanted you, he could take you—even from the old tower. But we'd be as safe sleeping here as in our own beds. He wouldn't hurt us."

"I wouldn't give it the chance to."

The boy said nothing more. They plodded back through the woods to the Sandybank Road, and then to Easthaven. Darkhair and Quiet were waiting for them in the Windinvoker longhouse. They urged Brightspear to stay the night, but he preferred to return home.

"There's an hour before full dark," he said. "Perhaps Goldarms will turn up along the road after all."

The rest of them sat in tense silence, picking at a cheerless supper. Near the end of the meal, Salal spoke sharply to Eyas:

"You farheard, boy."

"Yes, Grandmother."

"And you gave great strength to us."

"So did you and Mother Quiet to me."

"How far away was the giant?"

"About an hourmarch, or a little farther." Thinking of the distance made Eyas aware of dull, cramping pain in his legs.

"Not many can farhear that distance, and tell direction as well. You found the giant where you expected to?"

"Yes. . . . He was beautiful."

"I know. I thought so too, the one time I saw a giant. Long ago, long ago. But no Goldarms."

"I'll keep looking. And maybe the giant will see her."

Salal smiled wanly. "Giants don't concern themselves with humans."

"This one knows about the Goddess. He's seen her, where the sea has no islands and there are black cliffs."

Darkhair had been silent for a long time, staring into the fire. He looked up intently. "He told you this?"

"With his thoughts, yes. It was like remembrance."

"So it was with *my* giant," Salal nodded. "Well, well. A boy, and Sunnish-born at that, conversing with giants." She and Quiet exchanged glances, like two potters judging strange, fine ware.

In the days that followed, Eyas and Brightspear and many others kept up the search. But a month passed with no trace of Goldarms. One morning, when summer was near, Eyas arose to search again. The family still slept, but Quiet got up silently from Darkhair's side and followed her son. She stopped him by the family post.

"Stay, Eyas. Goldarms is dead."

"We don't—"

"She's dead. I dreamed of her last night. She's dead."

"You saw her in your dreams?"

"The ancestors told me. Believe me. They know everything, more even than the Goddess."

He would have argued, or at least protested her impiety, but her certainty and her sorrow were too great.

"We can't give her to the sea, but she must go into the family song." Quiet embraced him with shuddering grief. Eyas was ashamed to find himself thinking that she had not put her arms around him since he had been a little boy; then he thought of Goldarms lying dead in some lost thicket, and he shared his mother's sorrow.

A year later, two girls from Sandybank vanished within a month of each other. And a year after that, a young wife named Garnet Springbringer set out for Longstrand from her home in Easthaven and was never seen again. Darkhair began to dream of Admiral Thorn once more. He felt, as he had not in years, something evil coiling about the Gulf. Its strength was growing; it was testing itself, preparing itself. Soon it would be ready.

9

In high summer the centaurs came down from the mountains. They crossed the Bluemeadows River below the Great Cataract and cantered down the North Bank Road through the Valley. Farmers woke in the early sunrise to the rumble of hoofs and jingle of war gear, and the centaurs' deep sad songs like wind in high trees. Through dew-spangled fields the centaurs came, the dawn glittering on their spears. And the farmers hastily gathered their goods and followed the deep hoofprints down to the sea.

Their camp was east of Longstrand, on a gentle slope

overlooking the estuary and the Gulf. Here they unloaded their packs, pitched their tents, set out their wares of brass and iron, and waited.

The People often speculated on what female centaurs might be like; the males, at any rate, were impressive. From rump to forelegs, their bodies were well over a span in length; their tails, thick as a man's wrist and ending in a tuft of coarse hair, added half a span more. A tall man could just see over a centaur's back. The torso rose in a column, spreading into broad shoulders and long arms. The head was very human in shape and features, though larger and coarser, and a thick mane, growing from the top of the head to below the shoulderblades, made the head seem larger yet. Short, straight hair grew on the back, sides, and legs; it was usually brown or black, but sometimes auburn. The upper body was hairless except for the mane and a sparse beard on the heavy jaws.

On their travels the centaurs wore loose leggings of splithoof leather, but when they camped they went about as unclothed as the People. They carried their swords in ornate leather scabbards on their backs, and never removed them except to sleep. A man could lift such a sword, but none could fight with one; a centaur could swing it like a stick, and make it hum and flash like swarming bees.

That quickness was startling in brutes so indolent. Once camped, the centaurs ate, slept, and smoked resin in stubby clay pipes. Indifferent to weather, they lazed in sunshine or rain, rousing themselves only at dusk for an hour's swordplay and a night of songs and stamping dances.

In the summer of the year 256, when Eyas was fourteen, he met a young centaur named Boulder. Big for his age, with a gentle face, Boulder had never visited the Gulf before, and Eyas guided him around the village and the nearby woods. The centaur took more interest than most in the way the People lived, and the Gulf itself fascinated him.

"Never could I imagine so much water," he said one morning, walking back to camp with Eyas. "On the High Plains we have lakes, but they are so small. And all the trees! We must go days to find trees to feed our furnaces, and here you have them everywhere."

"I'd like to see your land," said Eyas. "It must be strange, with just grass and no mountains."

"Not much grass near Foundries Hold," Boulder grunted. "Just breadseed fields. In the wind, they ripple like the water here." He squinted off to the south, looking across the estuary. "I would like to see more of the Gulf."

"You'd have to go by boat," Eyas grinned.

"That would not be so bad." But centaurs were shy of water; they would wade, but could not swim, and Eyas could not remember ever hearing of a centaur going onto a boat.

"Would you like me to take you sailing?"

Boulder smiled down at him. "I would be frightened. But I would like to try."

"Then we'll go tomorrow, in *Whiteback*."

Darkhair was too surprised at the idea to object, and next day Eyas brought his grandmother's boat in from its mooring to the beach. While dozens of Longstranders gawked, Boulder splashed into the water and awkwardly climbed aboard over the side. The boat tilted under his weight; Boulder's mane swelled out, a sign of nervousness.

"Settle down just behind the mast," Eyas told him. The centaur obeyed, folding his legs under him. But it was not the easy repose of a resting browser: he was crouched to spring. One big hand wrapped itself around the mast. Darkhair, Netweaver, and several other men shoved the boat into deeper water; Eyas leaned on the tiller and *Whiteback* caught a breeze. People on the beach slapped their thighs in mildly ironic applause, while Eyas grinned and waved. Further down the beach, a dozen centaurs watched impassively.

"Where shall we go?" Eyas asked.

"The place called Mud Bay."

"Ah. Why there?"

Boulder looked over his shoulder at the boy. "I want a cannon."

Eyas's laugh was short and surprised. "Will you dive for it?"

"No, no. But if you find one and tie ropes to it, I will pull it up."

Eyas steered across the estuary toward Saltspring Point. "What an idea. No one's got anything from the wreck since I was a baby."

"I know. But we need a cannon."

The centaur's tone was grim. Eyas thought for a moment. "Are you fighting each other?" It might be a dangerous question; centaurs disliked discussing their own affairs.

"Men. We are fighting men." Boulder saw the alarm in Eyas's face. "Not the People. The Suns."

93

"But they're far off, to the south and east. You're in the north."

"They are moving into our lands. Many holds have been driven north, out of Transmontane into the High Plains. The Suns use cannons to take our land and keep it. It has been going on for years. They don't really war on us. Their farmers and herdsmen come into a hold, and then the soldiers follow them. Always a single hold each year, and the others hope that this time the Suns will have enough, so each hold must fight alone."

"Why not capture cannons from the Suns?"

"Some holds have done that. We hear the price was high in warriors' lives. But the Suns give the holds no time to make more cannons, or to learn their use. Foundries is far north; if we can master this new ironlore, we will have time to build all we need, and sell some to other holds as well."

"Provident as a centaur," Eyas said. "I'll strike a bargain with you, Boulder. If I help you bring up a cannon, let me go back to Foundries with you."

"I—I cannot strike such a bargain. Not without the word of Oldwalker, the Arm of Foundries. Your own family would have to allow it as well," he added quickly, as if glad of an additional argument.

"Then when you come back next year, bring me Oldwalker's word. If he refuses, I'll take the cannon's weight in iron goods."

Boulder rumbled with laughter. "And you call *us* sharp traders. Very well."

Eyas had no trouble finding the site of the wreck; remembrance had fixed it in his memory, and he had often sailed across Mud Bay. But the sandbar on which *Liberator* had gone aground was now largely washed away, and the water was dark with no hint of bottom.

"The last time anyone dived here, the ship was about three spans down," Eyas said as he dropped anchor. "It may be deeper. If we're lucky, the wreck should be fairly clear." He tied one end of a rope around his waist, and gave the other to Boulder. "If I'm not up in fifty breaths, pull me out."

Boulder clicked his tongue in assent. He did not look happy at the thought of being alone on a boat, far from solid land. "Good luck."

Eyas took a few deep breaths, stepped onto the steersman's bench, and knifed into the water. The rope uncoiled smoothly for a time, then stopped. Boulder watched a few bubbles break the dark, placid surface. The sun blazed down.

Then Eyas burst out of the water with a gasp, his black hair plastered over his face and shoulders. Boulder, mistrusting the boat's stability, leaned cautiously to the side.

"I think I've found one," Eyas panted. "More rope. A whole coil." Boulder tossed it to him, and Eyas vanished again.

Now the waiting was really endless. Boulder fingered the rope that Eyas was tied to, and at last decided to start pulling. But it went slack in his hands, and Eyas, dripping and exhausted, pulled himself in over the stern. The end of the second rope was gripped in one fist. For a long time he lay panting on the deck.

"We've got it," he said at last, sitting up slowly.

"Aha," Boulder growled happily. "How heavy?"

"I couldn't move it. The rope is tied through a ring on it."

"How big is it?"

"As long as my leg, and as thick as yours."

Saying nothing, Boulder stood up. His hoofs found careful purchase on the deck. Eyas handed over the rope. "I hope it's strong enough."

"I hope *I* am strong enough." From a centaur, this was flippant. Eyas felt a special liking for Boulder; he was almost as odd among his kind as Eyas was among the People.

The rope went over the side of the boat. Boulder began to pull it in. After a span or two of slack, the rope went taut. The centaur tugged once, then leaned back and hauled. Eyas wondered what he could do if the rope snapped and the centaur fell overboard. With a jerk, Boulder gained half a span and began hauling again. The boat trembled and listed.

It took less time than Eyas had expected. The cannon broke the surface with a dull splash and thudded against the hull. Boulder drew it carefully up and onto the deck. He dropped the rope and rubbed his hands on his flanks.

"So that is a cannon."

It was a barnacle-crusted cylinder, packed with mud in every crevice. A threeclaw scuttled from the muzzle. The rotted remnants of a wooden carriage were bolted to the underside. Eyas scraped a film of algae from the barrel and saw a dark glint of iron. "How could such a little thing be so dangerous?" he murmured.

"They can be made much larger. But this one is evil enough. It could throw an iron ball, bigger than a roundstone,

95

right through the hull of this boat. Your fathers and their men were lucky."

Eyas drew his hand from the cannon's metallic coldness. "It *is* evil," he said. "I can almost feel it. May the Goddess keep such things far from us."

"If She does not, the centaurs will." Boulder smiled, showing great white teeth. "We have done well today. Let us go back, before I remember how much water is under us."

"You are not like other centaurs," Eyas said as the boat neared Longstrand.

Boulder grunted. "Perhaps not like most, but like many. My grandparents were southerners, from Canyon Hold in Transmontane. The Suns drove us out when my father was young, and we took refuge in Foundries." As if thinking how much more he should say, he was silent for a time. "It is a hard thing for a centaur to be holdless, to have no place. My brothers and sisters and I are holded, for we were born in Foundries. But we remember our parents; they died in the camp of the holdless by the Swift River. I would not have Foundries suffer the fate of Canyon."

They brought the cannon into the centaurs' camp late that afternoon. The brutes gathered around while Boulder and Eyas cleaned it. Quiet conversations in the centaurs' language went on around them, too soft and rapid for Eyas to follow what was said. But he sensed their pleasure and excitement, and an undercurrent of vanity: they were eager to own such weapons as this, but not necessarily to use them. "A cannon wins no glory," one of them said.

A grizzled old centaur named Weedybrook, the leader of this year's traders, entered the circle of onlookers and spoke rapidly to Boulder. The younger brute let his mane go flat—a sign of respect—and answered in a few hoarse syllables. Then he turned to Eyas.

"The revered old one says I must leave at once for Foundries, with three others to help carry the cannon. It is wise. But I shall be sorry to leave you."

"I wish you could stay. We could do many things together."

"Next year." Boulder placed a hand on Eyas's shoulder. "When I bring you your welcome."

But Oldwalker would have no human in Foundries Hold, and the next summer Boulder brought instead a fortune in iron: tools, weapons, nails, and utensils. With his wanderyear still before him, Eyas possessed a fortune such as few People might gain in a lifetime.

Mothers all over the Gulf began to study their sons and daughters more critically, and more hopefully; daughters and sons wondered if their left arms would one day wear the Fisher tattoo. What would it be like, the girls wondered, to lie in the arms of a Sunnish-born man who had flown with windwalkers and swum to the bottom of the Gulf, who could speak with spiders and giants and call dabblers to perch on his shoulder? Could their breasts please a man suckled by the Goddess? The boys dreamed of the glamor of being husband to such a man, and threw themselves into mastering a score of masculine skills. Noticeably more families visited Longstrand that summer, to show off their eligible children and to study their competition.

If they hoped to interest Eyas, they were disappointed; he was rarely seen in Longstrand that summer. He was in the skyseed groves, visiting the family of Unsheath; he was in the tents of the centaurs, learning their smoking songs and genealogies; he was on the waters of the Gulf, fishing with his fathers and mothers.

10

The Gathering that began the year 258 was a disappointing one. The Goddess seemed not quite Herself. Remembrance was brief; the judgments were as fair and wise as always, but made in a mood the People sensed as weary patience, like a mother tiring of her children's dependence on her. Though Griptiller had resigned her Speakership, and Darkhair had been elected to replace her, the Goddess took no special note of the Fishers. She conspicuously failed to greet Eyas, who was young and vain enough to be hurt by Her neglect. It made him all the more impatient to say farewell to his family and begin his wanderyear.

After the Goddess had left, most of the People returned to their boats and prepared to sail for home. The Fishers instead waded to the beach, where they had pitched a tent, and began the meal of leave-taking.

"Sixteen years," muttered Griptiller. "They've gone like sixteen days. How did we ever fit you into one of those little reed boats, eh?" Her laugh was rough and phlegmy; her eyes, still dark and alert, were almost lost in wrinkles. Despite the blanket wrapped tightly about her, she still shivered after a long hour in the water.

Eyas shrugged, feeling doltish and awkward. He sat beside his grandmother, feeding her spoonfuls of thick, soured browser's milk. It was all she could keep down these days. When she had had enough, he turned to the salmon and berries in his own bowl, but ate with little appetite. He glanced down the beach; dozens of other families were bidding farewell to their children with meals as sad and cheerful as this one.

Darkhair and Netweaver said little, leaving their wives to give Eyas plenty of parting advice. Watching his parents' gentle smiles, Eyas saw himself through their eyes, and felt something of their sorrow. He was their last child, on the last day of his childhood. When he returned to Longstrand, it would be as a man, with a vote in Speaker's Hall and standing equal to his parents'. But it must be hard for them to look at their grown son when remembrance was fresh in their minds of the baby nursing on the belly of the Goddess.

Eyas put his heart into the ceremonies. He embraced his mothers and fathers and Griptiller with affection, making his grandmother wheeze. Firewing wept; Quiet, who had always taken less interest in him, pressed her cheek against his. With the same bowl his sisters had used, and Darkhair before them, Eyas walked to the water's edge. He dipped the bowl, returned, and poured it silently over the fire. Smoke and steam hissed together; the fire went out and then fluttered back to life again.

"Shall I get more water?"

Quiet shook her head. "Perhaps we've seen an omen." She smiled.

Almost before they felt ready for it, Eyas's canoe was loaded and in the water. He settled himself at the stern and held the craft steady by thrusting his paddle into the sandy bottom. He had spent the past year carving it from a bloodwood log, and felt pleasure in its balance and buoyancy. All along the beach, other young people were also embarking; not far away, his friend Old Yellowshaws, and beyond him Sky Dunehouse, whose beauty had already inspired clapstick songs. Family songs rose into the peaceful afternoon, blending rather than clashing. The westering sun blazed beside the Bridge of Heaven.

"Send us word of you," Firewing called, still sobbing. He nodded. Then he lifted his hand in farewell, pushed on the paddle, and set out across Gathering Cove. The Fishers' family song sped him on his way.

Most young People began their wanderyear by heading straight for a village, where they could find work and carouse with their fellows. Eyas chose instead to explore the western shores of the Gulf, where only an occasional beachcomber's shack could be found. The Westwall fell steeply into the sea, creating countless coves and inlets. Their beaches were narrow and rocky, formed by the outflow of fast creeks. In many inlets, driftwood clogged the shore; dabblers and waveskimmers nested among the dead limbs. Drier than the eastern shores of the Gulf, the mountains were still rich with trees and flowers.

For many days he hunted and fished, working his way slowly northward. He saw a few sails out in the Gulf, but felt no desire for companionship. At night he slept on empty beaches, watching the moon and the slow-shifting glow of the Bridge; when rain fell, he slept under his upturned canoe and listened to nearby dabblers and spitfars yapping about the weather.

Eyas supposed he was happy, and felt relieved not to be stared at, as he usually was at Gatherings. But the Goddess's neglect of him preyed on his mind and led him sometimes into morose reflections. One day he felt sure She had marked him for great things, and dreaded his destiny; the next, he feared She might have made a mistake, and he would spend his life awaiting an adventure that never came.

So passed a month and more. Rather than visit Northport before he wanted to, Eyas paddled eastward to Spider Island and spent a pleasant day fishing for redfin. Near sundown he pulled into a little cove and saw another canoe drawn up on the sand. Beside it, roasting a dabbler over a driftwood fire, sat a leather-clad man: Brightspear.

"I didn't know you wandered so far from home," Eyas greeted him, running his canoe ashore and stepping out.

"I've wandered farther in the past month," Brightspear said. He rose to greet Eyas with an open hand. "All the way to Northport and Rainfalling."

He was a tall young man of twenty-one and might almost have been Eyas's older brother. Both were broad-shouldered and slim, with long arms and legs; most of the People were stocky and short-legged. Both were dark-haired. Brightspear's beard was thick, black, and curly; Eyas's was sparse and fine.

"What brings you north?" Eyas asked. "Did you decide to take a wanderyear after all?" Brightspear at sixteen had stayed resolutely home, traveling only to hunt. Unlike other young men, he had never worked, preferring to support himself with his bow and snares.

"No. Is that a redfin? Gut it, and we'll have a fine meal."

They sat together on the sand, watching the sun sink behind the peaks of the Westwall. A wisp of cloud flared red and faded. After so many days alone, Eyas was slow and brief in speech. Brightspear talked idly of his journey, the weather, and the next day's hunting prospects. He piled more wood on the fire; the flames seemed only to deepen the darkness around them, and the air was chill.

"Well, then!" Brightspear said after a pause. "Are you enjoying your wanderyear?"

"Yes. More than I'd expected—it started badly." He described the Gathering. Brightspear, who had avoided the Gatherings for many years, was impassive.

"Sometimes I wonder about the Goddess," Eyas said. "Why She bothers with us. Why does She trouble to tell us how to live, and judge our quarrels? What does She gain from it but a few fish?"

"You've answered your own question."

"Have I?"

"The Goddess has power over the People of the Gulf. It must be sweet, to order humans about."

"Do you really think that?—Ah, of course. You've never felt Her, never had remembrance."

"What of it? I don't need to drink resin in wine to know it will fuddle my wits."

Eyas shrugged. Brightspear went on. "It's power, that's all. Just as the centaurs and windwalkers have power over the Nakeds, and the Nakeds think themselves honored."

"I'm a Naked too, Brightspear."

"You're Sunnish born, and Sunnish you'll die. It's not

your fault that you've been raised like one of them. But you've heard Silken talk about our own people. Our own land. Doesn't it quicken your blood to hear her tales?"

"In—in a way. But she's a good storyteller."

"Wouldn't you like to see the Dominance? Ride a sixfoot over the Grasslands, see the dawn from the walls of New Fort? Be among people who look like us?"

"What a thought!" laughed Eyas, just as Firewing would have.

"I mean it, Eyas."

"And what would someone like me do in the Dominance?"

"Whatever you liked. You'd be a Man, made a Man by the Sun."

Eyas burst into laughter. "Ah, ah! You're going back, and you want me to go with you."

"Yes. I want you to come with me, to bring my father's armies out of hiding, and take back the Dominance."

Now Eyas did not laugh. "Brightspear—I'm a Naked, whatever my birth. I couldn't live among people in the Dominance. They'd sooner befriend a walkingtree."

"They'd do as the Sun commands them."

"You're a Naked too, for all your leather trousers. How could you conquer a country you don't even know, when—"

"When what?"

"When you father grew up in it, and still lost."

Brightspear looked into the fire with eyes like stones. "I will do what I say I will do. I feel my destiny, Eyas. In my dreams I can see the great streets of New Fort, and thousands of people calling my name. I will go. If I stayed here I would die."

"So you will leave Silken."

"For a little while. Then I'll bring her home in triumph, and give her lands and herds and palaces. And I'll do the same for you, Eyas. You could be someone great. Not just a big threeclaw in a little tidepool, but a Man. You have skills with brutes—imagine yourself owning herds of sixfeet! Why, you could send them into battle without warriors, and they'd trample your enemies to dust."

"They would not be dust, Brightspear. They'd be dead men and women. Why should I want to do such a thing?"

Brightspear smiled. "Think about it, Eyas. Think of the glory, the adventure, the whole world at our feet."

"All I can think of now is the whole world under my

backside; it's hard. I'm going to sleep. Perhaps we'll talk in the morning."

Brightspear in the next few days said nothing more about leaving the Gulf, though sometimes he mentioned one or another of the stories Silken had told them. He appeared to Eyas a little abstracted; when Brightspear's gaze was focused on a splithoof in a salal patch, he seemed to be looking instead at some inner dream, some distant land. When he spoke, it was about immediate tasks, and usually in commands. He drew his bow with power and impatience, as if he yearned for a better target than a roosting dabbler or a grazing splithoof.

Eyas sensed something violent coming to the surface of Brightspear's mind, and did not want to provoke it. When Brightspear asked to accompany him at least as far as Saltery Bay, Eyas agreed though he would have preferred traveling alone. And he began to think it might be better if Brightspear did leave the Gulf; whether he lived or died, he would be safely away from the People.

—Or was Eyas simply rejecting the very destiny the Goddess had prepared for him? He had sometimes feared he would miss great adventures; would he miss them out of his own fear or laziness? Certainly there could be no adventure in the Gulf like those in the Sunnish epics; but the Gulf was real, solid, alive, and the epics were only words.

They island-hopped eastward across the Gulf, each in his own canoe; Brightspear's was fitted with a sail and outrigger, but he preferred to paddle alongside Eyas. In the good weather, their spirits rose. They sang paddle songs, fished, and, when the sun was too hot, rolled into the water to cool off.

Late on a bright afternoon, they rounded Kelp Point on Sandcliff Island. A girl called them from the shore.

"Hello! Come and help us eat some salmon." It was Sky Dunehouse.

Eyas waved his paddle and changed course; Brightspear followed.

On the beach below the high cliff that gave the island its name, Sky and Old Yellowshaws sat by a fire. Great chunks of salmon were broiling on an iron grill over the coals. The smell was pungent and savory.

Eyas gripped Old's hand. "I thought we'd meet eventually. How is your wanderyear going so far, you two?"

"A well-fed one, thanks to Sky." Old was a few months older than Eyas, and owed his name to the wizened face he'd had at birth. Though he'd lost his wrinkles, the name still suited him. He stooped; his hair was thin and dry, the color of grass in a dry summer. A broken leg, badly healed, had given him a half-limping, half-shuffling walk. He squinted, and muttered to himself like a doddering grandfather. Old was also unpleasantly intelligent—an odd child in a family as blandly handsome and dully prosperous as the Yellowshaws. He and Eyas had long been friends.

"So Sky is looking after you, is she?"

"What else can I do?" Sky smiled wryly. "The silly whiteback couldn't catch his tongue with his teeth."

She was a distant relative of the Fishers; one of her mothers was a cousin of the Windinvokers, and so related to Quiet. But the Dunehouses were an ordinary family of hunters and carpenters, with no special powers and little standing even in the small village of Easthaven. Sky was the only one of three children to survive infancy; with her marriage the Dunehouse line would end. ("Small loss," some neighbors muttered. The parents were considered a rough, unreliable lot, and the daughter an impudent brat with no respect for her betters.)

Certainly Sky showed no great respect for the sons of the Fishers and Yellowshaws, and no contempt for the singleton Brightspear. With quick gestures she plucked salmon steaks from the grill and tossed them to the newcomers.

"Ouch, hot!" Eyas grunted. Brightspear caught his portion and held it uncomplainingly as he sat down on a log.

They chatted as they ate; Old and Sky talked mostly to Eyas, and did not ask Brightspear why he was so far north. For the last few years Brightspear had been considered an embarrassment to himself—unmarried, without a craft or standing, a mere hanger-on of the Fishers—and therefore scarcely a person. Perhaps they sensed, as Eyas did, some latent violence in him, and preferred to ignore him rather than seek a safe topic of conversation. As the evening darkened, Old, Eyas, and Sky began a three-way mockery duel that sent them all into giggles and even drew smiles from Brightspear. At last they settled down for the night around the fire, but it was hard to get to sleep: one or another of them kept spluttering with laughter.

Eyas woke suddenly. The beach was dark blue under the

glow of the Bridge, and the fire had gone out. He heard a muffled cry, and the thump and hiss of someone's foot kicking sand.

They had eaten and slept in a clear patch of sand amid tangles of driftwood. The noise seemed to be coming from just beyond two big logs, in the direction of the water. Eyas lifted his head. Old was snoring softly under his blanket, his bare feet almost in Eyas's face.

Eyas sat up, his skin prickling with the chill of danger. His hand silently patted the sand until he found the knife that Sky had used to clean the salmon. Leaning against the logs, he lifted his head until he could see over them. A few spans beyond, two dark shapes wrestled on the sand. The smell of leather was strong.

Eyas's voice was a whisper like a blade drawn from its sheath. "Brightspear."

"Hush, Eyas." Brightspear's voice was thick, almost drunken. "We're coupling. We didn't want to disturb you."

Sky gasped as if half-smothered. *"Eyas—he's—I don't want to!"*

"Get away from her!" Eyas shouted, leaping to his feet. He heard Old's snores abruptly stop. The knife was slippery in Eyas's palm; somewhere just behind his eyes he felt his ordinary self yield to something else; he was becoming as much an instrument of violence as his knife. *"Now*, Brightspear, or Goddess look under you."

"Fuck your Goddess—I'll move when I'm done. Stay back, Eyas."

Eyas sprang from the logs like a prowl, gripped Brightspear by the hair, and snapped his head back. Brightspear lurched up onto his knees, looking both malevolent and foolish with his trousers down below his buttocks. His left hand lashed out, its edge striking a clumsy blow that was still hard enough to knock Eyas off balance; then Brightspear was up, tugging at his trousers. He crouched into a fighting stance.

"You never liked to play at axhand, did you? I always played too rough for you. Often I thought of killing you, Eyas, just to see what it would feel like. Now I will find out."

They circled each other. Brightspear shifted, ducked, and struck with startling swiftness; the knife spun away.

Eyas sprang back, his hand numb from the blow. Another step backward took him into the water; it glowed with phosphorescence around his ankles. The self behind his eyes watched but did not command; warlore ruled him. As Brightspear lunged, Eyas spun and rolled back onto the beach, flinging sand behind him. Brightspear, slowed but not blinded, spat sand from his lips and closed in again. His face in Bridgelight was stiff and pale, the sockets of his eyes lost in darkness. Wet sand hissed under his feet as he strode swiftly up against Eyas, hands poised for the killing stroke.

"Hoop!"

Old's hoarse cry, coming on his flank, threw Brightspear off stride. He barely ducked the whirring chunk of firewood that Old hurled at him. Then, as he straightened, Sky rose almost at his feet, her face a mask more terrible than his, and slashed him with Eyas's lost knife.

Brightspear drew a long, stuttering gasp that came out again as a shrill scream. He staggered back, his hands pressed against his face; blood spurted black between his fingers.

Sky pursued him, gripping the knife awkwardly and without warlore. She made a hesitant stab at his stomach, missed, and then cast the knife away. Taking up a driftwood branch as long and thick as her arm, she swung it with all her strength into his belly.

Brightspear vomited, a gush of stinking bile and fish, and doubled up. Sky lifted the branch again, and clubbed him across the neck. He fell into his vomit and rolled slowly onto his back.

They stood above him, not moving. Sky's panting breath was the loudest sound on the beach. Brightspear's upturned face was as pale as a dead man's, except for a black smear of blood across his left eye and cheek.

"Goddess, Goddess," Old whispered. "It was—"

"Rape," said Sky. "Not completed, but rape."

It was not a word the People had much occasion to use. Sexual violence against a woman was very nearly sacrilege against the Goddess. The last rape had been committed over forty years before: the man had been judged by the Goddess and exiled to Barren Island for the last few days of his life, but first the violated woman had gouged his eyes out, and her husbands had packed the empty sockets with salt. His name had not gone into his family song; he was remembered now only in grim ceremonies of the brotherhoods, when boys learned their responsibilities as men.

"Kill him," said Eyas, turning to find the knife. Sky held his arm.

"This is for the Goddess to judge," she said in a shaking voice. "And She told us to guard him, when you and he first came to the Gulf. Let Her decide his fate."

Sullenly, Eyas nodded.

"He must be mad," Old said. "He knows what rape is, and what the penalty is, even if he's not in the brotherhood any more. How did he think he could get away with it? Why, he'd have had to kill us all."

Eyas caught his breath. His warlore was yielding, but not to his ordinary self; a strange white rage filled his mind now. He sprinted to his canoe, found rope, and returned to bind Brightspear's hands behind him. Then he dragged Brightspear into the water.

Coughing and retching, Brightspear revived. Eyas sat him up in the blue-glowing water, gripping the front of Brightspear's leather tunic.

"Tell me this, Brightspear: Where is Goldarms? Where is my sister?"

From brow to chin, the left half of Brightspear's face was a clotted mass of blood, sand, and vomit. His right eye glared. He said nothing.

"You killed her, Brightspear. You found her alone in the woods, and you raped and killed her."

Brightspear grinned contemptuously.

"And the others—the two girls in Sandybank, and the woman from Easthaven. You killed them too." Eyas's voice was a growl, as deep and dangerous as a centaur's. He began to shake his captive like a spider killing a mouse, until Brightspear laughed crazily and spat.

"I am the Sun on Earth, Eyas. I do as I please, and I answer to no one."

"Answer me or I'll drown you."

"She hardly wept, Eyas. The others wept, but Goldarms only wept a little, when I cut her belly open."

Snarling, Eyas shoved him backward and held his head under water. Bubbles luminously broke the surface. At last Old pulled Eyas away and Brightspear sat up, coughing.

"Sky's given him to the Goddess, not to you!" Old shouted. Eyas said nothing, but the drunkenness of his white rage had not yet left him.

He gripped Brightspear by his bound wrists and hauled him back onto the beach. With clumsy force he tied his prisoner to a driftwood log, leaving just enough slack to

106

enable Brightspear to sit upright. Then he led the others some distance down the beach, out of Brightspear's hearing.

"I would gladly kill him, and take Her judgement on myself," he said. "But that judgement would fall on both of you as well. We must take him back to Longstrand."

"Good," murmured Old. "But it'll be dangerous. He'll be looking for escape every moment. And then to keep him a prisoner for almost a year, until the Gathering—"

"I'll guard him gladly every day," Eyas answered. "So will every other man in Longstrand." He was silent for a time. "He turned against the family that saved our lives. He was a brother to me."

At the sorrow in his voice, Sky and Old embraced him, as they would embrace someone grieving for the dead. Briefly and violently, Eyas wept. Then, almost calmly, he said, "We'll have to guard him all night. In the morning we'll start for Longstrand."

They nodded silently, and all three turned back down the beach. As they did, the rasp of wood on sand broke the stillness, and then a splash. Eyas burst into a sprint, the others following close behind; when they reached the campsite, Brightspear's canoe was already ten spans from shore, a darkness against the glinting water.

"Mock me for a fool," Eyas muttered. He found his rope in a tangle by the log. He had tied the knots too quickly, too sloppily. "Check the other canoes," he said.

They were intact; Brightspear had been too eager for escape to take the time to wreck them. But the paddles were gone.

"Well—a quick thinker," Old laughed bitterly.

Eyas found a hatchet in his canoe and cast about in the driftwood until he found a suitable branch. "Light the fire," he said, and began to chop at the branch.

"Can't it wait till morning?" Old protested. "He's got away, Eyas; you won't catch him with a whittled stick for a paddle."

"No, but if we reach Longstrand close behind him, we might be able to follow him and run him down before he gets into the South Hills."

"What?"

"He was planning to leave the Gulf; he wanted me to go with him. Now he'll have to go. He'd never be safe now, anywhere in the Gulf. His only chance is to slip away before we can get home."

"Well." Old had the fire going, and in its orange glow his face was grim. "I'd better find my own stick to whittle."

At dawn they were well out in the Gulf, headed for Rainfalling, where Eyas hoped to find a swift boat. The three of them sat in Old's canoe, towing the other two. It was slow; their improvised paddles were clumsy and inadequate.

As the rising sun began to brighten the clouds above the Eastwall, Sky sang an old Easthaven song, "Morning Rejoices." Her voice, sweet and clear, filled the blue dawn like the music of waveskimmers' wings when a flock takes to the air. Old picked up the song in a flat but energetic tenor.

"Why don't you sing?" Sky asked, turning to look at Eyas. It was light enough for him to see the wide bruises on her cheek, the swollen flesh around her eye where Brightspear had struck her. Her smile was so full of life that Eyas's anger weakened, faltered, and changed. He began to sing, knowing he had found a husband and a wife.

11

"What does she want?" Darkhair asked. The sweatbath was hot; he poured water on the rocks in the center of the hut, and steam sputtered up.

Winterberry Forester shrugged. "I don't know, Speaker. She came to the house this morning, and asked me to come and get you. She said it was terribly important, and you shouldn't tell anyone where you were going."

"Odd. How did she seem to you?"

The youth smiled unsurely. "All right. Maybe kind of excited." He wiped sweat from his face.

"Very well," Darkhair grunted. He got up and pushed open the door. After a quick run down the beach he dived into the chilly water, splashing and snorting. A few idlers on Traders' Beach waved to him as Darkhair waded out; he gestured vaguely in reply and began striding up through the muddy streets. Winterberry tagged along with him for a while, but left him at the foot of the cliff.

Darkhair wondered what Silken could possibly want. He hadn't seen much of her lately; she kept to her cabin, and his duties as Speaker kept him in town. Perhaps she'd heard some news of Eyas. Or the Suns had made contact with her, after all these years. It might even be something wonderful, like Goldarms back again, alive as ever after strange adventures.

The thought quickened his steps. Though his hair was gray and his beard had turned pure white, his body was still solid and powerful. He reached the tower at the top of the cliff without even feeling winded. Not bad for an old blackbeak in his fifties, he thought.

In the clearing, he paused for a moment. The cabin looked much as it always had, though perhaps a little more decrepit; Brightspear took no interest in keeping the place up, and the Fisher husbands had had no time. He walked through the vegetable garden, smiling at memories of many years, and knocked at the door.

Silken opened it. She wore a garment of silver-blue spidersilk, shimmering from her throat to her feet. It was so unlike her usual tunic and trousers that he wondered for an instant if it really was Silken. Then he remembered the red gown she had worn when she leaped from *Deliverer* into the turbulence of Ripmouth and the lives of the Fishers.

"Winterberry said you wanted to see me."

She smiled, and stood aside to let him enter.

"I haven't seen you in a long time." She took his hand and led him to the wide bench before the fire. "And it's been very lonely here, with Brightspear gone."

"Gone?"

"Oh—he's off sailing and hunting. He'll be back one of these days, and then go off again. He likes his freedom. . . . Tell me what you've been doing."

"Sailing and hunting. And being Speaker. I don't know how my mother stood it for all those years. But it fills the days. We miss Eyas."

"Yes. It must be sad, with all the children gone. I miss him too."

"Griptiller misses him most of all—she has no one to complain about now. But we all had our wanderyears, and he must have his. Before we know it, he'll be back, and soon we'll be grandparents again."

"I still can't believe Moonhorn and Harper are old enough

to have their own babies. Remember how they gaped at the boys and me when you rescued us? Time goes so swiftly—more swiftly for us than for men. We grow old so soon."

"You don't. You look just as you always have, and here am I with my old man's beard."

"Old man indeed. Darkhair—I've suddenly begun to feel as if my life were over. All these years alone, with just the boy growing up and—and not needing me much any more. Your women are luckier; they have their wives and husbands, and their children and grandchildren."

"I'm sorry. We've neglected you."

"Not at all. The others don't much matter, anyway. But I've missed you. And you've seemed very lonely yourself."

"A father doesn't get over a child's death."

"I know. Oh, Darkhair, I grieved for her, and for you. I wanted to comfort you then, but I didn't know how."

"No one does."

"I think I do now." Her green eyes were half-closed. Her hand reached out, touched his face. She leaned forward and kissed him.

"What—"

"Let us comfort each other, Darkhair. I want to make you happy, and nothing can make me happy but you, you."

Her shimmering garment had somehow opened, and her pale body seemed almost radiant in the dim room. It looked as beautiful as it had on that New Year's Day long ago; he had never forgotten that brief glimpse of her nakedness. Without his willing it, Darkhair's hand found her breasts. All his old desire for her, a desire he had never let himself admit, burned in him. They lay down upon the bench, their bodies hot and smooth together. Silken's desire seemed as hot and sudden as his own; she guided him inside her, and closed on him with a sigh. Her arms locked around his neck, her legs around his hips, drawing him deeper and deeper. They spent themselves with what sounded like a single cry.

For a time they lay still. Darkhair began to shiver. He got up, and sat on the edge of the bench with his hands on his knees. When he dared at last to look at Silken, her eyes held the glint of female intelligence he had seen at their first meeting. She had taken his measure then, had seen his weakness, and now she had exploited it. He did not know why, and did not want to know.

"I must go," he muttered.

Her hand caressed his thigh. "Stay."

"No. I must go." He got up and went out the door like a man walking in a dream. He did not speak again, but crossed the clearing and disappeared down the path.

Brightspear swung himself down from the sleeping loft. A slight smile softened his handsome, wounded face.

"You did well. I am pleased."

Silken did not look at him. Her hands smoothed the gown. "My life is in the service of the Sun," she murmured. "But this was the hardest thing I have ever had to do."

"Nonsense. You had a wonderful time—I watched you. And you've paid the Fishers back for all their stupid arrogance."

"Eyas must have done you a great wrong, for you to strike like this at his family."

"You see my face." He gripped her shoulders and turned her to him. The wound ran from his forehead to the middle of his cheek; his left eyelid drooped. The scab was thick, deep, and black. When it fell away he would carry a scar all his life.

"But he's always loved you, always. When he was a baby—"

Brightspear laughed unpleasantly and let her go. "If he'd stayed with us he might have had a proper upbringing; but he was raised by savages and now he's one himself—worse than that, he's half-savage and half-brute. I offered him a chance for glory, and he spurned it; let him stay and rot with the other Nakeds."

He began rummaging about the cabin, putting food into one pouch and traveler's gear into another: a spidersilk cape, an extra knife, some rope. From a box in a corner he took his father's yellow hood, and put it on. It fit him well.

"You're going now," Silken said dully.

"Yes. But I'll be back someday, soon. With an army and all the Dominance under my hand." He took her silence for skepticism. "I will do what I say I will do, Silken."

"I know. I have always known that."

He put the pouches and the copperheaded spear by the doorway and turned to look at her. She was sitting on the edge of the bench, bent over and looking at nothing.

"You've served me well. Now you'll serve me one more time before I go."

"Of course." She lay back and opened her gown. He fell upon her harshly, entered her, and spent himself with a shudder and a grunt. Silken was accustomed to his roughness; it reminded her of his father.

"You are the Sun on Earth," she whispered as he rolled off her and stood up. "Your will be done."

He pulled off the hood and tucked it into a pocket of his tunic. Then he gathered up his belongings and went out the door without a word or a glance back.

Quiet and Firewing had been bargaining on Traders' Beach when they saw Darkhair wade out into the harbor and swim out to *Waveskimmer*. He raised sail and steered swiftly out past Two Bows' Spit into the estuary.

The Fisher wives walked down the sand and up to the longhouse. Inside, Netweaver was feeding Griptiller a little sour milk. He looked up when they came in; the old woman hummed to herself, blinking at the fire.

"Where is Darkhair going?" asked Firewing.

"I didn't know he was going anywhere. He came in a few breaths ago, and said he needed to get something from the boat. He was Rocks Ahead by the look in his eye—"

Firewing hurried down to the boatshed, intending to get out a canoe and follow her husband. She found the Speaker's clamshell hanging from a peg inside the shed, and a note scrawled on a scrap of paperbark.

After she had read it, Firewing walked slowly up the steps, past the family post and under the grape arbor where Chirp's latest descendant rustled in her nest. Quiet, waiting in the doorway, took the note from her.

"We must get word to Eyas," Firewing said thickly, "before someone else tells him his father has banished himself for adultery."

12

In Rainfalling, Eyas's sister Harper heard their story, said a hurried farewell to her family, and took them aboard her boat, *Cloud*. Gales drove them south in a day and a half; now, on a raw and windy afternoon, Harper steered into Longstrand harbor.

"The place looks deserted," she said.

Traders' Beach was empty. To the east, in the distance, the centaurs' tents squatted under the blows of the wind. The houses of Longstrand showed little sign of life; their shutters banged in the wind.

Harper ran *Cloud* up onto the beach near the Fishers' boatshed. Eyas was ready to go straight to the longhouse, but his sister caught his arm and pointed to Speaker's Hall: the green-and-gold pennant of Longstrand flew above it.

"A meeting. The family will be there."

Inside the Hall the old murals leaped and danced in firelight, and the roundstones, set in the walls and pillars, gleamed like spiders' eyes. Eyas, Harper, Sky, and Old stood just inside the doorway, their eyes adjusting to the dimness. The benches were crowded, and everyone seemed to be talking at once. Eyas looked for Darkhair on the Speaker's stool, but the stool held only a clamshell on a thong. Behind the stool stood Givenlast Forester, looking uneasy as a temporary Speaker.

"I call silence, silence on Longstrand!" the old man cried out. The uproar subsided to a murmur like that between two breaking waves. Eyas saw his mothers now, sitting with Griptiller between them on the first of the women's benches. Across from them, Netweaver sat alone, looking at nothing. "Netweaver says Speaker Darkhair confessed to him that he had coupled with the Sunnish woman, Silken."

Eyas felt as if he were losing his balance, and locked hands with Harper and Sky. Behind him, Old growled wordlessly.

Givenlast turned to a shadowy corner. "Silken, do you deny this?"

Silken rose from the shadows, dressed in her familiar tunic and trousers. Her yellow hair spilled down over her shoulders and breasts. "It is true."

"Adultery is not to be judged by the Goddess, but by the People," Givenlast said. "The penalty is banishment, unless the wronged spouses forgive the adulterers." He rubbed his hands nervously. "Do the Fishers forgive Speaker Darkhair?"

"We do," said Quiet. The People gasped; to take Darkhair back, the Fishers would lose most of their standing.

"Do the Fishers forgive Silken?"

Before Quiet could reply, Eyas stepped forward. He stopped beside Givenlast, his eyes fixed on Silken. Under the babble that Eyas's appearance caused, the old man muttered, "You're breaking a serious rite, young fellow. You'd better have good reason."

"I do." Eyas gave his parents a faint, wry smile while Givenlast shouted for silence. Then Eyas said, "Silken is not the one to be forgiven or banished. Silken: where is Brightspear?"

The People clicked their tongues in surprise. Silken's face was calm. She did not reply.

"His face is scarred now, isn't it?"

Fear deadened her eyes. She nodded as if compelled.

"He came to you not long ago, didn't he, and told you to couple with my father."

"Why would Brightspear do such a thing?" Silken retorted.

Eyas drew a trembling breath. "Because a few days ago, Brightspear was on Sandcliff Island with Sky Dunehouse, Old Yellowshaws, and me. He tried to rape Sky." He paused, half-expecting an uproar, but the People were silent. "We stopped him, and Sky cut his face with her knife. I think he also raped my sister Goldarms, and killed her, and Garnet Springbringer, and the girls from Sandybank. He knew the penalty for rape, so he killed them."

Eyas felt rage build up again within him, like the Fastfoam River in late winter when it prepares to shatter the ice that imprisons it. He felt too the People's horror and dismay. "Brightspear wanted revenge, Silken—against me, against my family, against Longstrand. And he got it."

Her head rose arrogantly, with a flash of her youthful beauty. "Brightspear is a special man, with a great destiny. Why should he risk it all to couple with a silly girl—"

She saw Eyas's face darken, and stopped. Her arrogance faded, leaving her a frightened and lonely woman with a lined face and work-hardened hands.

"I ask again: Did he tell you to couple with my father?" The rage was alive in him now, pouring over her. She had never seen him possessed by such fury before, and she crumpled beneath it.

"Yes. Yes. Yes. He is the Sun, Eyas, the Sun on Earth;. I only did his will, as I have always done."

Now the People caught Eyas's rage, and their voices shook the Hall; they were on their feet, howling. Intoxicated by their wrath and his own, Eyas strode towards Silken, his hands remembering the feel of Brightspear's tunic. He would kill her with his bare hands, as he should have killed Brightspear. From far away he heard Sky calling, "No, no! Eyas, stop!"

Reluctantly, sullenly, the rage left him. In its place was only a wretched misery and sorrow for all of them. Silken sat back in the shadows and put her hands over her face.

Givenlast quelled the tumult by brandishing the clamshell. When silence returned, the room smoldered with hatred. "Do the Fishers forgive Silken?" he asked again, and his voice was dry and sibilant.

"Let Eyas answer for us," Quiet said.

"We do. But the duty the Goddess gave my family is at an end; Silken is no longer our responsibility. Let her go or stay; her fate is no longer our concern."

Silken showed her face to him, and now she seemed like a frightened little girl. "I would rather have died at *your* hands, Eyas, than those of some vengeful Naked. At least they were your words that have condemned me."

That night the Fishers argued for hours about what to do next. Netweaver was sure Darkhair would return in a few days; Quiet and Firewing thought he would hide himself in the Mistmarsh or some empty cove until he was found and brought home. Harper agreed with her mothers. Old and Sky listened but said nothing; they had grown close to Eyas in the last few days, but they were not members of the family. Eyas too kept silent. Griptiller, who had seemed to doze most of the evening, spoke at last.

"He'll leave the Gulf. If he can't be a Fisher, if he can't have his standing, he'd rather be nothing. He'll sail the Rip and never come back."

"That's madness!" shouted Firewing.

"I know my son. And he always was a little mad, or he'd never have let himself get between that she-prowl's legs."

"I give up," Firewing said. "Netweaver, tell her she's wrong."

"Maybe she's not," he said softly. "I remember something he said a long time ago. It was the day Eyas first talked to Chirp, when he was just a baby. Darkhair said he wanted to wander, to fight in wars and see the world."

"You never told *us* that," Quiet said.

"Husbands and wives don't tell each other everything," Netweaver said with a faint smile.

The argument went on. After a time, Eyas stood up. "I'm

going for a walk," he said. Sky and Old smiled at him; the others scarcely noticed.

It was one of those summer nights when both moon and Bridge were full, and darkness never quite fell. Hearing the rattle of clapsticks on Traders' Beach, Eyas turned the other way and walked down the gale-smoothed sand toward the fires of the centaurs' camp.

Boulder was there, cheerfully dizzy on resin and glad to see his old friend. The centaur was full-grown now, and even taller and heavier than most of his companions. He sat before his tent, swaying a little in time to a smoking song while Eyas told him what had happened on Sandcliff Island, in Silken's cabin, and in Longstrand.

"Strange are the ways of men," he said when Eyas was finished. "What will you do now?"

"I would like to follow Brightspear and kill him. But no one could find him in the hills. And I would like to bring my father home, but I think my grandmother is right."

"Griptiller is a wise woman. Even Oldwalker took counsel with her, in the summers when he came to the Gulf. But if Darkhair has gone to this place called the Rip, you could never find him."

"Not unless I could ride the wind." Eyas leaped to his feet. "Ah! That could be done."

"Where are your wings?" asked Boulder, grinning.

"On Unsheath's island. Boulder, I ask a favor of you. Go at once to Anchorwood, and ask Unsheath to send his warriors flying from here to the Rip. Let them search for *Waveskimmer*. I will sail in *Whiteback*; when they find my father, they can tell him to wait, and then they can guide me to him. Can you do this?"

"I can. But I cannot promise Unsheath will do as you ask."

"He will." Eyas took Boulder's hand. "Tell my family also; I've heard enough quarreling tonight."

"Go to your boat. I will leave at once, and tell your family when I return from Anchorwood."

Through the rest of that twilit night, Eyas sailed. Dawn came sooner than he expected, as he sailed along the Mistmarsh toward Big Harbor. Yearning for sleep, he stayed at the tiller. In midmorning a faint whoop came out of the sky. Three windwalkers passed far overhead, in V formation, and then three more. Their bodies were specks of white in a dark blue sky, moving with serene power to the northwest. Eyas dropped anchor near a nameless reef, and went to sleep.

A light thump on the deck roused him near noon. A windwalker had landed on the boat.

"Soarfar! It's good to see you."

Unsheath's son bared his teeth in a smile. His face bore new scars, the marks of his adulthood; he wore a black harness edged with red to show his status as heir of the Great Wing. The silver handle and iron hilt of a sword stood up behind his head from the scabbard on his back.

"I greet you, old friend. When the centaur told us of your troubles, Unsheath sent us out at once. We have found your father."

"Where?"

"Near the airfall you call the Rip. He is sailing straight for it. The tide is with him. By noon or a little after he will be in the Rip. We could not go down to him; the winds are treacherous there."

Eyas set to work raising sail. He was furious with himself for having slept, though he knew he could never have caught up with *Waveskimmer*.

"Can you try again, go down to him in the Rip?"

"He will be at the bottom of the airfall. We could not go down and return—unless riding a skyseed."

Soarfar was trying to cheer him up; that a windwalker could understand human feelings, and care about them, was consoling in itself.

"Very well. I'll have to take him the message myself."

Careful sailing put him off Blackrock Island not long after the tide had begun to ebb. Eyas had often been to Ripmouth with his family; he knew the tale of his great-grandparents' fatal return through the Rip, and in remembrance he had seen the wreck of *Deliverer*. In remembrance too he saw the face of his bloodmother, Peacebringer, as she let her baby fall into the turbulent sea. He often thought of her, and of his unknown father. Silken had not known him; she had known Peacebringer only as a pregnant servant who had joined Steeledge's followers at Copper Bay. That much Silken had told Eyas, and he did not think she knew more. Well, Peacebringer had gone into the sea, like the People's ancestors, and her flesh and bones had renewed the waters to sustain the People's children. Eyas dipped a hand into the dark water, honoring her memory.

The tide had taken hold of *Whiteback* now. The sail was furled; it would be worse than useless in the random gusts that swept the Rip. An airfall, the windwalkers called it—a place where cold rock and water drew air down and forced it out like the tide itself. Even now a clammy mist billowed over the boat, the ever-present fog that uncoiled from the Rip into the wider waters of the Gulf. Eyas turned for a last look at the green isles and blue water; then the fog thickened and he was in the Rip.

Black cliffs loomed dimly through the mist on either side, laced with foam where the tide struck them. In midstream the boat rode in a calm swiftness. Here and there, white water swirled across a drowned rock, like cloud flying from a mountain peak. Far ahead, the edge of the tidal bore rumbled and echoed. Eyas leaned on the tiller, guiding his old boat always toward dark water. The fog thickened until he could scarcely see the mast, then vanished. The cliff rose almost sheer, divided near the zenith by a narrow ribbon of blue sky. The canyon twisted and looped; in places the tide formed whirlpools in which enormous logs spun like twigs. The noise increased. Spray fell in a false rain. A half-submerged log, floating ten spans ahead of the boat, struck a hidden rock and rose straight up into the air. Eyas heaved against the tiller, sending *Whiteback* to the right, and saw the log smash down again just where the boat would have been.

The speed of the current increased, and the surface boiled white. The boat shot down a hill of roaring foam, spun completely around, and skimmed between two rocks with less than a span on either side. Eyas felt himself carried by a force that could shatter mountains, blind and unstoppable. But *Whiteback* still responded to his hand on the tiller, and delight beat in his blood with every leap and fall of the waters. Thunder off the cliffs drowned every other sound, but he shouted out the opening verses of the family song:

> "First was Two Bows, stone-born,
> And Anger, daughter of fire.
> These were their daughters:
> Salmon and Littlefoot.
> These were their sons:

Ax and Glittering.
Mothers and fathers of all the People,
Mothers and fathers of Fishers!"

Though nothing could hear him, though he could not even hear himself, the song became a part of the thunder, a pattern and rhythm that challenged the mindless crash of water on rock. From one rapids to the next, from one bend to the next, Eyas sang while his body shuddered with cold and his arms ached into numbness.

Imperceptibly, the Rip widened. The fog grew dense again, and the cliffs retreated into the distance. The tide began to slacken, and the surface calmed to an oily black. The echoes died away; in their place Eyas heard the fainter thunder of breaking surf, and the shrill cry of an unseen hawk. Wind blew the fog to shreds and left Eyas and his boat bobbing gently on the waters of the Great Bight. Far to the north and south, black cliffs heaved up into the densely forested mountains of the Westwall; to the west, the sea stretched unbroken and the sun rode low over a flat horizon.

" . . . That was Hemlock, of the Wreck Point Brewers,
A woman of kindness, a skilled sailor.
Her granddaughter Goldarms walked lightly in the morning;
In her beauty she fell, vanished like dew.
Yet still the family stands. Always the family stands."

The People knew little about the outcoast. North, said the windwalkers, were mountains buried in ice, ice that flowed into a cold sea they called Stormhome. Eyas felt sure that Darkhair must be following the southern shores of the Bight; perhaps he would seek refuge among the outcoasters, or sail all the way around Alland's End to Jadeland.

Raising sail, Eyas steered southwest while the sun sank in crimson. A few casts of his net brought him a finnet, which he ate raw, and several candlefish. These he placed in a holder and lit; burning in their own oil, the fish sputtered and glowed. Their light was not much needed on a summer night, but Eyas hoped that his father might see the yellow spark and know that another boat was out on the great sea.

For three days he sailed slowly southwest. He kept well offshore, for the surf was violent against the black cliffs, and he saw no safe harbors. The set of the current paralleled the

119

coast; at night he steered westward, deeper into the current, and slept as lightly and fitfully as a splithoof. Each morning he steered closer to land, searching for a sail or the smokes of a village. Once, on a wave-battered headland, he saw a blackened tower and the ruins of houses around it. Perhaps the Suns had built it long ago; its emptiness looked ancient.

On the third day the current took him past a long, sandy cape crested with wind-bent trees; then it carried *Whiteback* west, toward the empty horizon. Beyond the cape, Eyas saw the coast trend southeast, and he knew he had left the Great Bight. Far down the coast was a smudge of smoke: an outcoaster village at last. But the wind had died, and the current would not let him go.

Seemingly still, *Whiteback* lay in a flat calm while the jagged green-and-black mountains slowly retreated. Eyas wished he could invoke the wind as he watched the sun go down and saw only the faintest pink reflection of it in the east, glowing from the highest peaks. Somewhere beyond those peaks was Brightspear; perhaps he sat by a campfire, watching the crimson sky. Eyas felt an echo of rage again: if not for Brightspear, Goldarms would be watching this sunset from her husbands' longhouse, her children around her. Eyas himself would be paddling up some inlet where the scents of seaweed and flowering club were thick in the darkening air. He would be free to go where he liked, and to come home at last to sit by his own hearth. Instead he sat in dark emptiness, drawn against his will and strength into unknown waters.

In the silence he thought he heard a distant cry. Eyas sat up and then, only half-willing it, drew into himself and farheard.

It was not a cry; it was a gasping breath and a swirl of water against some smooth bulkiness. He heard it again and ran forward to the bow.

"Mother! Mother, I greet You!" he called, his own voice faint in farhearing. Far clearer was the sound of water stirred by great flukes.

The sun was completely gone now, leaving only a dark blueness in the northwestern sky. Under the white glow of the Bridge, the sea was silver. After a long silence, when even farhearing revealed nothing, the Goddess broke the surface within a span of the little boat.

Eyas, I greet you.

120

Enfolded by Her love, Eyas opened his mind and memory. For a time there was silence, and a sense that She felt sorrow at what was in his thoughts.

So now you seek your father. I sense him, but he is far away. Let him go, though you seek him out of love.

Reluctantly, Eyas bowed his head. "As You will it." Then, gathering his courage, he asked, "Mother, why did You not speak to me at the Gathering? Were You warning me, or have You turned away from me?"

A warning? Yes, perhaps it was. I am weary, Eyas. I have looked under the People for a long time, and soon that time must end.

"No—it can't end." He felt like a terrified child.

I have failed the People. I thought I could shape them, change them, save them from the misery men bring upon themselves. (He saw in remembrance the tower on the headland, as it had been one night long ago: grizzled men, soldiers in bronze and leather, fought by the light of the burning houses. A little boy screamed silently for his mother; a soldier irritably swung a red-smeared ax, killing the boy; a moment later the soldier too was dead.) *And the People are changed. They conceive when they wish, they taste the sea, they call the winds and hear spiders spin far away. They cherish their land, and live in peace with each other and with the brutes. But they are doomed.*

Eyas said nothing, but She knew his question.

I have only weakened them, as Griptiller in her love weakened Darkhair. She would not let him grow, and the child in him has destroyed the man he might have been. When the Suns came before, the People were already too much my children to resist them. I could not bear their suffering, and I fled from it. Not for centuries could I return to the Gulf.

Then I saw that the People must rise against the Suns or be destroyed. I sent poor beautiful Quickhand to his death, and all the others. When the Suns were gone, I thought the People might grow peaceful again, with remembrance to guide them if they must fight once more. But they are unready for what is coming, and time is short.

"If we are doomed," said Eyas softly, "why did You spare us when the ship was wrecked? Why did You suckle me, give me Your love, make me so different from everyone else?"

Her breathing was slow. At last Her thoughts entered his mind again.

All that lives must die, but death is not the same for all. I thought I saw a way to make from you what the People would have grown to become: a human strong against the human dead, with power in death as well as life. I changed you as no human had been changed before, not even my own ancestors who once walked the earth as men. At the least, I hoped you might bring new strength and wisdom to the People, and through your children spread your powers to all mankind. But I hoped most that you would break the grip of the dead on the living, and find a way between Hell's darkness and the other worlds of afterlife.

It is too late. I was too slow in changing the People, too late in changing you. I gambled against the human dead with your life and those of the People, and I have lost. The Suns are coming closer, faster, and with them the darkness; because of me, the People will go into it as they did before, and this time they will stay in darkness and sorrow forever.

I, who judged you, judge myself as well, and will pay the penalty for my meddling. I am the last of my kind. Soon I will go to join my ancestors in the sea of eternity, a better world than I deserve. They will not praise me for what I have done. . . . I ask forgiveness, Eyas.

"I can give You only love and reverence. And whatever the fate of People may be, it is my fate as well. I would return to them."

I send you home, Eyas. Farewell; may the time that is left be sweet to you.

The air chilled, and a wind began to blow out of the southwest. Eyas hurried to raise sail, knowing the Goddess had invoked the wind, and that it would carry him back to the Rip. The sail banged, and bulged taut; *Whiteback* sliced through a wave. Eyas took the tiller and steered by the Bridge for home, with the Goddess's sorrow and love as strong around him as the wind.

"Mother, Mother!" he cried out. "Is there nothing I can do to save the People?"

Not while Skyland hangs above the world.

She was gone. Eyas sailed on before the wind, and wept at the strange cruelty of Her last reply.

13

Whiteback came through the Rip more a hulk than a
boat, and Eyas had scarcely strength enough to keep it afloat
between the fury of the tide and that of a summer storm.
When the storm had passed, he slept fitfully on the tilted
deck of the drowning boat, and dreamed for the first time in
his life of Admiral Thorn. He had seen Thorn often in
remembrance, but never so vividly or so terribly as now. The
deep-set eyes were pits of blackness; the proud mouth curved
in a hungry grin.

*You are close to us, Eyas. We have devoured Hemlock, and
Goldarms, and Griptiller, and Silken. Soon we will taste
Darkhair's life. And we will feed well on you, Eyas....*

A wave washed across the deck, rousing him. He was alone
in the middle of the southern Gulf, drifting slowly eastward
just within sight of the Mistmarsh. As Eyas sat up he saw a
sail and recognized Harper's boat *Cloud* approaching. He
waved wearily; the boat's blue-and-white pennant dipped and
rose in reply.

Harper and Old and Sky took him aboard just as *Whiteback*
capsized and sank. "I owe my grandmother a new boat," he
mumbled as Sky wrapped him in a blanket.

"No," she said. "Griptiller died two days ago. And someone has murdered Silken. They cut her throat and burned
her cabin down." Her eyes were bright with tears. Eyas
nodded absently, reminded of what he already knew. He let
mourning settle over him like a second blanket and said little
on the return to Longstrand.

For centuries the pattern of the People's lives had sustained
them in sorrow as well as joy. Darkhair's crime had been
atoned for by his self-exile; Eyas's search for him had restored
the family's standing. The Fishers grieved in private, but
Firewing and Quiet could still celebrate the women's festivals
with the village sisterhood, and Eyas and Netweaver could
meet with the brotherhood, as if nothing had happened.

But patterns could also break. Eyas did not finish his wanderyear; he was needed at home. With Netweaver he built a new boat, *Second Waveskimmer*, and in it the Fishers went back upon the Gulf. Old and Sky resumed their travels, together with a merry girl from Last Soldier Cove named Violet Meadows, and the three of them were frequent visitors in Longstrand. Eyas often went hunting or fishing with them, and the four of them spent many nights in laughter and lovemaking. By autumn it was agreed that they should marry and become Fishers. At the end of the winter the marriage was celebrated with a feast, presided over by Speaker Givenlast, who drank too much and had trouble remembering the ceremonies.

On New Year's Day, 259, the Goddess did not appear in Gathering Cove.

The People waited in the water all day, while the year-gifts began to rot in unseasonably warm weather. That night the People spent sleeplessly on the beach or in their boats; all the next day they waited, but She did not come. The Speakers met that night and hastily concocted a new ceremony. Next morning the People waded out to Gathering Bar and pushed their little reed boats out into the empty water. The ebbing tide carried them into Deep Passage, and a breeze from the Westwall brought back the stink of rotting fish.

Almost guiltily, the People left Highdune Island and sailed for their homes. Instead of judgement, they had only the interim decisions of the Speakers, instead of remembrance, they had only the memory of silence, and sun glaring on the water.

"It's our fault," Firewing said as *Second Waveskimmer* neared Longstrand. "We offended Her. We should have done more than we did about Darkhair."

"No," said Eyas.

"What do *you* know?" she spat at him. "You're a man, and Sunnish at that!"

Eyas put a hand to his face as if she had slapped him. He had never spoken of his meeting with the Goddess, and he would not now—what She had told him would only drive his family deeper into despondency. But to hear such words from Firewing made him realize how frightening it could be, to be an abandoned child.

Springtime brought the traders and wandering youths, and the pattern of their lives sustained the People as it had the

124

Fishers. Only when two or three gathered quietly were the terrible questions asked, and answered in still more terrible ways. In the warmth of the nights, sleepers cried out, and woke grim and shaken. Haggling on the beach turned to quarrels and insults; mockery duels ended in fights. Givenlast tried to keep order and dispense justice, but he was an old man too fond of wine.

Eyas had his own problems. His mothers seemed to quarrel constantly, with each other and with Sky and Violet. Netweaver spent as much time as he could away from the house; when he had to be inside, he ignored the bickering with closed eyes. Old's sharp tongue annoyed all his in-laws, and it grew sharper still as he chafed at the tension in the household. Only in their lovemaking did the family seem like its former self.

Trade was poor that summer, reminding the Fishers that they were merchants as well as casters of nets. Not many flying islands came to the Gulf; Unsheath and Soarfar, despite their friendship with Eyas, drove hard bargains in the trading at Anchorwood. Eyas himself had to admit that the quality of the People's cloth and earthenware was poor. A month or so later, only a dozen centaurs came to trade, with little iron.

"We have little to spare," Boulder explained to Eyas as they sat in the centaur's newly pitched tent. "The Suns are foraying on our southern border. It will be a bitter war."

"Have you made any cannons?"

"Yes—of iron, and of brass. They look very beautiful on the wall around the Houses of Oldwalker. Other holds pay us well for cannons. But we do not use them much in battle."

"Why not?"

"They bring no glory." Boulder squinted through resin smoke from his clay pipe. "Once you said I was not like other centaurs. You were right; I am like Scall, the centaur who sold his sword to a goat."

Eyas laughed, knowing the centaur folktale, but he remembered how the thunderstorm had pursued him from the Great Bight to Ripmouth, unseen except as a darkening of the air, unheard except as a voice lost in the shout of the tide. Another storm was moving toward the Gulf; Alland itself was stirring.

Sky was pregnant by summer's end, and Violet by the autumn equinox. Firewing was overjoyed, and almost her old self, but Quiet was indifferent. She spent her time now in traveling: women in different villages were forming a new kind of sisterhood, whose purposes were secret. Quiet tried to interest her daughters-in-law in joining, but they were too involved in their men and their impending motherhood.

That winter Harper came to Longstrand to ask for food for Rainfalling. In Speaker's Hall she described how fishermen from Three Springs and Northport had taken most of a salmon run that traditionally went to Rainfalling; now they had neither food nor goods to buy any. The adults had been going hungry for weeks, and soon the children would be too. Harper herself looked gaunt and grim.

After long debate Longstrand grudgingly gave her three boatloads of dried fish and two of breadseed. Eyas would have been ashamed of the amount if he had not known how small the village's reserves had sunk. When the gift was voted, Harper bowed her head in thanks and then looked up.

"I was born a Fisher of Longstrand. I knew the fishing rights of every village, every family, before I could write my name. You will never again be asked by Rainfalling for your help, because next year the Goddess will affirm our right to the Bloodwood Creek run. —And if She doesn't come, we'll affirm it ourselves, with spears and arrows if needed."

The Goddess did not appear on New Year's Day of 260. Givenlast resigned the Speakership as soon as he got back to Longstrand; at the meeting to elect his successor, Quiet argued that the time had come for a group of Speakers, not just one, to run the village. She suggested the brotherhood choose a representative; so would the sisterhood and any other group with a special interest.

"I belong to such a group," Quiet went on. "We call ourselves the dreamwatchers; we believe—we know—our ancestors speak to us in dreams. They foretold to us that the Goddess would not return. They tell us now that a time of changes is coming to the Gulf and the People. We must be ready to heed our ancestors, or the changes will take us by surprise."

Eyas, hearing this, sent his husband and wives to confer with various friends and relatives. The hall was too still, especially the women's benches; Quiet had prepared for this, and her proposal might well succeed.

Givenlast, meanwhile, called a pause for discussion. He walked over to Eyas, who stood up in respect.

"Stupidest idea I ever head," the old man muttered under his breath. "Windinvokers always were a flighty bunch; just because they can do a few tricks, they think they know everything. Now this. Impious as well as stupid. The Speaker is the Goddess's voice, not some clapstick chorus." With the freedom of old age, he added, "Women's mischief!"

Eyas ignored the crudity. "How do you read the People?"

"Like children left alone in the house. They want to be good, and they want to play with the coals on the hearth. They just might choose to try this foolishness."

"And how would Griptiller have handled this?"

"I have no idea. The old prowl would never have let it get to the hall."

Eyas thought. "Perhaps you could tell them you'll consider the change if there are nominations first for a single Speaker, and no one wins a majority of the votes."

"Dangerous—we'll be stuck with her three-headed Speaker unless we get a strong candidate. But it's better than arguing all night."

He called the meeting back to order, and ruled as Eyas had suggested. Quiet and some of her allies exchanged quick looks before Quiet accepted the Speaker's decision.

"Good," said Givenlast. "Then who should wear the clamshell?" He held up the symbol of his office. Silence answered him. Again he asked, and a third time.

Old stood up. "My husband, Eyas Fisher, should wear the clamshell."

Givenlast Forester kept his composure, but many did not. Fishers had often been Speakers, but no one had ever heard of a youth of eighteen, not yet a parent, seeking the office. Even Harper had been in her twenties, and a mother, before becoming Speaker of Rainfalling. Besides, Eyas was Sunnish born—yet suckled by the Goddess—a friend of brutes—a smart trader—the adulterer's son—a sailor of the Rip—

The arguments crackled around the hall; Eyas ignored them and watched his mother Quiet. Her first surprise changed to swift private thought, and then to resignation. She met his gaze, smiled, and nodded slightly. Eyas relaxed.

It would be a bitter family quarrel that led parent and child to vote against each other. Eyas had not been entirely certain of Quiet's commitment to her dreamwatchers, or of her feelings for him, but her nod told him the family tie was still strong, and the dreamwatchers were still unsure of their own ability to hold power. When Givenlast called for the vote, Quiet's hand rose for her son; so did those of all the Fishers and their allies—as well as a few enemies, dreamwatchers who loyally followed Quiet's lead. The vote was a solid majority for Eyas.

In the ceremony of transfer, Givenlast whispered, "Well, now they can be good and still play with fire. I hope you know what you're in for."

Eyas could not remember a time when political intrigue had not been a daily topic of family conversation. His grandmother had said that politics was the art of getting along profitably with unlikable and ungenerous fools and tricksters; he found it so. Among the People, politics was a tangle of administration, gesture, and maneuver: if a job was to be done, it must be asked of the man or woman whose standing would thereby rise without giving serious offense to other candidates or their friends. The Speaker would thus enhance his own power and authority, but must not be too obvious about it. In many cases the award or withholding of a job or an honor was as tricky as plucking a firewing from a spider's web without rousing the spider.

But Eyas had judged the People's mood wisely. They wanted both continuity and novelty. To have a Speaker so young and unusual, yet still a Fisher, satisfied both desires. Longstrand was pleased as well by the stir the election caused in other villages, and stood behind him rather than risk unseemly quarrels that might cost it standing and lead others to question Longstranders' intelligence.

In the last days of spring, Sky gave birth to a son. She named him Gray, for his eyes were like Eyas's. He was a big, noisy, happy baby who delighted them all. Firewing cherished him especially, and even Quiet often withdrew from her long reveries to fondle her new grandson. With the birth in summer of Violet's daughter Golden, the household seemed restored to its former hectic self, full of shouting women, squalling infants, and cheerful relatives visiting from Yellowshaws, Easthaven, and Last Soldier Cove.

As the autumn days grew shorter, Eyas liked to spend his afternoons on the front steps with the babies napping in the cradles he had made for them; he enjoyed the warmth of the sun and the domestic clatter within the house. The warning of the Goddess was often in his thoughts, but only heightened his contentment: if this happiness could not last, he would savor it to the full while it did.

On one such afternoon, when the day had been crowded with ominous news, Quiet sat down beside him.

"What are you going to do about this feud Harper's started?" she asked abruptly.

"I'll offer to mediate; what else can I do?" Harper had ordered a raid on Three Springs after their fishermen had once again tried to take the Bloodwood Creek salmon run. Six men from Rainfalling, and five from Three Springs, had been killed.

"Send me to mediate."

"Would they accept you? You're Harper's blood-mother, after all."

"It doesn't matter. The ancestors warned me of the raid. They tell me I must go, and they will guide me."

"Will the brotherhood of Three Springs believe such a tale?"

"Three Springs has its dreamwatchers too—more than you think. They'll *make* the brotherhood agree."

"With five of their men dead, they'll be too vengeful to—"

"To listen to a few dithering old women?" Quiet looked steadily at her son. "I was not the first of us to understand the ancestors, Eyas, but now I do more than hear them. They have given me powers beyond farhearing and windinvoking. The men of Three Springs may be hotheaded fools, but they will listen to me. Watch—watch."

She stood up, arms at her sides, and closed her eyes. The late-afternoon sun seemed to darken, as if a cloud had crossed it, but there was no cloud. With unnatural speed, twilight fell upon the beach. The air chilled. In two or three breaths, a kind of night had descended. The chatter within the longhouse ceased; the babies in their cradles stirred and whimpered.

Fear fell upon Eyas as rapidly as the dark. He stood up and groped toward Quiet, now only a shadow in the twilight. "Stop it! Stop it!" he whispered. As if from far away, she replied,

"Not until you send me."

His hands found her shoulders. "No! Oh Goddess, give me light!"

A power rose in him, and in a white flash he saw Quiet's face. The darkness returned for an instant, then vanished for good. Sunlight warmed them once more.

Violet appeared in the doorway. "Is it going to rain? It got so dark—"

The babies were awake and crying. Eyas released his mother and picked up Gray, comforting him; Quiet did the same to Golden. Violet came down the steps.

"Poor things, they're hungry. Here, let me take them." She put Golden to her breast, and tucked Gray onto her hip. He squawked jealously. "Never mind, Gray, I can't nurse you both and still walk. Your mother's just inside—she'll be glad to see you. I never thought full breasts could be so uncomfortable," she added to Quiet, and hurried back inside.

"How did you do that?" his mother said softly.

"I don't know. It was like the first time I farheard. I just—I needed light."

"Sunnish born, yet you have such power. . . . Surely you hear the ancestors in your dreams, Eyas."

He hesitated. "No."

Quiet seemed to dismiss the matter. "You are the Speaker; you will decide for Longstrand what we should do. But next winter we will end the Speakership, and a group will decide."

"And when the Goddess returns?"

"I don't think she will." Quiet used the secular pronoun, as if the Goddess were any female. "It's just as well, perhaps. Now the ancestors will speak directly to us, not just through remembrance."

Sky appeared on the steps, with Gray happily nuzzling her. "The meal is ready." And the smile she gave him seemed brighter than the light he had invoked against Quiet's darkness.

Eyas sent Old to represent Longstrand in the peacemaking. Others, from almost every village in the Gulf, went also to the empty beach of Gathering Cove. The dispute was resolved by a complex exchange of gifts and apologies, but Old returned without gladness.

"It will happen again," he told the People in the Hall. "Each village will encroach on another. Nothing but battles will resolve these quarrels, unless we can remember the wisdom of the Goddess." The People nodded, but Eyas sensed only the habit of piety, not real understanding. His husband's words filled him with foreboding: next time it might be Longstrand at war with Big Harbor or Wreck Point.

The dreamwatchers increased their numbers. Their calm certainty attracted many, and they seemed truly in touch with something very strange and great. One autumn day, Quiet predicted the arrival of visitors from Northport; next day the visitors dropped anchor in the harbor. One of the Brewers' daughters, a child of twelve, woke to say a cousin in Big Harbor had just delivered a stillborn son with a purple birthmark on his face. Four days later a boat from Big Harbor confirmed the girl's story. Men, too, began to join the dreamwatchers, which was now much more than a sisterhood. An uncle of Netweaver's found a jade boulder in a Westwall creek after learning of its location in a dream.

Eyas kept his own dreams to himself until one rainy night on the edge of winter, when Violet woke sobbing beside him.

"The man, the man," she whimpered. "He said he was going to devour us."

"What man? What did he look like?" Eyas asked, holding her in his arms.

"Tall. I couldn't see his eyes. He had dark hair, I think, and he was so pale."

"Did he wear a—a blue robe?"

"Yes, yes."

"Admiral Thorn."

"Oh, Eyas, you've seen him too."

"We've all seen him, in remembrance. Darkhair killed him."

"That's right, I remember now." Then she added, "But you've also seen him in your dreams."

"What of it? I see you, and Sky, and the babies in my dreams."

"Thorn is different, isn't he? I can tell by your voice, and your skin."

"Yes, he's different."

"I'm afraid to sleep again."

"It's all right." He rocked her in his arms, lulling her, and watched the coals dying in the ashes.

"If you support us, we'll make you one of the village group," Quiet said to Eyas just before the election. "It would make everyone happier with the change."

131

Eyas shook his head. "The Speaker speaks to the Goddess for the People. The dreamwatchers reject the Goddess; I don't."

"The Goddess has rejected *us*. But the ancestors haven't. And they tell me they've spoken to you, Eyas. Don't bother to deny it. You're just being foolish and stubborn, clinging to the old ways."

He sighed. "If you have the votes, you'll get your way. But I think you're wrong, Quiet, and I won't help you. I must follow the Goddess, whether She visits us or not."

His mother stared scornfully at him. "What good did she do the People when she bound us to look after you and Brightspear and the woman? What did she give us but death and bitterness and sorrow?"

Eyas looked deep into his mother's eyes. In them he saw anger, but under it was no real hatred, only fear. Something had reached into her, into her living center, and now it ruled her through fear. That one so wise and powerful could be so ruled frightened Eyas in itself; and because she was wise and powerful, she saw what he felt and looked down. After a moment she turned and walked away.

The dreamwatchers won the election easily. In the Hall, Eyas removed the clamshell and placed it on the Speaker's stool. It was not picked up by anyone else; Quiet and her followers—two men and two women—were now the village group, and all spoke for Longstrand. They ordered a new house to be built beside the Hall, and left their families to live in it.

Netweaver and Firewing did not speak much about Quiet's departure, and when they met her in the village it was without rancor. But they drew together, consoling each other as Hemlock and Griptiller had after their husbands' deaths off the Mistmarsh. Eyas went about his late-winter chores, preparing *Second Waveskimmer* for its New Year's voyage. He played with the babies by the fire, read books, and sat joking in the sweatbath with his neighbors. Once, the family sledged up the frozen Bluemeadows River to spend a few days in Yellowshaws; but Old's mothers Ivy and Rose were dreamwatchers now, and too proud of their own victory over their village's last Speaker. Eyas, as a son-in-law, kept his peace, but Old lost his temper after three days and quarreled bitterly with his mothers. His fathers, pleasant men ready to sacrifice anything for domestic tranquility, tactfully suggested that

Gray and Golden must miss their familiar routine; the Fishers agreed and left next morning.

Not many boats left Longstrand harbor in the last days of the old year. The winter still lay cold upon the Gulf; snow fell thickly on the bloodwood blooms, and melted grudgingly. Eyas's family went first as always to Gathering Cove, and were not surprised to see only a handful of boats there. One was *Cloud*; Harper was still Speaker of Rainfalling, but when her family and Eyas's ate together on New Year's Eve she said the dreamwatchers would probably hold a meeting in her absence and vote her out.

"They can't!" Violet protested.

"But they will." Harper seemed tired but undiscouraged. "They know about Longstrand and Yellowshaws and other villages; and those who still love the Goddess are all here." She waved down the rain-soaked beach at the scattered tents and lean-tos. "A perfect time for them. When the Goddess doesn't come, half of us will give up."

Sky held her baby, wrapped in a blanket against the raw wind, and rocked him gently. Her face was sad. "What's happened to us? When I was a girl it was never like this. We were all so happy. When did it change?"

Firewing and Netweaver looked at each other, and said nothing.

On New Year's Day, 261, the Fishers sailed across Ripmouth. Eyas farheard the coming tide while Netweaver steered. The babies squealed with delight as the boat rode the tide, and the butterfly nets were heavy with fish. They returned to Gathering Cove under dark skies spitting rain and wet snow, and found only a few more arrivals. But the exhilaration of that swift race, and the familiarity of the old rites, kept up the family's spirits. In their tent they reminisced about other Gatherings, told jokes, and sang. The evening's high tide brought no sign of the Goddess, and they went to sleep early.

The Goddess did not appear on the next morning's tide, nor on the afternoon's. Several boats left the cove. The little reed boats, piled with yeargift fish, sat on the beach under a steady cold drizzle. Eyas and Harper exhausted themselves with farhearing, but there was no trace of Her. By the end of the third day of the new year almost everyone was gone from Gathering Cove. "We'll go home in the morning," Netweaver said, and no one argued with him.

It was a late spring, and a dull one. The village group ruled that Traders' Beach would be open only to visitors from villages also governed by groups. The brotherhood still met, but fewer attended each time; too many men felt pressure from their families and from the group.

One night just seven men, including Netweaver, Eyas, and Old, met in the brotherhood house. When Netweaver went to get the *Book of Longstrand's Men* for the reading, it was missing.

"This is a serious matter," he said. "Old—report it to the group."

In the house of the group, Quiet told him the book had been taken on the group's orders, and destroyed. He stared at her, for once unable to think of a suitable reply.

"We're ridding ourselves of all mention of the Goddess," Quiet said serenely. "All the books that deal with Her are being burned. I know, I know—many have much else of value in them. We'll have new versions made, better than the old ones."

"You had no right to enter the brotherhood house," Old said at last.

"The group speaks for Longstrand and acts for Longstrand. We have every right."

"How can the brotherhood meet if we have no book?"

"It's no concern of mine. The group doesn't think highly of the brotherhood anyway. It's too concerned with violence and war and male glory. We've seen where that can lead to—senseless feuds and killing."

"We'll protest this at the next meeting of the People."

"If you wish."

But Speaker's Hall stayed empty except for private meetings of the group. The brotherhood tried to regain support by quiet appeals to its lapsed members, and failed.

"They're not troubling the sisterhood," Sky said one night late in the spring. "Except for changing the songs that praise the Goddess. But it hardly matters. So many women are pregnant, we hardly have enough for the—rituals." She blushed; she had nearly mentioned things not to be spoken of in men's presence. Unlike their mother-in-law Firewing, Sky and Violet were modest women.

The pregnancies, however, could not be kept secret. It seemed as if every young wife in Longstrand had conceived, even those who already had two living children. But the ancestors, speaking through the group, had repudiated the Goddess's ancient commandment that no woman should bear more than two offspring.

"I'd love to be pregnant again," said Violet. "But I'll wait until this silly fashion passes."

Old gave her a mocking smile. "Wouldn't life be easier if you were a dreamwatcher?"

"No!" She looked at Eyas. "My dreams frighten me. Anyway, we're married to a man nursed by the Goddess; that's reason enough right there to have nothing to do with the dreamwatchers."

Eyas drank the last of his mug of beer. Violet's words disturbed him, though he tried not to show it. He had been special all his life, and took it for granted, the way Old accepted his bad leg and women accepted the powers of their bodies. But still it surprised him that others should feel he was worth any trouble—that his specialness, which had isolated him from the dreamwatchers, mattered enough to his husband and wives to make them choose isolation also.

He got up and walked noiselessly to the far end of the room, where the babies slept. Gray's knees were tucked under him, and his rump stuck up. Golden slept beside him, snoring a little, her thumb in her mouth. He touched each child, feeling their warmth and aliveness, and rejoiced in them. The Speakership, the brotherhood, the laughter of Traders' Beach—nothing else mattered while the children were safe and well.

"Let's go fishing tomorrow," he said when he returned to the fireside. "And make a little wanderyear of it—at least until Unsheath comes. Quiet's friends can't ruin the Gulf."

"Good," his father nodded. "Weather or no weather, it'll be better than watching Longstrand rot alive, like a spawning salmon."

14

Not long before dawn the next morning, the family woke. "Is it raining?" asked Violet.

"No," said Firewing, "but it sounded like thunder. Maybe an earthquake."

The sound rolled again from the direction of the cliff; then it was lost in the crash of shattered wood nearby. Voices cried out in another house. Netweaver got to his feet just as Old was starting to build up the fire.

"No light. Eyas and Old—get your bows, and all the arrows you can find. And axes."

"Father, what is it?" Eyas whispered.

"I think someone is shooting a cannon at the village."

Another crash shook the longhouse. The babies woke and whimpered; their mothers comforted them. After a fourth echoing roar, the noise blurred into a long, stuttering thunder, almost like spring breakup on the Bluemeadows River. The wall by the fireplace suddenly splintered, driving fragments of wood all over the room. Firewing gasped, struck in both legs by splinters. Netweaver gripped her shoulders. "Get to the boatshed," he ordered. "We've got to get the women and babies out on the water."

Furry, the current house spider, was squeaking with alarm as Eyas and Old dashed down the steps from the front door. They stopped short as something passed overhead with a sound like a gust of wind. An instant later, water sprayed up, gray in the dark-blue twilight, just beyond the beach. Eyas spun round and looked over the rooftops toward the cliff. Red flames shot out in three places along the precipice, and then houses shook under the impact of the shots. Eyas remembered the cannon he'd found for Boulder, and wondered if the centaurs had for some reason renewed their ancient war on the People.—No, impossible.

"They're Suns," he said to Old. "Goddess look under us." Two longhouses were on fire, and their orange flames were bright enough to show Old's unsurprised face.

"Suns or walkingtrees, they've got to be stopped," Old said. "I'll try to gather the brotherhood; you run the boat out." He shuffled into the darkness.

Eyas went to the shed. A cannonball hummed low overhead and punched through the roof. Then a second shot, and a third, fell on the shed. Sprawled flat on the sand, Eyas saw the shed door swing open; dust swirled out. He wanted to see if *Second Waveskimmer* was damaged, but fear of another shot kept him still. Something else hit the shed roof and shattered like a dropped earthenware pot. Fire sprayed across the roof and dripped down the wall. By its light, Eyas could see a gaping hole in the boat's side. Beyond the boat, a heavy beam had fallen onto the family's two canoes.

He scooped up his bow and quiver and ran back to the longhouse. More fires were breaking out; the Suns must have something like resin, that could be set ablaze and hurled from the cliff. Black smoke rose from many roofs.

"The boat's wrecked," he said when he got back inside. "So are the canoes. We'll have to try to get down the beach, away from the village. Mother, can you walk?"

Firewing, a shadow in the darkness, stood up. "Yes," she said, but it was more a sob than a word. Eyas picked her up. He felt the wetness of blood on her legs.

"Violet—Sky. Have you got the babies? Let's go. Where's Father?"

"Gone to rally the brotherhood," Violet said.

Longstrand was a tumult of screams and shouts and burning wood. As the Fishers went down to the beach, they jostled with others. Most were women and children, but a few were men. Eyas collided with one, a Weaver. "Find Old and Netweaver and join the brotherhood!" Eyas shouted, but the man ran off eastward down the beach.

Along with scores of others, the Fishers also went east, but more slowly. They were just past the last longhouse when three shrieking women ran back toward them. Then more came, stumbling in their haste to get back into the burning village.

"What's the matter?" Firewing asked faintly.

"The Suns must be coming down the beach." He turned and carried his mother into a boatshed; his wives followed. Eyas put his mother down as gently as he could. "Wait. I'll be back in a little while. Lie still, all of you." The shed was empty; its owners had already escaped. He took Sky aside. "Do you have a knife?"

"Two."

"Give one to Violet." He bent and kissed Gray, who was nuzzling his mother's breast, and then Golden, who had stopped crying and was looking around curiously. Then he went back out onto the sand. Three men hurried up from the center of the village, arrows nocked in their bows. They were Third Brewer, a veteran of Darkhair's attack on *Liberator*, Windy Coppersmith, and Summerday Forester, a son of old Givenlast.

"Eyas—Old sent us. Are the Suns coming?" asked Third.

"I think so." He fitted an arrow into his own bow and glared into the darkness. "Get up the beach, toward the cliff. We'll be easy targets here, against the fires."

Longstrand's little hill sloped away here, and the beach ran straight into a tangle of berries and young alders. The four men slipped into the cover of the underbrush and waited. Eyas felt the weight of his ax, dangling from the belt he had strapped on.

To the west, Longstrand burned. Cannonballs still crashed down, but the fires were doing far more damage. From the far side of the village, men's shouts rose above the noise; the Suns must be coming from the west as well. Eyas trembled with anger and fear. He heard the men beside him breathing fast, and calmed himself. Every arrow must count. A shaking arm would spare men who must die.

"Here they come," he whispered. "Wait till I shoot."

In a loose, open line, dark figures walked slowly down the beach. Some carried long spears, others shorter weapons that must be guns. None spoke. Firelight glinted orange off the iron plates they wore upon their chests, and off helmets crested with long hair like a spitfar's tail. One, in the lead, wore a dark cape and carried a sword. The soldiers' boots crunched on the pebbly sand.

Aiming for the swordsman, Eyas let fly and nocked another arrow. The swordsman halted and shouted something. The arrow had missed. But three more sang out, and then Eyas's second one, and the swordsman fell gasping. Another soldier collapsed, grunting with pain but not crying out. The rest dropped to the sand and called out to one another; Eyas could not make out their words, but their accents reminded him of Silken. One of them fired his gun toward the cliff. The shot was a wide miss, and the flash of red from the barrel made the soldier a target. One of the Longstranders shot back, and they heard the arrow strike flesh.

Eyas tapped the archer's back, warning him to move before the Suns fixed their enemies' position. Silently, the four men spread out through the alders. After a shot or two they moved again, while the Suns fired almost at random. As the flames of Longstrand spread, the soldiers became clearer targets. Eyas hit another one, but only after three misses.

Losing their leader had demoralized the Suns for a moment, but someone took command. With a shout, the soldiers fired a volley, dropped their guns, and charged toward the cliff with spears and swords. Eyas loosed his last arrow at fairly close range, but didn't wait to see if he had hit his man. He made a sound like two soft kisses, a signal to retreat back to the cliff. The Suns came up to the edge of the alders, found no one, and slashed a few hesitant steps forward before their new leader shouted, "On to the village! They'll be in there!"

But the four men were still among the trees. They watched the Suns turn away and retrieve their guns before plodding on. Three or four of them straggled behind, doing something to their guns, and Eyas remembered Silken's telling him that reloading was slow and awkward. Around the stragglers lay six bodies, only two of them moving. Eyas clicked his tongue once, then twice, and moved back down toward the sand. The other men, he knew, would be alongside him.

As they reached the edge of the trees Eyas saw that Third still had arrows. With a quick gesture, he ordered: Cover us. Third sucked in his breath, acknowledging. Eyas clicked his tongue again and ran onto the beach, drawing the ax from his belt. Beside him were Windy and Summerday, knives out.

The fight was brief, silent, and pitiless. At the end of it Summerday Forester and all four Suns were dead. The three survivors looked at each other in the graying light of early dawn. Eyas caught his breath and realized that he had killed men. It was much like the battles he had experienced in remembrance, except for the sounds of blows and the groans of the dying.

"What now?" asked Third.

Eyas looked up the beach. Despite the coming dawn, the flames were brighter than ever. The cannons on the cliff kept up a steady barrage that almost drowned out the sounds of battle in Longstrand itself.

"Back into the village," he said. "Through the trees at the foot of the cliff."

The sky was glowing with a spring sunrise by the time they slipped around the Suns' flank and back into Longstrand. The attackers had met resistance and were stalled among the burning houses at the edge of the village. Eyas would have joined the defenders, but first he must learn what was happening on the western and northern sides of the fight.

Speaker's Hall and the house of the village group were on

fire. Nearby, Old and Netweaver were ordering men to east and west, while cannonballs and firebombs crashed around them.

"We're holding them on the west," Old shouted. "What about the east?"

"Holding so far," Eyas told him. "But if the cannons keep firing, we'll be wiped out. I'll take some men up the cliff and try to stop them."

"They'll see you coming," Old protested. "The trail's exposed—"

"We'll go up the cliff, east of the tower."

"You don't know how many of them there are up there," said Netweaver.

"It doesn't matter. If we can wreck even two of the cannons, we'll have a chance. Goddess! How did they manage such a surprise?"

Eyas gestured to Third and Windy. Old found bows for them, and full quivers for all. Netweaver, carrying a double-edged ax, came with them. As they ran through the smoke, they met Quiet wandering down a muddy lane between two houses. Her face was blank with shock, and she would have passed by them without recognition. But Netweaver took her by the hair and swung her to face him.

"Did your ancestors warn you of this?" he snarled.

"No—no—they said nothing—"

He shoved her aside and glared at Eyas, who stepped back in alarm at his father's rage. "Get on, get on!"

Smoke concealed them as they went into the thickets at the base of the cliff. Eyas found a little-used trail, overgrown with blackberry brambles, and they followed it east along the cliff. About a hundred spans east of the tower, the four men began to climb.

The cliff here was almost vertical, with only occasional cracks or ledges large enough to support a hand or foot. In summer most children climbed it easily despite their parents' warnings; now, in a cold spring, the cliff was slippery with wet moss and slime.

At first Eyas concentrated on the climb, ignoring the crash of the guns above and the noise of battle below. Reaching a ledge, he paused and looked down. Longstrand looked like a lake of fire and smoke. Men and women ran from one burning house to another, or walked as aimlessly as Quiet had. To the west, the Suns were pushing into the village, dark figures moving with directness and efficiency from one lane to the next. Behind them lay brown bodies in the mud and ashes. On the east, the attackers had been stopped, just inside the outermost houses, and Eyas feared for his family in the abandoned boatshed. The Suns on the cliff were shifting their fire to that side of Longstrand. It was full daylight now, though the village still lay in shadow, and out on the water a few canoes and boats made for safety. Beyond them, the Gulf gleamed blue and green under a cloudless sky.

They went on climbing. If any Suns saw them from the village, none tried to warn their comrades on the cliff. When Eyas was near the top, he stopped at the bottom of a cleft, where a creek splashed out in a little waterfall. Above and to the left, a cannon bellowed. It must be right at the edge; if they followed the cleft, they could come out behind the cannoneers. But it meant scrambling over slippery stones in icy water, and somehow getting through a dense tangle of brambles and ferns without being noticed. He looked over his shoulder at the others, pointed at the cleft, and pulled himself up into the waterfall.

Twice he thought the force of the water would throw him back and hurl him from the cliff, but each time his hands found a hold. Once up into the cleft it was easier, and he helped the others get up past the worst part. After a moment's rest and whispered planning, they went on.

The creek, fed by winter snow and long spring rains, was strong, deep, and noisy, racing over a bed of smooth stones. As the cleft rose, it narrowed; dense banks of salal grew up on either side. Apart from the salal, little grew near the edge of the cliff, but the forest was dense within a hundred spans of the precipice. Eyas found a gap in the bushes and crawled up out of the cleft onto level ground. Cautiously he lifted his head.

Only ten spans to his left, five men in dirty black leather worked around a cannon. Like the one Eyas had salvaged from *Liberator*, it was not very large; but this one was mounted on big wooden wheels. Beside it were a sizable pile of cannonballs and several leather sacks of what must be gunpowder. The cannoneers loaded, fired, and reloaded with practiced efficiency and much joking and laughter. They were young men, sunburned and bearded, wearing no armor or helmets. Their hair was as black as Eyas's own, and long.

Farther along the cliff was a second cannon, and beyond

141

it—almost at the tower—a third, next to a machine that must be a catapult. It was hard to tell at that distance, but far more soldiers seemed to be gathered near the tower: reserves, perhaps, waiting to go down the trail when the cannons and catapult had done their work.

Netweaver came alongside him and saw the cannons. With his lips near Eyas's ear, he said, "We can kill these, but not all of the others. And if we stay, they will kill us."

"We don't need to kill them all—just wreck the cannons and the catapult." He slid back down into the cleft, where Third and Windy waited knee-deep in the stream. Eyas suggested a plan; all agreed. Then, while Third and Windy went up onto level ground, Eyas and his father went on up the creek a little farther. Long ago, the forest here had been logged off; alder and bloodwood were the second growth. Within thirty or forty spans of the cliff's edge the soil was too thin to support more than waist-high salal and an occasional tree, but beyond that the woods thickened and gave the Fishers good concealment. Moving silently, they reached a point behind the second cannon just as it fired and recoiled on its big wheels. Netweaver took Eyas's hand.

"Goddess look under us all. Eyas, you are my son and I love you. May we walk together on the Bridge of Heaven."

"Not until we walk together in Longstrand for many more years." Eyas kissed him and moved on alone toward the tower, the quiver heavy on his back. If anything went wrong, their lives would end; little loss, if Longstrand fell. How could the Suns have done this? To cross the Valley without an alarm being raised; to move men and equipment into perfect position, at night, in unfamiliar country—

"Ah," said Eyas softly, and was not surprised to see a tall man in a yellow hood among the black-clad soldiers near the tower. When the man turned, the new-risen sun fell on his scarred face: Brightspear was back in the Gulf after almost three years.

From hiding, Eyas studied him. The scar on Brightspear's face was dark purple, as if infection had settled in the healing wound. His features were much as Eyas remembered: handsome, regular, and impassive. In black leather, Brightspear's body looked thicker and more powerful than ever, and he moved with unconscious grace. The men around him seemed nervous and insubstantial beside his solid serenity: for all their dusty leather and gleaming weaponry, they reminded

Eyas of the fawning attendants of the old Suns in Silken's tales.

Brightspear was well within bowshot, but a cluster of trees shielded him; besides, Eyas was too near the Easthaven trail and therefore vulnerable to a quick response. He moved to his left until he found a clear line of fire between himself and the crews of the third cannon and the catapult.

They were clearly outlined on the edge of the cliff, standing against a coiling wall of black smoke from the village. Eyas took five arrows from his quiver and laid them on a rock. Deliberately, he nocked one on his bowstring, drew the string to his ear, and shot.

Two more were in the air before the first one struck a cannoneer in the small of the back. Off to his left he heard cries from the other cannon crews; Netweaver, Third, and Windy had been ready with their own arrows. One of Eyas's arrows missed, but another hit a Sun in the leg. The unhurt soldiers stared in amazement at their wounded comrades for a moment, then went on loading. Eyas admired their courage even as he shot again and saw his arrow strike one of the catapult crew in the face.

Brightspear saw the attack and shouted an order; soldiers broke ranks and ran to the cannoneers' aid. Trees screened the first cannon from Eyas, but he heard a distant crash: Third and Windy, having wiped out its crew, had pushed the first cannon over the cliff. Netweaver now broke from cover, though two of his crew were still on their feet. They saw him, and fumbled for weapons, but he was upon them too quickly. One fell with an arrow in his belly; Netweaver picked up the last man and hurled him over the edge. Then he began to wrestle the cannon toward the edge while Third and Windy ran to help him.

More soldiers were running along the cliff despite Eyas's accurate shooting, and some went past the third cannon to close with Netweaver. Others gathered around the cannon and catapult, raising shields over their crews, and a few came crashing toward Eyas through the salal. Eyas ignored them and shot twice more toward the cannoneers and their defenders. One soldier took an arrow on his shield; another cried out, too loudly to have been fatally hit.

Several of the soldiers going after Netweaver had guns. Eyas saw them stop, go down on one knee, and fire. Netweaver spun away from the cannon and fell. Third must have been in the line of fire as well, for only Windy reached the cannon. He heaved against it; it toppled over the brink. Two soldiers reached him a moment later and speared him to death.

Eyas aimed another arrow at the approaching soldiers, then slackened his bowstring and retreated into the woods. He had only nine or ten arrows left, and each must count. Somehow he must wreck that last cannon and the catapult, and then get back into Longstrand; a strong counterattack might drive the Suns back and give the People time.

Like a splithoof he ran deeper into the woods, then turned to intersect the Easthaven trail. As he had suspected, the Suns were all clustered near the tower, and none saw him cross the trail and circle around. On his belly, he crawled through the salal until he was close enough to the soldiers to smell them. He risked a glimpse.

The Suns were far more numerous than he had imagined—perhaps two hundred in all, most of them still standing in orderly ranks. Their attention was on their comrades farther down the cliff top. Brightspear and his attendants, concealed by the soldiers, could not be seen.

The cannon and catapult could not be wrecked; even as he watched, the long arm of the catapult snapped up, throwing a round black object that must be a firebomb. The best he could hope for now was to get onto the trail and back into Longstrand. If Old had at least slowed the attackers from the east, it might be possible to get the women and children into boats—even onto logs—and onto the water, while the men protected their escape. Most of the men would die, but the survivors could vanish into the woods to harass the Suns and warn other villages. Brightspear's greatest weapon had been surprise; deprived of that, his two hundred men with their single cannon and catapult could not hope to stand against the united warriors of the Gulf.

A breeze blew through the woods from the north, carrying the sweet scent of flowering club. And something else: dust and sweat and a rank odor almost familiar. Voices called out in the distance, and something bellowed in complaint. The waiting soldiers murmured and laughed at the sounds. Eyas heard the jingle of harness and the thud of heavy hoofs, and then a hoarse command.

He had heard of sixfeet before, but he had never seen one. Now he saw scores, each with an armored rider or pulling a high-walled cart. The brutes were something like centaurs, even to their smell; but the upright torso and head of the centaur were horizontal in the sixfoot. The head faced forward, twice the size of a man's; though humanlike, its features were huge, slack, and witless. The sixfoot's foremost limbs were simply an additional pair of legs supporting the heavy torso and great stupid head; occasionally one of the brutes reared up nervously and slashed at the air with hands whose fingers were mere claws jutting from a hooflike, calloused palm. The sixfeet's gray, furry hides were lathered and dust-streaked. They had been ridden hard.

Eyas thought he understood Brightspear's tactics now. Sixfeet, like centaurs, could not swim; to transport them across the Bluemeadows River must have meant building rafts. Rather than risk losing the element of surprise, Brightspear had ferried the cannons and catapult and foot soldiers across, knowing his main force would arrive in time to finish what the cannons had begun.

Despair ached in him. Deeply ingrained in the People was respect not only for centaurs but for their wild cousins the woodsrunners; it would not be easy for a warrior of Longstrand to strike at a centaurlike sixfoot even if its Sunnish rider was about to kill him. That, even more than the rider's advantages of speed and height, would ensure Brightspear's victory.

But despair also freed him. His father Netweaver was dead; perhaps the rest of his family were also slain. He could act without thought for the consequences, and boldness was as effortless as caution. Eyas crawled closer to the edge of the cliff, past the foot soldiers, until he reached the trail at the point where it curved round the base of the tower. Then he stood up, walked into the middle of the trail, and turned with his bow drawn. He had a clear shot at Brightspear, whose back was turned, and let fly.

Someone shouted a warning, and one of Brightspear's attendants leaped into the arrow's path. The shaft went through the man's upraised palm and then pinned his hand to his breastbone. One of the foot soldiers hurled a spear at Eyas, who spun around and ran down the trail. He might still get back to the village, warn them of the sixfeet, rally a last defense—

Six soldiers, coming up the trail, blocked his way. If they were surprised they gave no sign of it; two raised guns to their shoulders and took aim. Eyas plunged to the left, into the bushes around the base of the tower, while gunshots echoed off its stone wall. In a few breaths he found one of the two entrances to the tower, largely overgrown with blackberry brambles but kept open by children. He slipped through the empty doorway.

Once the tower had had four floors above the level of the cliff; only rotted vestiges of them remained, built into the walls. The basement of the tower was a tangle of bushes and stunted trees, open to the sky. The tower's other doorway was down in the basement, but even if he could reach it, it would only lead him back to the trail or down a vertical drop of over six spans.

Panting, Eyas admired the green of new ferns growing in the cracks between the stone blocks of the walls, and the blue of the morning sky. A dabbler flew overhead, its translucent yellow wings beating hard; it vanished, and a hawk stooped after it in a blur of brown and gold.

"A hawk at my coming, a hawk at my going," he muttered. The shouts of the soldiers seemed far away. But something else seemed to crowd around him, unseen, unheard, yet real. Presences surrounded him.

Smoke from Longstrand stung his eyes and stirred him from a kind of trance. Someone, brave but stupid, was crashing about in the bushes, trying to find him. He slung his bow over his shoulder and began to climb up the wall.

It had been easier in childhood: small fingers and toes found more purchase, and he had never thought then that he might fall. But he worked his way up to the narrow, uneven rim of wood that marked the second floor. It felt soft and rotten beneath his feet; he climbed again, until he reached the top of the tower. The ledge of wood here was just as rotten, but he sidled along it until he could pull himself into one of the windows. They were long enough to lie down in, so thick were the walls, and high enough to stand upright in. Without showing himself, Eyas could see the trail and some of the bushes near the base of the tower. The window was directly above the doorway, and he could hear the soldier slashing through the brambles.

A fist-sized stone came out of the powdery mortar of the window, and then a dozen more. Eyas judged the soldier's location and lobbed a stone; it struck metal with a clang, and the soldier yelped. Eyas threw a small volley of stones; now the soldier's cries of pain and fear were serious. The thrashing ceased.

Eyas turned his attention to the trail. He could see several soldiers and mounted troopers, laughing at the plight of their comrade. One, riding a very large sixfoot with a white mane, held a gun at the ready while he scanned the windows above the doorway. Leaning against the side of the window, Eyas shot an arrow at him.

At such short range, the impact knocked the trooper out of his saddle; the gun went off, and the sixfoot charged bellowing down the trail. It trampled two soldiers in its frantic rush toward the village.

The rest of the Suns withdrew up the trail. Eyas went to the opening of the window and saw the soldier lying face down on the brambles in front of the doorway. He dislodged a block of stone from the edge of the aperture, a block half a span long and a quarter-span thick. It fell and struck the unconscious soldier in the small of the back, killing him instantly. A shot echoed; the bullet cracked against the wall above Eyas's head.

Looking south, across the hollow interior of the tower, Eyas saw black smoke still rising, and the cannon kept up a slow bombardment. But to the north the trail was still empty; the Suns were temporarily stalled by his presence in the tower. It would not be for long. Brightspear would simply order his men forward and they would suffer as many losses as Eyas could inflict with his eight remaining arrows.

But nothing happened. Eyas backed out of the window onto the wooden ledge, and then climbed another two spans to the top of the wall. The masonry was completely weathered away here, and stones came away at a touch. He managed to peer over the wall, and saw the catapult being hauled by a sixfoot into a new position: it was aimed at the tower. A firebomb, a round black object like an earthenware pot, rested in the thrower; men rapidly wound the ropes. A soldier put a torch to the firebomb, and the catapult hurled it into the air. Smoking, the bomb sailed over the wall and shattered against the far side of the tower.

Fire splashed across the stone and dropped down into the bushes. It burned more fiercely than resin, with an oily smoke. The catapult was adjusted and another bomb smashed against the tower, this time right at the window Eyas had abandoned. Trickles of flame ran through to the inside, and set fire to the wooden ledge. A third bomb hit in the same place.

His eyes watering from the smoke, Eyas worked his way along the wall and climbed down to another window. This one gave him a view of the soldiers, but was far more exposed to their guns. He saw Brightspear walk toward the tower and cup his hands around his mouth.

"Eyas! You see what we can do. Do not hinder me, or I'll burn you out."

Eyas shot at him; the arrow fell short, but still reached the middle of the trail. A soldier raised his gun, but lowered it at Brightspear's gesture.

"Longstrand is dead, Eyas," Brightspear called. "You have nothing to fight for. Not even Nakeds throw their lives away. You have fought well; you can surrender with honor."

His only reply was silence. Brightspear strode down the trail, contemptuously kicking aside Eyas's arrow. "We're going down the trail. If you shoot again, you're a dead man." He stepped back, to the far edge of the trail, and waved to one of his officers, who shouted a command. In double file, the riders moved down the trail, their gaze fixed forward. Eyas saw a dozen foot soldiers take aim at his window. He drew his bowstring.

"Goddess look under me."

The riders screened Brightspear, but one sixfoot balked, leaving a momentary gap in the line. Eyas shot, snatched up another arrow, and shot again. The first arrow hit Brightspear's shoulder, staggering him; the second wounded the balky sixfoot, which screamed and threw its rider into the dust. The gunners fired as Eyas dropped flat. Bullets struck stone and shrilled off in other directions, and he felt a blow to his left foot. Looking down, Eyas saw blood welling from a ragged wound near his ankle. Dust was bitter on his lips. He was vaguely aware of shouts in the distance, and the growing hum and crackle of flames nearby. The wounding of Brightspear had confused his men enough to keep them from firing again.

Eyas backed out of the window, his unhurt foot reaching for the ledge. The Suns began shooting again, and an ill-aimed firebomb dropped into the center of the tower. Slowly Eyas climbed down the wall. He reached the next ledge, and almost fell when the rotten wood gave way beneath him. His bow and quiver impeded him; he let them drop. Under his breath, as he went from one handhold to the next, he sang the family song knowing he would never complete it. No one would be left to put his name in it, and he would not go back to the sea, yet still he sang while pain pulsed up his body and tears half-blinded him.

After a long time he reached the last ledge and hobbled along it to the doorway. Flies buzzed around the dead soldier. Eyas wrested a sword from the corpse's pale hand. It was a beautiful weapon, light, well-balanced, and keen. Delicate flowers had been engraved in the steel of the blade and the iron of the hilt.

Someone was approaching through the bushes, more cautiously than the first one had. Eyas stepped back into the doorway and leaned against the cold stone. Blood was sticky under his feet. He trembled, and the sunlight outside the doorway seemed very bright.

Suddenly a soldier stood outside the doorway, tall and expressionless. He carried a heavy spear. The soldier looked at him for a breath or two and then said, "Come out." Eyas only raised his sword. The soldier snorted and spat. "The Sun commands you to be taken alive."

"Let him come and tell me that." In mockery, Eyas mimicked the soldier's nasal accent.

"He didn't say not to hurt you. Come out."

The soldier lunged forward, the iron leaf of his spearhead aimed for Eyas's right hand. Eyas struck at the spear, deflecting it, and chopped awkwardly at the soldier's head. The man fell back a step; Eyas forgot his wounded foot and lurched forward, out of the doorway. Something moved in the corner of his eye, and he realized he had been tricked. A second soldier was lying in wait, and now struck him in the head with a spear butt.

Eyas collapsed across the Sunnish corpse. He dimly felt strong hands gripping him, lifting him; the trampled bushes and brambles were a blur of green. Again he sensed presences around him, a kind of hunger, like the flies buzzing around the dead soldier's blood. But there were only the two soldiers, puffing as they lugged him back to the trail.

They set him on his feet and marched him up the trail toward a cluster of alders. Eyas saw that the soldiers and troopers had not yet moved. The Suns watched him in baleful silence.

In the shade of the alders sat Brightspear. His leather tunic had been cut away, and a bandage tied over his wounded

149

shoulder and across his chest. A dozen attendants, some with drawn swords, stood around him. Eyas's captors forced him to his knees.

"You've hindered me," Brightspear said abruptly. "And cost me both good males and good Men. But for you, Longstrand would be ashes by now."

Eyas licked his lips and tasted blood. His sight began to clear, despite the throbbing in his temple.

"Perhaps it's just well," Brightspear went on thoughtfully. "You've taught my soldiers that Nakeds can fight well; they won't forget when we go against the next village."

"You can't conquer us all," Eyas mumbled.

"Of course we can. Do you think I came across the South Hills with just these few? Thousands more are following. Your Goddess is dead, and the People must know it by now—"

"Dead?"

"Two of my ships met with her a couple of years ago, off the Empty Coast. They used cannons on her. For a divinity, she bled like any brute, they tell me. Her flesh was very good; I had some of it myself that they salted for me."

Eyas leaned forward, propping himself on his hands. Brightspear nodded and smiled.

"The People will crumple just as you do. Eyas, I'm glad you didn't die. You can come with me now, to see the fall of Longstrand. It'll be quick, I promise you."

Eyas looked around, wondering if somehow he might break free and kill Brightspear before the Suns could stop him. His eyes met those of one of the attendants, a tall middle-aged man with a broken nose. The man stood with easy erectness, thumbs hooked in his belt, and looked at Eyas with undisguised interest.

"Admiral—" Eyas stopped himself. "No, you're not Thorn."

"I knew him well," the man said.

"You are like him."

The man laughed silently. "You honor me, Eyas Fisher."

"Enough," said Brightspear, getting to his feet. "Get my sixfoot."

Ignoring the pain of his wound, the Sun swung himself up into the saddle of a big, spirited brute. An attendant handed him his yellow hood, dark with blood where Eyas's arrow had pierced it. Brightspear pulled it over his head, but waved away another man who offered him a new tunic. He took the reins, which led to an iron bit in the sixfoot's mouth, and looked down at Eyas.

"We took the Foresters' longhouse last night. Before he died, Winterberry told me he murdered Silken. But all of Longstrand will pay for that, Eyas. Especially you and your family."

He ordered a mount for Eyas, and the tall man helped Eyas into the saddle; then he lashed his wrists to the pommel of the saddle. The brute stamped nervously, not liking the weight of a stranger on its back, until Eyas murmured soothingly to it.

"You do have a way with brutes," the tall man remarked cheerfully as he mounted his own sixfoot. "But don't try to escape. I'll be right behind you, with this." He drew a gun from a scabbard beside his saddle. Its narrow muzzle was not like the guns Eyas had seen in remembrance of the battle of Mud Bay; the Suns had improved their weaponry in twenty years.

"What are you?" Eyas asked quietly.

"My name does not matter. I am a Messenger. Now, follow Brightspear."

The troopers cantered down the trail behind Brightspear, Eyas, and the tall man. The foot soldiers marched along the sides of the trail, blinking and spitting in the dust.

As they rode down the cliff, Eyas saw that Longstrand was almost completely in flames. Speaker's Hall and the group house were gutted ruins; bodies lay everywhere in the muddy streets. But men with bows and spears still moved through the smoke, and Eyas saw Old limping among them.

No one barred the soldiers' way at the bottom of the trail; they paused to group themselves. Then Brightspear dropped his reins and drew his sword; it flashed in the smoky light, and he kicked his mount into a lumbering gallop up the little hill into the village. The Messenger poked his gun against the hindquarters of Eyas's mount, and it ran close behind Brightspear. The riders shouted; their mounts bawled and charged.

It was something like riding the tide at Ripmouth, to be carried helplessly into the battle. Eyas tugged at the thongs that bound him, but they held. An arrow whirred past. Guns banged. Men of Longstrand appeared from behind shattered walls, slinging stones and loosing arrows. Brightspear rode right over two of them as he slashed at a third; the defenders died or retreated, and the Suns pressed on into the center of the village. In the distance, other Sunnish guns cracked; the attackers on the beach were pushing forward as well.

Eyas rode through a wall of smoke into clearer air just above Traders' Beach. Three or four women, one of them Quiet, stood unmoving as the charge bore down upon them. Brightspear hurled his mount over them, and struck Quiet even as she raised her hands to stop him. Her face blank with shock, she stared past Brightspear at Eyas for an instant; then she fell back, breasts shining with blood.

The defenders were few and disorganized. Here and there, an archer brought down a rider before being chopped down or shot, but the Suns were not slowed. Brightspear gestured with his sword, and some of the attackers swung left, to the north side of the village, while he himself led the rest of his men onto the beach. Moving from one longhouse and boatshed to the next, the Suns drove out the women and children— and men, Eyas saw with rage—who had sheltered there, and pushed them along the sand.

When they came to the eastern edge of the village, the Suns who had attacked along the beach had already gathered almost twoscore prisoners, among them Firewing, Sky, Violet, and the babies. Some of the soldiers were bleeding from gashed faces or arms: the women had not surrendered easily, and looked more furious than fearful.

Sky and Violet clung to their babies. Eyas tried to call to them, but his voice would not obey him, and the women glared unseeingly at the wall of men and brutes around them.

Brightspear wiped his sword on his mount's flank, sheathed it, and leaned on the pommel of his saddle.

"Good day, Firewing," he called. "And Sky. Did you marry her, Eyas? Ah. And who's the other one with her? She's very pretty."

The woman stared in dazed recognition at Brightspear, then turned to see Eyas.

"Where's Netweaver?" Firewing screamed.

"Dead," shouted Brightspear. "And a fine warrior's death it was. You can be proud of him, and of Eyas, though *his* death will be slower and less dignified. Eyas—you see your family?"

He could only nod slowly, while something inside him cried out for the Goddess like a child wailing for its mother.

"You'll see them again, in Hell!" Brightspear's face went

pale and taut with a terrible eagerness; he sat up in his saddle and brought his hand down in a swift gesture.

The soldiers went to work with spears and swords and the butts of their guns. Eyas saw little Gray, frightened and screaming, recognize him and reach out just as his life was ripped from him. Between Eyas and Sky passed a look that carried all a lost life's love, a yearning that could shatter worlds, and then she too was dead, and Violet, and Golden, and Firewing with a broken curse on her lips. They fell in a heap with the bodies of the other captives.

A slingstone struck Eyas's mount beside its ear, and it reared up in pain and fright. Other stones fell, knocking some riders off their sixfeet, and then a volley of arrows thudded into the massed soldiers. Brightspear looked up from the massacre and drew his sword while the other riders turned and prepared to charge. Through the smoke, Eyas saw the grass-yellow hair of Old, and the forms of a dozen other men. The Longstranders charged silently down toward the beach, loosing another volley of arrows and then casting away their bows; now they held axes and spears, and their faces were those of nightmare.

An arrow thumped into the flank of Eyas's sixfoot, not deeply enough to kill, but the brute reared again and ran maddened down the beach. The Messenger, thinking Eyas was trying to escape, fired; the bullet grazed the right side of Eyas's head, with almost enough force to knock him from the saddle. Eyas gasped, swayed, and bent over the pommel. Behind him he heard Old's voice rise in a command and abruptly cut off.

Something had happened to the light. He seemed to ride in darkness, and the sixfoot's hoofs struck the sand without a sound. Dark figures swarmed around him, reaching out, and he knew they hungered for him. One drew close, and he thought he recognized Griptiller, her face contorted with greed.

"—Goddess, give me light!" he begged, and the darkness and its inhabitants shuddered and vanished in a white glare. Eyas heard again the thud of his mount's hoofbeats, the crack of guns and screams of dying men. Smoke roiled thickly around him in an acrid fog, and he saw his own blood soaking the sixfoot's gray mane.

Then a great voice cried out like a wave breaking on a rocky cliff, and the sixfoot's blind charge halted. Eyas looked up and saw a huge, gray-brown arm; its massive hand had gripped the reins and stopped the brute in its tracks.

It was Boulder, helmed in iron, his back and flanks covered in chain mail. His broad face was a mask of wrath; in his right hand he held a great sword almost a span in length. With a single slice he cut the thongs from Eyas's wrists. The sixfoot shuddered with fear until a word from the centaur calmed it.

"I came to warn you, but I came too late," Boulder looked down the beach at the burning village. "Stay. Suns must die for this."

They were just east of the village, about where Eyas and the others had fought at dawn. The village was lost in oily smoke; out of the smoke came five riders, each bearing a lance or sword. Behind them rode the Messenger, his gun sheathed.

The Suns halted when they saw Boulder where they had expected only a wounded, naked man. The centaur raised his sword. His hind hoofs dug into the sand, and he sprang toward the Suns with a roar. Their lances dropped to meet his charge, but his sword snapped them like a sickle cutting breadseed stalks. A swordsman stabbed at Boulder's flank; a backhanded swipe crushed the man's skull. Another rider's sword was knocked from his hand. Boulder reared back, and with a forefoot kicked the rider out of his saddle. The man shrieked as he struck the sand, and then lay dead.

In a few breaths all five of the Suns were dead and the Messenger was retreating back into Longstrand. Boulder picked up a Sunnish corpse by one leg and threw it contemptuously after him. Then he trotted back to Eyas, who had slid from his mount to the ground.

"What of your family?"

"Dead. Dead. Brightspear has done this." Eyas knelt on the sand, his hands supporting him. His voice was a whisper.

"I know. We heard on the High Plains that a new Sun had conquered Silvershield, and planned wars in the west. A month ago we took a Sunnish soldier who told us the new Sun was Brightspear, and I knew he must be marching against the Gulf. The snow was thick in the passes, or I would have been here ten days ago. Ah, Eyas, I grieve for you."

Slowly Eyas got to his feet. Blood painted half his face, and ran gaudily over the light brown skin of his chest. His wounded foot was swollen and black. He swayed and put a hand against Boulder's side to steady himself. "I must go to

Big Harbor, and then to Rainfalling, to my sister. To warn them, and fight beside them."

Boulder pointed out across the estuary at distant sails. "The People will be warned. But you cannot fight again until your wounds heal."

"The wounds don't matter," Eyas mumbled. "I can still draw a bow or sling a stone."

As easily as a father hoisting a child onto his shoulder, Boulder picked Eyas up and set him on his back. "Hold onto my mane," the centaur said, "and warn me if you feel too weak to go on. More Suns will come soon, with guns, and we must outrun them."

Under Eyas's legs, Boulder's chain mail was smooth and cool. The mane's softness and pungent scent comforted him with memories of the centaurs' camp on summer nights.

Shouts and the bellowings of sixfeet came out of the smoke. Boulder set off down the beach at a rapid trot.

"Where are we going?"

"Home, to Foundries Hold."

15

Between noon and nightfall they traveled far, but Eyas saw little. He was aware of the steady, untiring pace of the centaur, of the scents of blueblossom and club, of cold sunlight on his back. Once he heard Boulder shout, and roused himself. They were in the smoking ruins of Sandybank, and the centaur was smashing into a cluster of old men in Sunnish leather. Sixfeet bellowed as they lunged against their hobbles; a high-wheeled wagon overturned at a kick from Boulder, spilling sacks of food and gunpowder. They had intercepted Brightspear's supply train. The centaur swept up a food sack and a couple of coarsewoven blankets, tucked them under one arm, and ran on down the North Bank Road to the east.

Another time, late in the afternoon, they entered a farmyard. The family stood staring at them while Boulder cried: "The Suns are in the Gulf. Get into the hills; hide yourselves.

Longstrand and Sandybank are no more. Hide yourselves! They follow close after us."

A little girl started wailing, and Eyas whispered, "Gray, hush. Hush, it's all right."

But most of that first day's journey was a kind of trance for him, a dream without images. He woke at last in darkness, to the sound of wind in dense trees, and felt himself lying on the ground with blankets wrapped around him. Boulder was an unseen presence beside him.

"Where—?"

"Be silent. They are not far behind. We are near the river at Nightfire Bog. Will you eat?"

"Yes."

He was given two dry, smooth lumps of what must have been Sunnish bread. It was tasteless but filled his stomach. A true weariness replaced the trance; his wounded foot and head ached. Yet he fell easily into sleep beside his friend, and no dreams troubled him.

In the morning they went on, through empty meadows and silent thickets, with the great brown river close on their right. Eyas said little, but his thoughts hurt more than his wounds. Twice they paused at lonely farms to warn their families; at each, the farmers gave them food and drink.

"It's more than the Suns will get," said the wrinkled old woman who ran the second farm. "We'll burn it all down before we leave." She looked at her longhouse, orchards, and breadseed fields without a flicker of expression, while her family nodded.

"Why are the Suns following you?" asked the old woman's middle-aged son.

"Brightspear leads them. I am Eyas."

"Now I recognize you! We used to see you at the Gatherings; I was there when She suckled you." His face had been as hard as his mother's, but now it softened. "We're the Goddess's People, not dreamwatchers; we still revere Her. If you've been spared, it's Her will. Goddess look under you, and speed you to safety."

They dressed his wounds with feverbane. The women and girls embraced him while their men went to arm themselves. Eyas pulled himself onto Boulder's back and waved farewell.

"I should have stayed and fought beside them," he said as they looked back at the burning farm.

"You would only draw the Suns' full wrath upon them, and

do Brightspear no serious harm. Be patient. We'll see fighting enough before we're done."

If the farmers had opposed the Sunnish riders, it had not been for long: at midday Boulder stopped on a windswept hill and looked back to see a line of black dots moving rapidly along the road.

"At least twelve," he grunted.

"Is Brightspear among them?"

"No, but I see the one who escaped me when I killed the others on the beach."

Eyas shivered from more than the chill of the wind.

They went on into the empty fields of the eastern Valley, where the mountains of the Eastwall merged with the South Hills at the Great Cataract. Here the Bluemeadows River, swift and brown, fell fifty spans in thunder and mist. Above the fall, the river ran from the unknown north through a deep gorge, thinly wooded with dryland pine.

Boulder and Eyas followed the ancient centaur trail up the west side of the cataract; here and there, in the mud, the hoofprints Boulder had made on his westward journey could still be seen. The trail was steep, with many switchbacks, and in some places steps had been carved from the rock. It was slow going. Boulder climbed cautiously, but sometimes the way was so narrow that Eyas's wounded foot brushed against stone and he grunted with pain.

It was late afternoon. The slopes across the gorge turned golden in the westering light, and a rainbow glowed in the mist of the cataract. Eyas looked down and saw the Sunnish riders ascending the trail, slashing at their mounts' flanks to urge them on. One brute lost its footing and toppled screaming down the slope; its rider, leaping clear, abandoned it and climbed up behind a comrade.

Boulder paused and taunted the pursuers with a bellow that carried even against the roar of the falling river. He dug a stone, bigger than Eyas's head, from the side of the trail and hurled it down the slope. It missed, and the riders paused for only a breath before pressing on.

"Now I want them close behind," he growled. "So they think they need make one last effort to take us."

He went on at an easy walk, though the slope was leveling out and he might have run. The Suns were now hidden behind the curve of the hill. Boulder followed the trail along the high bank of the river, still climbing. The cataract was behind them, its thunder muted; the river, now more than ten spans below, ran heavy and swift with melt-water. The opposite bank was close.

In shadow, they made their way to a point where two tall pines stood near the edge of the bank. Thick ropes stretched from the trees across the gorge to a dense stand of pines; from the ropes hung a narrow bridge, floored with weathered planks. Boulder paused. Behind them came the heavy steps of the sixfeet. A voice rang out, and Eyas felt his throat contract with fear. The voice had a power and evil in it, and it was calling his name.

"Eyas!" the Messenger cried. "Eyas!"

He remembered Quiet's tale of the terrible voice she had heard at Ripmouth. Surely it had been a voice like this: whatever they were, Admiral Thorn and the Messenger were of a kind, and they were not human.

Boulder seemed undisturbed by the Messenger's voice, and only smiled as the riders appeared over the rise of the slope. Then he stepped easily out onto the swaying bridge and ran across it without troubling to hold the ropes. The Suns followed, but their brutes balked and screamed. The first rider whipped his mount forward, making the bridge heave and swing like a boat in choppy water. The others pressed on, and when Eyas looked back he saw the Messenger drive his sixfoot onto the planks.

Boulder half-climbed the far side, for the center of the bridge had sagged under the weight of the riders. More Suns followed the Messenger, but their facess were pale and taut with fear. As Boulder neared the end of the bridge, he reached behind him and drew his sword from its scabbard on his back. He gained the ground and slashed his blade down upon one of the support ropes. Its thick strands parted halfway, and Eyas saw the Suns staring up at them in startled horror. A second blow severed the cable altogether, and the bridge tipped over. A sixfoot and its rider fell screaming into the river. Another Sun dismounted and raced up the bridge, clinging to the remaining rope with both hands.

"Please, please!" he shouted.

Boulder turned and cut the rope. The tree that moored it lashed back and forth; the bridge dropped, throwing men and brutes from it. The Messenger shouted, but not in terror: it was a cry of frustrated hunger. Then he vanished with the others into the cold brown water. The Sun who had held the rope still clung to it, until the bridge struck the sheer rock of the opposite bank and he too fell.

Only three Suns—two of them mounted on a single brute—had not yet reached the bridge; they reined in at the edge of the bank and gaped at the rushing water that had taken their comrades. Boulder calmly got out his sling and flung a rock across the gorge. It struck the single rider, and he toppled to the ground. Without pausing to see if their companion still lived, the other two wheeled about and retreated the way they had come.

"They are hard to surprise," Boulder said. "But it can be done."

Eyas let himself down from the centaur's back and limped to the edge of the bank. He took the bandage from his head. The feverbane had done its work; already the wound was healing. He threw the blood-soaked cloth and leaves into the river, and watched them float swiftly for a moment before they sank. He had left the Gulf and the People. But now, if he should die in a strange land, at least his blood would be given back to the sea.

Leaning against a tree in his weariness, Eyas whispered words to go into the river as well: the last verses of the family song. He sang of Old, shuffling and brave, defender of Longstrand; of Sky, beautiful and wise, who rejoiced in the morning; of Violet, merry and strong, whose laughter was sweet as rain; of Netweaver and Firewing, and their grandchildren Gray and Golden, givers of joy.

When the song was done, he prayed to the lost Goddess to protect Harper and Moonhorn and their families. Then he turned and hobbled slowly to Boulder, who stood with arms folded across his great chest. The centaur made no move to help. It was darkening fast in the gorge; the trees merged into dim shadows, and the light had gone even from the highest peaks. Eyas paused, looked up, and saw a green spark hanging in the sky near the Bridge of Heaven. The old childhood rhyme came back to him: Skyland green, Skyland bright, grant the wish I wish tonight.

The Goddess named me well, he thought. I am a strange nestling, not yet fledged, and my nest is gone. But now my wings must grow strong enough to bear me up, and my talons must grow sharp.

159

He pulled himself onto Boulder's back, ignoring the pain in his foot. He spoke, and it was a command as easy, swift, and inarguable as the stoop of a hawk.

"Go on, while the light remains."

II

The Hawk Against the Sun

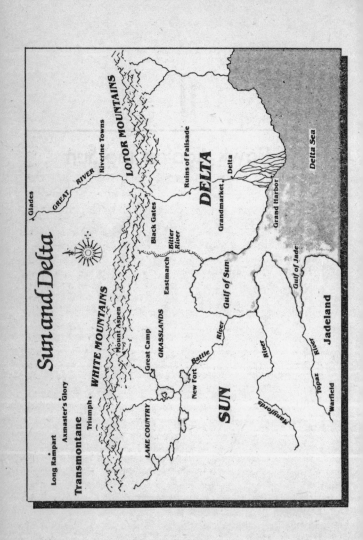

1

This was Wilderness, a land unchanged since Two Bows' time; Old Snow Woman still ruled the glaciers mantling the nameless mountains. Men had passed through these ranges long ago, but they had not stayed. Wilderness was the domain of animals and brutes. Mountain goats stepped daintily along high ledges; springbringers and firewings darted in the air. Woodsrunners bayed at night, their voices carrying far; the scent of giants was pungent in berry bogs, and walkingtrees left their strange tracks across silent meadows.

For days, Eyas and Boulder traveled from one valley to the next, through dark forests, across scree slopes still deep in snow, along streams raging turquoise-blue down from the glaciers in the first spate of spring. They came into country where bare hills rose above ice-bound lakes, and followed a strong blue river into valleys bright with aspens' green.

Eyas grew stronger, and soon he let Boulder carry him only where the way was steep or treacherous. Sometimes they paused to hunt for two or three days. Eyas made weirs and caught fish: gleaming trout, oily finnet, and others unknown in the Gulf but savory and filling. Boulder's sling and snares took splithoof and blackhorn whose flesh, with no seasoning but the smoke of a campfire, was sweet.

In those days at the end of spring, Eyas thought of little but the next step, the next task, and fell each night into a numb sleep. Boulder did little to draw him out of his lonely sorrow, though they spoke easily enough about the next day's route or the chances of good hunting. Eyas had known the centauric language since childhood, and now he mastered it; but their silences were longer than their words. Even as his wounds healed, grimness darkened Eyas's mind. Memories of that last morning in Longstrand returned. In his dreams, he held Violet and Sky again, and cradled his children in his arms, before he woke to the black emptiness of the night. Yet these were true dreams, and he almost yearned to be haunted.

They followed the trail around long lakes, shimmering in the spring like the Gulf, and over rolling hills gray with sagebrush and bright with wildflowers. Another range of mountains rose before them, mountains bare of trees and locked in ice, where the way was hard. But these too they crossed, and came into a great valley walled by sharp-toothed peaks. Here the trail ran between thick forests and a shallow braided river; Eyas saw moose and beaver, creatures mentioned in Old Stories but unknown to remembrance.

One morning he paused to drink from a pool beside the river, and in its reflection he saw himself: a gaunt face, scarred at the temple, with a blank look about the eyes. He put his hand into the pool, shattering the image, and tasted the water's clean strangeness. Longing for the Gulf burst in his heart, and for a time he knelt weeping on the rocks. Then he rose and said to Boulder, "I must go back."

"There is no going back."

"I have a war to fight. My own, not yours."

Boulder frowned. "You would hide in the hills and inlets, raiding Brightspear's soldiers. In a year, or a day, they would kill you."

"What of it?"

Boulder's huge hands clapped together, crushing a mosquito. "Would you die like that, Eyas? Or would you wage real war against the Suns, with an army of centaurs at your back?"

"A human among warring centaurs would be trampled."

"Not if he led them."

"I?" Eyas snorted. "Let the centaurs choose their own leader, one who can at least defend his own family."

"Centaurs alone cannot stop the Suns. We need men as well, and lotors."

Eyas smiled without humor. "Once you wanted to go sailing, when you really wanted a cannon. What do you really want now, Boulder?"

Boulder took him by the hand and led him to a patch of wet sand near the noisy river. The centaur knelt and with the point of his knife began to sketch a map in the sand.

"Here is the Gulf—and these mountains—and the High Plains. Here is Foundries Hold." He marked the spot with a pebble. "And the other holds that still stand against the

Suns." He put down just six more pebbles, all to the north and east of Foundries. "South of us are the conquered holds, and then our old lands of Transmontane. South of that are the White Mountains—" He made a crude slash, running east and west. "—And beyond them, the Dominance itself.

"Southeast of the High Plains lies the Yellow Desert, where the Bands wander with their herds. They are old cousins of the Suns, and their oldest enemies. Beyond the Desert is the Narrow Sea, the land of the lotors. From the Sea flows the Great River, south through the mountains into Delta. Just north of the mountains live the Riverines, men ruled by Delta; but they often rebel. The Suns have always wanted to conquer the Riverines. From the northern reaches of the River, they could move south through the Black Gates, between the White and Lotor Mountains, to strike at Delta's heart. The Deltans, for their part, push north against the lotors as the Suns push against us and the Desert Bands.

"If we could unite all these northern peoples, humans and brutes alike, neither Sun nor Delta could stand against us. But no centaur or lotor could command the warriors of the Bands and the Riverines; they despise free brutes even as the Suns and Deltans do. And no chieftain of the Bands or Riverines could lead us or the lotors. We need one who stands apart from all."

Eyas shifted restlessly, interested despite himself. "I know little about your people, Boulder, and still less about these others. They know nothing about the People of the Gulf. We would have nothing in common, no reason to unite."

"Desperation is reason enough." Boulder began to walk slowly back to the trail; Eyas followed, wryly amused at the centaur's attempted subtlety. "We are losing the war. In a year, or two, or five, Foundries will fall. Then the lesser holds to the north and east will fall, and we will all be holdless, wanderers like our ancestors."

"Holdless?" Eyas seized on the word; Boulder had spoken it with dread.

"When a hold falls to a conqueror, those who escape death or slavery must beg shelter from another hold. But they will never again be ... real centaurs. They are like your People when they have lost standing. Like your father Darkhair."

"And like your grandfather from Canyon Hold."

"Yes. He was holdless, and my father too, but I was born

165

on Foundries soil and so I am as holded as the Arm himself. I remember my father and grandfather, Eyas. I would not be like that."

"If the centaurs are desperate, why did they not ask for the People's help long before this? And if the others, the Bands and the Riverines and the lotors, are also hard pressed, why do they not forget their differences and unite? That's simple politics."

Boulder coughed with amusement. "The People love politics; centaurs love war. We love the fight for its own sake, win or lose, and we are jealous of our glory. We do not ask for help from our friends, nor mercy from our enemies. The Desert Bands are much like us in that. But I can see all our glory cast into the dust if we do not change. You were named and suckled by the Goddess, and given understanding of the brutes; if anyone can unite us with men, it is you."

The grimness in Eyas's mind turned and coiled upon itself, like the tail of a prowl preparing to spring.

"Very well," he said. "We will venture it."

In a narrow, wooded valley they came to an abandoned logging camp, a collection of crude sheds, steep-roofed and windowless. An enormous wagon, filled with logs, stood in the middle of the camp. Harnesses lay scattered in the mud around the wagonshafts; the pullers had left in haste. Fresh hoofprints ran along the trail to the east. Boulder halted and studied them.

"Sixfeet. The Suns have been here."

"When? How many?"

"This morning. It must have been a small patrol—five or six riders. The loggers escaped. A full-sized raiding party would have left this place in ashes."

"Why should centaurs flee a few Suns?"

"Workers are not warriors. Besides, these are not like the Suns who took Longstrand. Those were southerners by the look of them, accustomed to fighting only other men. These Suns of Transmontane are good riders, and they have fought us for generations. They know how to strike at a centaur and live to strike again." His mane puffed out, and he snorted softly. "They came up from the south, over the hills, and turned east to pursue the loggers. They will return this way, but they will not expect us."

"Will they have guns?"

166

"Perhaps. But a gun is hard to aim when you are in the saddle, and they won't have time to dismount. This will be sword against lances."

"I have my sling."

Boulder seemed startled by the implications of Eyas's words. "But—a centaur fights alone. Still . . . they would not expect a centaur carrying a man." He uttered his coughing laugh. "Well, it has never been done before, but if we are to fight against the Suns together, we begin now. Take this as well." He gave Eyas his broad-bladed knife. It was heavy, and balanced for a centaur's grip, but it would do. Eyas tucked it into the belt he had worn since the last morning in Longstrand, and made sure the belt's pouch had a good supply of stones. Boulder broke into a long-striding trot.

"We must hit them fast, while they're bunched together. If they can split up and attack from our flanks, it will be hard for us."

Eyas grunted. He wondered how accurately he could sling from the centaur's back; it would be worse than hunting dabblers from a canoe on rough water. But the thought of killing Suns filled him with dark elation.

They went swiftly down the trail—a road now, wide and rutted—while cloudshadow and sunlight passed over them. To the right, a long, logged-off hill rose gradually to a bare crest; to the left, a stream crashed over rocks, and beyond it rose another bare hill. They would have no cover, and little chance of escape if the fight went badly.

The road followed the winding of the stream. They rounded a sharp curve and saw the Sunnish patrol less than twenty spans ahead, coming toward them.

They were indeed unlike Brightspear's soldiers in the Gulf: their faces were squarer, big-nosed and cleanshaven. They wore hoods of chain mail, and round shields hung from their saddles. Even their brutes looked different. These sixfeet were brown-furred, with more intelligence in their eyes, and they seemed better-trained.

The leader of the patrol wore black and yellow ribbons on his shoulders; otherwise, all six of the riders were identically dressed in tunics and trousers of coarse black cloth. The leader and one other carried guns in scabbards beside their saddles, but they made no move to draw them when they saw Boulder. Instead, all six lowered their lances.

The leader kicked his mount's flanks; it shambled forward,

sidling to the stream side of the road, while two others moved to the opposite side. The remaining three came straight ahead.

Boulder halted for a moment. Eyas stood up on the centaur's back.

"Stop!" he shouted in the Gulf dialect—at the sixfeet, not their riders. The Suns' faces went slack with surprise; though they could have seen Eyas earlier, they simply had not noticed him, and they were dumbfounded when their brutes obeyed Eyas's command. Eyas hurled a stone at the Sunnish leader; it smashed his cheekbone, snapping his head back. He dropped his lance and swayed dizzily in his saddle.

Boulder charged the two attackers on the right. "Turn back!" Eyas cried out to the brutes. They reared up, and one rider fell heavily and did not rise. His companion turned aside with a frantic yank on the reins to avoid being kicked by the riderless sixfoot. In that moment Boulder roared, drew his sword, and swerved to turn upon the three riders in the center of the road.

They must have known they could not stand against his charge, and tried to split up, to repeat the flanking tactic. But Boulder's speed and strength were too great. His empty left hand seized a lance and yanked its owner to the ground, where he was trampled by his own mount; Boulder's sword snapped the other two lances in a single sweep. The two riders dropped their splintered weapons and tried to draw their swords, but Boulder killed one with a blow of his fist, and Eyas stabbed the other under the chin.

The centaur reared and whirled around, so swiftly that Eyas was nearly flung off, and renewed the attack on the first three Suns. The wounded leader had drawn his gun at last, but could scarcely aim. Boulder plucked the weapon from him and struck off his head. The rider of the rearing sixfoot, just getting to his feet, was slain with a kick. His companion had abandoned the fight, and was already halfway up the hillside.

"Take him, but don't kill him," Eyas said.

They overtook the rider at the crest of the hill, and Boulder yanked him from the saddle. His mount trotted on uncertainly, then halted and stared back blankly at its captive master. Boulder dropped the man, and put the point of his dripping sword at the man's throat.

Eyas slid off the centaur's back and squatted beside the soldier, who was gasping for breath.

"Do you understand me?" he asked the man in the Gulf dialect.

"Y-yes."

"Answer my questions. Are there more Suns nearby?"

"Our main force—a day's ride southeast of here." The soldier was young, perhaps even younger than Eyas.

"How many in your main force?"

"Thirty."

"A raiding party," Boulder said in centauric.

"Where are they headed?" asked Eyas. The soldier said nothing. Eyas held Boulder's knife where the man could see it. "Answer!"

"They go to burn the brutes' breadseed plantations along the Shale River."

"And where have you come from?"

The soldier seemed perplexed by Eyas's ignorance. "Three days' ride southeast. The town of Two Creek Fort."

"Do you serve Brightspear?"

Again the soldier's perplexity showed. "Of course."

"What do you know of him?"

"Only what everyone knows. How he came out of the west with his father's armies, and overthrew the usurper and restored the Sunteachings."

"Do you know where Brightspear is now?"

"They say he wars in the far west, conquering the Nakeds." Even as he spoke the words, the soldier looked at Eyas—who wore only a belt—with sudden understanding.

"They say truly," said Eyas without expression. "Tell me, have you always been one of the Vanquished?"

"I—I was born in the cult of Skyland, but I accepted the Sunteachings gladly when Silvershield was cast down."

"So you will go to join the Sun in Heaven when your time on earth is done."

Though he must have feared that time had come, the soldier replied bravely: "I may not speak of such things when I am not in swordshadow."

"You are in swordshadow now," said Eyas. "And in a way I am one of the Vanquished also."

"The Sunteachings may not be mocked, though I die to say that."

169

"Boulder—let him stand."

Cautiously, the soldier got to his feet. Eyas stood also.

"I give you your life, and your freedom."

The soldier looked almost as surprised as Boulder. Without a word, he went slowly to his sixfoot and swung himself into the saddle.

"Send word to Brightspear," Eyas called to him, "that Eyas Fisher still lives."

The soldier nodded, then spurred his mount into a trot down the far side of the hill. Eyas watched until the soldier was over the next ridge.

"Why did you not kill him?" asked Boulder as they returned to the road.

"He reminded me of Silken."

Boulder stripped the corpses of their guns and swords. While he tied them into a bundle, Eyas walked to the headless corpse of the leader, and from its waist unbuckled a leather belt and scabbard. He drew the sword, expecting a blade as elaborately engraved as that which he had taken from the dead soldier in the doorway of the tower. But this sword was bare and bright, and beautiful. He returned it to its scabbard and buckled the belt around his waist.

Boulder called the sixfeet to him, took off their saddles and harnesses, and sent them trotting up the road. "It is hard to war on our cousins," he said as he watched them go. "When we capture them, we set them free."

"Can they live in the wild?"

"Some do. Most return to their masters. But they are kin to us, as that Sunnish soldier is kin to you. This war has driven us to do evil, but we would not utterly forget our true nature." He looked at Eyas. "The sixfeet obeyed you. It was a help."

They washed themselves in the stream; its icy water calmed Eyas's spirit. He felt a tired pleasure, but also a sadness. Once Brightspear had promised him glory, the prospect of enemies trampled into dust, and Eyas had primly replied that they would be not dust but dead men and women. But now, when he looked at the bodies scattered on the road, they seemed indeed no more than dust. He recalled the vision of darkness that the Messenger's bullet had bestowed upon him at Longstrand, the awareness of hungry presences. The five Suns were in that darkness now, who had ridden in daylight and sweet air just a few breaths ago. Now they were only part of the dust in the road that Eyas must travel to reach Brightspear.

They walked side by side down the road, saying little. After they had gone about an hourmarch, Boulder paused and sniffed the air; then he burst into a run.

When Eyas caught up, he found the centaur standing by the bodies of four centaurs sprawled in a ditch beside the road. They were much smaller than Boulder, with auburn manes and brown hair on their hindquarters. Their breasts showed them to be females. Boulder stood singing his grief, while Eyas waited silently beside his friend until the song was done. Boulder turned and looked bleakly down at him.

"Workers, from the logging camp. If I had known of this, I would have slain the last Sun myself. Now we must build their pyre."

For the rest of the afternoon they cut wood and piled it beside the road. Then Boulder gently took up the bodies and laid them on the pyre. As it burned, Eyas tasted bitter smoke again and thought of Longstrand. When they left the pyre, the sun was low above the western peaks.

"What do your people believe about death?" Eyas asked.

"Our bodies return to mother earth; our spirits go to the misty land."

"And do those spirits ever return to this world?"

"Some say they are the lightning, and their hoofbeats are thunder."

"But do they speak to the living—advise them, warn them?"

Boulder almost smiled. "No more than we speak to the unborn in the womb."

"Our dead speak to us. They spoke to my mother Quiet, and sometimes to me."

"Strange are the ways of humans. You are creatures of marvel."

"Boulder—on the beach at Longstrand, when the Messenger shot me, I saw a place. There were people in it, or what were once people. One of them was my grandmother Griptiller, I think, but she was no longer human. She was hungry, hungry for me. She and the others reached for me, like starving people reaching for bread. I was frightened, and called on the Goddess, and the vision ended. I think I saw the land of the dead, but—" He paused, then went on:

"The Goddess taught us that when the People die, they go

171

into the sea, and if they have done good to others they go to dwell on the Bridge of Heaven. Griptiller was a good woman, surely. But if the Goddess was wrong, and if She died as Brightspear said She did, slain by cannons—then how could I call upon Her and save myself from that dark land? I do not understand the world anymore."

Boulder walked in silence for a long time. Then, hesitantly, he said, "Centaurs do not pretend to understand the world, only to live in it as best we may. But humans are—different. When I was very young, and saw my first humans, I felt that difference. We look upon you and we do not know whose world this is, yours or ours, for we cannot both belong in it. Only in the Gulf have I felt much in common with your kind—and even then, it was mostly with you."

"Is that why Oldwalker would not welcome me to Foundries before?"

"Yes. He owes you much, and he remembers your grandmother Griptiller with respect. But he will not rejoice to see a human in his hold, and he will want you soon gone."

"Simply because I am not a centaur?"

"Not only that—because you will bring change. He is well named, and in his old age he values little that is new. Even the cannon he accepted grudgingly, and only because his wives urged him. But many younger warriors can see how the war is going; they are ready to try something new."

"So I, the unwelcome outsider, must persuade him to make me leader of his armies."

Boulder looked wryly down at his friend. "If you fail, you can always return to the Gulf."

Eyas shook his head. The road ahead was long, but it would take him at last to Brightspear, before it led into the land of the dead.

2

Next morning, as they climbed a long hill, two gunshots rang out ahead of them. Eyas leaped onto Boulder's back, and the centaur broke into a gallop. At the crest of the hill they looked down into a little valley, hardly more than a boggy meadow, through which the road ran. In the valley, a battle had just begun and was already near its end.

Almost thirty Suns were riding west, spread out in a half-circle on both sides of the road. The bodies of two centaur warriors lay upon the road; five others, swords drawn, were running to engage their enemies. But each ran to a different part of the line, and the Suns awaited them with lowered lances and lifted guns. Smoke puffed out along the Sunnish line; by the time the sound of the volley reached Boulder and Eyas, three more centaurs lay dead. The two survivors reached the Suns, but the riders evaded them, then swarmed in on their flanks. It was all over in five breaths.

Eyas felt Boulder's muscles tense; the centaur drew his sword. With all his strength, Eyas punched Boulder's side.

"No! Stay here."

"My comrades are dead, and Suns still live. Do not stop me."

"Stay, Boulder, or we die like your mosquito."

"You saw how bravely they fought; I will avenge them."

Down in the valley the Suns were stripping their victims' corpses. Eyas slid off the centaur's back and stepped in front of him.

"Is that how centaurs fight?"

"Of course."

"Then the Suns deserve to conquer you all."

Boulder's face, already angry, darkened more. Eyas gave him no chance to reply.

"The Suns fought well, and each man helped the others. The centaurs fought singly. They should have run away, or charged the center of the Suns' line together, and broken through. They were brave, yes, but they were fools."

Boulder's grip slowly loosened on his sword; his tail lashed nervously.

"In a breath or two they will look up and see us." Eyas went back down the hill, through the trampled grass, and Boulder reluctantly followed.

"You have fought against high odds before," he growled. "Why are you now afraid?"

"I fear only that the Suns will return unharmed to Two Creek Fort. We will give them a surprise, and live to tell about it."

Boulder gave him a long look, and then sheathed his sword.

The raiding party left the road and struck out due south across the rolling green hills. The Suns made no attempt to conceal themselves; Eyas supposed they were trying to attract attention, to lure more centaurs into attacking them. He kept Boulder well behind, usually in the creek beds that ran below the level of the open prairie. As the afternoon waned, Boulder grew impatient.

"When do we surprise them?"

"When they camp for the night."

"You mean to fight them in the dark?"

"Yes."

"You think like one of them. Centaurs fight by day."

"Do they ever raid you at night?"

"Often."

"But they expect no trouble for themselves in darkness. Good."

"I do not like this—two against thirty, in the dark."

Eyas could not resist mockery. "Or will you return alone to Foundries after all?"

"We will do as you say."

Clouds had begun to spread across the sky from the west, and by nightfall the moon and the Bridge of Heaven were obscured. The Suns' campfires were all the brighter for the darkness surrounding them. Eyas led Boulder out of the creek beds; they settled in behind a clump of thorny bushes less than a bowshot from the camp. The Suns' voices carried clearly as they laughed and sang over their meal. Eyas crawled closer to reconnoiter.

The camp had been pitched on a slight rise, not far from a small stream lined with aspens. Eyas could hear axes: some of the Suns were cutting more firewood. The two campfires were perhaps ten spans apart; between them stood the sixfeet, penned inside a simple enclosure of sticks and ropes. The brutes were pulling up handfuls of grass and feeding themselves with grunts of pleasure. A single sentry trudged around the perimeter of the camp, a gun on his shoulder.

Eyas went back to Boulder. "When they go to sleep," he whispered to the centaur, "we make one run through the camp. The sixfeet are penned between the fires. If we go through the Suns to the right, perhaps we can drive the

174

sixfeet across the other group. But we must be quick—right through and out the other side."

"Good." For all his earlier reluctance, Boulder seemed eager now.

Before long the Suns fell silent and their fires dimmed. The sixfeet sometimes stamped and bellowed, until the sentry began a soft, monotonous song to calm them. Eyas was glad of that: he could locate the sentry more easily in the darkness.

When he had judged it to be past midnight, Eyas climbed silently onto Boulder's back. The centaur put down the clumsy bundle of Sunnish weapons he had been carrying since the fight the day before and rose from his crouch. They drew their swords, and the centaur walked into the darkness with silent steps. The sentry, still singing, was on the far side of the camp.

Most of the soldiers lay in a row between the fire and their mounts. Boulder sprang forward, straight across the sleeping bodies, his sword rising and falling. Eyas shouted to the sixfeet, "Danger! Run away!" They roused themselves and screamed; Eyas slashed at a Sun who was just sitting up; then the centaur turned and charged at the sixfeet with a roar. Their fright increased; they reared, broke through the thin ropes that penned them, and stampeded across the other campsite. Boulder was close behind, slashing and stabbing at the Suns who had escaped trampling, while Eyas defended his flanks and rear. A gun went off, sending a red flash into the air. The Suns' shouts betrayed their surprise and confusion; in the firelight, Eyas saw two of them attack each other, and one fall dying.

Then they were through the camp, circling back toward the thorn bushes while shots and screams filled the dark behind them.

"Where are you going?" Eyas shouted. "We must get away from here!"

"I cannot leave my trophies." Boulder stopped and groped about in the darkness until he found his bundle of weapons. He added a spear and gun to it; Eyas had not seen him take them. The centaur slung the unwieldy bundle over his shoulder and started off to the east.

"This was good vengeance," he growled contentedly. "And more. These trophies will earn me many wives."

They traveled east, then north, slept through the dawn in a mosquito-ridden wood, and reached the road in early afternoon. Before long they were in settled country; steep-roofed farmhouses stood upon the ridges, and breadseed grew in fresh-plowed fields. Herds of browsers, lean after the long winter and cold spring, grunted across meadows. Auburn-haired centaur females looked after the herds, and stared at the sight of Boulder and Eyas walking side by side down the road.

"The crops are slow this year," Boulder worried. "And the browsers won't give much milk until they grow fatter. It will be another hard winter."

The road began to seem very long to Eyas. "Perhaps you should carry me, and we can reach Foundries sooner," he suggested. Boulder looked uncomfortable.

"I do not want to carry you, now that we are among other centaurs. In battle, yes; we fight well together. But here I would be ashamed. No centaur has ever before carried a human."

"Because the sixfeet do."

"Yes. We will learn otherwise, when our warriors see how a human rider increases the centaur's might. But I feel awkward still."

"I understand." But Eyas felt a twinge of worry. He could imagine an army of men riding centaurs, an army more terrible than any Sunnish force. But reality was discouraging. Centaurs who fought without discipline or coordination, and took pride in vainglorious suicide, would not easily change their ways. Even if they did, who would ride them? The Desert Bands feared and despised centaurs; the Riverines, from what Boulder had told him, were no riders at all. Boulder's dream of an alliance of humans and brutes might well be so much resin smoke.

Near sundown they approached a small village, little more than a cluster of farmhouses, barns, and granaries. Eyas was surprised to see it unfortified.

"Centaurs need no walls," Boulder said. "Only warriors, like those." He pointed to a squadron of centaurs galloping out to meet them—the first males Eyas had seen that day. They carried long spears whose heads gleamed red-gold in the westering light, and they bristled in surprised hostility when they saw Eyas standing beside Boulder.

"Is this a Sunnish prisoner?" their leader asked. Boulder only grunted and glanced at Eyas.

"I greet you, Longleg," said Eyas in centauric. "I am Eyas Fisher. I met you in the Gulf, years ago. You were a great smoker, and danced all night when the moon was full."

Longleg's heavy jaw dropped. "Eyas! Well, well—humans look much alike, but now I recognize you. What brings you to the lands of Foundries Hold?"

"The Gulf has been conquered by Brightspear the Sun. I come to ask shelter of Oldwalker."

"You bring grim news. Come into the village for the night."

Longleg took them into one of the farmhouses, a single big room under a steep-pitched roof. Silent females, half-fascinated and half-repelled by the sight of Eyas, served them heavy loaves and a kind of cheese, along with enormous tankards of beer. Longleg and the other warriors listened with interest to Eyas's account of the attack on Longstrand and the journey across the mountains, and when Boulder told of the fights with the patrol and the raiding party the centaurs slapped their chests with excitement.

"Those hop-two-legs have scourged us well this spring," Longleg said. "More than twenty warriors died at Shale River not long ago, and the Suns left countless browsers slaughtered in their raids. At least they paid some price for it."

The talk turned to the course of the war, and their hosts were grim. Sunnish raiders from Two Creek Fort and other human settlements had been busy all spring, and the centaurs' counterattacks had done little damage except to themselves.

"At least," said one warrior with bitter ribaldry, "those of us who survive this summer will have plenty of widows to add to our families."

"Perhaps we can change matters somewhat," said Boulder. "But now let us sleep; we have far to go tomorrow."

They left before dawn broke on the first day of summer, and kept up a slow but steady pace. The countryside was ever more thickly populated, and news of their coming ran ahead of them, so that a crowd awaited them at each village. Always Eyas was struck by the number of females, and at last he asked Boulder about it.

"Two females are born for every male," the centaur said. "And more males die in infancy. When a male attains his youth, he must battle his fellows for place, and still more die;

177

those who survive to become warriors often die also in combat with the Suns or other holds. Only those who survive battle and prosper in trade may marry."

"So each male has many wives?"

"As many as he can afford." He managed to look both dour and pleased. "It is a costly business, for females produce all our wealth and they know their worth; a male must be renowned in war and rich in trade before he can think of marriage. I gained wealth through your cannon, and certain other dealings, but I have had little success in war. Now things will be different." He patted his bundle of weapons.

They saw Foundries long before they reached it, towering above the plain like a smoking hill. It was almost three thousand years old, and like Longstrand was built upon the rubble of itself. As Boulder and Eyas approached it from the west, the villages grew larger and closer together; many were bigger than Longstrand. Their inhabitants were mostly females, with a few adult males and many children as well. The children, in contrast to the warriors' dourness and the females' silent wariness, were lively and curious, eager to gape at Eyas. He in turn was fascinated with them: sleek and beautiful, they were often no taller than his shoulder. He even saw infants scampering like splithoofs between the legs of their elders, squealing with excitement. After the long loneliness of the journey, Eyas was gladdened by the bustling life that clustered around them.

As the road neared Foundries itself, it paralleled the Swift River, which flowed east through the hold. Along its bank were clusters of tents and crude shacks made of driftwood; many centaurs were crowded here between the river and the road, but few troubled to move from where they sat. They seemed almost like smokers deeply fuddled, though Eyas could smell no resin, and even those who straggled up to the road gazed upon him with dull eyes and blank faces. Many were warriors—or at least adult males—but they carried no weapons. The females stood with arms folded under their breasts, or holding infants who nursed fretfully. Eyas realized there must be thousands crammed into this camp.

"These are the holdless," Boulder said quietly. "Some have been here for years. My grandfather died in a tent like these."

"Is there no work for them? Many of the warriors look strong enough—or would if they were better fed."

"'Better to lose your life than lose your hold,' we say. These wretches chose to live in dishonor rather than die defending their own lands. Why should we honor them with our trust? Would they defend Foundries more fiercely than their own holds? Besides, you see them as they are—dull, broken, only half-alive, unfit for war or work. At least their children will be holded, those who do not starve. Come, let us hasten—this place angers me."

Eyas said nothing, but quickened his steps to keep up with Boulder. The stink of the camp was thick in his nostrils, but thicker, he suspected, in those of Boulder.

Beyond the camp they came to wide orchards bright with apple blossoms and buzzing with bees, and beyond the orchards were the first roofs of Foundries Hold. Where the road entered the hold, twenty warriors awaited them; Eyas recognized their leader, Weedybrook, who had been at Longstrand when Eyas and Boulder had retrieved the Sunnish cannon. He remembered Eyas well.

"The Arm has been told of your coming. He bids you to attend him at once."

"Does he intend to give me shelter?" Eyas asked.

"I know nothing of that. But I hope you find him generous." Weedybrook gave them an escort of ten warriors and sent them on.

Though he kept his face impassive and walked with gravity, Eyas felt dizzied by the size of the hold, and by its countless inhabitants. They followed their escort up a broad, cobbled street. The houses on either side must have been four or five spans tall; their steep, tarred roofs came almost to the ground, leaving narrow alleys between them. Most had deep porches and balconies, all crowded with centaurs. The doorways of the houses were large, indifferently carpentered by the People's standards, but adorned with metalwork of surpassing beauty: huge copper flowers, golden vines, and designs of meaningless but lovely curves and angles. No two doorways were the same. Eyas saw few windows, but those few held panes of windwalkers' glass.

As in the villages, most of the centaurs here were females and children, but these seemed more prosperous. The children were clean and well-fed; the females wore brightly

179

patterned blankets over their hindquarters, and adorned their breasts with many chains of gold and silver. But they stared at Eyas with the same astonishment, and looked aside in giggling confusion when he smiled at them.

They came into a quarter of warehouses, granaries, and smithies. The smells of hot iron, baking bread, and fresh-cut wood all mingled with a whiff of resin smoke. The air shivered with the roar of fires and the clang of hammers, and the wooden walls of the buildings were black with soot. Workers stood in the doorways of their shops and smithies, wearing trousers and aprons of leather or felt; their auburn hair was dark with sweat, and their strong arms gleamed like polished copper. Here and there, a warrior loomed dark and silent among the females, thumbs hooked in the sword belt slung over his shoulder.

Ascending, they crossed a bridge that spanned the Swift River and came into a crowded marketplace, where great loaves of bread were stacked, and piles of winter apples, and bolts of cloth. Yet even here Eyas saw little color; Foundries was a city of browns and grays, blacks and dull reds. He searched for green—a tree, a shrub—and found none. Even the blue of sky was dulled with smoke. Yet for all its drabness, Foundries was a place of power, of energy, where even the filthy water in the gutters ran quickly, and centaurs bred to run on the open plain had concentrated their strength instead on this mountain of their own making.

The street came at last to a wall, built of stone and mortar. It was old and neglected, covered with ivy and roses, but cannons jutted from its top. They were far larger than the one Eyas had found at the bottom of Mud Bay, and the first he had seen in Foundries.

"They are not much thought of," Boulder replied when Eyas remarked on them, "except as place-tokens. The Arm decorates his wall with them, and other holds buy them from us to keep their own place. But everyone sees them as defensive weapons, and centaurs prefer attack. Besides, each cannon requires several warriors to work it—"

"And warriors prefer to fight alone." Eyas nodded. He felt his confidence fade still more.

Before a gate in the wall stood a warrior in glittering mail, his hindquarters mantled in blue spidersilk that must have been a costly import from the Gulf. He gestured to

Weedybrook's escort; they turned aside to stand in the shade of a nearby building, leaving Boulder and Eyas to approach him.

"I greet you, Boulder," the glittering centaur said softly.

"I greet you, Foehewer. We come to attend on the Arm."

Foehewer, stroking his beard, met Eyas's gaze and looked away.

"Wait. I will inform him that you are here." He used the singular form of the pronoun, implying that a human could not be recognized as existing at all. Foehewer turned and clattered through the gate. Boulder fluffed out his mane.

"Ill-named fool!" he muttered. "Still, if the Arm sent him to meet us, we are considered important."

They stood patiently on the cobblestones, sweating under the hazy sky. The street below the gate was deserted except for the warriors in their escort; Eyas suspected that the street normally carried much traffic. He glimpsed an occasional bearded face peering over the wall, or through the doorways of neighboring buildings. But this place was very silent after the crowds and uproar of the lower streets.

Flanked by two attendants almost as gaudy as himself, Foehewer returned at last.

"The Arm welcomes you, Boulder. He will meet you and your . . . companion in the Smaller Garden."

"We will attend him gladly."

With Foehewer in the lead and the attendants behind them, Boulder and Eyas entered the Houses of Oldwalker. The air seemed brighter here, for the roofs were lower and farther apart, sheathed in copper weathered to a pale green. The streets were broad and smoothly paved; where they crossed, fountains splashed in stone basins. Apple trees and flowering vines grew in courtyards, offering the first bright colors Eyas had seen in the hold. Few centaurs walked the streets except for warriors, but Eyas sensed activity all around them.

They came to a house much like the others, but guarded by many armored centaurs. Its door was the most beautiful Eyas had yet seen. Across it ran iron centaurs in a field of golden grass and silver-stemmed flowers of jade and bloodstone and agate. One centaur ran before the others, clutching a broken sword; his eyes were black roundstones set in shell. His pursuers glared, grimaced, sneered, each face distinct

181

and individual. The fleeing centaur was naked; the others were splendid in burnished armor.

"Like a family post," Eyas whispered as they approached the door.

"Yes," answered Boulder. "Each Arm takes a great time from the lives of his ancestors, and renders it in the mark of his house."

"Oldwalker's ancestor is the one who flees."

"He was called Amethyst. The warriors of Coppermine Hold fell upon him when he was hunting, and nearly killed him. He escaped and returned to conquer them."

The guards swung open the door, and Foehewer led the way into a great dark room whose wooden floor boomed under the centaurs' hoofs. The vaulted ceiling was high and shadowy; on either side, doorways led to smaller rooms hung with tapestries and lit by candles. Foehewer went straight through the building to a doorway that opened onto a garden bright with sun and the glitter of water in fountains and pools. Plum and cherry trees, thick with setting fruit, made a green roof.

"Leave your weapons and trophies here," said Foehewer, pointing to a shelf beside the door. "None may carry weapons into the presence of the Arm." Eyas saw that the centaur was impressed despite himself with Boulder's bundle.

At the far end of the garden, sitting beneath a cherry tree, four centaurs awaited them. Three were middle-aged females, with plump, intelligent, and suspicious faces. Their auburn hair was too vivid to be natural; beneath rich garments, their flesh was heavy with too much food and too little activity. The fourth, sitting a little apart, was Oldwalker, Arm of Foundries Hold.

He was older than any centaur Eyas had yet seen. His hair was white all over his body; the skin on his chest and face was pink as a human baby's palm. He was not fat, but his flesh hung loosely on his bones, and his face was deeply lined. Under heavy white brows, Oldwalker's eyes were as bright and black as the roundstones, set in silver, that he wore as a necklace. His only garment was a plain gray blanket on his hindquarters. Though he sat unmoving, a bright and cynical glint in his eye made Eyas remember Griptiller.

Boulder paused, raised both palms toward Oldwalker, and bent his torso almost horizontal. Eyas did the same. The Arm beckoned them closer.

"Welcome home, Boulder. I greet you, Eyas Fisher." The old centaur's voice was a rough whisper; he spoke the Gulf dialect hesitantly. "Your presence here means evil news from the Gulf."

"The Suns have conquered it," Eyas replied in centauric. The females stared at him, but Oldwalker only smiled sadly.

"We feared as much. Sit beside me, and tell me everything."

While insects buzzed among the flowers, Eyas spoke quietly about the attack on Longstrand and his escape with Boulder. Oldwalker said little until Eyas described the fight on the road and their attack on the raiding party. He leaned forward then.

"So you rode a centaur into battle! Boulder, what of your place?" the Arm asked in amused mockery. Boulder looked embarrassed and said nothing.

"Alone, neither of us would have lived through that first fight," said Eyas. "Together, we avenged many centaurs' and humans' deaths. We were only the first."

"The first of what?"

"Of an army of centaurs and men," Eyas replied.

Hesitantly at first, but with growing eagerness, Boulder told the Arm of his dream of an alliance between men and brutes. The females looked at one another without expression as he spoke. Oldwalker only smiled. When Boulder had finished, the Arm was silent for a time. Then he said,

"Eyas, do you know of our pact with the Seagoddess?"

"No." He was surprised by the question.

"You know that we once warred on the People of the Gulf, long ago before we learned ironlore from the men of the southern lands, before we settled in holds. We wanted the Gulf for the resin of its bloodwoods, for the food it gives so easily. It was we who first planted breadseed in the Bluemeadows Valley, when the People were only grubbers of shellfish. But the Goddess came to us, and commanded us to make peace with the People. Some day, She told us, the People would come in a great army across Wilderness to aid the centaurs and bring long peace to Alland."

"I know of Aspen's Compact," said Eyas, "but not that the Goddess had a part in it."

"Aspen was a great warrior, the greatest since we were driven north from the Grasslands into Transmontane and the High Plains. He could have thrown the People over the Westwall and into the sea. But he obeyed the Goddess, and yielded the Gulf. After what you have told me, I think he made a bad bargain. The Goddess is slain. The People are conquered by the Suns. The army we were promised is a single youth with a wounded foot."

Eyas looked coldly at him. "It would be impolite to engage in a mockery duel with my host, especially when I could beat him at it. In your house Boulder has left a bundle of trophies; they are only tokens of what can be won when men and centaurs fight together."

Oldwalker coughed with amusement, while his wives looked scandalized. "A swift answer. I am glad you are not a centaur; you would stir up more trouble than Boulder. Well, well. You think you can teach us new warlore, and unite men and brutes. But I know my own warriors. Not many would give up glory in battle for a mere victory won with the aid of men. And not many would allow a human to ride them like sixfeet."

Eyas was tired, and his foot hurt. Oldwalker's words reminded him of times in Speaker's Hall when some old fool argued endlessly against the self-evident. His temper rose and his eyes fixed on the old centaur's face.

"Would your warriors attack the Suns at night, as Boulder did? Could they fight six Sunnish riders alone, and bring home trophies? Did Amethyst give up when his sword was broken?"

Oldwalker folded his arms and snorted softly. "You invoke my ancestor; I ignore the insult for the sake of your grandmother's memory. Now you will honor me with an act of kindness. You want an army that will obey you, and follow your warlore. My warriors will not, unless shamed to it. Give them a show of your might and guile, Eyas Fisher. Go into the camp of the holdless, speak with their leader Standaway Smith, gather your army there, and bring me a trophy from Two Creek Fort."

Boulder sucked in his breath, dismayed, but Eyas laughed.

"Griptiller often spoke of your tradelore," he said, "but she taught me one or two things about dealings with centaurs. I admire your offer; now let us bargain."

3

It took most of the afternoon, but at last each of them said, "I am pleased," and the bargain was made. Boulder and Eyas withdrew from the Smaller Garden, took their weapons and trophies, and left the Houses of Oldwalker. Their escort had gone; Foehewer alone bade them a sardonic farewell at the wall. In silence, the centaur and the man crossed the bridge into the lower hold and came at last to a house on a narrow street near the orchards that surrounded Foundries. A crowd of curious centaurs, mostly warriors, made way for them, and Eyas gazed in surprise at the door. In sheets of silver and bronze, it portrayed a stylized boat; upon its deck, a centaur and a human stood holding a cannon.

"This is my house," said Boulder unsmilingly. "As the son of a holdless centaur, I have no ancestors; I *am* an ancestor, or so I thought until today." Without ceremony, he pushed open the door.

The cool, dark, smoky interior, with its high ceiling and smells of cooking, reminded Eyas of home. Several young centaurs bowed to them, then clustered affectionately around Boulder.

"This is my family," he told Eyas. "My brothers Cirque and Agate; my sisters Dance Gaily Potter and Tillfallow Carpenter."

"I did not know centaurs had family names."

"Work names," said Dance Gaily with a shy smile. "Come— we heard of your return, and your meal is ready."

They sat in sweet-smelling straw by the rear door of the house, which opened onto a small garden; Eyas saw fireflies gleam in the dusk. Boulder's sisters brought food; the brothers served it to him and Eyas on wooden platters. In the Gulf, a reunion like this would have been full of shouting, laughter, and tears, a happy confusion. Boulder's family were quiet, but Eyas saw gladness in their movements. He also felt anxiety in them. They were all young, and though born in Foundries they were still strangers in it. What place they had they owed to Boulder; their fortunes depended on his.

Not until Boulder and Eyas had finished eating did the brothers sit to eat, and after them the sisters. When the meal was over, Tillfallow offered a tray holding resin pipes, but Boulder waved it away.

"We have too much to discuss," he said. He told his family of his journey, and of Oldwalker's subtle response to the proposal for an army of humans and centaurs. When he was finished, the long summer twilight was full dark; the sisters lit candles.

"We have made the bargain," said Eyas.

"But—an army of the holdless would be like a wooden sword," Cirque replied. "They will obey any holded centaur, true—but in battle they would only flee."

"Windwalkers' swords are made of wood,"—Eyas said,—"but they can cut as deep as iron. And flight is sometimes wiser than battle. Let us go to the camp of the holdless and seek out this Standaway who leads them."

"Now?" said Boulder. "It is night."

"I will not wait."

Boulder looked worried. "My brothers and I will go with you. You would not be safe alone."

"What—are the holdless dangerous after all?"

"Some of our unwed warriors go at night into the camp," Boulder explained, "to rape the females and practice swordplay on the males. It is a great scandal."

"The holdless are ours now," said Eyas as he stood up. "Your bachelors will have to find other amusements."

Under the light of the Bridge, the camp of the holdless seemed more alive than it had been by day. Centaurs moved about restlessly; the wails of hungry children blended with the melancholy songs of the adults, and the scent of resin hung in the warm air. Boulder and his brothers, their tails switching nervously, led Eyas from the road into the camp. Begging children put out their hands; females slipped away into the darkness. But Eyas was aware of many centaurs following them at a cautious distance as they went down a rocky lane through the tents toward the river. Suddenly their way was blocked by a dozen warriors carrying swords or clubs.

"What do you want here?" one of them called out.

"That's no concern of yours," Boulder growled. "Get out of our path."

A breeze carried the mixed smells of beer and resin from the warriors. One of them ambled closer, swaying a little.

"You challenge our place?" he asked. He lazily swung a club at his side. "Perhaps you want all the females for yourselves."

Eyas stepped forward, drew his sword, and knocked the club from the warrior's loose grip. The sword's point came back and rested under the centaur's ribs.

"A hop-two-legs has disarmed you, and holds your life. You have no place," Eyas said coldly. "Get out of our path, and out of this camp."

The centaur and his companions had not seen him in the darkness; the fuddled leader stared down at him in wordless horror, as if at some monster in a dream. Cautiously he backed away, while Eyas followed with the sword always on the centaur's skin. When they reached the other warriors, Eyas sheathed his sword and glared up at them.

"Oldwalker has given to me the care of the holdless in this camp. No warriors of Foundries may enter here again, unless I invite them, and no holdless centaur will be abused by any warrior. Get out, or I will make Oldwalker a gift of your tails."

The warriors turned and trotted away, their hoofs splashing in puddles of sewage.

In the darkness, the swords of Boulder and his brothers sang back into their sheaths. "I thought you surely doomed," said Boulder softly, "until I heard your voice. This is a better start than I had expected." He gestured to a holdless male who stood beside a driftwood shack. "We seek Standaway Smith. Do you know where her tent is?"

"Yes."

"Take us there."

"No need," said another voice. "I am here; I will lead you myself."

A small, thin female came out of the shadows and walked towards them.

"What do you want with me?" she asked.

"You are the leader among the holdless," said Boulder. "I am Boulder; these are my brothers Cirque and Agate, and the human is Eyas Fisher of the Gulf of Islands. We have a matter to discuss with you."

She came closer, and Eyas saw that she carried a long knife in a belt around her waist. Once she might have been beautiful, but want and hardship had made her grim. She looked at Eyas with impassive calculation.

"I owe you thanks. But I will let the debt go unpaid a little while. Come."

Her tent was near the river, a simple shelter lit by a single candle. Standaway settled herself at one end of it, leaving Eyas and the centaurs to crowd in as best they could. She regarded them silently. Eyas sat cross-legged on the sandy floor.

"I have been given a mission by the Arm, Standaway. He bids me to lead an army of the holdless against Two Creek Fort, and to bring back trophies."

"We obey the Arm in all things, for we live at his mercy. If he has given us to you, we are yours; if you take us to Two Creek Fort, we go."

Eyas grinned. "But will you fight? The holded despise you as cowards. Will you fight?" He used the singular pronoun, and Standaway seemed perplexed.

"I am a worker, not a warrior."

"You carry a working name, but the holdless are neither workers nor warriors—now. Where were you born?"

"Silverstream Hold."

"Is it beautiful, Standaway?"

"It was, before the Suns burned it."

"Would you like to go home? To rebuild your hold and live in peace?"

She looked away. "Do not mock me."

"I did not come across Wilderness to mock a holdless female. I come to teach your people my warlore, and to use it against the Suns."

He saw her dark eyes glitter. She leaned forward.

"What warlore could drive them out?"

"Their own." He held up a hand before her. "They are a single fist; centaurs are only fingers. Oldwalker himself said his warriors would change their ways only if shamed into it. So the holdless alone can save him, though he does not yet realize that."

She sat unmoving, her thin arms folded over her breasts. Her eyes met his.

"I will tell my people. Come tomorrow at noon, and tell us what your will is. Our males will try to learn from you."

"Will you try also?"

"I—a warrior?" She seemed almost shocked; Boulder looked sidelong at Eyas.

"You, and other females as well." He drew his sword and offered it to her. She reached out and took it with a faint smile, judging it with a smith's critical eye. A warrior's hand would have been too large for the handle, but hers was not. The blade shimmered red in candle light.

"It is very light," she said. "Well made."

"Keep it, then, and use it to win back your home."

"No. This is yours." She gave it back. "I will win my own."

Each morning, wagons brought Foundries' garbage to the camp of the holdless. At the edge of the road, the holdless waited while centaurs shoveled moldy bread and rotting fruit from the wagons; when the wagons were empty at last, the holdless scrabbled for what they could.

But this morning there were more wagons than usual, and they carried sacks of breadseed flour, boxes of fresh apples and splitroot, and jugs of fermented browser's milk. One wagon carried nothing but cheese; another, the dressed carcasses of domesticated blackhorns. The holdless did not fight each other for the food; Standaway and twenty other rawboned young males and females oversaw the distribution, while Eyas, Boulder and his brothers watched from one of the wagons. The only noise in the bright sunrise was the wailing of hungry children; as the morning went on, the wailing died away. Amid the stench of the camp, the smells of roasting meat and baking bread spread rapidly. When they had fed, the centaurs came hesitantly to the wagon to thank Eyas. He smiled and told them to go across the road into a large meadow.

By noon the meadow was crowded. Not far away, scores of warriors from Foundries watched with mingled curiosity and contempt. Eyas and Boulder left the wagon and walked slowly across the road.

"Will you allow me to stand on you?" Eyas asked.

Boulder looked at the watching warriors, then shrugged. "I wanted change, and now I have it. Very well. May those warriors have a good laugh; it will be their last for a long time."

Eyas sprang onto his friend's back, then stood. The warriors looked shocked; two or three even groped for their swords. The holdless stirred, surprised but interested as well. Eyas looked out across the silent meadow at thousands of faces, and drew a long breath.

"Standaway has told you of the will of the Arm—that you are in my care and will do my bidding. Will you come with me, to make war upon the Suns?" His own voice seemed thin and weak to him, but it carried across the meadow like a gliding hawk.

The holdless centaurs at first seemed surprised to be asked rather than commanded. Then, at first by ones and twos and afterward by hundreds, they answered him:

"Yes." Their voices, like wind under a hawk's wings, lifted him up. He drew his sword, raising it above his head so that it flashed in the noon like white fire.

"I am as holdless as you, but holdless I took this sword and holdless I shall use it until the Suns are cast down and I win my hold again. Will you come with me?"

"Yes."

"The way will be hard, and many will fall in blood and sorrow. Will you come with me?"

"Yes," and it was a single shout.

"Three times you have answered me. It is done. Look! The sun is at the zenith; it must descend. When it rises again, the world will be changed forever, and by our hands. Will you come with me?"

A fourth time they cried "Yes," and some of Foundries' warriors shouted with them, striding forward with waving swords and spears pounding upon shields.

"Goddess, look under us now," Eyas murmured. His exultation flashed out across them, a torch kindled in darkness, and reflected back to him from their eyes. He felt himself back in the Rip again, riding a current too great to be stopped or turned.

The holdless no longer sat idly in their camp. Now they rose at dawn each day, ate in the communal kitchens that Standaway set up, and gathered in the meadow to train. They wielded axes, spears, staffs and swords, even crude clubs. In squadrons of twenty, then fifty, then a hundred, they charged and retreated, and fought with growing skill. At first they were clumsy and disorganized, like children learning the steps of a dance. The warriors had to unlearn old habits; the workers, to learn new ones. The ten or twenty holded warriors who joined Boulder and his family were uncomfortable at first to be training alongside females—and Boulder himself was unsettled by the sight of his sisters swinging swords and hurling spears. But as day followed day, all became accustomed to the sight of females trading blows with males, and winning as often as not. Almost as strong as the males, the females were quicker and lighter on their hoofs.

Eyas worked from dawn to dusk, teaching his warlore to small groups who then taught it to others. Boulder was no longer reluctant to carry him, though some holded onlookers sneered at the sight, and the holdless vied for the honor of carrying Eyas. At night, the camp was lively with songs and children's laughter. Eyas lived among the holdless, now in this tent, now in that; he learned their genealogies and the legends of their lost holds.

In the heat of noon, the centaurs rested in the shade of the trees along the riverbank. Eyas was there one day, leaning against the trunk of an aspen while Standaway sat beside him, her legs folded under her, her tail switching at blackflies.

"How did you come to be leader of the holdless?" he asked.

"To care for my children."

"I did not know you had any."

"When the Suns conquered Silverstream, eight years ago, I was the oldest of three wives of a warrior named Opal. He was slain in the fighting. My sisterwives gathered in our house and set it afire, and died with their children. I—I was not afraid of death, for myself or my three sons. But I thought of the Sunnish soldiers walking on our ashes, scattering our bones. It was the disgrace of that which I feared. Better to be holdless, and at least die unconquered. My sons' sons would be holded, and could avenge us. So we escaped, and came to Foundries.

"The camp was smaller then, but worse than when you came. The holded warriors tormented us more. I saw that my sons would never live unless the holdless made some order. So I gathered a few others, and we made a part of the camp safe from thieves. We killed three in one night. More holdless came to find safety with us. And I made sure the children got their share of the food."

She paused; Eyas waited. When she spoke again, her voice was so soft it was almost lost in the sound of the river.

"Five years ago, in the winter, many starved. Boulder's

father died then, and his mother. At least his children were holded, and old enough to find place and work. Then pestilence came. Some died of it in Foundries, but in the camp we lost hundreds. All my children died. I burned them, and cast their ashes into the river. The Suns can never dishonor them now."

"So all the holdless are your children."

She nodded, then put her hands to her face. Eyas leaned forward and put his hand gently on her arm.

"Ah, Eyas—they were so young, and beautiful, and I loved them so!"

One night he woke, or thought he woke, and saw a dim figure squatting beside him. Though he could not see its face, he knew who it was: the Messenger.

We have found you, Eyas Fisher, said the Messenger silently. *We have fed on your family, and their lives were sweet. Soon we will feed on yours, soon you will be one of us in Hell. We have found you, and we will not lose you again.*

The voiceless words stirred Eyas not to fear but to rage. He reached out in wrath toward the figure, and the darkness vanished in a pulse of dazzling light. For an instant he saw the Messenger's face, pale and startled, and then it vanished.

Darkness returned. Eyas sat up, hearing the heavy snores of the centaurs whose tent he shared. The camp was tranquil, but he was a long time in calming himself. At last he got up and left the tent to walk along the riverbank until dawn.

That morning, Foehewer was among those who watched the holdless training in the meadow. Eyas, astride Boulder, came across the trampled grass to greet him. The centaur, surrounded by a retinue of six warriors, nodded haughtily in reply.

"You keep them well occupied," Foehewer remarked.

"They are doing well," said Eyas. "Many are still too weak or ill to be good fighters; they will do as bearers. We should have about two thousand capable of fighting the Suns, and another ten days will see them ready."

"Surely you do not expect them to succeed."

"The Arm does not expect them to succeed," Eyas said. "He thinks a month's feeding a small price to pay to be rid of them. But we will succeed. And once the holdless have human riders, they will be unstoppable."

Foehewer and his companions coughed amusedly. Eyas felt

Boulder grow tense. The dreamhaunting of the night before had left bitterness in Eyas's thoughts; Foehewer's scorn turned that bitterness to silent anger.

"Would you like to join us in practice?" he asked. "Just with staffs. Boulder and I can show you how we fight together."

Foehewer's smile faded. As a centaur of great place, he could not decline a challenge; but only a centaur of nearly equal place would dare to challenge him. Warrior protocol made no provision for a challenge from a human and centaur together.

"I will be glad to," he said expressionlessly. "And I will try not to hurt either of you."

A young female brought staffs, each a span long and tipped with iron to give extra weight. Foehewer swung his above his head, making it hum in the air, and then trotted out into the meadow. Boulder and Eyas, each with his own staff, followed. The centaurs faced each other at a distance of ten or twelve spans.

"I give you the honor of the charge," said Foehewer.

Boulder sprang forward, holding his staff horizontally in both hands. Eyas gripped his like a lance.

Foehewer's staff whirred down; Boulder parried and sidestepped while Eyas lunged out. The iron tip of his staff struck Foehewer in the belly, making him grunt. Boulder swung his staff like a sword and struck it against the back of his opponent's head. Despite the protection given by his mane, Foehewer staggered under the blow, recovered, and retreated. Boulder closed in, striking Foehewer's staff away, and Eyas—now at closer range—stabbed out again with the tip of his staff. Foehewer's front legs buckled, and he dropped his staff.

"Well done," he wheezed, struggling upright. "But it was two against one."

"Exactly," said Eyas.

"It is immoral and unwarlike."

Once Eyas would have laughed at such a remark; now he only looked contemptuous. Foehewer would not meet his gaze.

"We have business to attend to," the beaten centaur muttered. His retinue fell into line behind him as he trotted off with short-winded dignity, up the road to Foundries.

"He was much slower than I'd expected," Eyas remarked. "We should have been gentler with him."

"That's not what troubles him," said Boulder. "With real weapons, we'd have slain him in the first exchange. But he has lost place before his attendants—and before the holdless." He nodded toward a squadron of centaurs who had paused to watch the passage of arms. "Get back to work, you gawkers!"

The day passed in dust, sweat, and clangor. Late in the afternoon, the centaurs from Foehewer's retinue returned and walked slowly into the meadow. They found Eyas, riding Cirque, watching a swordplay drill.

"We bring a command from the Arm," said one of them.

He handed Eyas an object resembling a book: two thin, square boards, bound on one side by leather straps. On the upper board, a broken sword was inlaid in copper. Eyas opened the book and found not pages but a sheet of yellow wax poured into a shallow recess in the second board; the wax was incised with strange symbols. Eyas had been learning centauric script, but this was beyond him. Cirque took it and read, his lips moving. Then he looked angrily at the courier, who gazed stolidly back at him.

Cirque's face was dark as he turned to speak over his shoulder to Eyas. "The Arm gives you until tomorrow's sundown to leave for Two Creek Fort with the army. If not, he will revoke the bargain and expel you from Foundries. This is unfair! We're not ready—"

"Enough," said Eyas brusquely. "We obey the Arm in all things. Will you take a message to him?" he asked the courier. "Tell him he honors me by this command, and inspires us all to carry out our mission. We thank him for his confidence and trust."

The courier blinked, a little taken aback by Eyas's smiling acquiescence. "I will tell him."

Eyas returned the wooden book and beckoned to Boulder and Standaway.

The food wagons creaked out through the orchards at dawn next morning. But only a few score holdless—the crippled, the diseased, the aged—waited beside the road. Many of the tents were gone from the camp; the riverbank was deserted. Dew sparkled on the few surviving tufts of grass in the empty meadow.

The females pulling the wagons looked blankly at the little crowd of holdless. Then they unbuckled their harnesses, shrugged, and dutifully distributed the food.

For three days, messengers brought word to Foundries of the progress of the holdless army. Then the army passed beyond the last patrols, into rolling prairie long ruled by Foundries but now in the hands of the Suns.

Five days passed, then ten. The weather turned cold and wet; hail broke the breadseed plants in the fields and knocked ripening apples from their boughs. Foundries' warriors on the southern marches reported no word of the army and no contact with the Suns. For the first time since winter's end, a kind of peace had fallen over the lands of the hold.

On the eleventh day, five of the holdless appeared unannounced at Foundries. Only two were males, but all were warriors in arms, and one carried a large pouch slung over her shoulder.

"We come to attend on the Arm," she told Weedybrook. The old warrior had seen so many strange sights this summer that he only nodded and waved them through.

The warriors raced up the streets, through the market-places and across the bridge, leaving behind them startled crowds and a flurry of rumors. At the gate to the Houses of Oldwalker, they pounded rudely until a scandalized attendant admitted them. Foehewer, called from his noon meal, met the travelers outside Oldwalker's own house.

"You endanger yourselves with this unseemly behavior," he warned. The female carrying the pouch answered proudly,

"We obey the will of the Arm, that he be given a trophy from Two Creek Fort. Where is Oldwalker?"

"Follow . . . me."

The Arm was in the Smaller Garden, contemplating his ruined roses. The holdless warriors, remembering protocol too late, dropped swords and spears on the flagstoned walk as they approached him.

"We greet you, Oldwalker!" they cried together. The female reached into her pouch, bowed, and held out a trophy to him. Oldwalker took it and held it with trembling hands.

"What is this?" he asked brusquely.

The trophy was a twelve-pointed sun of hammered gold, larger than a centaur's hand, and set on a base of polished onyx.

"It comes from the temple of the Sun at Two Creek Fort," replied the female. "Eyas bids us tell you that he has left half the food in the Suns' granaries for the use of Foundries, and many weapons. He also bids us tell you that the army is now

195

bound east, to gather warriors from other holds and then to seek out the Desert Bands."

"Indeed," said Oldwalker tonelessly.

"If you do not require us, Arm, may we leave? We would rejoin our comrades as soon as we may."

Oldwalker nodded absently, fingering the golden trophy. The holdless left, scooping up their weapons as they went.

"Foehewer!"

The centaur almost leaped from the doorway into the garden.

"Send a hundred wagons, two hundred warriors, and five hundred workers to Two Creek Fort to empty the Suns' granaries and arsenals. And five hundred warriors will leave by tomorrow to join the holdless army; you will lead them."

Foehewer gaped in astonishment. "If the Arm wills it—"

"I do not will it. But I am an honest trader; I keep my word. You and your warriors had better prepare yourselves to bear the burden of human riders," he added. He laughed.

"Beaten! Beaten in a bargain by a hop-two-legs!"

4

Low brown cliffs ran east, scarred by gullies that dropped steeply to a sandy wash. To the south, beyond the wash, a rocky plain shimmered in the forgelike heat. Nothing grew there but clumps of tough grass and a few spiny bushes. This was the Yellow Desert.

The army of the centaurs was encamped along the base of the cliffs, which gave a little shade, and where a hole dug deep enough would yield a little brackish water. Eyas's tent was pitched under a rocky overhang; around it sat Boulder, Cirque, Agate, and other centaurs, patiently enduring the heat. Within the tent, Eyas shuddered and panted with fever while Standaway attended him.

He had lain ill for three days. The straw mat under him was soaked with sweat despite the dryness of the air. His fever would not break; Standaway could only try to cool his skin with damp cloths, and give him sips of water.

The dreamhauntings had come again the night before, and still went on though the sun was now past noon. Eyas could draw on no protective rage; he lay helpless before the taunts and threats of the Messenger, and Thorn, and others he did not know. Mingled with their grinning faces were fragments of memory, some new, some long-forgotten. He saw Chirp running down the sand; he felt the spark of pleasure the spider took from her game with him, and he heard the familiar but meaningless words of his fathers as they mended nets nearby. He splashed down the trail to Silken's cabin, looking for Goldarms. Men shouted and died in fire-streaked darkness—was it remembrance of the Sunnish tower on the outcoast, or a memory of Two Creek Fort? He was paddling up an inlet at sundown, with the scents of seaweed and flowering club thick in the air: a memory of a life that might have been.

Eyas. Eyas. Oh, Eyas, hear me.

He could not see her, but he knew her voice. "Sky—I hear you."

Find the cave, the cave in Mount Aspen. Go to Skyland. Oh, hear me, and remember!

"I loved you. I love you still, though you torment me like the others."

He sensed endless sadness and regret, and did not know if it was hers or his own. *We are past all love. Find the cave. Remember.*

She seemed to be calling from a great distance. He slipped into memories of her, and then of her death, and then the Messenger was back over him.

Soon I will be back on earth, Eyas. Twice you escaped me. But next time I will take you down into the dark and we will feed on you. We fed on Firewing and Quiet and Netweaver, on Old and Sky and Violet, on Gray and Golden, and their lives were good to eat. We have fed on Harper and her family, and on many others. Brightspear feeds us well. But your life will be sweetest of all.

Far away he heard centaurs' voices, and seized on them, pulling himself back toward life.

"He raves in his own tongue, as if he spoke with dreams."

"Is the fever still upon him?"

"I think it weakens. What if he dies? What shall we do?"

"Turn back, and seek safety in the far north. Build a new hold, if we can. But he must not die. He must not."

"Boulder—" Eyas's tongue was thick and dry. He opened his eyes to see Standaway and Boulder crouched over him, their faces intent on his. "Give me some water, and let me sit up."

The centaurs danced that night around their little fires, while Eyas ate bread and cheese and listened to their songs. Standaway sat with him.

"We will go on in the morning," he said.

"You should rest, Eyas."

"We have too little time. The Suns will seek vengeance for Two Creek Fort. They will strike hard at Foundries unless we distract them. We must find the Desert Bands soon." He fell silent, sorting through the memories of his fever. "But perhaps it doesn't matter," he added softly.

"What?"

"Nothing. Where is Mount Aspen?"

Standaway smiled. "Many mountains are so named. There is one near Silverstream, another at Coppermine. They are called after the mountain in the far south where Aspen himself was born."

"That is the one I mean." He did not know how he knew. "Where in the south is it?"

"I think it is in the southern ranges of the White Mountains, near the Lake Country where the Suns rule. We were driven from that land long ago, even before the Suns came."

She told him legends of the ancient days, when centaurs were newborn from mother earth and beloved of father sky, and they wandered freely across the Grasslands of the warm south. She told him of Whitemane, the female who though virgin gave birth to half-creatures, the first humans. For that crime, father sky took the gift of speech from her, and mother earth cursed her womb. Thereafter Whitemane gave birth to sixfeet, longfurs, and coursers, cousins of true centaurs but doomed to be slaves of men. She fled at last into the forests, where she bore the first woodsrunners, and changed at last into a mountain. Long afterward Aspen had been born on that mountain, and there he had rallied the centaur tribes when men beset them, and led the centaurs across the White Mountains into the green valleys of Transmontane.

Eyas listened in silence, and when she was through he said, "My dead wife Sky spoke to me today. She told me to seek Mount Aspen."

Standaway looked frightened, and glanced around to see if

anyone had overheard. "A dead human spoke to *you*?" she whispered. "To a male?"

"Yes."

"Strange are the ways of humans. Eyas, you touch on a great secret. Our dead speak to us—but only to females, and we do not speak of it with males."

"Do your dead guide you, warn you?"

"No. They come rarely to us, and only to share in life for a moment. They seem very lonely in the misty fields of death."

"Then you are lucky. The human dead—they seek to turn me from my path. I do not know why. But I will not turn, even if I die myself." His face was bleak. "Perhaps they think I can be slain more easily on Mount Aspen . . . . It is hard that Sky should be allied with them."

He sat up all night, unsleeping, while the centaurs' fires burned low.

The army marched across the rocky plain in a column more than an hourmarch long, moving no faster than its many high-wheeled wagons. The centaurs plodded through clouds of yellow dust all morning, paused for food and water at noon, and plodded on. They were a larger and more varied force than the one that had left Foundries to sack Two Creek Fort; prosperous holded warriors marched beside the holdless, and they came not only from Foundries but from Brokenhill, Tarsand, and other holds. Many were young enough to be considered children, but they bore the heat and dust as patiently as stones.

Eyas and Boulder roved up and down the column, silent but watchful for weariness or delays. In midafternoon one of the rear guards caught up with them. Like many females, she carried a long-barreled gun from the arsenals of Two Creek Fort; males' big hands and heavy musculature prevented them from using Sunnish firearms.

"A flying island is coming from the west," she said.

"Halt the column," Eyas commanded, and centaurs raced ahead to relay the order. The army stopped. Dust blew away, and silence fell. In the clearing air, Eyas could see the island approaching swiftly: a yellow-brown disc, trailing many ropes and flying low over the desert. It came abreast of the column, a little to the north, but close enough for its huge shadow to cover a good part of the column. Anchorstones and hooks dropped from it into the stony soil, followed by the white shapes of windwalkers, gliding down toward the waiting centaurs. Whooping, the windwalkers hovered, then soared back to the gondolas beneath the island. After a pause, a lone windwalker in a red harness descended swiftly to the spot where Eyas and Boulder stood.

"Eyas—and Boulder! I greet you, old friends."

"Soarfar! It is good to see you again," Eyas said.

"They told us in Foundries that we would find you here." Soarfar perched on a stone and flapped his wings to cool himself. His scarred face bore an expression of dull weariness. "I bring you bad news from the Gulf."

"Do the Suns hold it all?"

"Almost all. A few villages still resist, and some of the People have escaped into the Eastwall valleys. But most of the People are slain. The Suns take no captives. They have burned the villages, burned the skyseed groves." He glanced up at the island. "We will be lucky to reach home again. The nearest skyseeds are very far away, on the shores beyond the eastern sea, and the island grows heavier every day."

Now that it was so close, Eyas saw that it did look ragged: skyseeds were spread thinly under the great nets, and the island carried few gondolas.

"Where is your father Unsheath?" Eyas asked, though Soarfar's red harness had already told him the answer.

"Dead. We found one grove untouched by fire, and tried to harvest it ourselves. The Suns were waiting in ambush. Many died. Then the Suns tied torches to skyseeds and cut them loose, trying to burn our island. My father flew down to pierce one of the pods, and it exploded under him."

"I grieve to hear it."

"May I die so good a death. At Foundries they say you seek the Desert Bands. Not far to the east is the oasis of Bitter Spring. It is owned by the Hawks, the Band of Stormsong. They are good fighters—too good, perhaps. Their neighbors united against them last year, and made war on them. If Stormsong has not been beaten, she could be a strong ally."

Eyas nodded. "Good. We will seek her out."

Soarfar spread his long arms and took to the air. "We cannot stay. But I wish you well in your war, old friend. May we meet again in happier times. Farewell!"

Two days later, Eyas's scouts reported smoke on the horizon, and the tracks of many sixfeet and longfurs. Eyas shortened the column, putting more guards around the supply wagons, and pressed on. The land was a little greener here; mice and other scurrying animals darted through the scrub to escape the hawks that circled overhead. That night, sentries heard hoofbeats in the darkness; at dawn, riders could be seen in the distance on all sides of the army. They were short, dark men, dressed in trousers and loose tunics and wide-brimmed hats. Their sixfeet looked smaller but tougher than the brutes ridden by the Suns. The riders made no attempt to approach, but kept pace with the column as it resumed its march.

Eyas rode Boulder at the head of the line. The terrain was flat, covered with low, scrubby bushes. To the east, smoke rose from around a large grove of trees. North and south of the oasis, herds of longfurs wandered.

As the column came within a thousand spans of the oasis, scores of riders burst from among the trees; some fanned out to left and right, flanking the head of the column, while most came straight on. Eyas remembered the Sunnish patrol on the logging road, and held out his left hand. At the signal, swords grated in sheaths and spears rattled against shields. But the riders did not attack; they came to within fifty spans and halted. Lanceheads glittered; short, double-curved bows appeared. The riders' mounts caught the smell of centaurs and pawed nervously in the dust.

"They make a good show," Eyas said. "Let us go and greet them." To himself he added, *Goddess, look under us now.* These people looked far fiercer than any Sunnish soldiers.

Boulder strode forward until only a few spans separated them from the riders. Eyas raised both hands in salute. No one responded.

"I am Eyas Fisher of the Gulf of Islands," he called out. "I seek the Hawks, the Band of Stormsong."

"A nestling, are you?" answered a woman. Her words and accent were strange, in a dialect even older than the High Sunnish and Gulf tongues, but he could follow her well enough. "You're a long way from your own eyrie." The woman prodded her sixfoot forward a few steps. "A pretty sight you are," she laughed. "Baby-naked, riding a centaur."

Eyas laughed too. "You're a pretty sight yourself. Are you Stormsong?"

"I'm she." Like the other riders, she wore trousers and tunic of loose-woven white cloth, elaborately and beautifully embroidered in threads of red, yellow, blue, and gold. Her head was uncovered; her face was tanned, with high cheekbones and large eyes, and tattooed into a strange mask. Her black hair, thickly braided down her back, was adorned with feathers. Rings of gold and silver, set with opals, sparkled not only on her fingers but in her ears as well—something Eyas had never seen before. A curved sword hung from her waist. "What do you want?"

"Your friendship."

She laughed again, a harsh sound. "No stranger is a friend to us. Still less a shameless man with such a herd of thirsty brutes. Turn around. Go back to wherever you came from, or it will go hard with you."

"I will not."

"Then we'll feast on centaurs' flesh tonight, and I'll dance in your skin."

Eyas grinned. "The windwalkers told us your neighbors make war upon you—are they not enough to busy you, that you must seek new quarrels?"

Stormsong's eyes narrowed; she leaned forward, her arm on the pommel of her saddle. "What have you to do with flapwings?"

"They are my friends, as are these centaurs."

"A man, friend to brutes! You are shameless indeed." She glanced at the centaurs' ranks behind him. "Centaur cows with guns. Where did they get them?"

"From Two Creek Fort. The females have learned to use them well. One day we hope to make guns large enough for males; until then, they must content themselves with cannons. We have fifteen of those," he added.

". . . Do you try to frighten me?" Stormsong said contemptuously. "We could take your weapons with ease." But her hesitation had betrayed her unsureness.

"I see your riders, Stormsong. They look to be strong men and women. But even if you could beat three thousand armed centaurs, not enough of you would live to hold Bitter Spring against your enemies. No, I do not want to frighten you. I want to make a pact with you."

"A pact." She pointed to the sky, where a hawk hovered, shrilling. "What friend has he? We are people of the hawk; we make no pacts."

Eyas answered the hawk's cry: "Come, brother!"

So swiftly that Boulder ducked his head, the bird dropped from the sky, beat its wings, and settled lightly on Eyas's outstretched arm. Its cruel beak gently touched his face; he felt its wildness and pride, and honored it.

The riders froze into stillness. Stormsong's face became more of a mask than ever.

"Go to her, brother," Eyas murmured, and the hawk rose from his wrist and glided to Stormsong's shoulder. She closed her eyes and lifted a hand to stroke its feathers. The hawk struck at it, just enough to draw blood from a finger. Then it leaped up, with wingbeats like distant thunder, and was gone.

Stormsong sucked at her torn finger for a moment.

"Eyas; you are well named. Come into our tents."

"With gladness. I would come with some of my companions."

She frowned. "Do you fear treachery?"

"No. But if we make a pact, the centaurs must agree to it, and their leaders must have a part in making it."

"Brutes are to be herded, not flattered."

"When you befriend the hawk, you do not argue with him. And you expect some pain." He held up his wrist, showing her the little wounds the hawk's talons had made. Stormsong met his gaze with a faint smile.

"Bring your brutes."

While the column settled itself, Eyas and Boulder rode alongside Stormsong into the oasis; behind them came Standaway, Cirque, Foehewer, and the leaders of the contingents from the other holds. The oasis was larger than it had appeared. Set between two low, parallel ridges, it was perhaps a thousand spans wide and ten thousand long—an hourmarch or more. Its soil, watered by a chain of springs, supported an open wood of dryland pine. The trees were old and tall, scarred by sandstorm and frost, but they gave a pleasant dappled shade. Broad trails ran through the oasis, linking clusters of conical tents; dirty-faced children in ragged smocks came running from these little camps to see the strangers. Their parents stood watchfully gripping bows or swords as Stormsong and her guests passed by. Eyas saw no old people, and few adults who were not scarred or maimed: many lacked fingers, or an ear, or an eye.

The procession overtook a herder, who used his staff to clear a way through a milling mass of longfurs. These were the first Eyas had seen. Much smaller than sixfeet, the brutes walked on four hoofs; their torsos were erect, but their arms were no larger than a human infant's, almost-invisible vestiges in the thick, long white hair that covered them from shoulder to rump. The longfurs cried out nervously, in voices like children's, and seemed relieved to cluster together again when the humans and centaurs had passed.

"They are beautiful," Eyas said.

"The longfurs are our life," answered Stormsong. "They give us milk, blood, flesh, fur, hides—without them we would die."

The trail led to a small, green-scummed pond ringed by trees and tents. The place stank of excrement, rotting meat, and curing hides. Fires of longfur dung smoldered outside each tent, tended by bony children. Across the pond, sixfeet and longfurs waded into the water to drink; a herder, standing among his brutes, drank with them. Stormsong dismounted in front of a tent, found a cup of hammered gold on the littered ground, and dipped it into the pond.

"I offer you water," she said gravely.

Eyas slid off Boulder's back and took the cup. "I take it with thanks." The water was warm and sulfurous, full of strange tastes, but he drank it down.

"Your brutes may drink their fill if they thirst." Stormsong seated herself cross-legged by the flap of the tent. Five riders, who had followed them into the oasis, tethered their mounts and squatted nearby; they did not look at Eyas or the centaurs.

"Let us parley," Stormsong said.

Eyas spoke briefly of how he had come to Foundries, and of his bargain with Oldwalker. Stormsong listened without comment, but leaned forward with a show of interest when he described the sack of Two Creek Fort and the army's journey into the Yellow Desert.

"Serve them right to take a drubbing." She smiled grimly. "Their raiding parties foray too often into our ranges. We try to pay them back, but our own neighbors press upon us as well."

"It is the same with the centaurs," said Eyas. "We have shown that centaurs can fight well together, not just as a rabble of warriors. But they are too few, and too ill-equipped, to be a serious threat to the Suns. Better armed, and with human riders, they could throw the Suns back across the White Mountains; with the lotors and Riverines as allies, we could break the Dominance forever."

204

"And that is what you want of us? To be comrades to brutes?"

Eyas nodded.

"Then let us see how man and centaur fight together. I will duel you; if you can draw my blood before I draw yours or your brute's, I will consider a pact between us. But if I wound you first, you leave our land."

"A serious duel?"

"What other kind is there?" She sprang to her feet and untethered her sixfoot. "Come, show me your warskill!"

Reluctantly, Eyas and Boulder rose. The other centaurs looked alarmed, though not all understood enough of the humans' language to know what was happening.

"A duel," Eyas muttered in centauric. "If these people are no brighter than their leader, they'll make sorry allies."

"Command her brute," Boulder suggested. "Perhaps it will throw her."

"No—we can take no advantage that a Hawk riding a centaur would not have." He drew his sword as Stormsong trotted her mount along the shore of the pond to a clear space. She turned it with a tug on the reins and charged, sword high.

Though bigger than the sixfoot, Boulder could turn more swiftly. He slipped to one side, drew his own great sword, and slapped the flat of the blade across the sixfoot's face. It grunted with pain and broke stride. Eyas parried a slash from Stormsong; then Boulder gripped her sword arm and plucked her from her saddle. Furious, she dangled in mid-air. Eyas jabbed her delicately just enough to draw a spot of blood from her midriff. Then Boulder dropped her on her back and put one huge hoof on her sword arm before she could get up.

Stormsong looked up at them and laughed. "Too short a brawl! Get your brute's hoof off my arm."

"Let go of your sword first," Eyas grinned. Her eyes met his and glittered with perilous amusement. She obeyed; Boulder released her, but kept his sword poised. Stormsong stood up, slapping dust from her clothes.

"I like the way your brute helps you," she remarked a little breathlessly as Eyas dismounted and they walked back to the tent. The five riders who had followed them were still squatting in the dirt, as impassive as the centaurs near them. "Any two of these fighters, though, would have finished you."

"Any *one* of them, on a centaur, would be a match for five

ordinary riders," said Eyas quietly. Stormsong's eyes widened.

"Centaurs can't be tamed. You have some skill with them, but how would we break them to bit and saddle?"

"Break them? You'll be their partners, their equals. They'll allow you on their backs because I ask them to. You'll stay on their backs if you deserve to."

Her tattooed face was hard to read. "Then ask that centaur bull to carry me, and I'll try my skill against my own men."

"His name is Foehewer; ask him yourself."

"He understands me?"

"He speaks a bit of the Gulf dialect; he'll understand."

Judging from his baleful expression, Foehewer already understood. But he allowed her to mount. When she kicked his flanks, he jabbed her sharply in the belly with his elbow, and glared at her over his shoulder. "Ask," he growled.

One of the watching men croaked with laughter. Stormsong pointed at him, then at his sixfoot, and he hastily mounted.

"Foehewer, will you help me duel that man?"

"Yes."

"I thank you."

He burst into a long-striding gallop, down the shore of the pond, and then turned to charge the rider, who had pursued them. The man's face went gray under his tattoos, and he crouched low over his mount's shaggy back. Foehewer crashed into the brute, his fist cracking its jaw while his sword knocked away the rider's lance. Stormsong hacked at the man's face, but lost her balance and missed. The rider leaped from his moaning sixfoot and groped for his sword.

"Enough!" Eyas roared. "Don't strike. I won't see anyone slain who can fight the Suns."

Her face ablaze with excitement, Stormsong laughed, leaned down, and gave her opponent's face a cheerful slap. "By all the gods, what a ride! Foehewer, will you run with me?"

Eyas nearly burst out laughing at the mingled expressions on the centaur's face: embarrassment, pleasure, shame, and delight. Foehewer nodded and began to run, while his rider clung to his mane, howling with joy. The watching Hawks howled too, and clapped their hands in a quickening rhythm.

"Not a bad start," Boulder grunted, watching as Foehewer loped around the far side of the pond and longfurs scattered wailing out of his path.

It seemed, in the next few days, to be hardly a start at all.

Stormsong was the Warmaker of the Hawks, a rank roughly equal to that of a village Speaker; but she was responsible to the Aunts and Uncles, a council elected by all the band. This council met only at the Movings of spring and fall, when herds were gathered and driven to new ranges; Stormsong could not make a pact without the council's consent, and so must send messengers to summon Uncles and Aunts from all over the Hawks' territory—including some gone on raids against the neighbors to the north and east, or against the Suns to the south. The centaurs, meanwhile, were encamped outside the oasis in dust and heat, with little water.

Eyas stayed with his army, but spent much of each day with Stormsong and her attendants in the oasis. A kind of craze spread through Bitter Spring as more warriors discovered the pleasures of centaur riding. The Hawks slowly realized that a centaur was not merely a talking sixfoot, and could not be abused; but it took two tramplings, a broken back, and many minor injuries to make the point clear. When one Hawk dared to whip a centaur, Stormsong strangled the man with his own whip. Eyas did not interfere.

The Hawks yearned to take centaurs on reprisal raids against their enemies, the Scorpions and Prowls, but Stormsong forbade it. After seven days, the Aunts and Uncles were all gathered, and serious parleying began. It would have gone quickly but for Eyas's insistence that other bands be encouraged to join the pact.

"Give centaurs to the Scorpions! Those dolts can scarcely walk, let alone ride," one Aunt objected.

"Ally ourselves with the Prowls, after all their crimes?" snarled an Uncle.

"Why should we invite the Locusts and Pronghorns to share in the glory?" asked another. "They've done nothing for us."

Eyas kept his patience. "We need as many warriors as possible, and no band has nearly enough for three thousand centaurs. The Suns have been defeating the Bands because the Bands weaken each other, when they could lend each other strength."

At last the council realized Eyas was not making them a gift of the centaurs so that the Hawks could settle old feuds. Some grew sober at the thought of a united assault upon the Suns; others, dizzied at the sudden hope of loot and glory beyond their dreams, were all for an immediate march across the mountains to New Fort, which they thought would be only a few days' journey.

The centaurs, who had traveled farther across Alland than any of the Hawks, knew better. Boulder ended one long debate, when the sound of a brute speaking a human language was still new enough to carry a weight of its own:

"All the Bands, and all the centaurs in our army, are not enough. We must win the lotors as well, and the Riverines. For that, we must go east, away from the Suns, close to Delta."

"Who will guard our springs, our herds?" asked Stormsong.

"The alliance must be made swiftly," Boulder replied. "Then we turn west and south, into Transmontane, and take it this winter when the Dominance cannot send help across the mountains. Thus we protect your ranges, and our own holds, from the wrath of Brightspear."

"And then?" someone asked.

"Then we go east once more, to conquer Delta."

Along the shore of Stormsong's pond, where the council sat, silence fell. One young warrior pointed upward, to the Bridge, and said, "Would it not be easier to march up God's Bow, and drop rocks on the Deltans?"

Boulder snorted. "The White Mountains are the armor of the Dominance. For every Sun in Transmontane, there are countless more in the south. We could lose half our own numbers crossing the passes, especially in winter or early spring, before we ever saw the Grasslands and the Lake Country.

"If we want the friendship of the lotors and the Riverine men, we must help them fight Delta, and it will be an easy fight compared to that we face with the Suns. The Deltans are little more than slaves of their rulers; wipe out those rulers, and the people will be ours. Then we can strike against the Suns' flank while Brightspear still thinks us in the north. Let him send his own armies across the passes into Transmontane. Before he can recall them, we shall be knocking at his gates."

The Aunts and Uncles thought for a time, and accepted the plan—not because they thought it sensible, but because it seemed more ambitiously mad than any alternative.

"Very well," said Stormsong at last. "I will send envoys to the other Bands, and invite them to join the pact. Meanwhile, let us make ready."

The Hawk envoys made their best arguments simply by their arrival at the other Bandish oases, mounted upon centaurs armed with guns. A few duels demonstrated the advantages of riders so equipped, and the Bands were quick to send their own envoys to Bitter Spring. But summer was nearly over, and the nights were cold, before all had joined the pact. Following ancient practice, each Band gave hostages to the others; the hostages would remain with those who stayed to tend the herds. Many days passed in confused preparation, as hundreds of warriors rode into Bitter Spring, bivouacked near the oasis, and cautiously acquainted themselves with Eyas and the centaurs.

"It's worse than a Moving," Stormsong complained. The warriors of the Bands had to be trained to ride centaurs; sizable herds of sixfeet and longfurs were needed to supply the warriors; forerunners must be sent out to establish supply depots in the eastern wastes. When the army did at last leave the oasis, it was more like the slow rising of the tide than like the breaking of a wave.

In three long columns now, flanking the herds, the army moved east. Eyas rode usually at the head of the center column, accompanied by Stormsong on Foehewer and the Warmakers of the other Bands. For some time he had given up his nakedness for tunic and trousers, but he would not wear boots or a hat—they were uncomfortable, and made from sixfoot hide. Nor would he eat the flesh of sixfeet or longfurs, and more than once he had to calm the centaurs' anger about the diet of the Bands. He practiced the Bandish dialects, growing skilled enough in them to understand their jokes and to enjoy their chants and songs.

Much about his allies was hard to understand. They fought to the death over imagined insults. They mutilated themselves to cozen some trivial favor from their countless invisible gods. They sang songs about the beauty of their sixfeet, while slashing cruelly at their mounts with whips and spurs. Their proverbs praised poverty; their boasts were of the loot they had won; what wealth they had, like Stormsong's golden cups, was idly tossed amid dung and ashes.

But they rode with skill and fierce grace, laughed as merrily and sweetly as children, learned quickly, and endured hardship without complaint. One young Hawk, still

beardless, thought himself slighted by a companion's remark;
they dueled, and the youth was mortally wounded. In the
long afternoon he took to die, he joked, sang, and begged
Stormsong not to punish his killer. Eyas thought of dark
forms waiting for the boy, and shuddered between joy at his
courage and despair at his fate. When the boy was dead,
Stormsong herself cropped the friend's ears—not for murder
but for delaying the march.

The dreamhauntings came each night. After one long night
of little sleep, Eyas rode silently through the day; when the
army halted, he walked alone up a bare hillside. Stormsong
followed and sat beside him on a rock. Her tunic and trousers
were dark with sweat in the late-afternoon heat. She squinted
cheerfully down at the men and centaurs setting up camp,
and then east across the brown plain.

"We make good progress. But what ails you?"

He did not want to talk about the dreamhauntings; the
Bands knew of such things and had a superstitious dread of
them. "I think too much of my family," he said. "And of the
Gulf."

"What—think too much of a wrong done you? You are your
family's avenger. You can never forget your dead."

"No fear of that." He tried to turn the conversation to the
problems of the march, and for a while that contented her,
but at length she asked,

"What will you do when this war is done, Eyas, and you've
danced in Brightspear's skin?"

Both the question and the image it evoked made him
pause. "He dances in my skin already, and perhaps I in his.
But—I do not know. Perhaps I'll go home to the Gulf, and try
to rebuild Longstrand."

"Come home with us, if you like. Ah, we'll be rich with
loot and glory! And settling old scores with our new friends."
She nodded toward the campsites of the Scorpions and
Prowls. "Good fighters can always find good fights."

Eyas shook his head slowly. "We will feed Hell enough
dead men before we're through with this."

Stormsong covered her ears at the mention of Hell; then
her tattooed face twisted in a grin.

"No matter—finish your feud, then think what to do next."

Eyas reflected on her words. Yes, it was a feud—a personal
quarrel that had started on a dark beach on Sandcliff Island
long ago. If he and Old and Sky had slain Brightspear then,

how many would still be alive? Silken might still be weaving in her cabin, Darkhair sailing the Gulf with his husband and wives, the Goddess Herself still coming each New Year's Day. The wars and sorrows of Foundries and the Yellow Desert would be of no concern to the People, until perhaps the day came when they could fulfill the Goddess's promise to Aspen—

He turned from such thoughts; no use to look back at calm water when he was already in the Rip. Admiral Thorn, the Messenger, all the dark hungering shapes of Hell wanted Brightspear to prevail over the living; this war would feed the dark shapes, but somehow he felt sure his vengeance would thwart them—at least for a little while, until he himself sank down into darkness.

He felt sorrier for the Goddess than for himself and his companions. She had planned so long to save men from the miseries of life, not knowing the worse horrors of Hell awaited them. —Or had She known? She must have: the People's minds were open to Her, and the hauntings would have been no secret to Her. She must have planned for the People to strike not just at the Suns but at Hell itself. Eyas knew he was not the instrument She had intended to create out of the People, but an improvisation, a gamble. Very well; perhaps he would strike harder and deeper than even She had hoped.

With a soft laugh, Eyas stood, pulled Stormsong to her feet, and embraced her.

"Yes, I'll finish my feud," he said.

Stormsong, taken by surprise, endured his embrace for only a breath before breaking away. Her hand rose to strike, then paused.

"You're ignorant as well as mad," she hissed, "or I'd see your blood. Don't touch me again."

"I have blundered. I am sorry."

"Once we've been in battle, I'll bed you gladly. But not before."

Eyas had felt no desire since Longstrand, and he had put his arms around Stormsong out of very different motives than those she imagined. But he had enjoyed the slim hardness of her body, the sharp smell of her, and now he smiled.

"May that battle come soon."

Her eyes met his with no flicker of shyness. "May it come soon, and may we both survive it, or die together."

5

It was a tributary of the Great River, running southeast through a shallow valley between lines of hills. Rocky River, the lotors called it, but here it was only a wide brown stream, swift but untroubled as it neared its destination.

The lotors had once used a ford on the Rocky River, and villages had stood on either bank. They were ruins now; the Deltan raiders crossed the ford each year on their summer campaigns. The lotors' fields of corn and whiteroot were long gone back into grass; the road north to the Narrow Sea was only a rutted path.

Eyas lay on his belly on the crest of a hill above the ford, watching the Deltans cross the river. The autumn afternoon was warm and still, and the raiders' shouts and laughter carried well. They had good reason to laugh; the lotors had lost hundreds of dead, much of their harvest, and many towns and villages sacked and burned. The Deltans' wagonforts were crammed with grain, salt, paperbark, iron, and the half-cured hides of young lotors.

"You can smell 'em from here," muttered Stormsong, sprawled beside him. Just beyond her, a lotor raised his head and snarled silently as he caught the same stink.

His name was Forager. He was from Wall, greatest of the males' towns, and something like a Speaker or Warmaker. When he stood up, he could look Boulder in the eye, but his long frame was so thin that he weighed little more than Eyas. Like all lotor males, Forager had only the stump of a tail. His long torso was thickly covered in soft gray fur, shading to white on his chest and to black on his arms and legs. His hands were as wide as a man's but almost twice as long from wrist to black-skinned fingertips. His round head was furred in silver, with a broad stripe of black running across the eyes from one triangular ear to the other. The eyes themselves were large and dark, the eyes of a night hunter. The lotor's nose was a pink button on a short, whiskered muzzle above an oddly human mouth and jaw, in which sharp teeth gleamed.

He spoke purringly to Stormsong, who listened carefully and then translated for Eyas. Forager spoke a little of the Riverine dialect, which Stormsong knew; his own language was a blur of growls and snaps which Eyas was only beginning to understand.

"It's the whole lot," Stormsong said. "Three hundred riders, two thousand foot soldiers, fifty wagons, two big cannons."

"Are they all Deltans?"

"All the riders, and most of the soldiers. The teamsters are Riverines, and maybe four hundred of the soldiers."

"Remind him that we must spare the Riverines if we can."

"He knows, but he doesn't like it."

Eyas nodded. The lotors had once lived in peace with the Riverines, but for many years the Deltans' vassals had been helping to raid lotor country. Forager saw little difference between the stocky, fair-haired Deltans and the tall, black-skinned Riverines. Though he understood the purposes of Eyas's allied army, he was not himself an ally yet. He was a seeker of vengeance.

The lotor's reasons seemed to Eyas as good as his own. A month before, as the allies entered lotor country, scouts had come upon a swath of burned fields and villages, littered with lotors' corpses and the garbage of a human army. Eyas and Stormsong had first met Forager outside the rubble of a smashed village, and had nearly been killed by his archers. Only the presence of centaurs had saved them.

Slowly, awkwardly, Eyas had explained himself. Forager had been wary. Lotors respected centaurs, though the two peoples rarely met; but lotors hated and feared humans. The Desert Bands sometimes raided, and Delta had been pushing toward the Narrow Sea for many years. The Suns had never come this far northeast, and meant nothing to Forager. But if the alliance against them planned to strike at Delta, the lotors might join. First, Forager asked to see the allies test themselves against the Deltan raiders. The warriors of Wall and the lesser towns would watch, and then decide whether the alliance was worth entering.

Now, watching the Deltans, Eyas wished the lotors had been more trusting. The allies had been on short rations for a long time. This would be their first pitched battle—not like the night raid against the sleeping Suns at Two Creek Fort. If the allies did not win this fight, their alternatives would be grim: to retreat back into the Yellow Desert, or to seek winter shelter among the lotors, who would not welcome uninvited friends both hungry and beaten.

The slow march east had given Eyas some time to train his forces, but he was unsure of their discipline: they had had less than a season to unlearn old habits and acquire new ones. The warlore of the People, based on small fighting groups using water more than land, was of little use, and Eyas had had to improvise new tactics. Surprise had been his sharpest weapon so far; perhaps these Deltans had surprises too.

Their vanguard was across the ford now. Riders galloped up onto the bank, fanning out to form a protective screen for the wagons that followed, hub-deep in the muddy stream. The main body had been traveling in four columns, with wagons flanking foot soldiers. But in crossing the Deltans lost formation, and were slow in regaining it when they reached the right bank. Teamsters cracked whips over bawling sixfeet, trying to force a way through the milling soldiers.

Good; Forager had already described the impossibility of taking a Deltan wagonfort when it was fully formed up. The confusion on the bank would help.

"It's time," he said. The three of them crawled back to where Boulder, Foehewer, and several other centaurs waited with their riders. Farther down the western slope of the hill, men and centaurs hurriedly got up and formed two lines. Riders strung their bows or gripped lances. Centaurs drew swords or cocked their hammers of their guns. Eyas wondered whether he should have brought up the cannons after all; they and their crews were out of sight beyond the next ridge, helping to guard the noncombatants, the baggage train, and the much-reduced herds. But the allies had too little gunpowder to justify using the cannons in battle, and the crews were still far from expert.

Boulder let Eyas settle himself in the saddle. Like the other centaurs, he disliked being saddled, but the Bands had argued well that it was too easy to be dismounted from a centaur's bare back.

"If this goes wrong," Eyas muttered in his friend's ear, "remember it was all your idea." The centaur coughed amusedly and swung his sword in a humming arc.

"And if it goes well?" he asked. Eyas laughed.

Forager was standing beside Stormsong, while ten other lotors, his attendants, gathered around him. They carried

214

enormous bows, a span long, and quivers packed with arrows. Forager spoke to Stormsong, who turned to Eyas.

"He says his warriors should be following close behind the Deltans' rear guard. If we win, they'll join the attack. If we lose, they'll leave us to our own courage." She looked disgusted, but Eyas only nodded.

"They show good sense. Tell Forager that he and his archers are welcome to join us in the fight if they wish."

Forager understood and smiled evilly.

"He says he'll follow us, so the skins of the flayed children can be buried over the Deltans' corpses."

"Good."

Eyas drew his sword and pointed it south, toward a squadron of a hundred Scorpions mounted on sixfeet. They were flamboyantly garbed, gleaming with gold bracelets and necklaces of silver: bait for the Deltan riders. Ravine, the Scorpions' Warmaker, raised his lance in reply, and guided his warriors around the southern shoulder of the hill. They disappeared into a ravine. Lookouts, posted along their path, signaled their progress. But there was no need for the final message, that the Deltans had seen the squadron; Eyas could hear the Scorpions' war cries, and the distant rumble of hoofbeats.

Boulder took him up to the crest, and they looked down to see the Deltans milling about like startled ants. One of their cannons was in midstream, the other still on the far bank. Riders and foot soldiers were splashing across the ford. Meanwhile, teamsters drew their wagons into a semicircle, open only to the river. As they unhitched their brutes, foot soldiers crowded into the gaps between the wagons and formed close ranks. Pikes bristled out, a full two spans beyond the soldiers' leather shields. Gunners and archers clambered into the wagons. Each wagon had high sides and a pitched roof; soldiers could stand on the floor of the wagon and shoot through narrow slits in the wall, or stand upon a ledge and shoot through the gap between the top of the wall and the roof. The roof of each wagon extended well to the front and back, giving protection to the pikemen; hinged boards were let down to prevent attackers from crawling between the wheels. Within the wagonfort, more soldiers formed ranks, shields up to protect themselves, the teamsters, and the sixfeet. The Deltans still on the far bank formed a similar defense, though much smaller.

The Deltan riders stayed outside the wagonfort, forming a wedge-shaped line. Their red and green capes fluttered over mail shirts, and their lances were bright with many-colored ribbons that reminded Eyas of village pennants. A few of the riders seemed to be arguing about who should ride at the point of the wedge; one burly man finally claimed the honor.

The Scorpions had so far been concealed from Eyas; now they came into sight, charging straight for the Deltan riders. With a chanted cry, the Deltans lowered lances and trotted forward.

"Turn, turn," Eyas whispered. Some of the Deltans, eager for their enemies' gold, were already breaking formation; if the Scorpions too were caught up in the excitement, they would ruin the main attack and lose their own lives as well.

The Warmaker kept his head. He turned sharply to the left, while his warriors wheeled raggedly behind him. Even at this distance, their gold and silver glittered.

Now the Scorpions seemed to be in full flight, a raiding party that had underestimated its enemies' strength and lost its nerve. They scattered from the riverbank to the foot of the hills. Emboldened, the Deltans spurred hard after them, too fast to use bow or gun. In a few breaths they were far down the valley, half-ridden in dust. The Deltans in the wagonfort relaxed a little: shields came down, and a few pikemen broke formation to walk out and watch the riders' progress down the valley.

Eyas raised his sword again, brought it down, and led his main force over the crest.

The slope gave them speed and momentum. Stormsong screamed a war cry, and others answered. The Deltan riders were too distant to notice the second attack, but those within the wagonfort hastily organized themselves again.

A ragged volley of gunshots went off from the wagons, at too great a range. The gunners stepped down to reload; archers took their places. Scores of arrows whirred up and dropped among the attackers' first line. Men and centaurs fell dead. The first line fanned out along the whole length of the wagonfort. Riders shot arrows among the pikemen; centaur females fired at short range, then dropped their guns and swung clubs at the ironheaded pikes. Dust and smoke rose thickly around the wagonfort.

Boulder and Eyas held back, waiting for the second line. It was smaller and more compact, and aimed like a battering ram at two adjacent wagons near the north, upstream end of the semicircle. The pikemen between the wagons held their places, but their faces were pale with shock: few of them had ever seen centaurs before, let alone men riding them, and the implications were beginning to sink in.

The second line struck at the two wagons and the pikemen between them. The centaurs plucked away the pikes and turned them on the soldiers. Two or three Deltans were pulled out of the ranks, and flung over their comrades' heads into the crowded mass of men and brutes behind the wagons. Forager's archers had followed the second line; now, from a distant ridge, they dropped arrows with deadly accuracy and force among the Deltans inside the semicircle. But Eyas could see that archery alone could do little against a properly formed wagonfort: the walls and roofs of the wagons were too thick even for the lotors' heavy arrows.

Against the concentrated forces of the second line, the Deltan gunners and archers in the two wagons could do little. Standaway Smith had lost her rider, but as she came up to one of the wagons she stabbed upward with her lance, transfixing a gunner and yanking him from his ledge. Eyas thrust his sword through a firing slit; the blade came out red.

Several centaurs gripped the wooden skirts of the wagons and pulled them loose. Then they heaved at the wagons themselves, rocking them back and forth. One fell inward, then the other, while the men within them screamed. The centaurs and their riders sprang over the toppled wagons and slashed into the Deltan ranks.

Seeing their wall breached, the Deltans retreated, but were blocked by their own comrades. Frightened sixfeet reared and kicked, trying to escape, and prevented the soldiers from reorganizing their defense. The Riverines, dressed only in kilts and conical straw hats, could have been easily slain; but the attackers obeyed Eyas's order to spare as many as possible. The Deltans were chopped down without mercy.

Eyas and Boulder did not join the charge into the semicircle; instead, they turned and ran around the wagonfort to its southern end. Riders and centaurs had suffered heavy losses here, and their bodies were thick on the ground. Over the clash and clatter of the fight, Eyas roared, "Pull back! Pull back!"

Slowly, reluctantly, his warriors withdrew. Off to his right, Eyas saw the Deltan riders charging back. The centaurs and their riders trotted uphill a few hundred spans, out of bowshot of the wagonfort, while within it the sounds of battle went on. Before long, the Deltan pikemen and archers at the south end of the wagonfort were physically forced from between their wagons by their retreating comrades. Still disciplined, they moved as single bristling units, pikes held high as they marched along the riverbank to seek shelter behind the oncoming riders.

But they were followed and surrounded by a flood of teamsters, sixfeet, and terrified soldiers who ran blindly, colliding with the pikemen and the first of the returning riders. Overwhelmed, the pikemen's units began to break up. The riders, screaming unheard in the din, hacked at the desperate soldiers to try to clear a path.

Apart from a few stubborn groups, resistance had vanished within the wagonfort. The attackers burst straight through in pursuit of the fleeing Deltans; riders and centaurs outside the wagons turned to harry the flank of their routed enemies. A few Deltan riders cut their way out of the mob, and counterattacked. Forager's archers broke their formation with two quick volleys; centaurs and riders finished them off.

As the sun sank toward the hills, the battle became butchery. Some riders tried to surrender, perhaps assuming the victors would want ransom, but even those were slain. For two thousand spans downriver from the ford, corpses lay scattered in the trampled yellow grass. The Deltans on the far bank abandoned their wagons to come to the aid of their comrades, but few even reached the battlefield: Forager's main force, which had been watching from concealment, swept down on the smaller wagonfort, overran it, and killed the Deltans in midstream.

Calm spread across the valley under the reddening sky.

Eyas and Boulder traversed the field many times as they sought out the Warmakers and centaur leaders, and made sure that the allies did not undo their own victory. Bandish warriors looked to their wounded, rounded up the surviving sixfeet, and looted the Deltan dead. Centaurs took trophy weapons—even females, which amused Boulder and other males. Standaway, who had found a sword to her liking, showed it to Eyas with weary pride.

"I've lost my rider," she said. "But I've won my own sword."

Eyas reached out and touched her face, and felt her tears.

He left Boulder with other centaurs who were tearing some of the wagons apart for a great pyre. Smaller fires were beginning to glow in the dusk. The Bands were roasting sixfoot flesh as warriors admired one another's plunder and matched boasts. Songs and laughter filled the air, though many men sat silent and grim in the battle's aftermath. Eyas made slow progress: men and centaurs clustered around him, smiling, singing, clashing weapons together.

On the same ridge where he had stood with his archers, Forager greeted Eyas. The lotors' main force, almost a thousand strong, had cautiously encamped on the far bank, but scores of them had crossed to join their leader and tour the battlefield. Many of these latecomers were with Forager; when they learned who Eyas was, they saluted him by striking their bowstrings, filling the air with a strange, deep humming.

A young lotor, blind in one eye, stood beside Forager. He wore a caped hood of rough gray cloth, which marked him as a special individual called a priest—one who dealt with the lotors' gods. Eyas regarded him warily, knowing priests only from remembrance of the Suns' first conquest of the Gulf.

"I talk Bandish talk," the priest said. "You hear me?"

"Yes," said Eyas.

"My name: Blue." He pointed to the cataract clouding one eye. "My judge Forager joyous of you. He talk he go with you. Many lotor go with you. You hear?"

"I hear."

Forager spoke rapidly, with quick gestures of his long-fingered hands. Blue rubbed his own hands together, and then said, "He make honor gift of lotor food in skinface wagon. All lotor food."

A tactful gift, thought Eyas. To try to reclaim it might turn the victorious allies against the lotors. "Forager honors me. In return, I will feed Forager and all lotors who come with me. And all lotors will get much plunder."

When this was translated, Forager smacked his lips in assent, and spoke again. Eyas understood the gist of it, but waited politely for Blue.

"Forager talk he want blackskinface dead. All dead."

"No. But come with me, and we will talk to them."

Eyas and the two lotors walked down to the riverbank,

219

where the two hundred Riverine survivors sat close together, guarded by centaurs. Many were wounded, but none cried out.

"Who leads you?" Eyas called out.

"I do." A man, middle-aged and tall even for a Riverine, stood up.

"Do you understand me?"

"Well enough. I speak a little Bandish. My name is Peter Three."

"And mine is Eyas Fisher. Come, Peter Three, and speak with us."

The Riverine stepped slowly through the crowded prisoners until he stood looking down at Eyas.

"You and your men fought bravely."

Peter Three shrugged.

"This is Forager, who leads the lotors of Wall. His people are my allies now."

"I wish you joy of them."

Eyas clicked his tongue in annoyance. "Do not mock with me. He asks that you all be slain." When Peter Three said nothing, Eyas went on, "I refused him. You will not be slain."

The tall man's face did not change. "You are merciful."

"No, I am sensible. I want your people as my allies also."

"To what purpose?"

"The peace and freedom of all the peoples north of the mountains, human and brute alike. And the destruction of Delta and Sun."

Peter Three and Forager exchanged suspicious looks, while Blue muttered in Forager's ear.

"The Bands and centaurs fight very well together. What is your need of us?"

"We intend to conquer Delta, and then to march against the Suns. To reach Delta, we must sail down the Great River. Only your people have the boats, and the skill to take them through the Black Gates into Delta."

The Riverine smiled. "How old are you, Eyas Fisher?"

"Almost twenty."

Peter Three laughed, but his dark eyes gleamed with tears. "My oldest son was twenty. He lies out there, among the wagons; I saw him die. Now you tell me you will conquer our masters. How many more of my sons will die to put a new master over us?"

Eyas reached up and put his hands on the tall man's

shoulders. "I grieve for you, Peter Three. I am young, but I too have lost a son, and daughter, and all my family. We all go into the dark. But some of us die slaves, and some die free. You can choose for yourself, and for your other sons."

The prisoners nearby were listening intently, though few could understand.

"Choose? If we do not join you, you will kill us."

"No. If you refuse me, I will let you go home, and we will leave your towns in peace. I will have no slaves in my army. If you joined me only to save your lives, you would desert me when the chance arose." He smiled wryly at the Riverine. "Would you have fought us so fiercely if you had known we meant to spare you?"

One of the prisoners, understanding Eyas, laughed bitterly. But Peter Three did not. "We would have turned our pikes on the Deltans, perhaps." He thought for a while, and then chuckled. "You are a clever young fellow. If we go home, the Deltan soldiers in our towns will think we betrayed their brothers here, and they will put us to death. They would never believe you let us go without a price."

Eyas laughed. "Shall I go with you, to vouch for your honesty? No, do not think that I would lure you so to my side. Stay or go, as you like. Once you leave here, your joys and sorrows will not concern me."

"And if we join you?"

Eyas relaxed, looked up at Skyland rising in the east, and knew he had won the battle after all.

The Bands celebrated in a fog of cookfire smoke, boasts, songs, and Deltan wine. Eyas went to their fires to speak with Stormsong and the other Warmakers. The Hawks, drunk and jubilant, drew him into the circle where they sat singing and chanting around a large fire.

"Stormsong is readying herself to dance," one warrior bellowed in Eyas's ear. "Ah, she's a dancer, that one! None like her since her mother."

The warriors began a rhythmic clashing of sword against sword, a fierce and lovely noise. Women shrilled; men hummed and grunted. Attracted by the sound, other Band members, centaurs, and lotors gathered around the circle of swaying Hawks. The brutes' eyes reflected green or yellow in the firelight. The clashing quickened, then stopped abruptly at the edge of utter silence.

Out of the darkness, Stormsong sang. Her voice was low at first, then high and quick as a firewing's trill. Her song was an ancient one, half-prayer, half-lament:

> "God draws His Bow
> And we are His arrows,
> Drawn from the darkness of His quiver,
> Shot to the darkness of the sky.
> May we fly true, may we strike deep,
> May we please God with the song of our going."

A shape stepped into the firelit circle; seeing it, Eyas shuddered, thinking it a shape from Hell. It was pale, but streaked and blotched an ugly reddish-brown. Under matted yellow hair, its face was blurred, shapeless. The hair between its legs was clotted brown; though it had an oddly jutting penis, it was not a man. The shape began to dance like a dueling warrior, brandishing a sword. It sang. It was Stormsong, dancing in a Deltan warrior's skin.

> "He came upon me, strong and warlike!
> Our swords struck, struck again.
> Under his blade, my own searched out his heart.
> Out burst his blood, hot and bright.
> His soul leaped from his mouth,
> His eyes saw death.
> Brave was his coming, brave his going.
> He gave me the gift of his glory;
> I give him the gift of my dance."

Slowly she danced around the fire, while her warriors again clashed their weapons. She mimicked the Deltan's attack, his wounding, his death. As she fell, men stepped into the circle and poured water on the fire. Illuminated only by the pale glow of the Bridge, smoke uncoiled into the darkness and faded away.

The Hawks banged their swords together one last time and crowded cheering around Stormsong. Torches rekindled the fire; warriors lifted Stormsong to their shoulders. The centaurs looked at one another; Eyas saw amazement and horror in their seemingly impassive faces. The lotors seemed merely amused. Perhaps, thought Eyas, they saw justice in the flaying of one who had taken the hides of lotor children to adorn the Great Names who ruled Delta.

The excitement of the battle was gone now, and Eyas felt weariness fall upon him. Whatever he had wanted to say to Stormsong could wait till morning. He turned and made his way down to the river. For a time he walked along its sandy bank, listening to its swift whisper. It was dark under the sky, and tasted of marshes and meadows.

Quick footsteps made him turn. Stormsong was running after him. The Deltan's face and scalp were pushed back from her head like a hood; she smiled through blood-smeared tattooes.

"You saw me dance. Were you pleased?"

"No, not pleased. But I was in awe of you."

"I once said I'd dance in your skin. That would be even better, with your long black hair to wave about." She laughed, a teasing little girl stinking of blood and sweat.

Eyas gripped the skin below her throat and pulled, breaking the threads that held it together. It gave easily, and he peeled it down off her shoulders, her breasts, her hips and legs. Her body was wet, dark, and slippery with human grease; she did not resist him. Picking her up, he waded into the river up to his waist.

"I can't swim."

"Do you think I mean to drown you?" He lowered her into the water and began to wash her. Stormsong stood still, shivering a little, but patient as a child. Even when he scooped up handfuls of fine sand to rub on her skin, she made no protest. Across her breasts and down her belly, she was tattooed in a tangle of green leaves, red flowers, and yellow branches.

Solemnly she embraced him; solemnly he led her back to the riverbank and onto the dry, trampled grass still warm from the day.

6

Next morning, the Deltans were buried under a long mound of earth and rock. The Riverines beheaded their own dead and buried the bodies; the skulls would be taken south to adorn the ancestor-shrines of their towns.

The Locusts mourned their dead Warmaker by cutting off joints of their fingers, hacking off ears, and slaughtering many of their longfurs. Stormsong told Eyas the self-mutilations would lend strength to the dead chief, and the longfurs would keep him rich; proudly, she showed him her own feet, each lacking two toes, and the scars hidden beneath her tattooes, by which she had helped strengthen her own father. But she did not want to say much about her people's beliefs about death, and he did not press her.

The other Bands feasted, and experimented with captured pikes and guns. At noon, Eyas called a meeting of the allies' leaders.

"We have no time to lose," he began, "and we can't afford to feed an idle army. As soon as Forager brings more lotors to join us, we must start for Transmontane. The Suns will feed us, or no one will."

The Warmakers nodded with surprising docility, and Eyas realized that his new status as Stormsong's lover gave him greater authority than ever.

"We've taken great plunder," he went on, exploiting his advantage, "but we won't travel far with it. It must be taken back to the oases. Those who carry it will ride on to join us in Transmontane."

"Are we to conquer all the Sunnish strongholds?" asked Ravine, the Scorpion Warmaker.

"No. We raid and sack, and return to the Great River. At the end of winter we join Peter Three. By then he will have overthrown the Deltan garrisons in his towns." The Riverine smiled grimly. "When the ice is off the River, we sail through the Black Gates to conquer Delta itself."

"In spring we must move our herds," said Stormsong. "It's no easy task. Almost all of us will be needed."

"How long will it take?"

"From the first new moon of spring to the second."

Eyas shrugged. "It will have to be done with those who tend the herds for you. We cannot spare you; even if we could, you would have to find your own way into Delta over the White Mountains, and perhaps fight to reach us."

"Can you not wait until later in the spring?" asked Ravine.

"Delta must have no time to prepare for us."

Boulder said, "We do not like the thought of riding in boats."

"You rode in one," said Eyas.

"I did not like it, though the sea was calm that day. We know the River is dangerous in the Gates, and we cannot swim."

"Peter Three," said Eyas, "will your boats carry centaurs safely?"

"Yes. But I must warn you that the River is most dangerous just after breakup, and again in the summer flood. I cannot promise that all our boats would get through even during the late-spring slack."

Boulder and Foehewer looked impassively at each other, but Eyas saw the anxiety in their eyes.

"Let us worry about it when the time comes," he said. "We have enough to do for now."

The meeting turned to plans for moving the army southwest and to the building of a camp on the Great River for the allies to return to. But Eyas brooded over the centaurs' fears and the Bands' reluctance to leave their herds. Stormsong, sensing his worry, drew him back into the talk. He realized what she was doing, and touched her hand in thanks.

The next day the Riverines marched south, carrying their wounded on litters made from pikes and sixfoot hides.

"Send word if you need help," Eyas said to Peter Three as the column set off.

"I will. But we should do well on our own. You have done more than half our work for us already." He glanced at the long mound beside the river. "When we get into our marshes, we'll rouse all the towns at once." He looked down into Eyas's face. "If you do not come in the spring, the Deltans will come north and destroy us."

"We will come." He took the Riverine's hand. "I wish you a swift journey, and a good fight."

Peter Three's great black hand pressed his own. Then he turned and strode away. His son's head bounced in a sack slung under his arm.

The battlefield became a sprawling, noisy, temporary camp. Its numbers grew each day as more lotors came south from the Narrow Sea. Forager, who had left after the leaders' meeting, returned from Wall with five thousand archers. He and his lieutenants met Eyas, Boulder, and the Warmakers to bargain over the terms of alliance. Eyas had already gained some skill in the lotors' language, but the half-blind priest called Blue still acted as translator.

Long into a frosty night the leaders talked. Blue had learned Bandish as a captive of the Scorpions, and the other lotors shared the priest's distrust of humans. Arguments sputtered up like sparks from the smoky fire where the leaders sat, crouched under a makeshift roof between two wagons. At last Stormsong muttered to Eyas,

"Why should we put up with these quarrelsome brutes? Let's wish them well, and send them home."

"Peace. The Bands didn't join without bargaining, and the lotors are no more fools than you are."

"Small praise for either," she grunted. Eyas laughed.

At last the pact was made, and Eyas and Stormsong went back to their tent. The ground beneath their feet was crisp with frost. Like two white swords, the Bridge of Heaven rose to the edges of the world's growing winter shadow. Redspark was low in the west; Evenspark had set long since, but Skyland gleamed green at the zenith. Stormsong went into the tent while Eyas paused outside, watching the Bridge flow and ripple with light.

"They're good archers; I give them that," Stormsong said from within the tent. "But they couldn't turn back the Deltans on their own. I wouldn't count on them."

"They'll do very well," Eyas answered, still looking at the sky.

"—Are you coming in? Or shall I call some young warrior to share my blanket?"

"A lotor perhaps. Their fur is warm."

"Shame upon your mouth!"

He came inside, chuckling at the oddness of a woman who disliked ribaldry. Stormsong glared at him as she burrowed under a heavy gray blanket of longfur wool. Her eyes reflected the little fire in the center of the tent. Eyas undressed, glad to be naked despite the cold, and slid in beside her.

"Why do your people dislike the lotors?"

"They're brutes. Some say they were men who dreamed of becoming gods, and the gods punished them. But I think they're just animals that want to be men."

"They live in good country. Why haven't the Bands driven them out of it?"

"Too many of them, too few of us." Her answer was too quick; Eyas snorted. "... And they don't fight like us. They see well in the dark; they sneak out at night and attack when you don't expect them. Once, in my grandfather's time, some Scorpions went raiding toward Wall. Not one got home again. Even the Deltans didn't dare come this far north against the lotors until they got wagons and guns."

"The lotors sound like friends worth having, and dangerous enemies."

"For a time," she said grudgingly. "As long as you control them, they'll be all right. I don't know how you do it—keep us all from each others' throats. Your Seagoddess must have given you great powers."

"Once you accept the idea of fighting with the brutes, not against them, the rest is just politics." He was silent for a time. "The more we gain, the harder seems the way ahead. In the Gulf I thought the world was a simple place, but it grows stranger every day. I look at it and wonder who made it, and why."

"The gods made it."

"Which gods? Why did they make the Bridge, or humans and brutes? Why did they make the world so beautiful, and cruel? If they gave us life, why does death rule us?"

"Questions without answers. We're here. We live as best we can."

"You sound like Boulder."

She clicked her tongue in annoyance, slid onto him, and ended words.

Spring had been cold, summer brief; now autumn whirled away in early snow.

All across Transmontane, the harvest was in. It was a poor crop, but enough. The Limb of the Sun would receive his just portion, and the priests, and the army; the Men and Women who owned the land would fill their own granaries. Their stewards, the brutemasters, would complain about the bad weather and the laziness of workers, but they too would eat heartily. The males and females, for their part, quietly stole enough breadseed during threshing to see them through till spring.

In the garrison towns along the Northmarch of Transmontane, soldiers gambled and got drunk. They were lifetimers, committed to arms at fifteen; after twenty-five years, those still alive would take some land, a small herd, perhaps a brutemaster's job with some Man, and would drill the local males for the landguards.

Their officers, riders, were far different: sons of great families, or nearly great, winning rank for themselves. Many would leave the army after five or ten years to serve the Sun in the ministries of New Fort. Those who served well would take herds from the hands of the Sun or one of the Three Families—though the "herds" might be in the form of mines, smithies, mills, or shipyards. For that reward, even a few winters of garrison duty in the savage north were a small sacrifice.

Traders packed their goods and set off south, knowing that the soldiers in the frontier garrisons would turn to robbery for amusement before long. In the temples the priests gave thanks to the Sun Brightspear for a bountiful harvest gathered in peace. The inns fell quiet; few traveled the long roads south to the White Mountains. The sixfoot herds grazed in winter pastures, close to the farmsteads.

The raids began. Farms blazed up in the cold nights. Those who hurried to help did not return; those who came after daybreak found only ashes and corpses. The granaries were empty, the weapons gone, the herds vanished. Tracks, in mud or snow, were of centaurs and men in the heelless boots of the Desert Bands, and of strange longstriding creatures—lotors, some suspected, though no lotor had ever been seen in Transmontane before.

Alarmed, some of the Men of Northmarch sent their families into the towns; lesser freeholders followed their example, and soon even bonded males and females fled. In the towns, they crowded the temple porches and scavenged through the market squares. The priests grudgingly fed the first scores, but the later hundreds were driven out by soldiers to wander south. Some turned to brigandage, and worsened the winter's turmoil.

The sterner Men kept their families and servants at home, and called out the landguards. They might be simple country militia, but they made a brave show in the courtyards of the Men's mansions; the Men and their sons patrolled the fields on sixfeet, armed with swords and guns.

Still the raids went on, and the garrison soldiers came out into the countryside. They trudged north into the wind, from one burnt-out ruin to another. The riders scouted over the snowy hills, following centaur tracks; some riders vanished, though their mounts returned bawling with cold and hunger.

Troops quartered at Men's mansions soon heard alarming rumors from the veterans who led the landguards: in one camp, someone had silently slit the throats of a third of the militiamen in a single night, but left the rest unharmed. A large farmstead had been gutted, yet only food and weapons had been taken. The mansion's rich furnishings had been left to burn; yet Desert Bands had left their tracks, and the Bandish were famous looters.

The soldiers heard these stories and muttered among themselves. What were Bands doing this far south? And centaurs? Were they really allied somehow, or merely following each other? Were lotors really abroad in the land?

Unused to winter war, the soldiers marched and countermarched. They followed tracks that vanished under new snow; they saw no enemies. Impatiently, their officers split columns into patrols to cover more territory. Some of the patrols were not seen again. Couriers from the garrisons brought new orders almost every day: go here, a farmstead has been raided; go there, the raiders are reported moving north. Slowly the columns dispersed into the empty land beyond the marches. Snow flurries turned to blizzards, and the columns dug in to await better weather.

The first large settlement to fall was Axmaster's Glory, far south of the marches. The raiders attacked at night, in blowing snow; they killed the defenders and the priests, but no one else, and took little but food and weapons. When some of the survivors reached the nearest town, they brought confused tales of centaurs carrying men, or using Sunnish guns, and of tall shaggy monsters who shot arrows in total

229

darkness yet always struck their targets. The local commander, incredulous, put some of the survivors to torture with uncertain results. Then he dutifully sent word to the Limb of the Sun, in Triumph, the capital of Transmontane, and a request for more troops.

Two more towns fell, both far to the west of Axmaster's Glory. The columns north of the marches were urgently recalled despite the bitter weather. Many died of cold on the march back.

Most of the buildings in Long Rampart had burned in the fighting, so Eyas had made a sixfeet stable his temporary quarters. The smells of hay and dung mingled with that of smoke. The stable was cold, and lit only by a few oil lamps. Eyas sat on a bale of hay, between Stormsong and Boulder; Forager and Blue sprawled nearby, munching apples. Eyas handed a captured gun to Standaway Smith.

"We've found over thirty of these. What do you think of it?"

She ran her hands over the gun and found a catch that unhinged the barrel.

"It is beautiful. I see why they killed so many of us."

"They'd have killed more if we hadn't frightened them into running," said Boulder. "These guns have twice the range of ours. If the Suns can build cannons the same way, they can hit us from the other side of the mountains." He shifted restlessly in the hay. "Can we make such guns?"

"Not unless their gunsmiths show us how."

Three lotors came into the stable, slapping wet snow out of their fur. One of them gripped a human by the arms.

"We have caught one of their leaders," a lotor said in his own language to Forager. Eyas understood.

"Bring him in," he said.

The Sunnish officer's face was gray with shock. His right hand, sticky with blood, dangled oddly: a sword blow must have broken the wrist. The lotors forced him to his knees.

"Your name?" asked Eyas.

"Victor of the Marchwardens. Leader of the fourth squadron of the Northern Scouts."

"A Marchwarden?" Eyas repeated. "You bear a famous name. Are you of the Three Families?"

"I am."

"My name is Eyas Fisher. Do you recognize me?"

230

The wounded youth looked up for the first time. "You—"

"We met on a road far west of here, last spring. You and your comrades had just killed some centaurs. We did not yet know that, though, or Boulder here would never have let you go."

Victor stared at Boulder without recognition, and without hope.

"Did you send Brightspear my message?"

"I reported to my superiors. That is all I know."

"I thank you in any case. Tell me, how long have you had these guns?"

"Not long. They are called rifles, from the grooves in the barrel. Soldiers trained to use them were sent here from the Lake Country only a few days ago. They were trained for little else," he added bitterly.

"Rifles are new?"

"Yes. They are—I may not speak of religious matters here."

"Your gods inspired them? Or a Messenger?"

"We are not under swordshadow."

"You make a habit of fleeing into your religion like a rat into its hole. But you have told me all I need to know." Eyas leaned forward. "Does your wrist hurt?"

"Not much."

"Not yet. I will see that it is tended to, before you leave. You will bear another message for me, Victor of the Marchwardens."

Despite himself, hope sprang into the youth's face.

"Tell Brightspear this: he took revenge for Silken. I am only beginning my revenge for the Fishers and the People. Only beginning." He turned to Stormsong. "Have his wounds bound up; give him a place to rest, and food if he wants it. In the morning he goes free."

The others had not understood the conversation in Sunnish. "Free?" glowered Boulder. "His life is forfeit for those of the workers he killed."

"He will live a little longer, to carry a message for me."

"Why send him with your message? We have other prisoners."

"He is of a great family; he will be listened to."

"Is that your only reason?" snarled Stormsong. "If he is great, his death will be one more blow against the Suns."

"Boulder once freed some Sunnish sixfeet, knowing they would serve their masters again. I like this one. He loves his life."

"So do we all," she grunted. "So did all the dead Suns out there."

"Not like this one. He loves his life, but—he gives it. I sensed it when we captured him last summer, and I sense it now. He goes free; I do not want his life, and he will give it as willingly to the Sun."

Stormsong shrugged, got up, and stamped over to the youth. "Get up." She pulled him to his feet and dragged him past the lotors.

Boulder snorted softly as the two went out. "Did he tell you anything about the rifles? You spoke too rapidly for me to follow."

Eyas said nothing for a long time. "The priests of the Sun have made these rifles, or taught their gunsmiths."

"How would priests know? They're no smiths, and less warriors."

"The dead. The dead or their Messengers."

"Strange are the ways of humans." Boulder took the rifle from Standaway; it looked small in his great hands. "The first guns were used against us in my father's time. How would your dead know how to make even better ones?"

"I do not know."

Blue had been quietly translating as much as he could understand; the others had been speaking Bandish dialect, but the last exchange between Eyas and Boulder had been in centauric. When Eyas told him what they had said, Blue pulled his lips back from his sharp teeth. He spoke excitedly in lotor.

"Your dead speak to you? Teach you?"

"Yes."

"Marvel of all marvels! Fortunate then are humans above all other speaking creatures. Among us, a priest' may be granted one glimpse only of the other realm. I myself have yet to see our ancestors, but—"

"Lotors in Hell?"

"If that is the human name for it; we call it the other realm. My preceptor saw it three times: a land of tall trees, rich scents, much water—and all our ancestors, rejoicing in it. But your ancestors actually speak with your priests. A marvel."

"Your other realm is a marvel to me," said Eyas. "It sounds like our Old Stories about the good land on the Bridge of Heaven—or the Sunnish tales about Skyland. But they are only lies. For us, there is no heaven, no good land."

Blue's good eye fixed on him. "You speak with assurance."

"In Longstrand I nearly died. I saw Hell then—dark shapes, crowded in darkness and misery. Some of them can speak to the living, and even return to life themselves. They try to guide men's thoughts and actions. They favor Brightspear, or he would never have regained his father's throne."

"Favor him?"

"If the dead do not speak directly to him, they speak through creatures called Messengers. I think they are living people who have been—invaded by the dead."

Forager added another apple core to the litter around him, then stretched lazily. "Why should dead humans trouble themselves over living ones? Our ancestors leave us in peace."

"So do the centaurs' dead," Eyas said. "But ours seem hungry. When I saw Hell, the dead hurried to me, and I knew they meant to devour me. Perhaps they simply prey upon us, like prowls upon splithoof."

"Prowls favor the old and weak, not the young and strong," Forager objected. The luxuriance of lotors' language was mixed with an unpredictable literalness.

Eyas shrugged. "Whatever their motives, they favor Brightspear and they oppose me."

"You must die, and then they will win," Forager replied. "Why should they trouble over you?"

"Because I can do them some great mischief by warring against Brightspear. The Goddess made me for that mischief, and the dead themselves encourage me in it." He sprang up and took the rifle. "I do not know how the dead came to know gunsmithing—but I know why they teach it to the Suns. The dead fear us, Forager. They know our strength better than we do. If we strike soon and hard, a few rifles will make no difference."

Forager groomed himself, a sign of amusement or anxiety. "We are a long way from the Rocky River," he purred. "You have led us into a strange country, to fight against humans we do not know, and beside humans who were long our enemies. Now we find ourselves at war with your ancestors, which seems blasphemous." He glanced at Blue; the priest gestured vaguely.

"Theology has not addressed this issue," Blue said sardonically. "But it is no sin to war on humans in this realm."

"Spoken like a priest," hissed Forager, and turned again to

Eyas. "You see your ancestors' might raised against you, yet you rejoice. Even for a human, you are strange."

Eyas laughed, his breath white in the chilly air. "My ancestors see our might raised against *them*. Look at yourself, Forager—you are enough to frighten Hell."

The lotors' staccato barks of amusement mixed with Eyas's laughter; the centaurs, not understanding, blinked solemnly.

The raiders retreated north, struck farther west, and retreated again. Sunnish riders followed, their mounts struggling through drifts, and then turned back to their garrisons to await new attacks.

But Eyas led the allies east, across the empty plains between the Yellow Desert and Transmontane. The Bandish warriors rode on centaurs or on captured sixfeet, while lotor archers strode lightly across the wind-hardened snow. On sledges, the centaurs pulled weapons, food, bolts of cloth, and boxes of Sunnish books. Despite the cold, the army traveled swiftly through the short days and long, moonlit nights.

One night, as they lay encamped, Eyas sat up reading a Sunnish book about old wars with Delta, while Stormsong slept beside him. Suddenly she gasped and struck out. Eyas put his arms around her, and was startled by the coldness of her skin.

"My father! Where is he?"

"Gently—quietly. You were dreaming."

"He's out there—in the snow—it's no dream." She struggled against him. "He was here, in the tent. Let me go!"

"No!"

She sagged in his arms. "No. No, he's dead. Ah, but I heard him—I almost saw him."

"What did he say to you?"

She was silent, trembling. "He told me to go home. The herds are sick; the herders are too few to care for them all. Eyas—I've been given a vision. I must obey."

"Do you mean to take your people all the way north to Winterfields?"

"All of us, all the Bands. We must, or our brutes will die. Can't you understand that?"

"I understand. You believe this was a true vision?"

"Of course."

"I think it was a dreamhaunting."

234

"What does it matter what you call it? It was—"

"A lie, Stormsong. A trick, to draw the Bands away from the allies. The dead will do to you what they did to my mother Quiet—lure you, deceive you, and leave you helpless before your enemies. Go north, and you will find your herds well; but your father will come again, to haunt you, to keep you in your old ways until the Suns come and crush you—as they crushed the People."

She lay rigidly in his embrace, disbelieving. "It was my *father*, Eyas. I must go."

"Do this: Send couriers to Winterfields. If they come back with news of sickness in the herds, I will gladly bid you farewell, and we'll wait till summer, if we must, to take Delta."

Her indecision frightened him more than her willingness to desert the allies. "I have seen Hell, Stormsong. You trusted me when I called down the hawk. Trust me now."

"Perhaps—for a while we could go on—if the couriers are swift, they could be there and back in—how many days, twenty?"

"Good. We'll send them in the morning."

But in the following days after the couriers left, she spoke little to anyone, and her dreams woke her each night. Stormsong was not the only one to be dreamhaunted; all the Warmakers cried out in the darkness, and many other warriors as well. When they came to Eyas he reminded them of the couriers, and urged them to press on.

Now he drove the army hard. They marched from long before dawn until late at night, under the dim light of the moon and the Bridge. He himself slept little, and though he expected to be haunted he only dreamed—until Stormsong's cries woke him.

"This troubles us," Boulder said on one gray morning as the army plodded into a harsh wind. "The Bands are losing their resolve."

"And the centaurs?" asked Eyas.

"We fear no fighting. But we've come to like these humans, and we trust them in battle. If they lose heart, so do we. Besides," he added, "the journey down the River worries many of us."

"I know. But it must be made."

"Perhaps we should wait another year, strengthen our hold

on the north, before we attack Delta. If Brightspear sends his armies into Transmontane, we could return there, defeat them, and go south across the passes after all."

"No." Eyas's voice was as harsh as the wind. "The lotors and Riverines would face the Deltans' vengeance; the Suns would gain time to make more rifles, and learn to use them. We must go through the Black Gates, this spring, or give up the war."

"As you wish," Boulder muttered.

The winter seemed bottomless. Even as the days lengthened, the cold gripped harder. One storm followed another out of the north, slowing the army to a crawl. Some human warriors began to straggle, and a few deserted altogether. The Bands spoke of little but their herds and the return of the couriers.

"It's twenty-three days since the couriers left," said Stormsong as they broke camp in darkness. "If they don't return today, we go back tomorrow."

"Call the Warmakers together at the noon rest," Eyas answered.

By then the army was very near the Great River, halfway between the southernmost lotor settlements and the northernmost Riverine towns. The land here was hilly, lightly wooded with dwarf pine and a species of paperbark whose black, leafless branches stood stark against the gray sky. In a long valley the allied leaders gathered at noon around a fire.

"If Stormsong would go back to the herds, we will go with her," said Bitterwood, the Locusts' Warmaker. "I too have had visions, Eyas. They warn us. We have had great fighting this year, and will again next spring—fighting that will make us live in legends. But if we are warned, and heed not, what will become of us? A warrior without herds—" He spat into the snow.

"Eyas have no herds when he come to you," Blue objected in broken Bandish. The Warmakers glowered at him.

"Eyas had the greatest herd of all," Bitterwood retorted. "We respected him for it. And we'll gladly go to his wars again, once our own herds are safe."

Eyas stared at the smoky fire. In this desolate patch of snow he might win or lose battles still unfought. Yes, they respected him, enough to obey him if he commanded them to stay. But they would then be bound to him by a bond of mastery, not of trust. At every setback they would think again of their herds; when battle came, he would mistrust them and they, knowing it, would lose their trust in him. Yet could he dare to go against the might of Delta without them?

"Go to Winterfields if you will," he said at last. "I will not keep you against your wishes. If the Riverines give us enough fighters, we can take land in Delta and await your return by summer at the latest."

The Warmakers seemed only a little relieved. "You do not care if we go?" asked Stormsong.

"I care. But I will not force you to stay. I believe your visions are meant to lure you away, but I know how strong those visions are. Go, and quickly! Then come south more quickly still, and seek us among the Thousand Canals."

He saw shame in their tattooed faces; he was saying that Delta might be conquered without them.

"Not all of us need go," Bitterwood said quickly. "Let each Band leave a hundred warriors. We would not have it said that we betrayed you on the eve of battle."

"I accept," said Eyas before the other Warmakers could argue. "Those who stay will have plenty of fighting, but we will save a few Deltans for the rest of you."

The army went no farther that day. The Bands voted in the afternoon to choose who should stay; those who would leave the next day said farewell to their centaurs and readied their sixfeet. That night the camp was silent.

Foehewer came to the tent of Stormsong and Eyas, and knelt beside them in front of their fire.

"I will miss you," the centaur said to Stormsong. "We fought well together."

"And we will again." She took his hand, then leaned against his side, stroking the dark hair on his broad back. "I would not go if the visions did not command me."

"Strange are the ways of humans," Foehewer muttered, his dark face full of foreboding and sorrow. He rose and plodded away across the snow.

Eyas and Stormsong spent the night in love, sleepless yet untiring. As the camp began to stir before dawn, she said, "Make me stay. Tell me to stay, and I will."

"I am your lover, Stormsong, your friend, your ally, but I am not your master. Go; and when you return we will rejoice together. All will be as it has been."

Stormsong shook her head violently against his shoulder. "No, it will be different. But I will come back to you, wherever you may be, however hard the road."

* * *

Three days later, what was left of the army came to the Great River. The west bank here was a belt of open woodland that the lotors called Glades; it was to be the allies' base until spring. Lotors from Wall had built a sizable encampment near the shore of the icebound river, and the allies gratefully settled into the cabins and sheds. Smoke rose straight into the gray sky from a thousand fires; the smells of baking bread, hot iron, and fresh lumber hung in the air.

"Never in years has winter been so harsh," said Forager to Eyas as they ate with Boulder and Blue in Eyas's cabin. "Spring is only fifteen days away, but the ice on the River is still thick. Even a sudden warming could not bring breakup until well into spring." His breath fluttered frostily in the cabin's firelit dimness. "It will be another bad year for the crops."

Eyas stirred the kettle of beans that simmered over the fire, and did not reply. Blue crouched sleepily by the hearth, his fur fluffed out. Footsteps approached, cracking across the crusty snow: human footsteps.

"Hello, this house," a voice called out. "I am Peter Three; is Eyas here?"

Eyas bounded up and opened the door. Peter Three loomed in it; behind him stood two other Riverines, younger men. All wore heavy quilted jackets and trousers, thick felt boots, and closefitting caps of longfur wool. They bore no arms.

"I greet you, Peter Three! Welcome. Warm yourselves, and share our supper."

"Gladly." They came in, stamping snow from their boots. Peter Three nodded to the two lotors and Boulder; the younger men stared.

"My sons, Oakhaft and Another." They were boys, gawky and ill at ease, but they had a measure of their father's solemn power. A levelness in their gaze told Eyas they had seen battle.

He served them bowls of beans and chunks of centaur bread. Little was said until the meal was over.

"We hold the towns," Peter Three began. "The Deltans fought hard, at least in the beginning. Afterward they refused battle, and retreated."

"Through the Black Gates?" asked Eyas.

"Above them. The road above the gorge was still passable.

We followed them to the first fortress; then they drove us back."

"A road?" said Boulder. "You told us of no road."

"A trail, centaur. The fortresses on it are small, but they hold the trail. And now the snow is too thick to cross. It is a road for the Deltans, and only in spring and summer."

"Better that than the Black Gates in little boats," Boulder grunted.

Eyas ignored the remark, and asked, "Is the winter hard in the south?"

"Bitter hard. We rode all the way up the River on the ice."

"You rode sixfeet?"

"No, they pulled our sledges."

"How far is the river frozen?"

"Past the Black Gates. Ah, I hear your thoughts. You would go south on the frozen River."

"Yes," Eyas said.

"Men have done it, but not many have lived. The River drops steeply in places. Avalanches often block the gorge, and many blizzards blow through it."

"We will do it again," said Eyas.

Boulder stroked his sparse beard—a gesture of relief. The lotors muttered and purred to each other, while the Riverines shrugged. Eyas stood up.

"I will go to speak with Ravine." The Scorpion was the only Band Warmaker left with the army. He was a brave and intelligent man. But Eyas wished, not for the first time, that Stormsong were still beside him.

7

On New Year's Day, 262, the allies left the frozen Riverine marshes and entered the Black Gates. The great canyon dividing the White and Lotor Mountains was little wider than the Rip, but its sides were higher and steeper; upon the rims, snow lay ten spans thick, dull white and overhanging the narrow canyon floor. The wind blew ceaselessly from the north, piling snow in thick drifts behind each bend in the canyon.

The centaurs, four thousand of them, marched in the van, pounding down the snow into a road. Behind them and the sledges they pulled were the Riverines, six thousand men and boys, and the five hundred warriors of the Bands, mounted on sixfeet. In the rear of the column were eight thousand lotors.

Even in the rare intervals when the roar of the wind died away, the army was silent. The only sounds were the scrape of feet or sledge runners on hard-packed snow, the clank of pikestaff against shield, and the occasional groan of a sixfoot. When snow cascaded hissing from the cliffs, the marchers paused to see if a full avalanche was coming; then they trudged on, their breaths whitening the air.

It was dark in the canyon, but at noon the strip of sky brightened above the cliffs. Eyas, riding Boulder near the head of the column, looked up. The western side of the canyon was less steep here, and snow mantled it. At the canyon's rim was a wall.

"The first of the fortresses," said Peter Three, who rode beside him on Boulder's sister Tillfallow.

"Can they see us?"

"If they trouble to look."

"And what could they do to us?"

"I do not know."

"Can they send word to the other fortresses?"

"Not until spring thaw."

Eyas nodded. "Then we go on."

The column marched onward, but Eyas and Boulder paused at the foot of the eastern cliff, where they could see the Deltan fortress more clearly. It seemed deserted: no banners, no one on the wall, no smoke—unless it was hidden in the gray mist scudding above the canyon. For what seemed a long time, nothing happened. Then a bell rang out faintly, and Eyas saw tiny figures appear on the wall. He beckoned to the nearest Riverine centenary.

"Halt your men where they are. Pass the word down the column: Halt until I give the order to move."

The centenary obeyed. The units ahead of his kept on going. Without warning, a dozen javelins dropped into the widening gap, burying themselves in the snow.

Peter Three and Tillfallow rejoined Eyas and Boulder. Ravine rode up, with Forager and Blue close behind.

"Now what?" asked Ravine.

"The Deltans have seen us," Eyas said, pointing to the javelin shafts. "They must be using catapults, and not many of them. If they have cannons, they can't train them on us."

"What of it?" snorted Ravine. "We'll just march right through. They can't get many of us."

"They'll get none of us if I can help it." Eyas and Boulder went across to the waiting Riverines and summoned their centenaries.

"Can your men run?" he smiled.

"Like this cursed wind," one answered.

"Good. Each hundred will run from here to the next bend in the canyon—one group on the east side, the next on the west. Keep open formations, and don't let your men bunch up or stop. When each group comes abreast of me, it'll go where I point."

The first hundred floundered through the drifts along the eastern cliff. Another volley of javelins fell, but only a couple of them reached the cliff and no one was hurt. Eyas sent the next hundred along the same side; the Deltans had the range now, and the javelins killed two men. The third hundred ran for the western cliff, and were safe before the Deltans could adjust their aim.

It went on through most of the blustery afternoon. Before long, the Deltans were shooting only two or three javelins at a time; then they began hurling stones and lumps of ice. Darkness fell in a snow flurry, and under its cover Eyas moved the rest of the army.

Standaway Smith came back to find him. "All are well. We're making camp not far beyond the next turn. We've lost only eight dead and twenty wounded." She looked more closely at Eyas in the deepening gloom. "Do you weep for them?"

He rubbed his cheeks with a mittened hand. "For all of them, Standaway."

She reached out and put her arm around him.

"I wonder if anyone is at Gathering Cove," he whispered in Gulf dialect.

"I do not understand."

"No matter. Come—it has been a hard day."

They walked down the frozen river in darkness and stinging snow.

Twice more, in the days that followed, the army passed within range of Deltan fortresses, but a blizzard concealed them from one and the other they passed at night. Men and brutes died of cold, and in avalanches, but the army did not slow.

Eyas slept little. He waited for dreamhauntings, but they came instead to Bandish warriors and Riverines. The Riverines, at least, seemed undisturbed by the dead.

"Yes, they come to us—more now than usual," said Peter Three one morning when a blizzard kept the army within its tents. "My son Another is visited almost every night. But they are only a nuisance. Once a head has been properly placed in a shrine, our duty to the dead is done." He grinned. "We honor our ancestors, but I confess that they seem silly and malicious when they pester us. I think they envy the living; is that not foolish?" He waved at the unsavory mess of breadseed cooking on a small fire, and at the frosted fabric of the tent. Eyas laughed, taking heart from the Riverine's good cheer.

"Tell your son to speak with me when the dead come to him next. If they war upon us, we should know what they say."

The smile faded from Peter Three's face. "Do you really believe that, Eyas?"

"I know it."

"You choose strange foes."

"They chose me."

Later that day, when the blizzard died away and the army was breaking camp, Ravine came to see Eyas.

"We must turn back, Eyas."

"Why?"

"I . . . do not like to speak of such things, but if we go on into Delta, we will be destroyed."

"Your dead tell you this?"

Ravine looked away, at the dark cliffs. "Yes."

Eyas pulled his cloak closer around him. Strange foes indeed. They knew what he was doing; no doubt they dreamhaunted the Deltans, warning them. Eyas half-shared Ravine's fear: perhaps they should go back, fight a defensive war or none at all—simply retreat, retreat into the northern wastes.

"—Do your ancestors love you, Ravine?"

"Why, I do not know."

"Do the dead warn you so that you might escape to enjoy long years of peace?"

"They do not say; they only warn of destruction."

"The Riverines may be wiser than we. They say their dead are foolish. Perhaps ours are too. Why should they warn us of the destruction they mean to bring upon us?"

Ravine shrugged.

"Because they are not sure they *can* destroy us, Ravine. They try to frighten us, because they fear us. I rejoice in their threats, and so should you."

The Scorpion stared at him. "I do not know whether you are the bravest man in Alland, or simply mad."

Eyas laughed. "And who led the first attack on the wagonfort at Rocky River? Was that brave, or mad?"

Ravine grinned awkwardly. "Ha! Well—we have cast our lot with you and the brutes. Lead on, and we follow. One can die but once, in Delta or the desert." But he did not look happy.

In a gray, gusting dawn the allies broke camp and prepared for the last stage of their march through the Black Gates. Eyas sent for Another Three, who came running lightly through the windblown drift. He was wrapped in a bulky cloak of longfur wool, with a hood to protect his face.

"I greet you, Another," said Eyas, who walked alongside Boulder toward the head of the column. "Your father tells me the dead visit you in dreams. Did they come to you last night?"

"Yes, Eyas." The youth kept his eyes downcast as he watched his step. "They say we should turn back, or leave our heads unhallowed in foreign earth."

"Do you believe them?"

"They are frightening sometimes, Eyas. But we do not listen to the dead."

"Good. And did they tell you how the Deltans will beat us?"

Another hesitated. "No—just that they will be too strong for us."

Eyas said nothing for a moment. "Very well; go back to your hundred. You're wise not to believe what the dead tell you."

When the young Riverine was out of earshot, Eyas said to

243

Boulder, "He was told more than he told us. But he was not afraid."

"Strange are the ways of humans," grunted Boulder.

"True. Sometimes brutes are easier to understand."

Near noon they came to the southern end of the Black Gates. The cliffs here were far lower, and not far ahead Eyas could see a flat gray horizon under a dull overcast sky. He called a halt.

"I'm going to farhear," he said to Boulder. "If the Deltans know of us, they may be hiding above those cliffs. It would be a good place for an ambush."

Boulder nodded. Eyas squatted on the snow, drawing into himself, feeling dizzy as he called upon the power after so long.

. . . Yes. On both sides of the River, he farheard the clank of metal, the snort of sixfeet, men muttering to one another in Deltan rhythms, the crunch of boots in crusty snow.

Boulder was watching him intently. Eyas sighed and stood up. "Call the leaders."

They accepted his warning with surprising readiness, though farhearing was a skill unknown to them. But the leaders argued over how to respond. Forager suggested a dash through the ambush, as they had done below the first Deltan fortress.

"The River's too narrow here," Ravine objected, "and the Deltans are on both sides. They may have cannons as well as catapults—they could chop us up before we ever get out onto the plain." Eyas remembered how boldly Ravine had argued for marching past the first fortress; the dead must have been eating at his courage.

"I see no other way," Forager replied through Blue. "If we could get to the top of the cliffs, we might drive the Deltans away." He pointed to the low but near-vertical face of the western cliff. "We are good climbers, but even we cannot ascend such a slope."

"Then we'll go through at night," Boulder said.

"The Deltans will surely have a screen of soldiers on the ice," said Eyas. "If they sound the alarm, the ones on the cliffs can fire down into the darkness—" He paused. "If they *can* sound the alarm. Forager, could you send some of your warriors ahead, to slay any Deltans hiding on the ice?"

"Easily."

"Let it be done."

That night the allies muzzled their sixfeet and wrapped rags around anything that might clank or squeak. Then the column moved slowly forward, sledge runners scraping softly over the snow. The sky was deeply overcast and gave no light; the air was still. Men and centaurs groped through the blackness, while lotors guided them. Forager and Blue walked at the head of the column, on either side of Boulder. Eyas sat on the centaur's back, but could not even see his mane.

As they reached the last bend in the canyon, the lotors paused. Eyas heard footsteps almost as light as dry snow falling, and then Forager tapped on Boulder's flank. Whispers fluttered in the darkness: the lotor scouts were back.

"We found ten humans on the ice," their leader said to Forager.

"All dead now?"

"All dead, in silence. No others remain. The Deltans on the cliffs must have sentries, and we saw the glow of campfires."

"You please me." Forager murmured the news to Eyas, who listened patiently to his broken Riverine and then said, in lotor,

"You please me. Let us go on."

The army came around the bend; now Eyas could see a dim pink glow above the cliffs on either side. He shook his head. The Deltans were slovenly ambushers, or else did not really expect their enemies to move at night. If the dead were aware of the Deltans' clumsiness, they must be furious.

The silence was so deep that Eyas kept glancing back to see if the column was indeed moving. Only an occasional scuff of hoof or foot could be heard. Slowly the head of the column came abreast of the pink glows, and then moved beyond them. Eyas began to breathe more easily. Let nothing go wrong, and they would be past the ambush well before dawn.

Far behind him, in the middle of the column, a voice cried out—the cold voice of a Messenger.

"Deltans! Awake! The enemy is here! Awake!" Echoes carried the cry into the darkness, bouncing from cliff to cliff until the canyon resounded with a gobbling howl.

Boulder spun round, knocking Blue down. The centaur would have charged blindly up through the column, but Eyas yanked at the scabbard hanging on Boulder's back.

"Wait. The lotors must guide us. Forager—find the man who cries out, and silence him. But do not kill him; bring him to me."

Forager and the half-blind priest hissed softly and vanished. The cries went on, and now Eyas heard rapid, stumbling footsteps, sobbing breaths, the clash of metal against metal. The Riverines were breaking, running in terror through the darkness away from the terrible voice. Farther back, the Band warriors began to sing battle chants, but uncertainly. On the cliffs, the glow of campfires dimmed. Men called out; horns brayed. A burning arrow soared up and fell to the ice, sputtering and flashing an eerie red. More followed; they were easily dodged, but they kept burning, illuminating all around them. Eyas heard the rattle and thump of a catapult, and then the crash of stones.

The centenaries, regaining control of their men, drove the Riverines forward at a jog trot, while the centaurs took advantage of the fire-arrows' light to round up the men who had broken ranks. Javelins and stones fell into the column, but no one was left behind; the killed and wounded were lifted onto the nearest sledge.

Boulder and Eyas moved steadily toward the rear, urging the hundreds to move quickly. Eyas heard the Messenger's voice, off to the left, as if he were planning to scale the western cliff and join the ambushers. Boulder heard him too, and trotted out in pursuit. Behind them, firebombs began to burst, splashing flame and shadow across the canyon. Eyas remembered Longstrand, and felt old rage and sorrow flood through him.

A tall figure appeared in the dimness ahead, unmoving. It was Another, Peter Three's son.

"Get back to the column!" Eyas commanded. "And hurry—we can still get through."

Another looked up at him and smiled.

"We meet again, Eyas Fisher—and Boulder."

It was the Messenger they had slain at the Great Cataract, grinning out of the youth's dark face. Eyas drew his sword.

"Shall I give you news of Sky, and Violet? Of Old, and Gray, and Golden? Firewing and Quiet, Netweaver, Hemlock, and Griptiller? No need; soon you will be with them."

Shuddering with fear and rage, Eyas saw without caring that the fires on the ice had dimmed. A deeper darkness than night's was falling. Even the lotors were blinded, and called out to one another in startled trills. Boulder lunged forward, slashing, but the Messenger only laughed.

"I should have called darkness upon you at the bridge," he said. "Now it is upon you forever, Eyas."

Eyas roared with fury, his voice as terrible as the Messenger's, "*Goddess, look under me!*"

As if the River itself had exploded in white fire, the Black Gates filled with light. Eyas could not see its source; shadowless, it was everywhere. Before him stood the Messenger in the youth's body, a spear aimed at Eyas's chest, but the light seemed to daze him, and he stepped back. In that moment a long lotor arrow sighed past and struck the Messenger's eye with such force that his body was knocked sprawling.

Dazzled by the glare, Eyas shut his eyes; when he opened them, the light was fading swiftly, leaving only the scattered red and orange fires that the Deltans had flung down. No more came. The Deltans' cries carried clearly on the still air, and the bellows of sixfeet. But they grew fainter with every breath. The ambushers must have been terrified by the light, and perhaps even by the Messenger's voice. In the dark silence that sank back upon the ice and mountains, torches flared; men and brutes called out, seeking comfort in each other's presence.

Eyas dismounted. He smelled Forager nearby. "Bring me a torch. And send for Peter Three."

Four lotors bearing torches came out from the column and stood around the body of Another. It was again the boy, not the Messenger; Forager's arrow had flung both into Hell, and the dark face held only a strange, surprised look.

Peter Three was there, looking down at his dead son. Eyas turned and embraced him.

"One of the dead possessed him, and gave the warning. I grieve for you again, Peter Three."

The Riverine shuddered. "Possessed . . . At least it was not for long. When I saw him last, he was still my son. Forager has done me a service." He knelt beside the boy, touched the black hair and the thin beard, red with blood, along the line of the jaw. Then he plucked out the arrow. "Oh, my son," he whispered. "What shall I say to your mother?"

Eyas pulled himself into the saddle, and Boulder turned back toward the column. Blue and Forager strode easily alongside, leaving the torchbearers to watch over Peter Three's mourning.

"Where did that light come from?" asked Eyas.

The lotors chattered with surprise. "From you," said Blue. "You were too bright to look upon. You are a divinity, Eyas, a seen mover."

"No. But I think I am used by a divinity."

"Yes, yes. An unseen mover moves through you. I did not say you were a *great* divinity."

Boulder coughed. Eyas would have laughed as well, but he thought of Another Three, and was silent. The unseen mover, if there was one, seemed very far away.

8

The village of Miller's Newfield was twenty mud-brick huts and sheds, clustered on the bank of a narrow canal and sheltered by a row of willow trees. Sitting on a bench outside one of the huts, Eyas could look south across the half-frozen surface of the canal, past the leafless trees, to a muddy field where children grubbed for any whiteroots that might have been missed in last year's harvest. The children often paused to look west, where lotors and Riverines marched south along the top of an earth dike. Though the air was cool, the morning sunshine was bright.

Beside him on the bench sat Peter Three; facing them was an old man, squatting comfortably on the hard-packed yellow dirt. His wife, flat-nosed and white-haired, knelt at a grinding stone in her doorway, making flour from a handful of breadseed. At a respectful distance behind the old man stood the village's fifteen young men and women. All were dressed in thin, colorless shirts and knee-length trousers.

"This is a great gift you would bestow upon us," the old man said when Peter Three had translated Eyas's words. "Too great for nameless ones like ourselves. Only a Name may own land, and this land belongs to the Great Name Bald Miller."

"Your Great Name deserted you," Eyas replied. "He is gone; he has no claim on the land or on you."

"Then it is the conqueror's. Names have often warred on one another, and taken land and nameless ones by violence."

"I have no need for land, or for slaves. That is why I make the land a gift to you."

"No land here is a gift, unless from Guardian himself. But land may be paid for. How should I, old and poor as I am, pay for all this land?"

"Lend me your sons and daughters, to fight in my army. They will share in the wealth we take from Delta, and bring it home to you. When Guardian and the Great Names are beaten, your line will own this land forever."

The old man looked as if he wanted to laugh. "We are peasants, not warriors. The Names are the fighters, and their mercenaries—not we."

Eyas grinned. "We have come two daymarches from the Black Gates, and have yet to see one of these fighters. They flee before us."

The old man hesitated before he spoke again. "Perhaps they had good reason to flee. We have heard tales of monsters in the Black Gates, and demons clothed in fire."

"Do we look like demons?"

"No. I think you are a man. The Riverines we know, and we have heard of the Desert Bands. It is strange to see a lotor skin with the brute still alive inside it. The centaurs we have heard of. When the Great Names realize you are not monsters, perhaps then they will stand and fight. And if they defeat you, what will become of us?"

"Your masters will return and take away your land. They will take revenge. All the more reason for your sons and daughters to know how to fight."

"All the more reason for them to keep close at home, if you will allow me to say it. No, no; we nameless ones are made to till the soil and feed our masters, and nothing more."

"Have you no name at all?" asked Eyas.

"Newfield Sixty-Three, my Great Name calls me. Some call me Father, or Grandfather, or Seventy Summers; nameless ones may be called anything."

"Then I will give you a name to keep."

The old man looked surprised, and the young people stirred.

"I will name you Willow Newfield. You look as tough and old as your trees."

The old man cackled. "I planted those, in the days of the Great Name's grandfather. Willow Newfield . . . Will you give names to the young people also, and to my good wife?"

249

"Name them yourself, or let them choose their own."

"Revere the gods! I feel like a sixfoot that's got into a field of ripe breadseed. Well—I, a Name. It is done. We will take what you offer, and give what you ask. But I will come too."

"Are you sure? It will be a long march, and we will see hard fighting soon."

"No matter. I have never been off this land, and I would like to see the great city before I die. Besides, a Name owes his strength to his master, and I am now a Name."

Each day, as the army marched south, Eyas and Peter Three spoke in little villages like Newfield, naming the peasants and giving them the land they had worked upon all their lives. Each day the army grew, swollen by peasant recruits. Shy and awkward, armed with little more than axes and hoes, they trudged south behind the main force; in the evenings, Bandish and Riverine warriors trained them for combat. The peasant youths were clumsy, but strong and obedient. The thought of returning rich, to land of their own, gleamed in their eyes.

But they saw no fighting. The villages lay half-deserted, undefended; the towns and garrisons were empty. Centaurs and riders often saw Deltan scouts in the distance, but never closed with them. A few bridges had been burned, and most of the granaries hastily emptied by the retreating Deltans; in those places, the peasants who remained were quick to join the allies simply to be fed. Old people and children followed the army, slowing it down. Boulder grew irritable at the delays.

"By the time we reach Delta City, the Great Names will have remembered their courage," he complained to Eyas.

"I hope so. Better a quick battle than a long siege. . . . What is that?"

They were near the west bank of the River; ahead, a long ridge lay across their line of march. The top of the ridge looked like an immense fortification.

"The ruins of Palisade," said Peter Three.

"Palisade!" Eyas remembered Silken's tales of the ancient times, when Palisade had conquered the first great empire three thousand years ago. Even the Suns' legends honored the Allseers, the dynasty that had ruled from the Dawn Coast to Jadeland until northern nomads had come over the mountains. "We will camp there tonight."

The Deltan peasants would not climb the ridge, fearing the

ruins as the home of evil spirits, but the rest of the allies settled cheerfully among the broken walls and headless pillars. Lotors bobbed and swayed through the streets, holding torches; Riverines sang old war songs around their fires. The centaurs marveled at the stonework, intricate carvings worn and softened by millennia, yet still as beautiful as any door in Foundries.

"It's said that the nomads who overthrew this place were driven south by centaurs," Boulder said as he and Eyas settled down for the night after long wanderings through the endless ruins. "But I do not believe it. How could those who built such splendor be conquered by a few warriors with bronze swords?"

"We will do the same," shrugged Eyas.

"If Delta is as great a city as this was, I hope we do not leave it like this."

Eyas burrowed under a blanket, missing Stormsong. "It will all be the same in the end, Boulder."

The centaur's eyes glowed in the firelight. "It is all in the manner of dying."

Sky spoke that night in Eyas's dreams, for the first time in many months. Her voice was far away and full of sorrow.

They fear you, Eyas. They are afraid. Seek the cave on Mount Aspen.

"What is there?" he murmured in his sleep.

Their downfall, their end, peace, peace, an ending. Seek the cave—

"Sky—show yourself to me. Oh, I love you still."

No. I cannot. Only seek the cave. And remember me. Remember me.

—He was awake, looking up at the black outlines of pillars rising against the glowing Bridge. The crescent moon was high in the sky. Boulder snored softly on the far side of the dead campfire.

"Goddess," Eyas whispered, "tell me: what am I to do? Why am I in the world?"

Nothing answered.

"How can so many people live so crowded together?" asked Ravine. He stood on a dike beside the other leaders, looking south. The land was growing green again, despite the persistent cold, and the canals reflected a bright blue sky. Villages stood everywhere, none more than half an hourmarch from

251

another. More widely spaced were the deserted strongholds of Great Names, with stone walls and red tile roofs. Only in the far distance could smoke be seen, rising from settlements not yet abandoned by the Deltans. The peasants were going with their masters now; the Great Names had seen the peril in leaving them behind.

"They'll be more crowded than this in Delta City," said Eyas. "Perhaps it's just as well they've taken the peasants. More mouths to feed, and we might encourage a revolt inside the city."

"It would be more warlike to fight in the open, but even with all these clodkickers we're sure to be outnumbered," answered Ravine. He sucked his teeth. "The Deltans plan a trap."

"Do your dead warn you again?"

Ravine looked grim under his tattooes. "No. They leave us in peace now. But it has been too easy. I wish Stormsong were back with us."

"So do I."

By night, lotors ventured out in search of enemies, and came back only with news of still more empty villages. By day, the columns of the army moved south, pausing only to repair bridges or to forage for supplies. Once or twice, Bandish warriors riding centaurs skirmished with Deltan scouts, but could take no prisoners. The silence of the land was irksome and frightening: it was like a fog through which the army groped.

Spring was well advanced, but still cold, when they reached the city of Grandmarket, a dense mass of whitewashed buildings at the junction of two large canals. The city must have held many thousands, but only rats and spiders wandered in its narrow streets. Eyas kept the army outside the city walls and sent in patrols. They returned in excitement.

"Not much food," said Boulder's brother Agate, "but we found resin, Eyas, and beer, and wine! The houses are full of fine carpets, gold and silver—it's a city of treasure."

"Tell no one," said Eyas. "We'll go around the city."

Boulder and Agate stared at him. "We've had no resin since we left Foundries," Boulder protested. "It would be—"

"It would be a trap," Eyas interrupted. "They hope to fuddle us, and burden us with plunder. We'll have time enough for that when Delta falls."

Reluctantly, the centaurs agreed. The army marched around Grandmarket, preceded by lotor scouts who searched the villages for Deltan gifts. They found plenty of them, but lotors did not like resin or alcohol, and cheerfully threw the bait into the canals. Rumors spread through the army; some grumbled, but the march went on.

The weather was clear, but cold. The Deltan recruits looked worriedly at the unplanted fields, where even the weeds seemed stunted. "Windwalker weather," Willow Newfield called it. Eyas overheard and asked the old man what he meant.

"When the spring is cold, the windwalkers come from the northwest; they raided us last year. May all their islands fall upon the mountains!"

Eyas smiled and said nothing.

The army's route sometimes took it along the west bank; now the River was so wide its far side could scarcely be seen, and its brown expanse was broken by low green islands. Warships, much like the ones Eyas had seen in remembrance, cruised up and down the River; sometimes they fired a cannon shot or two at anyone venturing to the water's edge, but they made no attempt to attack. Peter Three spoke with grim respect of the Deltan marines. They had been the first to conquer the Riverine towns, and maintained order throughout the Great River Valley and the Deltan coast. Eyas, seeing sails again, yearned for a fair wind and a deck under his feet.

Westward, the canals branched and branched again: human hands had turned the valley into an extension of the Delta, a bewildering archipelago. Here the army found towns still occupied, castles bristling with armed men; but no one offered combat. From the town walls and castle towers, blond-bearded men with ruddy faces glared down at the long columns; the allies stayed out of cannon range, and the Deltans made no sorties.

"They mean to fall upon our rear when we reach Delta City," Forager remarked as the army passed one castle.

"I know," said Eyas. He sent out centaurs to guard the army's rear, and to burn bridges. The Deltans would not be able to strike quickly. And if they did come south, they would find lotor archers hidden within bowshot of every road.

The morning mists burned away. The allies had spent the night in a cluster of hamlets not far from Delta City. A narrow, treelined canal cut across their route, with a single bridge. Centaur scouts, led by Boulder's brothers Agate and Cirque, had crossed the bridge the night before to protect it; now, as the mist cleared, the centaurs shouted an alarm. Eyas and Boulder, followed by a hundred centaurs with riders, left their camp and crossed the bridge.

Ten or twelve warriors were riding up the road from the south. They wore cuirasses, wide-brimmed iron helmets, and knee-length boots with long white fringes. Their leader held up an unstrung bow. He was a burly, round-faced young man with a drooping red moustache but no beard. His companions halted well out of bowshot; he kept on, sitting very erect on a large sixfoot, until he was less than ten spans from the centaurs and riders.

"You speak the Deltan tongue?" he called out in a strange accent. Eyas had learned enough of the language to reply.

"I speak a little."

"No more do I. I'm a Homelander by birth. Godhonor's the name. Who leads your army?"

"I do. I am Eyas Fisher."

"Good morning to you. My master Guardian sends me to speak with you under an unstrung bow."

"I listen."

The Homelander lowered his bow and leaned easily on the pommel of his saddle, but his wary glances at the centaurs belied his brave show. "The old man's right unhappy with this invasion. Spring flood's just days away, and not two handfuls of seed in the fields from the city to the Black Gates. The city's so crowded you can hardly see the Pillar. All manner of brutes and outlanders trampling about his countryside, and the people wetting themselves with tales of demons and evil spirits. Ah, he's an unhappy man indeed."

"We all bear sorrows in this world," Eyas replied.

"An easy oath to that! Now, someone's going to bear sorrows in plenty if you keep on as you have, but it won't be Guardian. He loves peace; we could have fought you far north of here, but the old man wouldn't have it. 'See if it's plunder they want,' he says, and we left you a whole city full of it. You wouldn't trouble yourselves to take it and go home, so—" He spread his arms helplessly. "We're to give you one more chance, the old man says. Turn around now. Help yourselves to Grandmarket; keep the peasants you've taken, and go back over the mountains. Even the Riverines will be forgiven, and left in as much peace as you leave us."

"Tell me, Godhonor," said Eyas, "does Guardian have many mercenaries in his service?"

"Close to thirty thousand, and he's sent away for more."

"If I gave you the plunder of Grandmarket, would you and the other mercenaries come over to our side?"

Godhonor leaned back, eyes wide. "You'd bribe us? And with our master's own wealth! No, no—we're paid, not bribed, and by Guardian and the Great Names, not a pack of bandits and brutes."

Eyas laughed. "Then you'll earn your pay."

The mercenary shrugged and sighed. "So be it."

"Tell me this: why were you sent, and not a Great Name—or at least a native Deltan?"

"What—honor brigands? I was sent to bargain, and Great Names only command. You'll see plenty of them if you keep on."

"I hope to meet you again."

"I don't. You're a likable fellow, for a barbarian, and I'd not rejoice to be the one to take your head." He raised his bow in salute, then turned his mount and trotted back to his companions. They wheeled and galloped off.

"They'll have some treachery planned," Boulder said when Eyas had told him of Godhonor's offer. Eyas grunted agreement, then gestured to Cirque and Agate.

"Take a hundred centaurs with riders, and overtake those warriors. Capture them unhurt if you can; then send scouts ahead. Be quick. The whole army will be on your heels."

The scouting party was scarcely gone before Eyas summoned the allies' leaders.

"We're within two daymarches of Delta's walls. Tomorrow night we'll camp outside them. No doubt the Deltans plan traps and ambushes, but they won't expect a sudden advance after the way we've crept along. Leave the baggage train, the old, the children, the sick. Leave the cannons, and the wagons, and just enough warriors to guard them. The rest of us will run. Make haste!"

Across the fields and marshes ran a sound like summer thunder. Firewings and blackbeaks rose squealing and moaning from their nests; stray sixfeet and longfurs ran from the sound.

The army's scouts charged through villages crowded with terrified peasants, and slaughtered Deltan patrols in sudden skirmishes. Where bridges had been wrecked, the centaurs waded across, or chopped down trees. Ambushers were betrayed by captured peasants, or betrayed themselves when nervous soldiers fired too soon.

North of a wide, shallow canal, a wagonfort defended a major bridge; the army went around it, found a ford, and splashed across. The Deltans, fearing they might be cut off, abandoned the bridge and wagons and raced south. They collided with units marching north; the panic spread. Officers saw their men throw down their arms and run, and could not rally them.

The roads themselves seemed to carry the message: peasants felt the ground tremble, and abandoned their villages. Herders frantically drove their longfurs across fields and roads, seeking the safety of the nearest walled town. Deltan riders, blocked by peasants and their brutes, slashed and stabbed to clear the way; mercenary pikemen slaughtered hundreds, and retreated south over the bodies.

Nightfall brought no respite. Exhausted Deltan soldiers paused for a bowl of half-cooked grain; lotor arrows whirred out of the darkness, and the deep shouts of centaurs drove the Deltans on, staggering through hedgerows and orchards. Here and there, in the crowded countryside, a hamlet burned; but that was the only light. Men groped in ditches on hands and knees, until lotors' long fingers gripped their hair and lotors' knives cut their throats. Wagonforts took sudden volleys of arrows out of the darkness, and answered with futile gunfire; if riders left the shelter of the wagons, they did not return.

By morning, most of the towns and villages north of the city were in flames, and the dawn mist was acrid with smoke. The only Deltans left on the roads were peasants too tired or injured to keep moving. They stared at the columns of trotting centaurs, at Riverine pikemen, at longstriding lotors with curious eyes and sharp teeth, at peasants from the north bearing axes and clubs.

Eyas and Boulder had fallen far behind, seeing to the safety of the slower-moving baggage train and camp followers. Now, in the sour gray dawn, they hurried to catch up. As they ran alongside a narrow canal, they found a young peasant couple with a wailing child. Eyas halted the centaur. The

Deltans, shivering in thin cotton smocks, bowed their heads. The child, a yellow-haired girl of about three, went on crying while her mother rocked her.

"What's the matter?" asked Eyas. "Is she sick?"

"No, master," whispered the young father. "Hurt. The Great Name riders drove us off the road last night. One struck at us, and hit our little girl."

Eyas slid from the centaur's back. "May I see her?"

The mother expressionlessly held up the child, as if in sacrifice. Eyas gasped. A swordstroke had slashed the little girl's face open from eyebrow to jaw. Her head and chest were dark with crusted blood.

Gently he took her, and rocked her in his arms. "Goddess, look under her, and bear her up," he said. The child went on dully wailing. Her parents squatted by the roadside, casting wary glances up at the inscrutable centaur and the grieving young man.

A hundred Riverines came up the road, their pikes like a leafless forest above their heads. Eyas beckoned to their centenary, who hurried over.

"Have you any good healers in your hundred?" Eyas asked. The centenary nodded.

"A pretty fair one, Eyas. For the little one?" He turned and bellowed, "Hyacinth Ten! Get over here!"

The healer, almost as tall as a lotor, strode out of the ranks. He studied the child's wound, then rummaged in a leather pouch.

"I cannot save the eye, but I can close the wound and give her something for the pain." He took out a small glass vial wrapped in moss, and put it to the child's lips. Her wails quietened; she seemed to doze. Hyacinth Ten worked unhurriedly, whistling under his breath, while Eyas held the child.

"That's as much as I can do. If they change the bandage every day, she should be all right. Poor little thing."

Eyas gave the child back to her mother, and told her what the Riverine had said. "Care for her well, and when the war is over, bring her to me, to Eyas Fisher. She will want for nothing in her life."

The father met his eyes for the first time. "Why?"

"Because this war is none of her doing."

"No, master. Why was she hurt?"

Eyas said nothing. The Riverines resumed their march at a

257

jog trot, their centenary chanting the step. Eyas gently touched the child's forehead, and her parents'.

"You are nameless? Then I name you: Asking, and Silence, and Golden. From this day you are named and free. Go among your people, give each a name, and tell them that they too are free. When the war is done, come and seek me." He pulled himself onto Boulder's back, and from a saddlebag took two small loaves of bread and a whiteroot. He gave them to Asking, and waved farewell.

"You have not forgotten yourself," Boulder said as they trotted south.

Above the smoke of burning villages rose the city of Delta, old and great. It sprawled across three islands at the point where the Great River began to divide into countless branches. Its eastern side was a maze of docks on the main stream of the River; to the north, west, and south, it was armored by a stone wall five spans in height, with towers half again as high. Within the walls were stinking alleys and broad thoroughfares, ten thousand whitewashed houses of mud brick, and the Hundred Palaces of Guardian and the Great Names.

Looming over the city was the Pillar. It had been built over two thousand years before, with the labor of a whole generation. The priests of an ancient religion, the Brightness Cult, had ordained it; its completion had marked the founding of the Hand of the Templars, an empire that ruled for a hundred years from the Dawn Coast to the Grasslands when the Suns had been ignorant herders in the Yellow Desert. The Hand had fallen, and empires after it, yet still the Pillar stood, indestructible, a narrow cone over one hundred spans high. On its flat top a fire had burned for centuries, a beacon and a reminder of Delta's power.

That power had been used against the allies only to scorch the land for a daymarch around the walls. The canals were black with burned wood. Rats scuttled through the ashes of granaries and into the untended fields. Yet even here, whether through incompetence or the peasants' reluctance to destroy their few possessions, some houses still stood and a few herds of sixfeet and blackhorns wandered aimlessly. The allies, sweeping around the city, found enough to feed themselves.

The leaders stood on the high porch of a temple in an abandoned village. Not far to the south was the city, its walls screened by nearby palm trees but its palaces, and the Pillar, clearly visible.

"Why don't they resist?" muttered Boulder. "Are we so fearsome that we can simply walk in?"

"They plan a trap," Forager said through Blue. "We can cut off the city from the land, but not from the River." He pointed to the east, where several white-sailed galleys were moving north, rowing steadily against the current, to watch the invaders and perhaps land marines to harass the allies' rear. "If we stay outside the walls, we must starve or lift the siege to find food. If we attack, they can pick us off from the walls. Or they could even let us in, and crush us in the streets."

"Their whole army must be in there," Ravine nodded. "If they need reinforcements, they can bring them in from across the River or from the south. The lotor speaks wisely."

Eyas said nothing at first, but only watched the galleys in the distance. Then he asked for the prisoner Godhonor to be brought to the temple. The leaders settled back, curious to see what Eyas planned.

Godhonor, his hands tied behind him, was prodded up the steps by a squad of Riverines. On the porch he sat cross-legged beside Eyas. The Homelander's face was puffy and bruised: the centaurs had not been gentle in capturing him. Eyas ordered the captive's hands freed, and sent for food.

"What will the old man be thinking?" he asked.

"Ah, he'll be powerfully furious, he will; an easy oath to that. You and your trained animals have made a great nuisance of yourselves."

Eyas laughed. "He's not so mad that he'll come charging out to chastise us."

"No, no. But he'll rally the west, and east, and south. The havens alone will send enough men to crush you against the city walls, like a pot against an anvil."

"Likely enough, if we wait for the hammer." A Deltan recruit came up the steps with a tray of food: dates, spiced breadseed paste, a peppery stew of beans and blackhorn flesh. With a cautious glance at the centaurs and lotors, and a glare of hatred of the mercenary, he put the tray before Eyas. "Eat your fill, Godhonor."

"You've not gone to all this trouble just to cheer me up—though it's a rare view we have from here, and a

259

passable meal." He began to scoop up paste on two dirty fingers, slurping noisily.

"An easy oath to that," grinned Eyas. "When you're done, you join our side."

Godhonor finished the paste and started on the stew. "Do I, now? What good would I be, when you can march to Guardian's front door and I can't even keep out of your hands?"

"You can draw a map of the city, and tell me where the soldiers are."

"A high price for a meal, and the wine not even here yet."

"A small price for your life."

"Ah. It's that way, then."

"Your comrades will watch you die, and they'll follow you, one by one, until one of them shows some sense."

"By the waters of Holywell, some of those rogues would draw your map in their mothers' blood. Well, and what else? Will you want a proper tour of the city as well?"

"I'll want your company, yes, and that of your men."

"And just what are we to get out of this shameful treason?"

"A few more hours of life, if we lose. A great war, if we win."

Godhonor spat out a date pit. "This isn't war enough for you?"

"If all goes well, this war will be over very soon."

"If all goes well, it'll be the first time it ever did in Delta."

Next day, skirmishers probed toward the walls of Delta, testing the city's defenses. The Deltans made no sorties; the allies did not often come within range of the occasional cannon shot or catapulted firebomb. On the walls and rooftops, countless Deltans crowded for a glimpse of lotors, and of men riding centaurs. Most saw only peasants, jogging raggedly in the distance with axes and spears on their shoulders.

Behind the siege lines, men and brutes tore down bridges, fortified villages, and gathered whatever might be useful: pots, cloth, tools, wagons, even flocks of redcrests, dabblerlike animals with clipped wings, that waddled along canal banks ahead of whistling peasant soldiers.

While most of the army dug itself in north of the city, Eyas led a small force to a village at the intersection of a canal and the River. Its largest building was a two-story warehouse, built on the canal's edge where a loading dock jutted out into the water. The centaurs and their Band riders, forty altogether, went into the first floor of the warehouse; sixty lotors went upstairs.

Eyas walked out onto the dock with Godhonor and the ten other captured mercenaries. Like their leader, they were redheaded Homelanders. They had taken their enforced change of sides without much complaint and even seemed to look forward to carrying out Eyas's plan.

"The River patrols are fairly regular," Godhonor said. "We should see one of them before long. They'll want to get safely ashore in the city before nightfall." It was late afternoon; the shadows of the men on the dock extended far out across the rippled brown water.

He was right; a Deltan galley, oars flashing, soon came round a spit of land to the north. It was well offshore, but Eyas could see its officers on the high afterdeck, scanning the riverbank. Two small swivel-mounted cannons were mounted at the stern rail, each with its cannoneer; on the forward deck, ahead of the thirty rowers, stood a squad of marines.

Godhonor raised a scrap of white cloth on a spear and waved it quickly over his head. The galley pulled in closer; Eyas, wearing a mercenary's broad-brimmed helmet, waved with the others. As the Deltans approached the mouth of the canal, an easy bowshot from the dock, the mercenaries gestured still more urgently. The galley's captain, a fat man with a pointed white beard, ordered his rowers to enter the canal. As the galley came closer, Godhonor called out,

"Quickly, captain! The barbarians could be upon us at any moment!"

"What unit are you?"

"Sixth Foreigners. We were cut off when the barbarians advanced. Ah, it's good to see a friendly face!"

"How many are you?" The galley was nearly at the dock; a sailor made ready to cast a line.

"Just ourselves, and ten wounded in the warehouse. With a little help, we can have all aboard in no time."

One of the mercenaries caught the line and made it fast; the rowers shipped oars. The galley came to rest with its leftboard midships just below the end of the dock. Crewmen hoisted a gangway and scrambled up at the captain's command.

The sailors followed the mercenaries into the warehouse. Bandish warriors knocked the Deltans unconscious.

"Now," said Eyas.

The wide doors of the warehouse burst open; on the second floor, lotors with drawn bows appeared at the windows. The centaurs and riders charged over the dock and down the gangway; once aboard, they spread out forward and aft, clubbing anyone who resisted. The oarsmen leaped from their benches, then cowered down as centaur swords hummed over their heads.

The marines on the foredeck were quickly overpowered and disarmed, and the captain surrendered. The fight had taken only a few moments, and no one had been killed.

Eyas came up onto the afterdeck. "I greet you, captain. You have a fine craft here, and I'm sorry to take it from you. The oarsmen will stay aboard. You and your officers, except for the steersman, will go ashore with the marines."

"Why not kill us outright?" the captain asked bitterly. "What hope have we here, with barbarians everywhere about?"

"Lie low for a day or two, and you'll be back on duty before long." He grinned at the captain's incredulous stare and then gestured to the gangway. "Make haste, captain."

The twenty centaurs crouched on the narrow walkway between the rowers' benches. The centaurs ignored the rowers' horrified gaze, but their manes fluffed out; they did not like the feel of a deck beneath them. The lotors were eager to explore the galley, but Eyas ordered them below, into the hold. With them went the Bandish riders, whose appearance betrayed them as foreigners, except for a few who put on marines' armor and helmets. Their leader, a Locust named Obsidian, curled his lip at the captured Deltan weapons.

"Only four guns, and none of them any good. The crossbows are fair, but I wouldn't wager my life on them. It's no surprise the Deltans ran before us, if these are the best arms they have."

"The cannons on the afterdeck are serious weapons," said Eyas. "They'll suit our needs. Send some men belowdecks to bring up the gunpowder and shot."

The sun was down; with oarsmen rowing and the River carrying it, the galley ran swiftly south. Other ships were dimly visible, most of them making for haven in Delta while a few were bound for the distant east bank. To the west, the land was dark under a red sunset, with only a rare fire to be seen where soldiers or peasants cooked their suppers, or a hut burned.

As they neared the city, the galley's steersman changed course to clear a long mole that protected the docks. Once around it, he turned into the manmade harbor. Lanterns glowed on anchored ships, and at the end of each dock, but the city itself was strangely dark and silent. But the fire burned as always at the top of the Pillar.

"Do as I tell you and no one will be hurt," Eyas said to the steersman. "You and the rowers will stay where you are after we've docked. Do not raise an alarm, or try to signal for help."

"Yes, master." The Deltan, no older than Eyas, looked sick with fear.

Eyas went down the walkway, repeating his instructions to the rowers in a low voice. They grunted or nodded in reply. As the galley drifted up to a dock, they shipped their oars; men on the dock waited to take the lines. At Eyas's signal, Bandish warriors in marines' armor stepped off the foredeck onto the dock.

"And where've you lads been?" one of the dockmen called out cheerfully. "You give off a stink like a herd of sixfeet." A warrior punched him in the stomach, then chopped him across the neck as he doubled up. Three other dockmen were disposed of, quickly and silently. The warriors doused the dockmen's lanterns; in almost total darkness, most of the raiders left the galley. Many carried kegs of gunpowder as well as their weapons.

Boulder came up to the afterdeck with a keg under his arm. The steersman flinched away, but the centaur ignored him. By the light of a small lantern, he loaded the two small cannons. He worked carefully, making sure each charge was tamped down properly. Then he put a scrap of slow match in the lantern flame. Blowing softly on the glowing red tip of the match, he waited.

Out of the darkness came the sounds of creaking wood and slapping water. Voices drifted with odd clarity from craft moored out in the harbor. From the darkened buildings along the waterfront came laughter and curses, and the wailing of a bagpipe. The rhythmic thud of soldiers marching in step echoed off the high walls of the buildings. Behind those noises was the low hum of the city itself.

The warble of a firewing carried faintly down the waterfront. The cry came again, from the opposite direction, and then a third and fourth from close at hand. Eyas answered with three short trills. Boulder turned one of the cannons on its swivel, and put the slow match to the touch hole.

The shot crashed into the third-story window of a building overlooking the waterfront. Bricks and glass erupted; fire flared through smoke and dust. Shouts and screams were drowned out by the second shot, which blew a hole in the next building's front.

"All right—everyone onto the dock!" Eyas shouted. The steersman and rowers clattered over the side. Boulder and Eyas leaped to the main deck; Boulder jammed the slow match into the gunpowder keg and dropped it down a hatch. Then they too went onto the dock, and Eyas swung up into the saddle.

"Get away from the ship," Eyas commanded as Boulder charged through the Deltans. They ran up the dock behind the centaur, and scattered into the darkness. With a muffled thump and a geyser of orange fire, the galley exploded.

Up and down the waterfront, other explosions thundered. Docks and sheds burned, and in their red light lotors and centaurs came running to assemble. The Homelanders stood nervously waiting in an alley, swords drawn.

"Now for the northern gate," Eyas said to Godhonor. The mercenary nodded and pointed up the alley.

The raiders moved in a solid mass behind the mercenaries: centaurs and riders, then lotors. People crowding the streets vanished, or ran terrified ahead of the raiders. Pale faces stared down from dark windows, until lotor arrows drove them away. More fires broke out as Bandish warriors hurled torches through doorways knocked down by the centaurs' hoofs. A squad of Deltan soldiers blundered into the raiders, and ran away up a side street without striking a blow. Arrows swarmed after them.

As they pushed deeper into the city, the streets grew wider and more crowded: many peasants, seeking shelter in the city, were sleeping in gutters and doorways. Those who could not escape stood passively, eyes cast down at the cobblestones, as if awaiting death. The raiders passed them by.

They burst into a wide thoroughfare, lined by tall tenements with columned porches where lamps burned and hundreds of Deltans crowded away from the raiders. Eyas saw people trampled in the crush, and their screams were like blows. "Faster!" he shouted to Godhonor.

Pairs of soldiers had been patrolling the avenue. Most vanished; those who offered combat were chopped down. The raiders moved north, into a darker and less crowded stretch of the avenue, until they came to a circular intersection with a fountain at its center. On the far side stood a mass of pikemen. They blocked the avenue, and Eyas was sure that Deltan riders waited in some side street to smash into the invaders' flank.

He turned and shouted to the lotors, "Shoot over our heads—beyond the fountain!" Arrows sang swiftly. The pikemen, who could not even see the archers, began to drop where they stood. "Again!"

The second volley opened real gaps, and the Bandish riders charged in. Their centaurs knocked pikes aside, or pulled them like grass stems. The Deltans broke formation. Those who escaped into alleys or doorways were ignored; those who ran up the avenue were trampled. Eyas heard shouts from the rear, and the bawl of sixfeet: the ambushers had not expected a rush on the pikemen, and were grouping for pursuit.

The raiders met no more serious resistance until they neared the northern wall of the city; an occasional brick fell from a rooftop, but that was all. They ran through stinking streets, slipping now and then on the wet cobblestones, while dark figures receded into shadows. To Eyas it seemed almost like the vision of Hell he had had at Longstrand, made worse by the noise of terrified children and howling warriors.

Winded, the raiders slowed to a walk as they approached the city wall. Gunshots rang out from the parapet, wounding several centaurs and knocking a warrior dead on the street.

"The gate is a good five hundred paces to the left," said Godhonor. "They'll chop us to bits if we go on up the avenue and along the wall. We'll have to use the side streets and then rush the gate."

"Good," said Eyas, and followed the mercenaries into a lightless lane. The houses here were low, little more than huts, and showed few signs of life: a scent of cooking, a baby's wail. In the distance a bell rang steadily, and men shouted from the city wall. More faintly came the deep cries of centaurs and the shrilling of lotors. Gunfire crackled far to the north. Eyas took a deep breath: the assault from outside was underway.

At an intersection, Godhonor turned right and Eyas saw

the northern gate, a dark square against the yellow-gray brick of the towers on either side of it.

"To the gate, quickly," he ordered, and Boulder leaped past the mercenaries.

Between the northernmost houses and the gate stretched an empty space many spans wide. The raiders charged silently into the gap, while Deltan arrows and bullets fell among them. But the attackers outside were distracting the soldiers on the wall, forcing them to disperse their fire. Boulder reached the gate, a double door two spans high and built of heavy iron-bound timbers. Two great beams secured the doors; Boulder and another centaur heaved one out of its great iron bracket, then the other. The doors swung inward a little, and Eyas glimpsed dark figures advancing from the north: centaurs and riders, Riverines and peasants, while lotors launched covering barrages of arrows. Cannons boomed along the wall, filling the air with the stink of gunpowder. The doors swung wider.

Eyas looked over his shoulder and saw Deltan riders clattering north out of the dark streets, toward the raiders clustered about the gate. Lotor arrows dropped some of them, yet the Deltans came on, lances lowered. If they were not stopped, they would trap the raiders in the gateway; if the raiders scattered, the Deltans could shut the door against the assault from outside. He drew his sword and pointed to the Deltans:

"Attack! Keep them away from the gate until our warriors can reach us!"

The raiders turned with a roar and charged back across the flagstoned space, while spears and arrows sliced among them from the defenders on the wall. The Deltan riders' sixfeet slowed a little at the sight and sound of their centaur cousins, but the riders whipped their brutes onward.

Eyas, at the head of the raiders' counterattack, saw Godhonor running alongside. The Homelander met his gaze for an instant, then halted as if unable to keep up with Boulder's long strides. Then Godhonor swung his pike over the centaur's shoulder and down hard across Eyas's chest.

The blow knocked Eyas out of the saddle with such force that he scarcely felt the second shock of the stone pavement. His sword was gone; he gasped for air. Godhonor dragged Eyas to one side, while the other mercenaries, seeing what had happened, fell in around their leader and his captive. A

Deltan rider bore down on the mercenaries, his lance gleaming.

"Go by, go by!" brayed Godhonor. "We're Guardian's men, you great dolt! Make room, let us by!"

Eyas heard the crash of Deltans and centaurs colliding, the buzz of arrows and the cries of dying men. Even Boulder's great shout of rage and despair seemed very far away.

9

For a long time he was carried and dragged, struck and kicked. Torches and faces swam out of darkness and receded again. Once he was aware of being marched down a dim corridor. He lay on damp stone, tasting his own blood. Hands gripped him and released him. Men laughed and cursed, their voices echoing. It was very quiet.

Eyas blinked and squinted in bright sunlight. He was lying on his side on coarse gravel, his hands tied over his stomach. He drew a breath and winced at pain in his side, his face, his legs. His ankles were hobbled by a short length of braided leather. Water trickled busily somewhere nearby. As his vision cleared, Eyas saw a small plant, a sort of shrub, growing out of sandy soil. Its leaves and branches gleamed in the sunlight. It was made of silver.

He sat up. He was in a small garden, surrounded by windowless walls twice the height of a man. Overhead was blue sky and the dark loom of the Pillar. All around him were plants, flowers, and trees; all were made of silver and gold, with blossoms of precious stones. A golden dragonfly perched on a flower whose petals were polished jade. A willow trailed golden branches in a pool.

The gravel path on which he sat led from a shadowed doorway to a table of marble in the center of the garden. There sat a thin old man, beardless and shaven-headed, in a heavy red cloak. He was eating cakes and dried fruit with quick gestures, and he chewed noisily.

"You're awake, are you?" The old man beckoned to him. "Come and break your fast. But move slowly, or you will die."

Eyas got to his feet and shuffled down the path. His legs

267

trembled, and he sank heavily onto the bench across the table from the man.

"The honey cakes are very good, and the apricots. Butter, jam, syrup—" He waved a bony hand over a tray of delicate enameled bowls. "And strong tea."

Eyas ate hungrily, savoring the rich and unfamiliar flavors despite his sore jaw and cracked lips. The tea, dark and astringent, warmed him. The old man watched him eat.

"Now to talk. I am Guardian. You are the leader of the rabble outside the city."

"I am a prisoner. I lead no one."

"Don't play the fool. You are Eyas Fisher. Godhonor said you come from a land by the western sea."

"Yes."

"And you intended to conquer this land before waging war on the Suns."

"Yes."

"Well, well. You have come a long way for such modest ambitions. Why not march up the Bridge of Heaven to conquer Skyland and the moon?"

"I have no quarrel with Skyland."

"Nor with me, yet here you sit, with your army outside my gates."

"The Riverines and lotors are my allies, and they have quarrels enough with you." Eyas looked coldly at the fur trim on Guardian's cloak: lotor fur, set with small roundstones. "And I knew I would need all of Delta's strength before I could attack the Dominance."

"No doubt you would. The Suns grow in power with every breath they draw. Some day they will try their strength against us. We will defeat them as we are defeating you, by drawing you in and crushing you. But it will be a terrible war; may it not come in my lifetime. Yet you think you could conquer them with a few brutes and a mob of nameless ones."

"I know I could."

"To what end? Would you establish a Dominance of the brutes over men?"

"No. But each people would keep to its own land, and live in peace."

"And live in peace. A fine dream, especially in a warrior. But who would rule? Who would enforce such peace?"

Eyas knew he was being mocked, but had no heart for a duel. "Each people would rule itself as it chose. Perhaps there would be new wars, but they would be costly. We northerners know we could never fully conquer the south, even if we wanted to. And if the south attacked us again, we could defend ourselves; we know how to now."

Guardian snorted and shook his head. "Perhaps barbarians can afford to rot in their hovels, but we cannot. We are too many; we must take new land. Our nameless ones breed too fast—so do the Names, for that matter—and the land yields less each year. If you yourself ruled Delta, you would soon be warring on your old friends, or seeing your new subjects starve. And if they chose not to starve, they would overthrow you and put someone in your place who would win new land for them."

"If they had no Great Names to support, my subjects would eat as well as you and I have." Eyas nodded at the remains of the breakfast.

"Would they indeed! Do you know that I am the twentieth Guardian? My dynasty has ruled for over three centuries—because we know how to rule, we and the Great Names. Without us, the nameless ones would die. They are stupid and ignorant; they would use next year's seed to make a keg of beer. Look how they followed you, trusting as baby longfurs led to the slaughter. The fields go unplowed, the orchards unpruned. The canals will soon be clogged with weeds; by summer the northern provinces will have no food at all. It will mean famine. Even if your followers left at once, and the peasants went back to their fields, fifty thousand would still die. Another twenty days of this war, and twice as many will starve. Yet you would deprive them of their rulers, and doom them, to no purpose. Eventually someone would seize power, restore the Great Names, and found a new dynasty. It has happened before: rulers went soft, the canals went untended, and new rulers took over. But it will not happen now."

"No," said Eyas. "An easy oath to that."

Guardian smiled, surprised. "You sound like Godhonor. A fine young fellow, for a foreigner. I wish I could have trusted him."

"So do I. I was sure he had come over to us."

"Oh, he had. Do not think he plotted to betray you. But he saw how the fight was going last night, and thought to buy his way back with you." The old man slurped his tea. "He and his fellow mercenaries bought themselves a quick death, and that was something. You will envy them before long."

Eyas ignored him, drew into himself, and farheard. It was like stepping into a waterfall: his perceptions whirled past the breathing of the hidden guards, past the clatter of a kitchen, past the monotone wail of someone in a stone-walled room, past the cacophony of the crowded city, to the sounds of cannon fire and guns, the shrill cries of lotors and the shouts of Bandish warriors.

He came back to himself. Guardian had stood up, overturning his bench, and was brandishing a dagger; four tall soldiers stood in front of the old man, spears poised at Eyas's chest.

"You are in no danger, Guardian. At least, not from me. My army is busy near your northern gate."

The guards looked dismayed. Guardian snorted and spat phlegm on a golden flower.

"A clever trick, and an easy guess. Will you now clothe yourself in fire, or strike terror in me with your voice?"

"What will *you* do, Guardian? Will you kill me, and hope my army loses courage? Perhaps they will fight all the harder. Will you spare me, and bargain with barbarians? Centaurs drive hard bargains. Will you hold out until more mercenaries come? Can you feed this city for long?"

"Be still." Guardian slowly sheathed his dagger. "A place has been prepared for you. The guards will take you there. Your friends will not know your fate unless I choose." He brushed absently at a jam stain on his cloak, turned, and walked away.

The guards carried Eyas out of the garden, down long flights of stairs, and dumped him in a cold room. It was lighted only by a small window high in one wall. A pile of moldy straw was the bed; the walls were slimy with damp. The door shut silently behind him.

Eyas rolled onto the straw and watched a narrow slit of sunshine on the wall opposite the window. The bellow of a sixfoot came faintly from outside, and the shout of a human. From very far away came a sporadic thumping: cannons. He listened, while the sunlight moved across the wall, and took a strange comfort from the sounds of life. At last he fell asleep.

That night the beatings began.

Men burst into his cell, struck him with iron-tipped batons, kicked him with practiced skill. When they tired, one of them propped Eyas against a wall and shouted,

"How many in your army? How many men? How many centaurs? Lotors?"

Eyas gasped for air and said nothing.

"How many? What weapons? How many weapons?"

The questions and beatings went on all night; the men were too adept to let him escape into unconsciousness. All that day he drowsed, waking when clotted blood filled his mouth. That night the men returned.

It went on, a dream without escape, until he lost track of time. He never saw his attackers' faces. Sometimes he heard, even over the shouted questions, a low, monotone wail; perhaps it was himself. When he slept, the dead crowded around him and whispered silently in his head, jeering and mocking. Then, as if losing interest, they ceased to haunt him; in his sleep he called out to Sky, to Old, to Netweaver, but silence answered him.

One morning he woke to see the stripe of sunlight far lower on the wall than he had last noticed: summer must be here. He was warm. A blanket had been thrown over him. Beside him was a wooden bowl; instead of the usual breadseed paste, it held fried whiteroot and steamed vegetables still warm from the fire. For a dizzy moment Eyas wondered if he had finally answered their questions. No; but perhaps they feared he might die.

The inside of his mouth was badly cut, and his jaw was stiff and swollen; he had to break the food into morsels and chew them slowly. His hands, swollen by the bonds on his wrists, fumbled awkwardly. It took a long time to empty the bowl.

The door opened. Two stocky men, in leather tunics and dirty kilts, came in and lifted Eyas to his feet. They hauled him out into the corridor, up a flight of wooden stairs, and into a high-walled yard. They cut his bonds and pulled off his filthy clothes. One of them threw a bucket of soapy water over Eyas, tossed him a sponge, and let him clean himself.

When he was dry, the men gave him a rough, colorless shirt and knee-length trousers, of the sort worn by peasants, and took him back into the building. They went up several flights of stairs, along corridors with tile floors and paneled walls, and at last into a room overlooking a small garden. The air was sweet with incense. Sunshine streamed in through large glass windowpanes. Not far away, someone was playing a stringed instrument, filling the room with a simple, pleasing tune.

"Stay here," said one of the guards—the first words they had spoken to him.

Eyas sat down on a beautifully carved chair by the window. He looked down into the garden, bright with flowers and trees growing heavy with fruit. Apart from the music, he heard nothing.

"I greet you, Eyas Fisher."

A woman had entered from an adjoining room. She was young, dressed in a white robe embroidered with gold; her yellow hair fell over her shoulders in thick braids. With a grace that reminded Eyas of Silken, she crossed the room and sat facing him. She studied him with a mixture of sympathy and distaste.

"They have not treated you well. But that is all over now."

"Is it?" His own voice sounded harsh and strange to him.

"The Great Name Bronze commanded that you be tortured. He and his faction are no longer . . . in favor. I am the NameWoman Whiteflower; I speak for another group. We now have the ear of Guardian—"

"Whiteflower," Eyas interrupted. "The lotors revere a NameWoman Whiteflower."

"The lotors?"

"She went alone to the Narrow Sea, two thousand years ago—during the brutes' war against the Hand of the Templars. She killed herself to show the lotors and centaurs that her people wanted peace. The Suns have a poem about her."

"Indeed. I did not know that. Well, I too seek peace. I hope I can gain it without . . . that." She licked her lips. Eyas realized she was frightened of him. "I must tell you that the siege goes on. The fighting is terrible."

"That is why I am still alive," Eyas said.

"I cannot say. But I am glad that you are. Now that Guardian listens to wiser counsel than Bronze's, we may bring the war to a quick end."

"How?"

"A bargain: we will release you if your army raises the siege. All will have safe conduct back over the mountains, including our own nameless ones who choose to stay with you. Guardian will sign a treaty of peace and friendship with the Riverines and the Bands."

"But not with the brutes?"

"Well—"

"No matter. Go on."

"Each of your soldiers will be given ten gold pieces. Twice as much for your—officers. A thousand for each of your generals, and ten thousand for yourself. In addition, you are welcome to the treasures of Grandmarket."

Eyas felt weariness ache in him. He slumped down in his chair and rubbed his swollen face. "Guardian does not bargain."

"He does now."

"Then he bargains too late, and his offer is too low."

She shrank at the harshness of his voice, then wrapped herself in cold reserve. "May I ask—?"

"I want his whole army. If he wants to keep his throne, he's welcome to it. But I want his army."

"I see. Bronze's men have not broken your spirit."

"Do not mock with me, Whiteflower. I have not come all this way from the west to be bought off with a woman's smile and an old man's bribes. Let him kill me, or yield to me."

"Eyas, I beg of you—think! If you will not deal with us, Bronze—or someone worse—may gain Guardian's ear. If your own life means nothing to you, think of your allies. Will you throw those lives away in a futile war?"

"My allies are out of my control; they can fight or flee as they choose. Think yourself of Deltans' lives." He rubbed his wrists. "I do not think Guardian is the old fool you say he is. I think he alone ordered me imprisoned, and he alone ordered me brought here. You do his bidding, not he yours."

She looked down at her hands. "You are a very strange young man. Are all your people like you?"

"My people were destroyed by the Suns. Now my people are the men and brutes outside your walls."

Her blue eyes met his gray ones. "I will tell Guardian your answer. He will not be pleased. You have been standing on a precipice, Eyas, and now it has given way beneath you."

Eyas said nothing. Whiteflower stood, bowed gracefully, and left the room. A few moments later, four soldiers came in from the corridor.

"Come with us."

They did not fetter him, but he walked with swords at his back and sides. His guards took him down into the garden, through doors and along hallways, until at last they came to a lane where a team of four black sixfeet stood hitched to an open wagon. The guards put Eyas in the back of the wagon. Chains, bolted to the sides, were locked around his wrists. A pole between his legs kept him standing.

A guard gripped Eyas by the hair and slashed his forehead with a dagger. Eyas felt hot blood run down his face.

"You didn't flinch. Good. Don't cry out, no matter what happens, or you'll be dying for days. Keep still, and it could be over by dawn." He slapped Eyas's arm companionably.

A young soldier, heavily armored, pulled himself onto the driver's bench. His face was a red-and-yellow mass of sores and pimples, and he wiped a creamy discharge from the corners of his eyes. After giving Eyas a dull-witted grin, the driver turned and shook the reins; the brutes lumbered down the lane. Ahead of them went an escort of riders, pounding drums and shaking rattles.

They came out into a crowded street, where foot soldiers used clubs to clear a path. A mass of faces glared up at Eyas: some amused, some angry, some hateful, but most only curious. Few were well-dressed, and all looked thin and underfed. Someone threw a stone that clanged off the driver's wide-brimmed helmet. More stones flew out of the crowd. A bottle crashed against a wheel; a lump of sixfoot dung struck Eyas's shoulder. Blood, clotting on his eyelids, made it hard to see. The roar of the crowd reminded Eyas of the waters rushing through the Rip.

In a whisper, he began his family song, while stones pelted down upon the wagon. The sixfeet, struck by occasional stones, bellowed; Eyas called out to them, and they quietened. Their driver turned to squint at him, then slapped the reins. The brutes broke into a trot, and Eyas went back to his song. More stones struck him, but he was deep within himself and did not feel them.

At last the shouts lessened and the stoning ceased. The wagon began to climb. Blinking, Eyas saw that they were ascending a ramp. He looked up and saw the Pillar, dark against the warm blue summer sky. The ramp spiraled up it, broad enough for two wagons. Soldiers stood motionless along the sides of the ramp, staring at Eyas but ignoring the long line of half-naked slaves who bore loads of firewood. A few soldiers called out cheerful insults to the pimple-faced driver, and he answered in kind.

The ascent seemed longer than the journey through the streets. A chill wind gusted from the northwest, but on the south side of the Pillar the sun was warm. As the ramp wound high above the red-tiled rooftops, Eyas looked out and saw fields untended but bright with the green of early summer. Not far beyond the city walls he saw the raw yellow earth of the allies' camps and trenches. Now and then a puff of smoke bloomed above the earthworks, followed by the dull thud of a cannon.

The defenders made no reply, but Eyas saw soldiers massed behind the northern gate, as if preparing for a great sortie. Thousands must have been crowded into the open space before the gate; they spilled over into nearby streets and lanes. Rooftops were dark with people watching the soldiers, and the whole city hummed like an immense hive.

So they would kill him, and announce the fact to the besiegers—perhaps fling his head into their trenches. Then they would attack while the allies were still shocked and demoralized. In Guardian's place, he might do the same. The scheme would probably work, but at a greater cost than the Deltans imagined: the allies would make one last vengeful assault and only then retreat. Eyas grieved for the useless deaths his own death would cause. The lotors, at least, had the prospect of the other realm, and perhaps death would be no endless sorrow for the centaurs. But for the Bands and Riverines and Deltan peasants, only Hell awaited. When he himself had died and been fed upon, the remnant of his soul would perhaps feed upon his friends, as hungry and pitiless as any Messenger.

Near the top of the Pillar, a downdraft brought the smell of smoke, mixed with a putrid stink. Eyas looked up. Projecting well beyond the rim of the Pillar's top were a number of wooden beams. At their ends hung human bodies, wrapped in chains. Blackbeaks flapped about the corpses, or clung to the chains while they pecked and tore at the bodies. A lump of carrion fell from one body; a diving blackbeak snapped it up.

The wagon reached the top, a flagstoned platform perhaps twelve spans across. In its center burned the fire, under a conical roof of blackened iron. The wind blew its smoke away to the southeast, across the city and the misty river. Soldiers and slaves stood watching as the wagon halted by a low, flat-roofed building—little more than a hut—of stone and mortar. Its door opened, and Guardian stepped out.

"Did he cry out?" he asked the driver.

"No, Guardian. Just kept up some barbarian song, and once he calmed the sixfeet."

"Well enough. He does well to make peace with his gods." The old man turned his gaze on Eyas. "You were offered peace and riches, and you rejected them. Now you will live just long enough to see your army smashed. After that I will give you a quicker death than you deserve."

He nodded to a soldier in splendid armor, who bowed and undid Eyas's chains. Others pulled him from the wagon and dragged him to the base of a beam. The chains were a sort of cocoon, into which they thrust him. Leather straps were buckled tightly across his chest, his stomach, and his legs. A soldier hauled on a rope, and Eyas was carried out to the end of the beam, five spans from the edge of the Pillar. His hands were free; he wiped clotted blood from his eyes and looked down. Directly below was the smooth, steep-sloping side of the Pillar, dizzyingly far. If he fell, he would strike the wall and then the ramp. He might undo the straps easily enough, but would have no escape except by traversing the rope beneath the beam. The soldiers would have plenty of time to put a bullet or crossbow bolt in him, or simply to free the rope and let him fall.

The wind gusted, swinging him like an apple on a bough. The blackbeaks circled him, moaning and yapping, before returning to their meal.

"Can you see well?" called Guardian. "We will signal the attack soon, after our heralds announce your whereabouts to your army." A soldier, holding a disc of polished copper, reflected a flash of sunlight toward the northern gate.

Almost at once, a group of riders went out, across the scarred and trampled land between the city and its besiegers. The cannon fire slowly ceased; even the hum of the city seemed to lessen. The tiny figures of the heralds approached the siege line, and halted. Eyas saw a party of centaurs and riders go out to meet them. After a brief pause, the centaurs turned and ran; the heralds withdrew at an easy trot.

Eyas could see the news traveling along the siege line: men and brutes came out on their earthworks, and even their shouts could be heard on the wind. Centaur war songs rumbled like distant waterfalls, full of grief and wrath.

A sudden cannonade erupted from the city walls, sending up geysers of smoke and dirt along the earthworks. The northern gate swung wide and the Deltans charged out, cheering, in a musical clatter of harness and armor. They paused only to form a broad wedge. They were a mass of color and glitter, flashing with pennants of blue and yellow and white, and they moved with grace and precision as they advanced on the besiegers.

"Wait. Wait," Eyas muttered. "Wait for them."

Lotors loosed volleys of arrows. As Deltans and their mounts were struck, the wedge slowed a little, then went on. The volleys had been weak, and now they ceased altogether. Eyas saw the siege line empty as men and brutes retreated. The Deltans quickened their pace, shouting.

Just as their vanguard approached the earthworks a cloud of fire and smoke engulfed the point and center of the wedge. Three more explosions went off along the line, doing little harm but disrupting the Deltans' attack. Even at this distance, Eyas felt the concussions.

The wind soon cleared the smoke. Hundreds of men and sixfeet lay dead or dying, while the rest of the Deltans milled about, fearing more explosions if they crossed into the besiegers' trenches. The besiegers themselves were gone. At last, driven forward by their officers, the Deltans advanced.

Guardian stood near the edge of the platform, by the scaffold that supported Eyas's beam. Flashes of reflected sunlight winked in the distance; the soldier in gaudy armor translated the messages for the impassive old man. The siege was ended; all around the city, the trenches were empty. Riders had pursued a handful of invaders to the northwest, but had been halted at a demolished bridge. It was obvious that the allies' main force had left some time before, perhaps several days, leaving only enough warriors behind to maintain the illusion of a siege.

The sun began to sink, and the wind grew chillier. Guardian wrapped himself in a cloak of lotors' fur and spoke at last to Eyas.

"Your friends have deserted you, it seems. So much for the loyalty of brutes and barbarians. But your stubbornness was a favor to me, Eyas; this victory is cheaper than the compromise I offered you."

"Victory?" Eyas laughed, feeling light-headed and remote from himself. "Your own men lie dead before your gates, Guardian. My people are unbeaten. They will retreat to the northwest, away from the garrisons you left along the River, and hide in the White Mountains. Your army here will not be able to overtake them."

Guardian smiled and pulled his hood over his shaven head. In the light of the setting sun his face looked like a golden mask. "My army will pursue them, yes, but only to herd your rabble. If they retreat to the northwest, so much the better; Brightspear will finish them off for me."

Eyas gripped the web of chains. The wind seemed colder in the dusk. "The Sun."

"He crossed the Bitter River at Grand Forks ten days ago, with a great army. Obviously he thinks to conquer us after we have been weakened by you. I will turn his own strategy against him. Your followers will blunder into his army soon. They may fight valiantly, but your rabble cannot stand against trained Sunnish troops. When the Suns are weary and off guard, my own army will fall upon them."

"You knew he was coming. You knew, yet your woman tried to bribe me to go away." For the first time since the night in the Black Gates, Eyas felt rage boil within him. "You old fool—my quarrel is with Brightspear, not with you. I would gladly have made a pact with you, and marched with your armies."

Guardian's face was unreadable now in the deepening dusk, but his dry chuckle was full of mockery. "I make no pacts with brutes and barbarians. I too have a quarrel with Brightspear, but mine is the just quarrel of a whole empire, not of some sulking young savage. We have watched the Suns grow in arrogance over the centuries, and we knew that some day we or they must rule Alland. I told you once that I feared the coming of that day, but that was before I saw how your rabble might be useful as unwitting allies. Now I see that we shall win after all; shall I share the glory with a mob of bandits and brutes, and a young fool? We have no need of your friendship. The gods speak to our priests; they foresaw your coming, and told us to let you come unhindered to my walls. Now they tell us we shall conquer the Suns as well."

"Did your gods foretell that the Black Gates would be filled with light?" asked Eyas. "Did your gods send an army to lie in wait for us, only to run in terror? You are a fool indeed, Guardian, if you believe your gods."

The old man shook his head. "You defile yourself with blasphemy in your last hours. Pray to your own gods to intercede with ours, whom you have offended. I will speak with you in the morning, before you die." He turned and went into the hut.

With their master within earshot, the soldiers on the platform made a show of themselves, pacing rigidly about the fire, snapping orders to the woodbearers, and striking poses along the low wall. Down in the city, lights burned, revealing endless lines of soldiers marching through the gates of the city. But by midnight the lights were out again, and quiet fell. On the platform the only noise was the steady roar of the fire; from the city came occasional sounds of celebration or sorrow, a drunken cheer, a woman's scream. The wind blew, humming through the ropes and chains.

Clouds scudded across the Bridge, dimming it; the moon had long since set. Eyas shifted his weight in his web of chains, while the wind turned him one way and another. He ached, and his body longed for sleep. At last, despite himself, he dozed.

Something landed with a light thud on the beam above him. Eyas woke and looked up. The sky was completely, unnaturally dark overhead. But in the orange flicker of the fire he saw a windwalker crouched on the beam. It was a male, bearing a glass-edged sword and clad in a harness of red leather.

"I greet you, Eyas," the windwalker whispered.

"I greet you, Soarfar."

"Once you saved me on the ground; now I save you in the air."

Eyas looked up, beyond Soarfar, and realized that a flying island was moving slowly over the city, blotting out the sky. Pale shapes dropped from it, warriors gliding down toward the Pillar. An anchor whispered out of the dark and clanged against stone; it scraped across the platform and caught on one of the brick columns supporting the roof over the fire.

Soldiers sat up, shaking sleep from their heads. A slave cried out at his first glimpse of the windwalkers. Someone shouted an order. A sentry outside Guardian's hut went in to rouse him.

Three more windwalkers settled onto the beam; above them was a cluster of skyseeds, weighted by a stone. Almost casually, perched on the beam like firewings on a branch, they held the skyseeds steady while Soarfar hung upside down with his long prehensile toes curled round the rope that ran under the beam. His sword sliced through the leather straps that held the chains together around Eyas's body.

"Climb up to the skyseeds."

The chains were open, but Eyas clung to them. His arms trembled. As if in a dream, he saw soldiers grapple with windwalkers, slaves run toward the ramp, Guardian emerge from his hut in a long yellow sleeping robe, a dagger in his fist.

"Climb, Eyas!" Soarfar extended one long arm and let the wind lift him back to the beam. The same arm then reached down to Eyas; he grasped it and climbed. Something grazed his leg. He looked down and saw a short spear caught in the chains.

He pulled himself up onto the beam. Soarfar stepped off to clear Eyas's way to the windwalkers holding the skyseeds, but Eyas waved them off as well. While the windwalkers clung to the rope or hovered close by, Eyas crawled the length of the beam and jumped to the flagstones. Guardian saw him and shouted for help, but all his soldiers were locked in combat.

Eyas wrested the knife from the old man's hand. "One more chance, Guardian. I offer you alliance. Together we can break the Suns."

"No. I trust in the gods, not in brutes and renegades." He met Eyas's gaze. "Kill me; it will make no difference."

"You are right. You make no difference now, so your death would serve no purpose. Live, Guardian." He threw the dagger away, turned, and stepped to the low wall on the edge of the platform. A windwalker slipped a loop of rope under Eyas's arms, and tugged at a knot. It released the stone, and the skyseeds lifted him into the wind. Soarfar whooped twice. His warriors broke away from the Deltans, spread their arms, and lifted off the platform into the night. One or two Deltans fired guns at the attackers and were answered with a rain of glass-tipped darts.

The gondolas of the flying island were not far above the Pillar. Eyas saw windwalkers soar and hover about him, guiding his skyseed to one of the gondolas. A windwalker on the roof of the gondola caught Eyas and freed him from the rope; a hatch opened and Eyas slid through it into the room within.

It was dark, and smelled of straw and windwalkers. Several females and infants clucked and cooed around him, stroking him. One of them put a round fruit in his hand; he ate gratefully, tasting again the tart flavor of the fruit which Unsheath had given him long ago—perhaps in this same gondola.

Through the open windows came distant shouts, the bawling of sixfeet and the clang of bells. The gondola jolted a few times, and soon Eyas's ears began to ache. He realized the island must be rising. The sounds of the city faded away, and he heard only the creak of ropes and the cries of windwalkers.

Soarfar came through the hatch. "You are well? You are fed?"

"Yes. Ah, Soarfar! It is good to be here with you."

"We rejoice to have you." His long fingers stroked Eyas's face in the darkness.

"You must have known where to find me."

"The centaur Boulder told me yesterday."

"Boulder? Where?"

"Near the mountains. We crossed them last night, and in the dawn saw a great army marching northwest—your army. Boulder told me you were a prisoner in that great stonepile, or perhaps slain. I thought we might rescue you, or at least avenge you. Now we climb to a northflowing airstream. In the morning you will be with your people."

Eyas touched his friend's arm. "I will plant the skyseed groves again, and look for your coming each year."

"So may it be."

"Tell me, Soarfar—how did the army come to be where you found it?"

"Boulder said he could see no quick end to the siege, yet more and more humans were joining your army—too many to feed. He and the others chose to retreat to the mountains, and prepare for more fighting in the spring."

"Did you see another army as well? Suns?"

"We saw dust not far to the west of your people. It may have been herders, going up into the hills. But I told Boulder of it. If the Suns are that far east, it is a great wonder. They have not warred on the canal diggers for many generations."

"I think they come to war on me, not on the Deltans."

"Then they owe me much for bringing you away from the stonepile."

"Stay with us, and collect your debt."

The windwalker smacked his lips, amused. "If the winds will it."

Eyas had stripped off his dirty, bloodstained clothes, and now burrowed into the straw to keep warm. Several windwalkers, adults and infants alike, crowded around him in the darkness. The island seemed to hang unmoving for a time, and then swayed a little.

"We are in the northern stream," said Soarfar. "Soon we will pass over Delta again, or near it; not long after dawn we should reach your army." He was silent for a time. "We were in the Gulf not long ago."

"Tell me what you saw."

"The People are not completely conquered. Their villages are gone, but many escaped. We found some in the hills above Northport—and a fine stand of wild skyseed."

"Do they war against the Suns?"

"No. They hide. But the Suns do not hunt them much. Since Brightspear left the Gulf, his soldiers choose to stay in their forts. Someday the People may strike back, when the dreamwatchers bid them to."

"Dreamwatchers. Still they follow dreamwatchers." Shivering, Eyas fell asleep. Sky spoke to him, urging him to seek Mount Aspen, but he was not sure if it was a haunting or only a wishful dream. He woke, saddened, in the chilly darkness of the gondola, and was comforted by the nearness of his sleeping friends. Then he drowsed, waking often, until the windows glowed at last with blue-gray light. The infants, squeaking sleepily, crawled to their mothers' breasts; Eyas rose and went to a window. Soarfar joined him.

The island had descended again, and was flying roughly southeast. Not far to the north, the peaks of the White Mountains glowed pink in the dawn. Below the island, under scattered clouds, the land was a mottled surface of plains and hills, too dry for settled farmers but supporting a few wandering herders.

Eyas and Soarfar watched the sun come up, filling the gondola with a golden glow. Now the hills below were a dusty yellow-brown, casting long shadows across the valleys. Not far ahead, smoke or dust rose into the clear air.

"That must be your army," said Soarfar. "They are early on the march. I must see to the descent; eat with my family, and soon you will be safe on the ground." He bared sharp teeth in a grin, and hauled himself up through the hatch.

While Eyas ate fruit and hard, sweet bread, the gondola jolted and swayed. The windwalkers took no notice, and seemed untroubled by their ears, but to Eyas the noises of the island and the whoops of warriors were muted by growing pressure of air. At last his ears cleared, and he heard distinctly the sounds of battle: the thump of cannons, the cries of men and brutes.

He stood up quickly, grunting at the pain in his legs and back, and reached for the rim of the hatch. From the roof of the gondola, clutching a rope, he looked down.

The island had descended by release of many skyseeds, and was now only fifty or sixty spans above arid, rugged terrain. Rocky slopes plunged into waterless gullies that widened into barren valleys. Directly ahead, a chain of low hills overlooked a dry lake bed that extended west into a canyon. On the hills an army was massed, looking at this distance like swarming black ants. Hundreds of riders and thousands of foot soldiers waited behind the crests of the hills, where cannons fired steadily to the south. Wagons hastened between the cannons and a camp north of the hills, carrying shot and powder. Obviously the attack had just begun, and had been prepared in haste.

Even from this height, Eyas could not see clearly into the lake bed; smoke and dust obscured it. But he knew his army must be there, for the army on the hills was Sunnish. Somewhere down there, perhaps beneath one of the countless black sunburst flags, stood Brightspear.

10

From the ground, the approach of the flying island must have been awesome and frightening, but it was no surprise. The Sunnish cannons kept on firing, while soldiers and riders watched the island bearing down upon them. Here and there, riflemen raised their weapons; the Suns could not tell whether the windwalkers meant to attack, or simply to fly over the battlefield, but they were taking no chances.

Soarfar glided down to stand beside Eyas. He grinned ferociously. "More fighting! We cannot stay long, but we will hurt them while we can."

Anchorstones dropped, and grappling hooks, mooring the island at a height of about fifty spans over the hillside where the Suns' main force was concentrated. The soldiers' ranks broke in places as the stones and hooks thudded down among them. Some tried to chop through the ropes, but were driven off or killed as glass darts fell glittering upon them. The musical sound of glass striking iron was almost drowned out by the cries and shouts of the Suns as they sought shelter under the shields of their pikemen.

"I must get down to my people," said Eyas. "This is the battle I came to fight."

"In time, in time. First we must take prizes, and slay the cannon men." Soarfar drew his glass-edged sword and barked a command; more darts fell, most thickly upon the cannon emplacements, and scores of warriors swooped from the island. They dropped with arms at their sides, swift as stooping hawks; then, just above the cannons, they slowed their descent and glided with terrible grace upon the cannon crews. Rifle shots sputtered; a few windwalkers fell dying from the air. But most, with swords dripping, soared up over the lake bed and returned to the attack.

A great shout came out of the dust and smoke on the lake bed as the allies saw the windwalkers. The wind freshened, clearing the air, and Eyas saw a thick line of centaurs charging up the hillsides towards the cannons. Bandish war cries shuddered on the air. Behind the centaurs and their riders came pikemen, lotors, Deltans, advancing up the slopes.

More dust blew away, and Eyas shouted with amazement as the rest of the allied army stood revealed. The men and brutes who had come through the Black Gates were many, yet they seemed few compared to the vast numbers of Deltan peasants who now began to follow the warriors towards the Sunnish line. It was not an army; it was a people, a nation of countless tens of thousands. Plodding behind the army's warriors, they bore few arms. Most carried only a few possessions, or pulled handcarts, yet they were more awesome in their strength than the centaurs charging ahead of them. As they came up out of the lake bed they sang until their voices drowned out all else. Two or three Sunnish cannons still fired, slicing long rifts in that mass, rifts that healed themselves between one breath and the next. On they came, their songs a celebration; the allied warriors seemed to take strength from those songs, and quickened their pace as they neared the crest. Lances gleaming, swords high, they smashed against the Suns.

The first rifle volley was the only one. It did great slaughter among the Bandish warriors and the centaurs, but the riflemen could not fall back to reload; their own men, harassed by windwalkers' darts, had pressed forward and gave no room. Trapped against their comrades, the Sunnish riflemen died bloodily.

Behind the crowded foot soldiers, Sunnish riders hurried east and west, seeking the flanks of the allies. But the riders found no flanks: where the centaurs' line ended, pikemen or lotor archers advanced. Beyond them were the Deltan peasants, as unstoppable as the tide. Here and there, riders plunged into that moving mass, killed a few, and were pulled down. Their comrades turned back toward the Sunnish camp. Foot soldiers, perhaps thinking retreat had been ordered, fell back also.

What should have been a slaughter on the lake bed was now a near rout on the hills. Centaurs charged again and again; lotor arrows whirred into the Sunnish ranks; windwalkers swarmed down, their swords swift. The Suns gave way, stumbling over the bodies of their comrades as they retreated toward the low earthwork around their camp.

Soarfar flew back up to the gondola, with a human ear clutched in each long-toed foot. "Good fighting," he panted. "But now we must raise anchors. The airstream will change direction soon; we must take it while it still leads out to sea and the homeward stream. First we will put you back on the ground."

Directly beneath, the Suns were retreating, but the nearest of the allies were still well to the south, along the crest of the hill. Eyas pointed to them.

"Can you put me down among those centaurs?"

"Yes."

Once more, skyseeds were brought down and Eyas was suspended beneath them. A warrior pierced one; with three windwalkers guiding him, Eyas began to drop away from the gondola.

"Next year I will seek you in the Gulf," Soarfar called.

"If the winds will it. Farewell, Soarfar."

The skyseeds dropped him swiftly—too swiftly, for the wind had slackened a little. A Sunnish rifleman looked up from the melee and fired at Eyas as he drifted over. The bullet sang past, piercing a skyseed and wounding a windwalker just above it. The other two gripped the rope above Eyas's head and tried to slow his descent, to steer him to the crest. They failed.

He landed with a thump on the hillside, a hundred spans or more from the nearest centaurs, and among a startled group of Sunnish riders. Windwalkers suddenly swarmed around him, slashing and stabbing at the Suns to give Eyas room. A centaur, looking down from the battle on the crest, pointed his great sword at Eyas and plunged into the Sunnish ranks; bullets cut him down

Eyas shrugged off the rope. He was naked and unarmed amid his enemies, yet joy roared in him. Nearby, a rider fell from his mount, his throat gushing blood from a windwalker's thrust; Eyas climbed into the empty saddle. Sunnish riders closed in on him as the windwalkers rose.

"Go back!" Eyas shouted to the sixfeet. "Danger! Run away!"

The dull faces of the sixfeet contorted in terror; bawling, they reared and wheeled, striking out blindly with their clawed forefeet. The riders swayed in their saddles, cursing and slapping their frightened brutes. Eyas's mount, after a brief shudder, was calmed by his hand on its midshoulder. Eyas tugged the reins and wheeled, seeking a gap but finding none except to the north: between himself and the centaurs the Suns were packed like bricks in a wall.

To stay meant death. Eyas kicked his mount's flanks and rode it toward the Sunnish camp at a gallop, evading riders and foot soldiers who tried to bar his way. Somehow he must break out, circle the Suns, and gain safety. Again he shouted, and sixfeet scattered out of his path across the bodies of screaming soldiers.

Where were the windwalkers? He glanced up and saw them ascending to the island. An anchorstone heaved out of the earth, swinging dangerously as it rose. Others followed it. Then, from the island's ballast platforms, stones began to fall.

Beneath that bombardment, the Suns died in hundreds. Stones the size of a man's head crashed down on them like a hailstorm on breadseed stalks, and the army's discipline collapsed. Men ran maddened, stabbed one another, or fell praying on the ground only to be crushed by their comrades. The island's shadow moved away, but slowly, and it seemed a long time of blood and screaming before the stones no longer fell.

Eyas rode through carnage, right to the edge of the Sunnish camp before he was able to turn west. Behind him, the survivors of the bombardment were running toward the camp, while centaurs and pikemen pressed forward over the bodies of the dead and dying.

A rider trotted out from the camp, observing the rout with cool distaste. He looked at Eyas, and changed at once from a calm warrior to a gawking youth. Eyas recognized the face half-hidden under the rider's helmet: it was Victor of the Marchwardens, whose life he had spared on the logging road and again at Long Rampart. Victor reined in, then gathered his wits and drew his sword.

"To me! To me! It is Eyas Fisher! Hasten, hasten!"

More riders came from among the tents and wagons. Eyas said softly to his mount, "Now run—fast, fast." It obeyed, breaking into a jolting gallop that carried Eyas past Victor, past the perimeter of the camp, and out into the open country to the west. Victor pursued him, followed by twenty or more other riders.

The island was high over the lake bed now, gleaming like a green-gold cloud. The allies had broken over the hills, but the Suns' retreat was slowing. Officers rallied their men, resisting the assaults of the centaurs while the main force of the Suns began to form ranks near their camp. Beyond the camp to the east, the Deltan peasants flowed down the hillsides in dark rivers.

But they had not come over the hills to the west. The slope of the terrain and solid masses of Sunnish troops forced Eyas still farther from safety into gully-scarred hills. Victor and the other riders had fanned out into a long line; to try to turn into a gully and seek the canyon to the south would mean being intercepted.

The hills, low and rounded near the Suns' camp, grew steep and rocky. Eyas's sixfoot settled into a steady trot; sweat gleamed in its coarse black hair as it scrambled up one hillside and down the next. Eyas sought a thicket, a ravine— anything that might conceal him—but the hills offered nothing but clumps of yellow grass and scattered thorn bushes, and he was never out of sight of his pursuers for long. Carrying armored men, the Suns' mounts tired more rapidly than his own; each time he looked back, Eyas saw the gap widen. But he knew they would take him in the end, and they must want him alive: more than once he had been in easy rifle shot, but they had not even tried to fire.

The late-morning sun glared down out of a white sky; the air shimmered with heat. As he topped a hill Eyas saw that the southernmost riders had found an easier path and were overtaking him more rapidly. He would have to turn north, toward ever-higher hills beyond which he could see the sharp white peaks of the mountains. It would be harder going, and already his mount was near exhaustion, its gray tongue lolling.

The sixfoot suddenly snorted and shied. Eyas caught the scent as well: the scent of a giant, pungent and unmistakable, bringing with it memories of the day long ago when he had sought Goldarms. The scent came from the north; what had brought a giant to this dry, treeless country? No matter—where a giant was, water must be nearby. He turned his mount to follow the scent. The sixfoot whined and moaned, but obeyed.

They came down into an empty streambed, whose white sand reflected the heat like a mirror. The scent was a little stronger here, mixed with that of water. The sixfoot's thirst made it forget its fear, and it shambled more quickly up the stream.

To the south, Eyas saw the Suns reach the streambed and turn into it, with a few taking the rougher terrain along its banks. They were no more than seven or eight hundred spans behind; he and his mount would be lucky to get more than a mouthful of water before they must go on.

The sides of the streambed gradually steepened, until he rode between stone walls twice the height of a centaur. The air buzzed with insects; a spider scuttled across his path, carrying a mouse in its jaws. The smell of water was strong now, that of the giant almost gone. In its place Eyas caught a whiff of something strange, a sour-sweet odor.

He followed the stream round a sharp bend and glimpsed a water hole under the steep east bank. At that moment something slapped his chest and arm. The sixfoot howled and bolted as Eyas swayed, gasping for breath, and fell heavily onto the hot sand.

He was lying on his back, and could feel little but a distant tingling on his chest. The sun blazed into his eyes, but he could not blink without a conscious effort. Each breath seemed to take all his strength.

Off to his left, next to the water hole, something moved. He glimpsed a blurred white shape striking out toward him, and heard it slap on the sand near his feet. At last he realized what had struck him: a walkingtree.

It scraped forward, and he could see it from the corner of his eye: a squat, bulbous trunk, mottled gray and brown and almost two spans high, its top covered with white, whiplike branches that half-concealed the vertical slit of its mouth-stomach. One of those branches had hit him, injecting its venom from the sting at the tip, and now it was trying to loop a branch around his leg and drag him across the sand.

Almost lost in the white glare of the sun, a hawk soared serenely overhead. Eyas tried to call it, but could not speak. It did not matter. Guardian had planned his death for dawn today; he had won a few more hours, enough to see many Suns die. That was something, and perhaps Brightspear himself had fallen by now under a centaur's sword or a Riverine's pike.

Hoofbeats drew near, and a voice called out in warning. Close by, someone dismounted and ran up to Eyas, gripped him, and dragged him across the ravine into a patch of shade. He saw black-clad warriors, sweating, warily approach the water hole with lowered rifles. Disturbed, the walkingtree rustled its branches and drew back on its roots against the far wall of the ravine. Hands that Eyas could not feel propped him up. He wished he could laugh: it seemed funny that the tree should be cheated of its prey.

"Step aside," a voice commanded quietly, and the soldiers around Eyas hastened away. A warrior walked into Eyas's field of vision. He wore no armor, only a black tunic and trousers tucked into boots. His dark hair fell into the folds of a yellow hood pulled back upon his shoulders. It was Brightspear.

"So, Eyas." Brightspear stood before him, thumbs hooked in his belt, sweat glistening on his scarred and sunburned face. He looked older, harder, and wearier than when Eyas had last seen him. "I might almost think the Goddess herself arranged this meeting; on a battlefield we would have had little chance to talk." He seemed to struggle to keep from smiling. "Has the venom robbed you of speech? Well, well; all prayers are answered in time. When you were very small, and used to follow me about, I often wished you would give me a moment's peace from your prattling."

He sat down beside Eyas and wiped his face. "Ah—the shade feels good. It has been a hot day's work—a battle, and then a long chase. Your windwalkers cost me a victory, but it doesn't matter; they brought you to me, after all."

His mood darkened a little. "Who would have thought your army would be so great? The Messenger told me it would lie in my path, but he said it was only a rabble of brutes and peasants. And a storm in the Gulf is only wind and water," he added with a snort. "Ah, you have done wonders, Eyas! The People would have to make clapsticks out of whole hemlocks to honor you properly. —You, there! Bring water."

A soldier hastened to the far side of the water hole, out of reach of the walkingtree, and returned with his helmet brimming. Brightspear took it and held the rim of the helmet to Eyas's lips. Most of the warm, brackish water dribbled from his mouth, but he managed to swallow a little. He could taste something that must be giant; it had come recently to drink, unafraid of the walkingtree. Brightspear took a long swallow, then poured the rest of the water over his head.

"Mmph. That's better. You know, when you escaped from Longstrand I knew somehow that you would find your way to me again. If a centaur would carry a man, that man was dangerous—and of course I already knew of your power over brutes. The Messengers cared little about you, but they are concerned with men, not animals. Their wisdom is great, but they have their limits. We had one with us today, but a dart slew him; the battle would have gone very differently if he had lived. Well...after this, perhaps they will heed me more, and command me less.

"We were beaten this morning, Eyas. You must have seen much of the battle. Beaten. What is left of my army follows close behind." He laughed almost silently. "It is an orderly retreat. Many of my men fought for my uncle when I first went back to the Dominance, and I gave them plenty of practice in retreating. Your forces seem slow to exploit their victory, so we should get across the Bitter River without trouble. If your officers are wise, they will go north, back to their homes. That will gain them a year or two of peace, while I recruit new armies and conquer Delta. Then—" He clicked his tongue. "I will destroy all the northerners, humans and brutes alike, for what was done today. All of them,

Eyas. Do you doubt me? I always do what I say I will do. Do you remember how Silken taught us *Redsandal's Glories*? I did not know it then—or perhaps I did—it was a prophecy:

> "'While the Bridge shall stand
> The Sun will rule with much might.
> His sword will slay cloudbrutes.
> His lance will fell centaurs.
> He will cast down all rebels.'

"I will have more than swords and lances, Eyas. The Messengers promise new weapons, deadlier than rifles. We will fly like windwalkers, and ride iron wagons that go without sixfeet. I will scourge Alland, and rule it from the Gulf to the Dawn Coast. The Messengers tell me that there are other lands, far across the Sea of Reefs, and they say my destiny is to rule them also."

He snapped his fingers. A soldier brought a pouch of salt meat and whiteroot.

"Soldier's fare. I eat what my men eat, live as they live, and take them into great danger. That's why they love me, Eyas—and why your army loves you. Did you hear the peasants singing? 'Eyas, Eyas, giver of names, giver of land!' There is a dangerous deed, teaching courage to peasants."

Brightspear rambled on, his voice soft and rapid, speaking of his adventures in the western mountains, the overthrow of his uncle and his triumphant entry into New Fort. It was as if he had spoken to no one for a long time. Eyas listened, but the words seemed faint and far away. As the venom began to weaken, he could feel a growing ache all over his body, distracting him from Brightspear's words.

"... I said, I have Darkhair."

With an effort, Eyas turned his head, and Brightspear smiled.

"Ah, you are still with me. Yes. He joined some Jadelandic pirates, and was captured a year ago. I had him brought to New Fort; he is imprisoned there, in good health. We have spoken together a few times, and he knows something of your adventures. He is proud of you, Eyas. I saw his smile when I told him how you held us off in the old tower on the cliffs."

A warrior, riding up the ravine, shouted something in a dialect Eyas could not understand. Brightspear sighed and stretched, lithe and powerful as a prowl.

"The brutes are pursuing us, and I must see to my army. I will tell you one more thing: I am glad you did not come back with me to the Dominance. You would have done too well. But as my enemy you have been useful; I will never have an enemy as great again."

"Only yourself," Eyas whispered, but Brightspear did not seem to hear. He stood up and nodded to two soldiers nearby.

"The tree has waited long enough. Give him to it. Goodbye, Eyas."

They gripped his wrists and ankles. Eyas spoke again: "When I come to you in your dreams, will you rejoice?"

Brightspear's eyes clouded. Eyas remembered the fear he had once seen in his mother Quiet's eyes; the same fear now lived in Brightspear.

"Be quick about it!"

They swung him twice, then threw him onto the sand near the walkingtree's roots. Its branches coiled smoothly around him and lifted him up. For an instant, poised before the tree's yawning white mouth, Eyas stared down at Brightspear and the others; they seemed shrunken, misshapen. Then it was over.

11

In darkness he saw; in silence he heard.

They were upon him at once, reaching for him. He heard their voices though they could not speak, saw their hands grope toward him though they had no substance. Cold enfolded him. Within himself he felt a spark, like an ember among ashes, and knew it was that which they hungered for.

Goddess, look under me! he cried without a mouth.

The ember pulsed, swelled, and flared. The shapes recoiled, drew into themselves, crying out in something like terror and something like joy. Light struck them like spears, driving them back yet holding them near.

He was in a place. What its real nature was he did not know; it seemed much like the ravine, but its dim outlines shifted and blurred, rose and sank. The dead were crowded everywhere, and if they had the forms of men and women he knew it was because he could not see them otherwise.

We burn, we burn. We feed, we burn, we feed.

They were writhing, swelling, battening on his light. Eyas called out again: *Sky, come to me! Violet, Old, Golden, Gray—all, all, come to me!*

A shape stood before him, larger and clearer than the rest, a man with hands outstretched. It was the Messenger he had slain at the Great Cataract, the Messenger who had died again on the ice in the body of Another Three.

We have hungered for you, Eyas. Now we feed well.

But the Messenger came no closer. Like the others who swarmed around Eyas's light, he seemed almost trapped, unable to seize his prey or to escape. Eyas spoke to him:

I am dead, but still I deny you.

You cannot. We feed on your light and heat; you burn with life like a fire that does not cool.

The dead were all around. His light nourished them, hurt them, drew them close yet kept them back. They swirled like dust in an unfelt wind; their silence wept in his mind. Without substance, they still felt hunger and cold. Each face was sharp, distinct, a person's face, yet in their multitudes the dead were like snowflakes falling in the night.

Yes, we are many. Men have sprung from the earth for ten million years and more, yet Hell is infinite and eternal, and holds us all.

Still I deny you!

Only Hell is real, Eyas.

Yet you must feed on the living. Without them you are nothing.

Without us, the living would not exist; they would be less than nothing. Their bodies are only matter, drawn together for a little while, to live and decay in the same instant back into unlife after they have formed their undying souls. Men would long ago have vanished from the earth, given it to the animals and brutes, if not for us. We are tillers of the earth, raising a crop that would never grow without us.

Only to devour us?

If the breadseed would open its leaves to the sun, it must yield at last to the harvester.

I cannot accept; I will not accept.

Eyas, your life still burns hot in you. But soon, soon it

*must fade; soon you will feel cold and hunger as we do, feel
your mind begin to dwindle. Then, when a new soul appears
within your grasp, you will seize it, and feed as we do.*

I will not.

*Here only the weakest do not feed. They are the wraiths;
eternity for them is only endless hunger, unappeased forever.
Would you wane to that when you might be strong, aware,
able to sense the living, able to guide them—even to walk
among them once more?*

. . . To return. As a Messenger.

*It is not easy. You must feed on many lives, and then seek
out a human whose hold on life is weak.*

Like Another Three?

Like him. And like your father.

Eyas's light grew hotter, and the Messenger retreated a
little.

*He was a simple man, a soldier. When Steeledge fled to the
south, he sent your father with the army into the west, and
took your mother as a servant to the Woman Emerald. Your
father was still in the mountains when Brightspear came from
the Gulf, and it was then that I entered your father's body.*

*You were the Messenger at Longstrand, the one who pursued
me to the Great Cataract.*

Yes.

And where is my father now?

*Those possessed by the dead carry no spark of life into
Hell; they are consumed. He is among the wraiths. Do not
grieve for him. At least he has not vanished utterly, like the
soulless ones.*

That would be better than this horror.

*Would it? The soulless live a brief life, ask questions and
learn no answers, and then wink out like snuffed candles. Not
many man are so cursed; something in them is too close to
brutes and animals. And not many of the dead would choose
the nonexistence that some fools yearn to bring upon us all.
Yes, Eyas: Hell has its politics, its factions, its wars.*

And Sky is of those who would destroy all Hell.

*Your wife—yes. But here there is no wife, no husband, no
son or daughter. Attend me, Eyas! You held a little power in
life, for a few brief days, and found it good. Here you may
hold power beyond imagining, forever. Do not despise what
you cannot change. This is real; this is what is and must be.
You are strong, strong as the greatest of us who have fed*

*upon millions since men first walked upon earth. Your place
is with us. We who rule Hell rule earth as well, eternally. If
our foes ruled in our place, mankind would vanish soon from
the earth. But is it a bad thing that men live to rejoice in
each morning? Would you deny to children yet unborn the
joys you knew, the sweetness of strength and the salt of love?*

*You denied my children, Messenger! You robbed them of
their lives, fed upon, and boasted of it in my dreams. You
destroyed my family, my people, my Goddess, like so many
weeds in your field. I warred against you in life, and I war
against you still.*

Eyas's rage rose like a fountain of white fire. He burned,
and with burning hands seized the dark form of the Messenger. Like a kindled straw, the Messenger pulsed with light,
cried out, and dwindled into wailing silence. Eyas's hands
gripped nothing; all that remained of the Messenger was a
faint, endless cry, like an echo resounding from distant cliffs:
a wraith.

Under a black sky, through the mists of Hell, Eyas walked.
His light made darkness visible; his wrath was a tumult. He
strode into shadowy palaces and laid burning hands upon
Hell's rulers. His face shone in silent forests where no wind
blew and the dead slipped whispering among dark trees,
seeking the firefly souls of the dying; he stood upon the peaks
of mountains long since gone from earth yet remembered in
Hell, and walked in fire across the crowded desolation of
enormous plains.

How long he journeyed he did not know, nor how far;
perhaps he stood still, like some great stone, while Hell
poured over him like a tide. But at last he stood within a city,
greater than any now on earth yet no more solid than the
memory of a mist. Once, he knew, these towers must have
stood upon earth; now those who had built it, and thronged
its streets, and died within its walls, kept its shadow around
them.

In a dark street within the city, he saw Sky standing among
the murmuring dead. A look had passed between them once,
on the bloodstained beach at Longstrand; now it bound them
once more.

*Oh Sky, you are beautiful. Come close to me; let me touch
you again.*

*I dare not. I would not feed upon you. Even now I feel
your warmth, and I hunger for you against my will.*

Let me give you what is left of my life; let me warm you for a little while.

No. Look around you, Eyas. Do you see how all stay far from you? This is the City of Ending. We who dwell in it are the enemies of the Messengers. We would overthrow them, and end Hell itself. Yes, we feed on the living, but only to sustain the strength to war against the Messengers here and on earth.

Sky, Sky! All I can give you is my life, and you will not take it.

No. You have more to give. We had hoped you would find the way to Mount Aspen, and from there to Skyland. There is the true power of the Messengers, Eyas. There must someone go, someday, if this horror is to end.

It is too late.

No. You still burn with great strength; go to a living man in his dreams, bid him take up the journey, and guide him on it. It can be done.

Another form stood beside her, a man. He looked at Eyas, but did not approach.

It can be done, the man echoed. *Eyas, I greet you, and ask this of you: go and find a man upon earth to seek the cave in Mount Aspen. Tell him to place his hands upon the golden circles of the door in the cave. Once he is inside, he must lie upon one of the beds he will find. When he reaches Skyland, he must say to the one he meets: I come from your maker, and I claim all your service and all your wisdom. Let the man do that, and he will gain the power to destroy Skyland.*

Eyas saw, like an image in remembrance, the mountain: a tall, snow-mantled cone with a flat summit, brilliant against a blue sky.

Why did you not tell me this before, when I might have gone to the mountain?

We have little strength; we could not enter your dreams for long. And we feared that you would think our pleas only another trick of the Messengers.

How do you know that Skyland can be destroyed?

I built it, long ages ago, before Mount Aspen first rose in fire.

If it is so old, let it last a little longer before I seek its destroyer. Sky—where are our children?

In the indifference of her face he learned one more of the

horrors of Hell. *No children endure the first embrace of the dead. They are wraiths. The others—Old, Violet, Netweaver, Firewing, Quiet—all feed with the Messengers.*

He searched for rage within himself, rage to burn and smash Hell and all its countless dead. Instead he found only sorrow, an emptiness as great as this dark realm itself. His light dimmed; Sky and the man beside her, and the other dead in the phantom street, faded into darkness.

Eyas—what is happening to you? she called. *Oh, burn again! I would not feed upon you, but your light—your light—*

He is not dead, her companion cried out in wonder. *Life calls him back. Eyas, remember! Destroy Skyland—destroy Hell—and end this misery forever.*

Eyas reached out, his hands pale and cold as ashes, but Sky would not come nearer. She faded; the city was lost in darkness.

12

He drew a deep breath, and smelled sagebrush and redthorn. Other smells hung in the cool air, familiar odors of men and brutes. One scent was close in the darkness.

"Standaway?" he whispered, his own voice strange in his ears.

"I am here."

"Good. Good." He was warm beneath a blanket; he sensed her lying near, and fell asleep into dreams filled with the dead.

Dawn woke him with its first blue light. A hand touched his cheek. He opened his eyes and saw Standaway, her head bent over him. He was still in the ravine, lying by the wall where the walkingtree had waited near the water hole. A crude tent had been rigged over him; Standaway sat with her legs folded under her, at the opening of the tent. She did not smile, but he knew she was happy.

"Are you thirsty?"

He nodded, and let her lift his head so he could slip from a bowl she held. It was the same brackish water that Brightspear had given him, but now it tasted sweet.

"What has happened?"

In the blue light, Standaway was still and beautiful. She answered softly; it was not yet sunrise, and Eyas was aware of many sleepers near the tent. "We saw you come from the flying island, and then escape the Suns. We followed as soon as we could, and found tracks up this ravine. Foehewer was the first to reach you; you lay here, by the water, and beside you was a walkingtree, split in two. Foehewer saw great footprints in the sand—like a human's, but larger than a centaur's."

"A giant. It was near—I smelled it."

"I have heard of them, but never seen one. You—we thought you were dead. It looked as if you and the walkingtree had fought, and that you had somehow slain it. But there were the great footprints, and the tracks of sixfeet and Suns. We knew only that some terrible fate had befallen you. Then I saw the skin move over your heart, and knew that you still lived. We waited here for three days now, to see if you would live or die."

"I live," said Eyas, reaching out to take her hand.

But his own hand hesitated. He turned it, looking at back and palm, at wrist and forearm. With a grunt he sat up and cast off his blanket.

"So we found you, Eyas. You were bathed in the bitter juice of the tree."

His skin and hair and beard were white, white as hoarfrost. Where the Fisher tattoo had been on his right forearm and hand, he now saw only the dark blue web of veins beneath the skin. In the brightening dawn he seemed almost to glow.

Eyas stood. In Hell he had walked untiringly, wrapped in fire; here he tottered, less sure on his feet than when he had played with Chirp on the beach at Longstrand. Standaway rose too, and wrapped the blanket around his pale shoulders. Leaning against her warm side, Eyas looked about.

The ravine was crowded with tents; sleeping men and brutes covered the sand. Atop the steep banks of the ravine, lotors paced gracefully, tall and dark against the brightening sky.

"Is all the army here?"

"No. The Deltan peasants, and the warriors too wounded

to fight again, have gone north into the mountains." She herself, he saw, bore bandaged wounds on her legs and flanks. "But the Bands have come at last." Standaway pointed to a sleeping figure close by, wrapped in a coarse blanket.

Eyas walked carefully over and knelt beside the sleeper. He smiled to see the tattooed face, its fierceness softened by sleep.

"I greet you, Stormsong."

Her eyes flashed open; the tattooes came to snarling life. Then surprise and fear contended in her face.

"Eyas . . . are you alive?"

"Yes."

She could not speak for a moment. "I saw you yesterday, when we reached here—but I thought that when you woke you would be as you were." He reached out, touched her face and brushed aside a wisp of hair; she did not flinch. "You look so strange."

"Like a shorn longfur."

Her fear vanished in a guffaw. "Not far different! Well, hawk-caller—brown or white, you're alive. I won't leave you again." She sat up, embracing him. "You were right. The dreams were a deception, and our herds were well. We came back as quickly as we could, but we had to find a way over the mountains. We passed through some Deltan villages, and heard rumors that the allies were coming north. But we knew nothing of the Suns, and didn't hurry. When Boulder told me yesterday of the battle, and your return, I nearly sliced my nostrils in penance."

"I am glad that you didn't."

The sleepers were waking. They saw him, shook others awake, and came slowly across the sand: kilted black Riverines, yellow-haired Deltans, gray lotors, centaurs black and brown and auburn, tattooed Bandish warriors. The sentries on the high banks of the ravine turned to their companions, camped out of sight, with urgent gestures; soon hundreds stood looking at Eyas and Stormsong and Standaway.

No one spoke. The only sounds were the shuffle of feet, the clop of hoofs, the clink and rattle of armor. It was full day now; though the floor of the ravine lay in shadow, the warriors along the banks were splendid in the morning sun.

Stormsong had been sleeping in only her trousers; now, remembering her modesty, she cursed and yanked on her tunic. As Eyas stood, swaying a little, she sprang up, took his arm, and steadied him. He smiled at her. Then he turned to the warriors and raised a white hand in salute.

A thousand swords rose in answer, flashing in the sun, and a thousand spears. Like the first rockfalls of an avalanche, gunshots cracked, and then were drowned out by a thousand voices crying Eyas's name.

Slowly he walked down the ravine, with Stormsong's strong arm around his waist and Standaway following close behind. The cheers went on, louder with each breath, as warriors woke and learned that Eyas lived. The ravine thundered and echoed like a drum.

He stopped. "Get me back to the water hole—to the tent. Quickly."

"Are you ill? You're weeping."

"Get me back. And send . . . for Boulder . . . and the others. If they still live."

Ravine was dead, slain when Boulder and the other raiders were fighting their way out of Delta; many of the other leaders bore new scars. But they were well, and still exhilarated by their victory over the Suns and Eyas's recovery. Now they gathered around the little tent, eager to see him yet unsure of what to expect. Forager and Blue groomed themselves nervously. Peter Three, a bandage around his head, sat with unnatural stillness. Foehewer was there, despite a serious wound in his right foreleg, but he kept his mane flat, as did Standaway. A Deltan named Flinty Meadow, leader of the peasants, stared unabashedly at Eyas. Stormsong, sitting at Eyas's right hand, drummed her fingers on her leg; Boulder, on Eyas's left, was impassive. When Eyas met his eye, the centaur smiled a little, but he seemed as unsettled as the others by his friend's transformation.

"I am glad to see you all," said Eyas softly.

"This is the happiest day the world has ever known," said Flinty. His round face, sunburned above a bristly beard, was boyishly cheerful.

"May it know even happier," Eyas smiled. "Tell me now what you plan."

No one spoke at first. "Your plans are ours," Boulder said.

"You know far more than I. First tell me this: how did so many Deltans come to join us?"

Flinty looked surprised. "It was your doing, Namegiver. The man you named Asking, and the woman Silence, went about the countryside to give us our names and freedom, as you commanded them. For those gifts, we choose to give in turn our service, until you release us."

"And where are Asking and Silence now, and their daughter?"

"Still in Delta, Namegiver. They go from village to village, south toward the havens on the coast. They say they will not cease until each nameless one is named and freed."

Eyas said nothing for a time, and Flinty's cheer turned to anxiety. "Does this news displease you?"

"No; but if I had known the might of the nameless ones, I would have shrunk from setting foot south of the Black Gates. Boulder, what of the Suns, and the Deltan army?"

"You know of Guardian's army?" Boulder seemed surprised. "We learned of it only yesterday. They are three days' march to the southwest. We can fight them if we must. But Delta can wait. It is Brightspear who must be destroyed."

"The Suns are almost out of reach," Peter Three objected softly. "We would have to pursue them into the Dominance, and fight them on their own land."

"We beat them once," Boulder said.

"Only by luck—with the help of the windwalkers and the courage of the peasants. Now the peasants seek food and shelter in the mountains, as we told them to, and the windwalkers are gone."

"The Bands are here," snapped Stormsong. "If the Suns are in disarray, we can crush them—even on their own grass."

Forager spoke. He had mastered the Bandish dialect that the leaders used, but turned often to Blue for help with a word or phrase. "We have not done what we intended to do. Delta is weakened, but not conquered. Brightspear has escaped. Winter comes. The lotors think of their families, their fields. If we do not take land and food for the winter, we must cross the mountains."

"So you wish more fighting?" asked Eyas.

"We must, or seek our home." Forager's long black fingers rubbed together. "We can beat the Deltan army, but the peasants emptied the granaries when they joined us. If we return to Delta, we will starve there. The Suns will have plenty of food, but they will be bitter foes. Yet we will do as you wish: send us to fight the Deltans, or the Suns, or send us home."

The others assented. Eyas was silent for a time.

"We came south to break the power of Delta and the

Suns," he said at last. "Forager is right; we have failed in that. Now we must fight to survive, or go north. Will the peasants find enough food in the mountains?"

Peter Three shook his head. "Enough for a time—wild whiteroot, small game—but not enough to last them all winter. But the mountains are better than this desert."

"And many would die if we took them north across the mountains. Well, let them shelter there until we can win them land and food for the winter. Delta's northern provinces offer us nothing. So we must go against the Dominance, not to destroy Brightspear but to protect our own people."

"It will be hard," said Boulder, "but with you leading us again we can do it."

"You must do it without me, Boulder. I cannot lead you."

The centaur looked carefully at him, while the other leaders tensed. "Not lead us, when Brightspear himself is within our grasp? Are you still weak? We can wait until your strength returns—"

"No. I have another task, a journey I must take. If I succeed, the powers that uphold Brightspear will be overthrown, and he with them."

"Where would you go?"

"To Mount Aspen."

"That is far to the west, deep in the Dominance," Boulder objected. "How will you reach it without an army?"

"If the allies cross the Bitter River, Brightspear will gather all his forces there, in the Eastmarch. I will travel alone through the hills while his attention is turned to you. He will not fight you with the respect you deserve—he thinks us a rabble. And he thinks I am dead; he saw me thrown to the tree."

The leaders cried out, enraged. "So that is how it happened," growled Peter Three. "Then we have one more reason to conquer Brightspear. His death will be a slow one."

Boulder spoke slowly, unsure of his words: "This journey, this task—were you given it in Hell?"

"Yes."

The leaders' anger vanished in stillness.

"I will not ask you what happened there, Eyas. But the human dead have warred on us, plagued us, warned our enemies. Do you trust those who gave you this task?"

"It is no deception. Yes, I trust them. One of them was my wife Sky."

302

Stormsong touched his arm. "Don't speak of these things, or you will draw the dead around us."

His gray eyes, palé in his white face, met hers. "They are around us now, countless as dust. They suffer, but perhaps I can end their suffering."

As if to ward off the unseen shapes he spoke of, she hunched her shoulders. Boulder still frowned.

"Strange things have happened to you, Eyas. You are changed, and more deeply than your skin. But you are my friend, and if you must go then I will not keep you. What of those dead who rule Brightspear, who deceived the Bands? Will they not warn the Suns that you still live, and tell them where to find you?"

"They may. But only the rulers of the dead are strong enough to speak to the living. I destroyed many of them; Brightspear may sleep for many nights before they come again in his dreams, or send more Messengers to counsel him. If they do warn him, what of it? My task will not wait."

The leaders were silent. Eyas saw fear in the faces of the humans, grim alarm in the centaurs' frowns, and something like pity in the black, deep eyes of the lotors.

"Make your plans," he said, "and march west when you are ready. I leave tonight."

"Not alone," said Stormsong. "I said I would not leave you again. I will go with you."

"And I," said Boulder.

The others burst out in protest; Boulder raised a hand.

"You chose me when Eyas was captured, to lead the allies until his return. He has returned, and goes again. Choose another leader."

Eyas smiled. "Once, Boulder, you said that only I could lead an army of brutes and men."

"We have learned much since then," the centaur replied.

"Must you leave us, Namegiver, and the centaur, and the wild woman?" asked Flinty. "We came to fight for you, to fight beside you."

"We do not all fight upon the same patch of ground, or with a single sword," Eyas told him. "If we go, we go as arrows, to strike the Suns where they do not expect it."

"A good archer retrieves his arrows," said Blue. "We will find you, Eyas, when we have won our battle and you have won yours."

Again Eyas smiled, but they saw grimness and sorrow in

303

him. "If I am not found, remember my promise to the daughter of Asking and Silence. I would have that promise kept."

"It will be kept," said Peter Three.

13

Four of them left that night: Eyas on Boulder, Stormsong on Standaway. Slowly they rode through the army's camp; hands reached out to clasp theirs, and eyes gleamed in firelight. Eyas remembered the camp of the holdless outside Foundries, the dull sorrow and hunger into which he had walked. They were all holdless still, these brutes and men, but they were proud; the humans were loud in laughter, and the centaurs stood with manes erect. Some warriors asked Eyas to stay; a few joked about his pallor; most only wished him a swift journey, and raised hands in farewell.

At last they passed the sentries and went southwest, down a long hill to a plain, dark with cactus and spikeweed. The night was clear and bright: Evenspark had set, but Redspark burned in the east and the full moon shone just below the Bridge. Harsh the land might be, but it was still lovely and full of life. The hills and plain glowed dark blue, and nightwings filled the air with their quick trills. Spiders wove webs from bush to bush, or scuttled across the sandy soil after mice and longpaws.

The centaurs loped almost soundlessly across the plain. Stormsong and Standaway spoke quietly together, accustoming themselves to each other; Foehewer, troubled by his wounded leg, had reluctantly stayed behind and Standaway had insisted on carrying her.

"Will you speak now of your task?" Boulder asked after Eyas had been silent for a long time.

Eyas hunched himself inside his jacket of longfur wool, shivering in the chill air. "Not yet."

Near dawn they came upon the tracks of Brightspear's retreating army, and followed the rough trail west until dawn; then they camped in a gully and slept through most of the long day, each a little way from the others. Eyas's sleep was light and restless, filled with strange dreams: often he saw Mount Aspen, and seemed to climb a rocky trail to a cleft in snow-mantled stone. But always he woke, shivering, before he entered the cleft.

Late in the afternoon they rose, ate a hurried meal, and resumed their journey. Stormsong and the centaurs spoke of what happened since the departure of the Bands, but Eyas said little. When they halted to camp again, on a grassy hill, Stormsong took his hand.

"Lie with me. I am not a stranger to you, am I?"

As dawn began to break they took comfort in each other's closeness; now Eyas slept deeply, and heard Sky's voice in his dreams.

They know. They know, Eyas, and they are warning Brightspear. You must go quickly.

Behind her silent voice he sensed fear, and a strange tumult like a skyseed grove in a gale: a frenzied motion without release. The cries of the dead woke him to the cool light of a morning on the edge of autumn. Wind hissed in the dead grass.

Stormsong slept. Eyas got up and saw the centaurs sitting nearby, speaking softly. He went to them.

"The Suns know. The dead are very frightened of us."

"Good," grunted Boulder. "Your task will do them a great mischief."

"Yes. But I take no pleasure in it."

The centaur put a hand on Eyas's shoulder. "It will be well."

Eyas nodded and went back to his blanket. He could almost see the dead swarming around him, hear their voiceless cries: Hell was shaking, tensing, reaching out to slay him yet afraid of his return. Somewhere, hungers keened that once had been his children: their terror and pain never ended, and never would while the Messengers ruled.

He lay down again, listening to the whisper of the grass. The wind had blown over hillsides for long ages, longer than the Old Stories said, longer than remembrance taught. When Two Bows left his canyon to seek the Gulf, the dead were already as numberless as the snowflakes of a thousand winters. They were older than the Goddess, older than the Bridge. They had walked through the dreams of the living, and looked again through living eyes on the windblown grass.

305

Their power was old and vast and remorseless; yet it sprang from hunger and despair. They ruled to no purpose but the endless prolongation of their own misery. Dying in the tree, he had invaded their shadowy palaces, struck terror in them; alive, he saw more clearly how little he had done, how little he could do.

Stormsong drew closer to him in her sleep, her eyes moving behind their lids. Her breathing quickened. He shook her, calling her name.

"—Ah! Oh, you are still—they said—"

"The dead?"

"They said you would leave me, desert the allies—join the Suns."

Eyas embraced her. "They will say worse. The dead war upon each other; if all goes well, we will win that war for one side and overthrow the other, forever."

"How... how can the dead make war? What more could happen to a dead soul?" Then she covered his mouth with her hand. "Don't speak! I don't want to know. Better a thousand enemies in life than even a glimpse of what comes after."

He rocked her back to sleep, smiling a little, and then slept himself, with the smells of centaurs and dry grass sweet in the windy air.

That night they reached the Bitter River. The Suns, invading, had destroyed several Deltan forts on the east bank of the shallow stream, and sacked the villages that supported the forts; retreating, they must have killed or captured any Deltans left in the region, for the ruined settlements showed no signs of life. Crops almost ready for harvest were trampled flat or burned black. The villages were piles of rubble.

The centaurs carried Eyas and Stormsong north along the riverbank, seeking a ford well to the north of the one the Suns had used. At dawn they found one and waded across into the lands of the Dominance. In a grove of oaks they sheltered for the day and then hastened west into the hills.

It was greener country than they had seen since leaving the Great River. South of the White and Lotor Mountains, much of Alland was dry, but the grasslands of the Dominance were in the path of spring and summer storms from the Delta Sea; here the hills were forested, and laced with streams.

Farmsteads and logging camps were scattered through the woods, linked by rutted gravel roads.

Though scarred by logged-off hillsides and abandoned mines, it was a pleasant, quiet land. The companions saw no sign that the people here were at war: the roads by day had no military traffic, and only a few riders and teamsters seemed armed. At night the farms and hamlets sparkled with lamps, and drunken laughter carried far on autumn mists.

For three nights they traveled swiftly along the roads, sleeping in woods or thickets during the day. No dreamhauntings came to Eyas, but Stormsong gasped and moaned in her sleep, and woke sweating. She would not speak of her dreams, but grew grim and haggard.

One morning they lay concealed in a wooded canyon, not far from a bridge. Autumn was truly in the air now: maples were turning red, and the trunks of paperbarks were losing their mottled green as the outer bark died and prepared to peel off. From a Sunnish village not far to the east, the wind brought the stinks of smoke and dung.

Eyas, the only one awake, heard hoofbeats and silently roused his companions. Through a screen of leaves they looked up at the bridge and watched a Sunnish patrol rumble across the planks. They were no bumpkin soldiers, but veteran riders armed with rifles and lances. They had a look of tired, dusty competence, and some bore half-healed wounds. Eyas and Boulder glanced at each other: these were warriors from Brightspear's army, sent north to find them.

The patrol rattled away to the west. "How close are we to Mount Aspen?" Eyas asked.

"I do not know," answered Boulder. "It stands somewhere to the north of Great Camp."

"We have many days' travel left," said Standaway.

Eyas squatted down among dying ferns, chin on his knees, and stared at the decaying leaves that littered the canyon floor. It was impossible: the dead knew where he was, and he could not evade their unsleeping eyes. How many of Hell's rulers had he destroyed? Ten, twenty? Millions more must have sensed the tumult and turned their attention to him.

He looked at his white hands. Well, let the dead do what they would. He might well escape the Suns; if he did not, Hell would feel his wrath again, and its rulers would flee him or be burned to wraiths. Then he would find a living man to finish this journey: a Riverine, a Band warrior, a Deltan—even a Sun. One way or another, Skyland would be destroyed. "Let us go back to sleep," he said. "We have far to go tonight."

The journey now was a run and a wait, sudden gallops down empty roads and long pauses in hiding. Patrols were suddenly everywhere; the farmers and herders began to carry spears or axes, and to travel the roads in groups. The land here was more thickly peopled, less wooded; only a few days' travel south lay the great cities of the Lake Country, the heartland of the Dominance. Yet they managed to go unseen; though the dead might mark their passage, they could not warn the Suns in time.

In a gray dawn the companions settled for the day on a hillside above a large town already awake and clangorous with smithies and furnaces. Wagons rolled down a broad, paved road; sooty smoke hung in the mist. The town was a mass of solid brick buildings, dominated by the terraced pyramid of its main temple.

"It smells like Foundries," said Boulder. "Every town does, and the towns get larger. The Suns are too many."

Stormsong grunted agreement. "If our people don't fall upon Brightspear soon, before he can catch his breath, he'll be unbeatable. . . . At least they have plenty of food." She bit into an apple from an orchard they had passed through in the night. "If only they catch him in time. What do you seek at Mount Aspen, Eyas?"

"A door in a cave."

"And what's behind the door?"

"I don't know."

"Something that can overthrow all that?" She waved the apple toward the town's smoking chimneys.

Eyas had blackened his face and hands and hair, to make himself less visible; he smiled now with a flash of white teeth. "All that is clatter and stink. The Suns are strong because they . . . they believe in themselves and their world. They quarrel about cults and Sunteachings, but the dead make sure that one faith or the other seems true—whichever suits their purposes for the time. The Suns are rich and mighty, but if their faith is broken, their wealth and might will be like armor on a man in deep water."

"Perhaps. I have seen good fighters die of broken faith."

"I saw my whole people die that way."

Stormsong lay down beside him; young alders and brambles rose around them, their leaves already browning.

"Would you go to Mount Aspen even if it wouldn't hurt Brightspear?" she asked quietly. Eyas put his arms around her.

"Yes."

"Then what is this all about, if not to ruin Brightspear? Why are we risking our necks?"

"The Bands are afraid of Hell."

"No shame in that."

"No, none. If all goes well, I will destroy Hell itself with what lies behind the door."

She stared grimly at him. "If you're not mad, and you do destroy Hell, what will happen to us then when we die?"

"Perhaps we will find out." He felt her shudder against him, and held her tightly.

That night, patrols were everywhere. Every field, every trail, every wood was alive with riders. Their dark shapes moved through the blue brightness of a clear night. Eyas, crouching in the shadows, farheard to find a way among the Suns. He heard them muttering among themselves, against their leaders' commands—soldiers' complaints and snatches of rumor. Some said Brightspear had slaughtered the brutes' army down in the Eastmarch; others, that he had marched in secret to Delta. But most seemed sure that Brightspear followed close upon the couriers who had ordered them out of their comfortable garrisons to search the countryside.

"Wild centaurs in the Dominance," Eyas farheard one soldier snort. "What next, an embassy from the windwalkers?"

"I was in Transmontane last winter," another said. "It was no joke."

"Say what you will about old Silvershield," the first one muttered, "in those days we never had brutes daring to war on us on our own soil."

"Hush! Get us both flogged for your blasphemy."

Eyas led his companions around the patrols and north, into narrow mountain valleys where only herders wandered. They traveled by day and night now, sleeping briefly and hurrying on. The air smelled of winter here, at the feet of the mountains, and the streams were scummed with ice at night.

Fourteen days after crossing the Bitter River, they came onto a broad plateau, walled by low hills, and paused to eat and drink by a slow-flowing creek. While the others slept,

Eyas walked up the stream to seek a ford, and came upon two children: a boy of ten or so, and a girl of seven. They were dressed in coarse smocks and barefoot despite the chill in the air. They looked up with interest but no alarm as he neared them; the boy drew a fishing line from the pool where he and the girl squatted.

"I greet you," Eyas said.

"I greet you," the boy answered. The girl—his sister, no doubt—stared at him with wide, dark eyes.

"Why is your hair so white?" she asked.

"I'm very old—see my white beard? What is your name?" He sat beside her at the edge of the pool.

"Little Peacebringer. My brother is Copper Bell."

"Peacebringer! That was my mother's name. I am called Fisher."

She giggled. "We're fishing, too."

"Where are your mother and father?"

"Up there," the boy said, pointing north. "With the herd. It's a big herd." Eyas listened, and caught the distant bellow of a sixfoot.

"Do you live here?"

"Only in the summer," the boy answered. "Soon we'll go down to winter pasture. We work for Brutemaster Sand," he added importantly.

"Ah."

"He's a Man."

"Of course."

"Who owns you?"

"No one."

"Ooh!" the girl squeaked. "You must be a Man too."

Eyas laughed. "No, just a wandering fisher. Tell me—do you know where Mount Aspen is? A mountain with smooth sides, covered with snow, and a flat top."

Copper Bell looked almost pityingly at him. "Everyone knows Mount Aspen." He pointed across the stream, to the notch between two of the hills on the edge of the plateau. In the notch, Eyas saw the flat-topped white summit of a mountain.

"What a silly," the girl said. "You must not know anything."

"You're right," Eyas smiled.

A woman's voice called from somewhere upstream, and the children scrambled to their feet. "We have to go," said Copper Bell.

"We didn't catch any fish!" his sister wailed.

Eyas stepped softly into the pool, and winked at her. Then he reached into the water, paused, and brought out a fish something like a large finnet. It squirmed in his hands; he gave it to Little Peacebringer, who held it in the front of her smock. The children gaped at him.

"I told you I was called Fisher."

"Thank you, Fisher," they chorused. Their mother called again, more sharply. "Coming!" shouted Copper Bell. "We got a fish, Mother!" his sister screamed, and they ran swiftly into the trees.

Eyas watched them for a moment; then he turned and walked slowly back to his companions.

Stormsong woke at his footstep. "Why do you look so sad?"

"It's nothing. Wake the centaurs. A herder's family is close by—and Mount Aspen is just over the hills."

Late that night they crossed the hills and looked west, across a broad and forested valley, to the white cone of Mount Aspen. Its summit glowed in Bridgelight, seeming to float in darkness.

"We come upon a holy place," said Boulder. "Aspen himself may have stood upon this spot, and wandered in this valley."

Eyas remembered what Standaway had told him, long ago in the Yellow Desert, about the birth of the centaurs' greatest warrior on the slopes of this mountain, and the rallying of his people here when humans had driven them from the grasslands of the south. Out of an ending, Aspen had retrieved a beginning; looking now upon the mountain, Eyas saw only an ending.

On that day in the desert Standaway had told him also of the secret that female centaurs kept: the sad returns of their dead to look again at the sweetness of life. She had never mentioned it again. But why should men and brutes share this world yet not eternity? Why should lotors rejoice in their other realm, while men and centaurs suffered in theirs?

The Messenger had said that only the soulless ones were doomed to ask unanswered questions, but perhaps the dead were only a little less ignorant than the living. The dead cared nothing for the brutes and seemed not to know that centaurs and lotors survived death as humans did. They had not recognized the power of the Goddess, though the power She had given to Eyas had thwarted them on earth and

311

destroyed them in Hell; to the dead, even She was only a brute.

He knew he had no answers, only a stubborn faith in a dead Goddess. As if afraid of where too much thought might take him, he said, "Let us go on. If we hurry, we can be on the mountain by nightfall."

Boulder looked doubtful. "The valley will be full of Suns."

"I know, and the mountain too. Better to evade the ones in the valley by daylight, and attack those on the mountain at night."

Standaway drew her rifle from its sheath and carefully loaded it. A dangerous smile curled on Stormsong's lips.

By dawn they were well down into the valley, and soon struck a deep-rutted wagon trail. They followed it north for a time, then left it to bypass a village and its fields. The woods were second growth, alder and maple and paperbark, too recent to have crowded out the underbrush of ferns, berries, and brambles. Trails ran everywhere, dotted with the little tracks of splithoofs. Many trees were turning: the canopy overhead was more red and orange than green.

Apart from the village, they saw no signs of men until noon, when they nearly blundered into a squad of Sunnish riders in a meadow. The riders were sitting by a creek bank, eating a meal and cursing the mosquitoes while their mounts browsed on the long grass. Eyas was tempted to farhear, and perhaps learn how many Suns were patrolling the valley, but impatience drove him on; they circled the meadow and crossed the creek upstream.

The western side of the valley was less wooded; farmsteads and villages were scattered along the lower slopes of the mountain, linked by roads showing signs of frequent traffic. Most of the roads ran down the valley to the south, but in midafternoon the companions found one that led due west.

The centaurs trotted steadily up the road, sniffing the air. For a long time they saw only trees and occasional clearings; then they came into a broad field and passed within twenty spans of a log-walled farmstead. A team of harvesters, cross-ing the road with a hay wagon, scattered at the sight of them; a woman screamed in the farmhouse door.

"Now we'll have to stretch our legs," said Boulder, and broke into a gallop. Soon they were in woods again; from behind came the clanging of a bell. Boulder and Stormsong drew their swords, and Standaway her rifle; after a moment Eyas drew his own sword. It felt strange in his hand.

The road rose in a series of switchbacks, with trees close on either side. But it was easy to hear the thud and clatter of sixfeet, and the jingle of harnesses: a patrol was coming toward them.

"Fight or hide?" Eyas asked.

"I hear six at least," Boulder answered.

"Then we hide."

The centaurs swung off to the left, in a stand of paperbarks, and crouched behind a vine-tangled deadfall. Moments later the patrol came past: eight young riders, blinking in each other's dust as their mounts galloped down the hill. Stormsong covered her mouth and shook with suppressed giggles. Boulder and Standaway snorted.

"They're only boys," said Stormsong. "We could have handled them easily."

"May they live to be old men," Eyas answered.

"If that's the best the Suns can put against us," she grinned, "we'll have no trouble."

Eyas shook his head. "Real warriors will be waiting for us on the mountain."

The climb was gradual, and the centaurs ran without tiring. Once, a gap in the trees showed the Sunnish patrol far below, returning in pursuit; their mounts must have been winded, for they moved slowly. Eyas called a halt, and farheard. The pursuers' voices came to him, but ahead were only the sounds of wind and falling water.

The road ended at an abandoned mine, a few rotting cabins around a deep pit. Fresh ashes and sixfoot dung showed that the patrol had camped here before descending to the valley. Beyond the mine, the trees thinned to a scattering of pines on a steep, stony slope. Snow glinted farther up, and a banner of cloud trailed away toward the south from the unseen summit. It was very quiet.

"Somewhere up there is a trail to the cave," said Eyas.

They climbed first to the north and then to the south, scrambling over frost-cracked stones and through clumps of flowering club. Rivulets trickled through patches of moss and beds of withered wildflowers. The trees were wind-gnarled, their roots clutching at the scanty soil.

Eyas and Stormsong walked beside the centaurs; no one

313

spoke, and they often paused to rest. If the patrol still followed, they saw no sign of it. The valley below was tranquil, a mass of reds, greens, and yellows in the golden afternoon. To the north and east the horizon rose in glittering peaks; to the south, hills rolled down to a great plain, hazy with distance, mottled with cloudshadow and dark lakes. The sun was descending to Mount Aspen's shoulder, casting the eastern slopes into shadow.

Boulder touched a stone as large as himself, crusted with gray and orange lichens. "They had to look from here at their lost lands," he murmured in centauric. "After that, the crossing of the mountains must have seemed little hardship."

All the valley was in the mountain's shadow when they came at last upon the trail. It was half-buried in dirty snow, a path marked by small cairns.

"No footprints," said Standaway. They looked up, their breaths fluttering white in the evening chill. The trail wound away into the darkening snow. Far above, the cloud streamer at the summit was a banner of fire.

"They'll be there," said Eyas, "guarding the cave."

"We'll have to fight our way in," Boulder said. Eyas looked at him in surprise.

"It's my task to enter the cave—not yours. Once we reach it, you must get back down the mountain and seek the army."

The centaur folded his arms and stared calmly down at Eyas. "When you were a captive in Delta, I did not know if you lived. Whatever happens now, I will not endure that uncertainty again. I go with you."

"And I," said Standaway.

Stormsong said nothing until Eyas looked at her.

"Try to keep me away, hawk-caller."

"We are going against Hell, Stormsong."

"I know, I know!" Anger and fright contended in her voice. "Go on, while the light lasts."

Eyas stood very still, remembering the thunder of the Great Cataract and the darkening forests above it. His hand touched her cheek.

"All right."

Through a long twilight they climbed. The night was clear, the Bridge bright; Skyland was an emerald at the zenith. Wind hissed across the snowfields. In the valley, lights twinkled in scattered villages, but they seemed very far away.

Near midnight Eyas halted in the lee of a low cliff, as much to escape the wind as to farhear. Cold and weariness made it hard to draw into himself; when he did, the sounds of men were sudden in his ears. Feet scuffled in snow, hands rubbed against each other, voices muttered softly; someone growled about the cold. He heard no sounds of sixfeet: they did not trust their brutes. Footsteps resonated oddly—someone was walking slowly in a narrow place that must be the cave.

He came out of himself and heard only the wind. Carefully he followed the trail up to the edge of the cliff where he could look uphill.

The trail wound back and forth across an empty snowfield until it was lost against a stony escarpment. The Suns were there beneath the escarpment, most of them just outside the cave and a few within it. All were close together; his farhearing had gone well beyond the cave, but he had sensed no one else.

Silently he went back to the others.

"They are about two hundred and fity spans above us, near the mouth of the cave. The trail is in full view of them."

"How many?" Stormsong asked.

"Between fifteen and twenty-five. Most of them just outside the mouth of the cave."

"Can we get on their flank?"

Eyas chuckled. "Better than that."

After a few moments' whispered planning, they left the trail, moving back down the slope and then turning left, toward the north. The terrain was rough, treacherous with last year's hard-packed snow, but it shielded them from the Suns. A step or two at a time, they circled well around before climbing again. Here the winds had scoured the stones bare, and they moved more quickly. Once or twice a pebble rattled away under a foot or hoof, and they stood still for long moments, waiting to see if the Suns were alerted.

The mountainside narrowed into a sharp ridge, with snow on its eastern side. They climbed cautiously across the hard crust, span by span, working their way back to the eastern side of the mountain. Eyas halted them. A hundred spans below, the blue-white of the snow was broken by an irregular black line: the rocky edge of the escarpment.

"Stay here until I return," he whispered. He pulled off his felt boots, his trousers and tunic, and left his sword with

Stormsong. She tried to protest, but he was already gliding down across the snow. Within a few steps he seemed to disappear, to fade into the whiteness.

Stormsong stood shivering between the centaurs, cursing under her breath. The wind increased; even Boulder and Standaway shuddered now and then as gusts struck them.

As suddenly as he had gone, Eyas returned. He dressed himself with cold-clumsy hands, speaking softly as he did.

"A hundred spans south, then straight downhill. There's a ledge outside the cave. It's a drop of about a span and a half from the top to the ledge. If we land behind the Suns, we can get into the cave without much fighting. I don't know how deep the cave is, but once we reach the door I think we'll be safe from them."

The centaurs looked briefly at each. Boulder murmured to Standaway, "If we live to return, will you honor me in marriage?"

"Gladly, and be honored as well."

Eyas snorted softly, and pulled himself into Boulder's saddle. As Stormsong sprang onto Standaway's back, Eyas drew his sword.

"Now."

The centaurs' broad hoofs slid on the hard snow, but the moan of the wind hid the sound. Gently, swiftly, they came down the slope. The black line of the escarpment was close; now they saw the ledge before the cave, crowded with dark shapes crouched down against the wind. A pale face turned up toward them, its mouth a black circle of surprise.

Boulder and Standaway leaped, shouting, and crashed upon the black stone of the ledge. A man cried out, struggling to draw his sword from beneath his cloak; Boulder's sword chopped him almost in half. With a shriek, Stormsong slashed at another. Blood gushed black and streaming in Bridgelight. A rifle banged uselessly at the sky.

The centaurs wheeled, almost colliding, and found the dark mouth of the cave.

"The leaders are inside—no more than three of them," Eyas said. "Quickly!"

Side by side, their heads almost brushing the roof of the cave, the centaurs charged in. Shouts echoed; hoofbeats resounded like an avalanche. A spark flashed in the blackness, and a torch burned yellow. It was held by a Sunnish officer, standing between two others with raised rifles.

316

At close range, Standaway shot one, then flung her rifle at the others. It struck the torchbearer, who fell back with a gasp. The torch fell at the feet of the other rifleman; flame climbed his black cloak. He fired wildly just before Boulder ran him through.

The man's own body smothered his burning cloak, and blackness fell again, but in the brief torchlight they had seen that the cave ran level between straight, smooth walls: it was actually a tunnel, made by men. Boulder strode ahead, his sword before him, while Standaway followed with a hand on his flank. The Suns were still shouting and cursing behind them; one fired his rifle, and a shot screamed off the ceiling.

"No firing!" another screamed. "You could hit one of the Men, you dung beetles! Get the Men out to safety first."

The tunnel seemed endless. Soon the Suns would get their officers, dead or alive, out of the way; then they could follow, shooting into the dark until they hit their targets. Eyas thought of invoking the Goddess and perhaps drawing light from its unknown source within him. No: the light would give the Suns a target. This time he must grope in darkness.

Boulder's sword boomed against metal. He thrust out his free hand to slow himself.

"It must be the door. What now?"

Eyas dropped from the saddle and reached out blindly. Cold metal numbed his hands. The gold circles—where were they? His fingers swept across the door, from one wall to the other. Behind him the Suns' voices were an echoing babble, coming closer.

There! A raised surface, barely noticeable, its edge curving. He kept one hand upon it, reached out with the other, and found the second one. His hands pressed against them.

"Hurry up, Eyas!" Stormsong snarled. "They'll be on us—"

Between the two circles the door split into two panels and swung inward. Light flooded the tunnel. Eyas plunged in, squinting against the glare, with the others on his heels. A shot cracked, glancing off one of the panels as they began to swing shut. Before they closed, Eyas saw their outer surface was a dull silver, set with many golden circles; only touch had revealed the ones that opened the door.

Now they shut. The tunnel continued, gray walls and floor lit by glowing white hemispheres set in the roof. The air was warm and faintly scented. Boulder touched the nearest of the glowing lights.

"This is a great marvel," he said. Eyas nodded impatiently.

"Come on. They may find the courage to try the door, and the luck to open it."

Stormsong, panting, looked warily down the tunnel. "I don't like this place. It's strange."

Eyas pulled her from Standaway's back. "Come on, I said!"

The door thumped. As if waiting for that signal, Stormsong and the centaurs followed Eyas at a jog trot for almost a hundred and fifty spans, and then came to a second door. It was a featureless gray, like the walls, and swung open at their approach. Stormsong raised her sword.

"Put it away," Eyas said. "It'll do no good in this place." He went through, into a room much wider than the tunnel. It was sparely furnished with tables and chairs of some gleaming black substance, like enameled iron. The walls were white; the whole ceiling glowed softly, and the floor was covered with a green fabric.

Eyas paced about the room. It was silent, meaningless: a room within a mountain, a room filled with unnatural light and sweet-scented air. Though it was clean and free of dust, it seemed unimaginably old and long deserted. Despite the warmth, Eyas shuddered.

In the far wall, a circle of green began to glow. Eyas went toward it, and a door opened beneath the green circle. Within, he saw a short passage, and part of a smaller room. With a glance at his companions, he went on. They followed, the centaurs ducking their heads.

This room was circular, perhaps four spans across, and furnished with six low couches radiating from a central column. Walls, floor, and ceiling were covered in a smooth, slightly resilient white material. Four glowing circles in the ceiling gave light. Six squares of dark gray glass were set in the circular wall; between each of them was a shiny black hemisphere like a roundstone.

"I like this place still less," said Stormsong quietly. "What is it?"

"I don't know," Eyas answered. He walked around, searching for another exit. If they stayed here, they would be trapped if the Suns got through. As he returned to the door, it silently closed. Stormsong cursed and gripped her sword. The floor began to tremble. From somewhere in the ceiling, a musical note chimed.

"I was told to lie on a bed," Eyas said. "Then somehow I

would go to Skyland." He sat cautiously on one of the couches; its white fabric yielded slightly. Stormsong also sat. The centaurs settled themselves warily on the floor, their dark eyes on the door.

The chime sounded again, and they were pressed gently down. Shaking, Eyas stretched himself out on the couch. It was raised where it met the pillar, and he faced one of the glass squares. Suddenly the square turned a deep black, with pale streaks moving swiftly down them. The glowing circles dimmed. Eyas felt his limbs grow heavy. The blackness and moving streaks vanished; he looked out upon the mountains, and cried out in wonder.

The mountains were shrinking, falling away, turning into a mottled pattern of blue and gray and black. It was like rising under a skyseed, but at a terrifying speed.

Now the pattern shifted, tilting, and blackness slid over it. A band of light moved slowly across the window, and Eyas realized he was looking up, at the sky and the Bridge of Heaven.

The room must be part of a flying ship, like a gondola beneath a windwalkers' island; it was lifting them far above the earth, but Eyas could not understand how it worked. The Bridge slid away, and again he looked out on a dark pattern of mountains, rivers, and clouds. One river stood out, a gray ribbon on a dark plain; it must be the Great River, fraying into the patchwork of its delta. The ship was moving east, climbing higher; he must be looking straight down, yet his body was still pressed against the couch.

Boulder and Standaway were sprawled on their sides, hands touching, eyes shut. Stormsong was struggling to rise from her couch.

"Stay!" he commanded. She obeyed, relaxing with a gasp.

"What's happening to us, Eyas?"

"We're flying—like windwalkers—but higher and faster."

"What if we fall?"

"We won't."

"Promise it!"

He laughed. In the window, part of a long peninsula was slipping by; it must be Homeland, Godhonor's country in the far southeast of Alland. Clouds obscured the sea beyond it. Eyas wondered if they would see the windwalkers' land, far around the world.

Sunlight flashed into the room. The clouds below were still

dark, but soon they turned dawn-pink and then white. Below them, the sea shone blue in the morning.

"Has dawn come already?" asked Stormsong.

"I think we have flown to meet it."

His heaviness began to lessen. In a few breaths, his weight was normal. Eyas sat up. His eyes met Boulder's; the centaur was not afraid, but he looked grim.

"Once you kept me from returning to the Gulf," Eyas said. "Do you regret it now?"

"Not if you can still play mockery games." Boulder got up. Standaway rose with him, and followed him to one of the windows. It showed a scattering of clouds along a green coastline, and a great yellow-brown desert east of the sea. "I look down," said Boulder, "yet down is also under my hoofs."

"More human strangeness," said Standaway. "Look—the edge of the world."

The horizon curved in a blue arc against darkness. In the windows on the far side of the room, the sun shone in, its brightness oddly dimmed so that it could be looked upon. Near it ran a thin band of light that must be the Bridge of Heaven, but narrower than they had ever seen it before.

"The Bridge looks wider in the Gulf than it does in Delta," Eyas said, standing beside the centaurs. "We must have traveled still farther south, and the Bridge must be almost directly above us."

They went from window to window, watching the earth dwindle. Sometimes they saw light flashing among the clouds—lightning, Boulder guessed. Before long the sun set behind the curve of the horizon; the flashes went on, throwing light here and there across the darkness.

Now the Bridge began to expand again; it seemed to be breaking into countless sparks, winking and flashing almost as brightly as the lightning below. Beyond the Bridge they saw the moon, a crescent of white and gray.

The chime sounded. In the pillar above each couch, a little hatch slid down, revealing a tray bearing flat yellow cakes and a bottle of water. They ate and drank, finding the food strange but satisfying. Other hatches opened at the base of the pillar between the couches, and hollow-centered seats slid out. Eyas examined one.

"It's a privy."

"About time," muttered Stormsong.

After a time they drowsed, Eyas and Stormsong on a single

couch, the centaurs on the floor. When they woke, the images in the windows were confusingly shifted. Some showed only blackness; others glittered with hundreds of sparks, moving slowly upward.

Eyas got up and went to a window, and realized at once that the ship must have turned while they slept. At the top of the window he saw the world, half-hidden by the icy white haze of the Bridge's inner edge. It seemed almost solid at that distance, but the nearer regions thinned to distinct points of light; at the bottom of the window Eyas saw only an occasional glint or flash. The Bridge was a vast ring of scattered dust and fragments, a field of fireflies over which the ship soared like a nightwing.

"Eyas—look." Stormsong, on the far side of the room, was staring at the bottom of a window. There, bright with cloud and green, was the rim of Skyland.

It was as beautiful as the Gulf had been on that summer day when Eyas had carried Soarfar back to Unsheath's island. Blue lakes gleamed in the sun; plains as green as jade stretched to the edges of dark forests or faded into the dun of deserts. It looked like the Gulf as the Goddess had shown it to the People in remembrance of the days when the ice had just left the land; yet it was a made thing—a disc, not a globe, an island higher and vaster than windwalkers ever dreamed of.

As the companions watched in silence, Skyland seemed to expand, filling all the windows while its rim retreated into a misty horizon. The ship trembled, and fell more slowly. Clouds loomed closer and the sky turned from black to dark blue. The chime sounded twice, startling them.

"Should we lie down again?" asked Standaway. Eyas nodded. Reluctantly, they left the windows. From his couch Eyas could see only the sky, dotted with clouds. He felt the trembling cease; the chime rang three times. Only then did they realize that they had come to rest as gently as a baby placed in a cradle. The door opened.

Smiling at his own needless caution, Eyas stood and went quickly through the door onto a platform at the top of a ramp. His gaze was drawn upward, outward; he swayed, and put a hand against the door to steady himself.

The horizon was very far away, yet higher than any on earth. It was as if he stood at the bottom of a great bowl, and looked up toward its edges. Streams, lakes, and forests extended up the sides of the bowl, distant yet distinct in the clear air. Above the horizon was the dark blue of sky and the whiteness of the Bridge—all the Bridge. Wide and diffuse, it arched away from the horizon and receded to an impossible height. Within its ellipse of light hung the blue crescent of the earth; beyond the Bridge's far, narrow edge was the white crescent of the moon.

The others joined him on the platform, and stared upward at the splendor of the earth within its ring. They did not speak.

Eyas tore his attention away and looked around. He saw the dimensions of the ship: a tall white cylinder, tapering to a point far above the door. The ramp wound down around it, a substantial structure almost as wide as the ramp on the Pillar. Somehow the ship had settled as smoothly into its resting place as a knife into its sheath. The ramp spiraled round the ship's hull four times and ended on a broad paved circle. Low buildings, of the same dark stone as the pavement, stood at the edges of the circle; beyond them were woods and fields.

The air was warm, and held the perfumes of strange flowers. Eyas wondered how the streams would taste. He looked again at the dark sky, the two worlds and the ring of light, and the fierce glare of the sun.

"Let us go down," he said quietly.

At the foot of the ramp they paused, unsure where to go. Then, fifty spans away, something moved from the doorway of one of the buildings.

It looked at first like a centaur. But though it was a four-footed creature with the legs and body of a centaur, it had no human torso—only a thick neck ending in a long, narrow head like that of a splithoof. It was covered by short, glossy brown hair; its neck was adorned with a slender black mane, and it bore a long-haired tail. The creature came to within a span of them, then stopped and regarded them with large, dark eyes. Though its mouth did not move, somehow it spoke in soft Bandish.

"Name yourselves."

The centaurs replied, then Stormsong and Eyas.

"You are greatly changed, Eyas Fisher, since I last saw you."

Eyas was silent, not knowing what to say.

"By what right do you come here?"

322

"By the will of the maker of Skyland."

"The maker has been dead for ten million years."

"Yet you do his will," Eyas answered, "as do I. He spoke to me in Hell, in the City of Ending, and sent me here."

"You are in great peril," the creature said. Eyas stood very still; the creature's quiet voice seemed to come from nowhere, and he did not doubt that it could destroy them as mysteriously as it spoke. "Have you words of passage?"

"I come from your maker, and I claim all your service and all your wisdom."

As if surprised, the creature lifted its head.

"Many have come to Skyland with other words of passage, and I have given them what their words permitted. Others have come with only their questions, and those I have slain. Only you have come to claim all, and you claim it in the maker's words. I obey you as I would the maker."

Eyas took a slow breath. "Tell me your name."

"I am the Archivist."

The word meant nothing. "You said you had seen me before—where, and when?"

"Whenever you were near a roundstone, I saw you."

"A roundstone—" Eyas glanced at Boulder, who kept his impassive gaze upon the Archivist. "Do you know why I have come here?"

"If you come from the maker, you come to destroy what he made."

"I do. Tell me how."

"You claimed my wisdom as well as my service. You will need both, if you would destroy Skyland."

"Then teach me."

"I do your will. Come with me."

Stormsong touched his arm. "We go with you, Eyas."

He hesitated, looking at his companions and then at the patient creature facing them. He knew that power awaited him: the power for which the Goddess had made him, the power for which he had lost his family, his people, his life. Stormsong's eyes met his. What was she? A superstitious, tattooed barbarian, who would dance in an enemy's skin to forget her own dread of death. And the centaurs: what had they to do with Hell and the sorrows of humans?

Boulder looked down at him, a faint smile on his dark face. Standaway pressed her hand against a still-unhealed wound on her flank. She never spoke of pain, but Eyas remembered how she had wept for her dead children, long ago on the bank of the Swift River near Foundries Hold.

The Goddess had made him for this moment, but so had these three, and a hundred thousand others. He served Her purposes, but also those of brutes and Bands, Riverines and peasants. Many had died for him, and would not return to earth. The Goddess had made him, yet his mother Firewing, holding him to nurse on Her belly, had sensed Her sadness, the sadness of a mother who knows she must make her child strong enough not to need her anymore. If he would be true to Her, he must decide for himself.

"Come with me," he said. They followed the Archivist into the building.

14

They lay, as if asleep, in a small room; yet they seemed to be on earth again, standing on a stony hillside with the Archivist. The creature spoke in a soft voice, dispassionate as the wind, while they sensed a subtler wind blowing silently through their minds.

"This is the earth as it was when Skyland was not yet made," the Archivist said. "But men are already masters of the world."

They looked up at a sunset sky. The moon was half-full. Where the Bridge of Heaven should be, they saw only a few white sparks.

"Those are the manmade worlds. They circle the earth, as Skyland does now. Millions live within them."

At once the earth vanished, and they drifted within an enormous closed space, a vast cylinder. Above and below them were buildings, trees, and fields, like Skyland curved upon itself. Eyas saw children splashing in a pond, and heard their screams of delight. The cylinder seemed open in three long gaps; even as he looked at them, he realized without knowing how that they were windows, sealed against airless space. He saw the sun shining through one window, saw the earth hanging in another, and understood the complex system of rotating mirrors that sustained the illusion of immobility when the cylinder was really rotating.

"The first of the great civilizations built this little world, and a hundred like it. Ships traveled here from the earth, and went on to the moon and beyond. Here they built greater ships—larger even than this cylinder—to take them to the stars."

"What are stars?" asked Eyas.

They were back on the hillside. Night had fallen, and the sky glittered with countless points of light, from horizon to zenith. Stormsong caught her breath; the centaurs sighed.

"They are suns like our own, but very far away. Men hoped to reach them, to find new earths and other races. A few ships began their journeys out before the dead could stop them."

Now they hung in space, outside a manmade world. Its hull receded into distance, turning slowly. A flash of light, brighter than the sun, erupted from the hull. Debris gushed out in clouds of frost; the world broke up in a silent explosion. In the star-filled darkness, other flares burned suddenly and briefly.

"In those days," the Archivist said calmly, "the dead were still learning how to control the living. They found that those who died here, far from earth, did not enter Hell. They vanished, like soulless ones.

"The dead saw that soon more men would live in space than on earth. Their souls would be lost to Hell. To save themselves, the dead lured the living into a great war against one another. All the manmade worlds were destroyed, and millions died on earth as well. After that, the dead allowed no more travel into space for a thousand years."

The hillside was changed: centuries had passed over it. In the night sky, the Bridge glowed against the stars. It seemed less regular than it should be, and Eyas realized that its fragments were not yet as small or as scattered as they would eventually become.

"The dead feared that someday men would return from the stars, and lead humanity away from earth again. It would not be hard; the war had poisoned much of the planet. The second civilization was slowly growing, repairing what it could, inventing what it could not repair. But many species had been destroyed, tools were lost, and the soil was almost barren. The dead restored lost knowledge, hurrying to forestall the return of the starmen.

"So men journeyed into space again, and dreamed of living there as their ancestors had. The maker was one of them. He had invented two things unknown to the first civilization, the gravitator and the Shield. The first could be used to power spacecraft, and to build earthlike satellites like this one. The second was a field of force that nothing could penetrate. The dead sent Messengers to him, and taught him what he needed to know to build Skyland. With a Shield around it, it would be safe forever, a place where men could live in peace while the earth healed itself. The maker thought that worlds like his could also go out to the stars."

They saw Skyland as it had been then: raw and new, its fields brown and unplanted. Strange buildings stood abandoned near a ship like the one that had brought Eyas and his companions here. A man burst from one of the buildings, running toward the ship. Eyas recognized him: the maker, a tall man with horror in his face. Three others pursued him, seized him, and carried him to the ship.

"The dead deceived him," said the Archivist. "They used his knowledge to build a great Shield, a barrier that closed off not just Skyland but the sun and inner worlds. Not even a grain of dust, or a ray of light, could pass into it, and from outside the sun seems no more than a dying star. If the starmen returned, they would think that the earth had been destroyed, or that they had lost their way."

The maker and his captors disappeared inside the ship. The Archivist went on: "He had little time before they took him, but he commanded me to await his return, or one who would come in his place to destroy Skyland."

The ship rose silently into the sky.

"The Messengers took him back to earth, and there he died. Other Messengers came. They filled Skyland with plants and animals that might be needed on earth after later wars, and they used me to store knowledge. At times a new Messenger comes to take that knowledge."

"And you have waited ten million years?" asked Eyas.

"Yes. I learned about Hell, and the rule of the dead. I learned that the maker was in Hell but still seeking to overthrow it. Not only Messengers have come; some men have been sent by the maker. Most never reached the hidden ships which the Messengers keep. One did, but Messengers were waiting here for him."

"Why didn't you destroy Skyland yourself?" Stormsong demanded.

"I am a machine for recording information."

Eyas realized that knowledge had come to them while the Archivist spoke; it waited, like memory, to be called into awareness. But he knew what he knew. He knew the structure of Skyland, and the physical laws that governed it. He knew every machine in Skyland, and how to use it. He understood all that men had learned about life; he knew that every living thing gained multidimensionality in its creation, and that Hell was the dimension in which human life persisted: a function of humanity's genetic nature, coexistent with the dimension of life. If it was a realm of misery it was also natural, as inevitable a property of humanness as any physical trait.

Like a waking man remembering a dream, Eyas saw all that the Archivist had seen in its long watch over the earth. He saw civilizations rise, flourish, and fall in war and famine. He saw the shape of the land change, saw deserts turn green and mountains wear away under grinding ice. He saw men who could create new kinds of life, saw the first centaurs step unsurely from mechanical wombs, saw small nocturnal animals transformed into tall lotors.

Again and again the dead harvested the living. When the survivors were few, the brutes they had created built civilizations of their own. But always men regained their powers, and drove their rivals into the woods and deserts. New cities rose on forgotten ruins; priests called to gods with a million names and were answered by the voices of the dead with the formula for gunpowder, the secret of the steam engine. Nations grew and contended until one ruled all the world's billions; then the priests heard nothing in their dreams, or heard their gods call for punishment and purification. Empire after empire crashed in fire and blood; in Hell the dead swarmed hungrily upon the dying.

Not all accepted the endless cycle. The dead had their wars too, silent and savage. The Archivist knew little of these, except what it could glean from the Messengers it served. Some, the Raiders, could not wait for a harvest and stirred up wars among primitive states. Others, the Refusers, like Sky and the maker, dreamed of breaking the link between earth and Hell, and finding oblivion in starvation. But the Messengers had always won. The Raiders and Refusers could only haunt the living; the Messengers, greatest feeders, had the strength to return to earth.

Some of the living had also sought escape. Once, when Hell was locked in a war, a whole civilization had chosen to give up its humanity and to seek a different fate. Its children, transformed into the first cetohumans, vanished into the seas and into their own unknown dimension when their long lives ended. Others learned of the soulless ones, and tried to discover the genetic flaw that blessed its possessors with extinction; but the Messengers crushed all who ventured in that direction.

As great and helpless as the tide, humanity had ebbed and flowed. Not even catastrophe could disrupt the cycle: ice ages came and went, plagues swept the world, and once a planetoid trapped within the Shield struck the icebound antarctic continent, but always the dead preserved the living. The cycle would go on for uncounted millions of years, unless it were broken. Someday, the dead knew, it must break. Some disaster would destroy mankind, or mutate it into a new species, or rouse it from its long trance to overthrow the rule of the dead. Then the infinite hunger of Hell would be unappeased, and the dead would dwindle into wraiths, perhaps even into the nonexistence that Sky hoped would end the misery of Hell.

The futility of it ground against Eyas's mind. All the suffering, only to sustain yet more suffering: the blind clawing of the dead for the souls of the dying, who struggled in turn to be fed with the souls of their children—how could the dead accept it?

They were in the little room, rousing themselves. The domed ceiling above them was a mosaic of fading colors. In a corner stood the Archivist—or what they now recognized as an extension of the great machine hidden beneath the surface of Skyland. They looked at one another with silent surprise, bound by the knowledge they shared.

"Let us go outside," said Eyas.

They walked, unspeaking, to the shore of a small lake near the buildings. A herd of deer gathered curiously around them. Eyas knew the name for them, as he knew that they had been extinct on earth for almost nine million years. He knew as well that only a very few lived and bred naturally here, though their genetic templates were stored with those of thousands of other lost species. The animals and plants of Skyland were there simply to sustain its ecosystem as the maker had intended, against the day when men might have to seek haven here.

The centaurs waded out into the lake to bathe. Stormsong and Eyas sat together, stroking the deer. The Archivist stood silently nearby, unblinking in the bright sunlight.

"Destroying the Shield generator means destroying Skyland," Stormsong said.

"Yes." Like her, Eyas could visualize the structure of the generator, built into Skyland's core. The satellite's artificial gravitation powered the generator; both would have to be destroyed. Skyland would suffer gravitational collapse, within moments. "But Hell will be unharmed. Men will still live and die on earth, and feed the dead."

"We can build new Skylands, and go out to the stars in them. If all of us left, Hell would have nothing to feed on."

He smiled wryly. "It would take centuries, even with the knowledge the Archivist has given us. Not all would want to leave, and the Messengers would have time to thwart us—even put a new Shield around us. Besides, we don't know what happens to those who die away from earth; perhaps they simply go to another Hell. So—"

"What?"

"The Shield need not be destroyed. It can be refocused, so that only the earth and moon are inside it."

Stormsong looked at him. "You'd destroy all life on earth. The planet would freeze."

"All would die, and then Hell would begin to dwindle. The Messengers would have no one to possess; they would be trapped and destroyed as well."

"And we with them!"

"We will die in any case." He rubbed his pale face wearily. "I do not like it, but it must be what the maker intended. Nothing else would work."

Her face was unreadable under its tattooes. "What about the others—the lotors, the centaurs, the windwalkers? The canids on the other continents? The animals who could yet evolve into thinking brutes? Can we destroy them as well?"

"The lotors will know eternal happiness," said Eyas. "Perhaps the canids will too. The centaurs' afterlife is not much better than our own. What does it matter? All will end someday; let it be now, and be done with it."

Stormsong's fist exploded against his jaw, knocking him flat. Before he could recover she was on him, her knees pinning his arms, her knife against his throat.

"The dead warned that you'd desert us, and they were right. Or did you go mad in the tree? Have we come all this way only to kill ourselves?"

"Stormsong, I have seen Hell."

"And I've seen life, you great fool. Why do you think we Bandish fear death? Because this life is good. Death is a high price for it, but not too high."

"What would you have me do, then?" With sudden power he threw her onto the grass, twisted her knife away, and flung it into the lake. "Shall I admit defeat? Let the Messengers build another doomed empire on our bones? Shall I tell the brutes to go home and await the slaughter? The Goddess made me for this, Stormsong."

"If she did, she was an even greater fool than you." Her mouth twisted in contempt. "She made you a man like no other, a man who makes the rest of us glad of our lives and willing to give them up for your sake. But you were made to end our lives, were you? To give us hope, and then turn the world to ice. What will the difference be then, between earth and Hell?"

Eyas stood up. "I will do what I say I will do."

"Do it, then! Let your child die in me, and not know what a madman its father was. Let it join the other wraiths."

The centaurs splashed out of the lake, their bodies glistening in the sun. Standaway's arm was around Boulder's waist, and she was smiling. Eyas looked at them and rejoiced in their beauty. He took Stormsong's hand and drew her up; she glared unsurely at him.

"Beaten!" he snorted. "Beaten by a single blow and a few words, and the smile on Standaway's face." He put his arms around her, and after a moment she returned his embrace.

"Have you been quarreling?" Standaway asked.

"Fighting a battle," answered Stormsong. "The grimmest of all."

A small machine rolled across the grass to them. Within it were trays of food like that in the spaceship; they knew now that it was synthetic, but it tasted just as good as before. While they were eating, the Archivist spoke:

"Five ships have left their stations on earth. They will reach Skyland within twelve hours."

Eyas nodded, knowing that Mount Aspen was only one of ten spaceship stations scattered around the world. "Messengers?"

"Yes. Seventeen of them altogether, all from other continents. They intend to kill you."

Eyas knew without asking that the Archivist could not destroy the ships, nor even kill the Messengers when they landed unless they failed to give it the proper words of passage. The ten landing sites, scattered all across Skyland, were each near a small armory; the Messengers would be well armed as soon as they arrived. It would be impossible to kill them all; even if he and Stormsong and the centaurs hid in the forests, the Messengers could bring in reinforcements and eventually capture them.

"Our only chance is to destroy Skyland just before we leave," said Boulder. His eyes seemed deeper and darker with new knowledge. "A timed disharmony in the gravitator will do it."

"We can't throw away ten million years of wealth and knowledge," Standaway protested.

"We'll take much of it with us," said Eyas. "The Archivist, and the genetic templates, some of the robots and other machines—"

"And weapons," Stormsong interrupted. "All we can get. We have a war still to win."

Eyas nodded reluctantly. "Archivist, where is our army now? Do your roundstones show it?"

"Yes. It is in retreat."

"Retreat?" shouted Stormsong.

"Your allies crossed the Bitter River seven days ago. The Suns withdrew before them, and then attacked in force. Your allies broke out of an encirclement; they are fighting their way back to the river. The Deltan army awaits them across the river."

Eyas looked at the others. "Now we must hasten."

Below the green hills of Skyland was another world, of metal and glare and endless tunnels. Into this world Eyas descended, finding his way as readily as he had once walked from the Fisher longhouse to Speaker's Hall. He sat within a kind of boat, a wheelless vehicle that rode a magnetic stream into the core of Skyland. All he saw was strange and new, yet familiar; he could remember every stage of Skyland's construction, he knew the function of every circuit; the vehicle controls were as comfortable in his hands as the paddle of a canoe.

He went alone, while the others looked to the salvage of Skyland's riches. On that long journey through bright tunnels, he thought about the maker's motives: he had not needed to give Eyas the words of passage that would grant him all human knowledge, all history. Other words would have commanded the Archivist to yield the simple secret of refocusing the Shield. But the maker had wanted to make sure that it was done, that Eyas would act to suffocate the world. The maker had judged him well; the sudden memory of ten million years of suffering had been enough.

But Stormsong's love of life, and her callous indifference to others' pain, had thwarted the maker's plan; had he come without her to Skyland, Eyas knew he would still be going on this journey to the heart of mankind's greatest machine, but it would have been a journey with a far different ending.

The vehicle slowed and stopped inside a large room, a hemisphere of dull metal. At its center was a plain white chair facing a narrow column a little more than a span high. Eyas walked to the chair, sat, and raised a hand before the column. Symbols suddenly glowed in the air, projected onto his optic nerve. They told him the state of the gravitator's energy flow, and the strength of the Shield.

He gestured; the symbols pulsed orange, then yellow, with a warning that he did not heed. Swiftly, silently, his hand commanded the machine to destroy itself. It obeyed.

When the process was begun, Eyas returned to his vehicle and sent it back up the long tunnel. Behind him, a machine was in the last moments of a ten-million-year existence. Its molecules had endured that long in a kind of trance, immune to time, as the earth itself had been. Now the machine would waken into death. He wondered what men and brutes would waken to, and began to understand the vast increase of his ignorance.

For the return journey only the centaurs and the Archivist stayed in the passenger compartment, amid boxes of genetic-template cylinders and piles of laser rifles for which there had been no room in the cargo hold. Though Skyland was chiefly a repository of information, its robot factories could produce

332

almost anything devised by the maker's civilization; the Messengers, however, had rarely exploited those factories, preferring to guide each succeeding civilization at a gradual pace. Thinking of what Bandish warriors might do with the destructive power of laser rifles, Eyas respected the wise husbandry of the dead even as he despised their complacent arrogance: had they recognized early what a threat he posed to them, they could have armed the Suns or Deltans with weapons that would have eradicated the allies in an instant.

He and Stormsong were up on the control deck, lying on couches facing a bank of screens and optic projectors. Though the Archivist had already received the total information storage of its central computer, it remained connected to that computer: it would monitor the Messengers' ships and all information sent by roundstone to Skyland until the satellite's destruction.

Eyas overrode the ship's automatic systems with a gesture and, with another, commanded it to lift off. On the screens, the landing site dropped away.

"The nearest ship is three hours from landing," the Archivist's voice murmured in Eyas's ear. "The farthest is five hours."

"Can the Messengers take control of their ships?"

"No. They have never needed to before, and do not anticipate the need." It filled a screen with glimpses of the Messenger ships' cabins: men and women lying on couches or staring silently out at space. They had come from other continents, but apart from their strange clothes they looked like ordinary Allanders—some fair, some dark. Only in their eyes did their true natures show; Eyas remembered the tall man at Longstrand and rubbed the gunshot scar on his temple.

"What will you do when Brightspear is beaten?" asked Stormsong.

"Teach others as we have been taught—everyone in the world, men and brutes. Then we can decide what to do. Perhaps we can change our genetic patterns, as the cetohumans did, or go into space as the maker hoped to. When men and brutes all share our knowledge, we may find a way to overthrow Hell without destroying the earth."

"Maybe the lotors will let us enter their other realm."

Eyas laughed. "After all the strangeness of this day, that

333

doesn't sound strange at all." He looked at her and took her hand. "To be a father again . . . it will be a long wait until next summer."

"Longer for me than for you."

The first Messengers, all men, reached Skyland without incident; Eyas and the others watched the three of them hurry to a building near their landing site. They encountered another Archivist, gave it words of passage, and went inside. A few moments later they emerged, riding in a small, open car, and set off toward the landing site that the companions had left. Monitors followed their journey. On a road through a wood the car began to slow, then stopped. The Messengers got out, grim-faced and gripping laser rifles. They moved awkwardly, heavily, and after a few staggering steps they fell. Trees cracked and toppled around them. The monitor went dark.

Eyas sighed and lay back. The gravitator's field was strengthening, drawing Skyland in upon itself. From space it still appeared as a bright green circle, dappled with clouds and streams, but the symbols flashing in the air before Eyas's face told him of failing girders, snapping cables, spreading power failures.

The remaining Messenger ships were near enough to be drawn swiftly down into Skyland's destruction. Their gravitator drives too weak to overcome the sudden pull, the ships went out of control and began to fall, tumbling end over end. The men and women within them were flung about their cabins, screaming.

Before they struck, Skyland crumpled like a flower in a great unseen fist. The green circle darkened, split, and shrank; lightning flashed in the condensing atmosphere for a few moments. Then Skyland flared like a small sun and vanished into darkness. The monitors on the Messengers' ships transmitted chaotic red-orange patterns of light, and then nothing.

"Gravitational collapse is under way," the Archivist said. "Skyland will become a black hole in approximately twenty hours. It will circle the earth seven more times in a decaying orbit for the next ten days, and then evaporate. The Shield has already broken down. Light from outside should reach us within ten minutes."

The ship skimmed across the Bridge of Heaven. The sun

sank behind the rim of the earth. A few breaths later, the stars shone.

Around the broad black circle of the earth, beyond the rim of the Bridge, they saw a greater bridge: a band of light, still and serene. Within it were single stars brighter than Evenspark, shimmering clusters, clouds that glowed. Somewhere out there, Eyas thought, were the starmen. Already the sun's light was going out to them, a call from their lost home. Some day they would answer that call.

He turned his thoughts to the earth and called the Archivist. "Where is the allied army now?"

A diagram of a battlefield glowed before him. The allies were in a narrow valley; to the north, west, and south, the Suns held the high ground, and to the east was the Bitter River. Arrayed on the far bank was a line of wagonforts and behind them stood Guardian's army, ready to slaughter any who crossed the river. Now a roundstone in a centaur's necklace showed the hills to the north, dotted with puffs of cannon smoke. The valley bottom was strewn with corpses of men and brutes, but the allies' artillery still returned fire, and Bandish warriors rode centaurs in a counterattack up a shallow ravine. Another image: a swirl of black-clad soldiers, seen from the roundstone in the pommel of a Sunnish rider's sword; then a glimpse of the allies' main force, behind walls of wagons and Riverine pikemen. In the distance the river gleamed in the afternoon, and beyond it was the glitter of sunlight on Deltan armor. Now a Sunnish officer's face appeared; he spoke excitedly to his commander, describing casualties and requesting orders. Eyas heard Brightspear's voice reply,

"Press the attack."

The ship fell through the night, curving around the earth toward day. It passed over the Dawn Coast, over the eastern provinces of Delta; the sun rose at last, and the sky overhead was a clear autumn blue. Brown hills slid by close below, casting long shadows eastward. Locked onto roundstone signals, Eyas guided the ship to the valley where the allies slowly retreated before the cannons and riders of the Suns.

Smoke and dust rose thick above the battlefield. With the setting sun in their faces, the allies did not see the ship hovering above them; but their enemies did, and cried out in wonder as it sank tail-first, gleaming and silent, onto the

335

yellow grass of the valley floor. Guns and cannons fell silent on both sides. The haze of battle began to clear. Like one of the ruined pillars of Palisade, the ship stood between the armies, ancient and strange, an augury of unimagined power and terrible change.

The sun was low in the west, a red circle above black hills. Eyas triggered the ship's loudspeakers, and his voice rolled across the valley.

"Lay down your arms, men of Sun and Delta."

With the ship's senses, he scanned their faces in the red twilight. They gaped, frowned, shook their heads, put hands to their ears. Their brutes bawled in surprise at the noise of Eyas's voice.

"The Dominance and Delta are overthrown. Lay down your arms. No man or brute will harm you, unless you resist."

—There was Brightspear, on a hilltop overlooking the narrow western end of the little valley. He sat astride a big sixfoot, with a retinue of riders and foot soldiers about him, no more than a thousand spans from the ship. His face was shaded by the rim of a silver helmet studded with roundstones; his expression was calm, almost serene.

"Lay down your arms. I am Eyas Fisher, and I promise safety to all who yield."

A sound rose from the allies, like a farheard tide rising in the Rip. In the last red light of evening, pikes rose glinting; arrows shot jubilantly into the darkening sky. Men and centaurs and lotors ran out past the corpses of their comrades and enemies, toward the ship.

A boy on a hillside threw down his pike; another did the same, and sat wearily down on the grass. Swords clinked and clattered as they fell upon each other. But many of the Suns still gripped their weapons as if entranced. They looked from the ship to the hillside where Brightspear's black and yellow banner flapped against the purpling sky, awaiting an order that did not come. Eyas could see officers speaking urgently to the Sun, but Brightspear sat motionless upon his mount.

"He's not going to surrender," said Stormsong. "But we can kill him from here with a laser bolt."

"No." Eyas smiled almost sadly. "He knows me well. I'm going out to speak to him."

She looked alarmed but did not argue. Eyas went into a

little elevator that lowered him to the passenger compartment.

"I'm going out to take Brightspear's surrender," he told the centaurs. Boulder shook his head.

"He'll try some treachery, Eyas. We'll cover you."

"Very well. But shoot no one who puts down his weapons."

Standaway nodded, and took up a slim black laser rifle. She and Boulder followed him to the door; it opened, and a platform folded out of the hull. When Eyas stepped upon it, it lowered him gently to the ground.

Night had fallen, but the hull of the ship gleamed with lights. The allies, hastening forward, paused when they saw Eyas walk away from the ship toward the hill where Brightspear waited. They murmured uncertainly; then their faces turned to the sky, and they cried out in surprise.

The stars were coming out. And in the Bridge of Heaven there was a great gap, a slash of blackness—the empty wake of Skyland. As it spiraled toward the earth, the collapsing satellite was drawing the ring into itself.

Eyas walked past a line of Sunnish riders, past cannon crews and foot soldiers who parted ranks to let him through. They stared at him with fearful curiosity: a tall young man, with a pale face and snow-white hair and beard, dressed in dirty Bandish tunic and trousers and felt boots. A few warriors still held rifles or lances, but none offered him violence. In the cold, still air, Eyas's footsteps seemed loud.

At last he came to the hilltop, where dark shapes waited. He recognized Brightspear, and approached him.

"I greet you, Brightspear."

"I greet you, Eyas."

"Our war is over."

Brightspear chuckled in the darkness. "Is it?"

"You told me not long ago that you would rule while the Bridge still stands. It stands no more. Skyland is destroyed, and the Messengers' power is overthrown."

"Is it?" Brightspear asked again. "Their power is not of this earth."

"Let them rule in Hell; here life rules. It was in my power to destroy the world, and Hell with it, but life forbade me."

"So you would be the Sun, and rule in my place."

"There are no more Suns, no more Guardians. Only men and brutes, and our cousins out there. Look up, Brightspear! Those lights are stars, suns like our own, with worlds like

337

earth. Men went to them, long ago; we shall go too, and perhaps to a better destiny than Hell. Yield, and come with us."

"Give us light," Brightspear commanded, and torches were kindled. In their red flicker, Eyas saw Brightspear's face above him.

"I know what the stars are," Brightspear said in Gulf dialect. "But men will not go back to them, to be lost in nothingness."

His eyes gleamed in the torchlight, but it was Admiral Thorn who looked out of them. Eyas recognized him, and stepped back in amazement.

"You have possessed him."

"His hold on life was always weak," Thorn murmured. "When we told him you had survived the tree, he went mad. If you dreamed of revenge, Eyas, you are cheated of it. But you have dealt us a bitter blow, and caused us much trouble. We too have cause for revenge, and we shall take it." He gestured to the soldiers. "Kill him."

The warriors stepped reluctantly forward, swords drawn, and then retreated from the white glare that burst around Eyas's body. The sixfoot reared up with a shriek as Eyas grasped the Messenger's wrist and pulled him from the saddle.

"To me! To me!" cried the Messenger in the voice that Quiet had farheard long ago, but no one moved. Eyas's hands closed around his throat; the Messenger struggled, screamed, and slumped to the ground.

Eyas released him, and felt his rage dwindle with the light. As if from a long distance he heard men shouting and weeping, but he ignored them. He knelt, and in torchlight saw Brightspear reappear in dying eyes.

"Brightspear. Brightspear." The Sun's hands groped up, seeking something unseen, unseeable. Eyas grasped them. "It's over now."

Brightspear's breath rattled in his crushed throat and escaped in a puff of frost. His hands were cold; they tightened, then pulled away from Eyas to grope again in the darkness. Then he was dead.

Eyas stood up. If this was vengeance, vengeance was only another word for sorrow and pity. He looked at the men around him: they had conquered half the world they knew, yet they seemed only frightened boys.

"Throw down your arms."

Some wept as they obeyed. One, braver than the rest, said, "You are our master now, Eyas. What is your will?"

"To make you men who need no masters. Go, look to your men; tend your wounded and bury your dead. Make camp, and rest. In the morning we will speak with you, and with the Deltans." He looked more closely at the warrior who had spoken. The young man met his gaze. "Victor of the Marchwardens—you and I have journeyed far. May we next meet without a battle."

He turned and walked back down the hill. The ship, wreathed in its own lights, was surrounded by silent warriors of the allied army. A chill wind hissed in the dead grass around his feet, quieter than his footsteps. He heard it even as he went among the lotors, the centaurs, the Bandish warriors, the Riverines, the Deltan peasants; he heard it even as they began to cheer and sing.

At the ship he found Stormsong and Boulder and Standaway, singing with the dusty soldiers crowded close around them. "We are holded now," Standaway shouted over the jubilation. Eyas nodded. He stood with Stormsong between the centaurs, his arm around Standaway's waist, Stormsong's hand stroking Boulder's mane. It was good to have a family again.

The Tower at Longstrand

On a summer afternoon in the Year of Freedom 312, Eyas Fisher came out of the family longhouse and stood for a moment in the shade of the arbor. Dense bunches of ripening grapes, purple as amethysts, hung amid the leaves. Chirp—the latest in a long line with that name—leaped from a vine onto his shoulder. He patted her absentmindedly while she clucked and chirred in his ear.

Golden followed him out of the house and leaned against the door, which was covered with a picture in hammered silver: a man and a centaur standing in a boat, holding a cannon. At fifty, she still looked like a buxom adolescent; her yellow hair fell over her tanned shoulders and breasts, and all that remained of the scar she had suffered in infancy was a deep dimple in her cheek. Her regrown eye was a slightly darker blue than the other. Long life, extended youth, and healing of damaged tissue had been among the gifts of the Archivist.

"Leave the door open," she said. "There's not a breath of air inside." The aroma of baking bread came from the house. Golden squinted out at the sun-dazzled waters of the Gulf. "Are they still out there?"

"Yes—see, there's the sail." Eyas pointed to a white triangle, one of many dotting the estuary. Darkhair was with one of his younger great-grandchildren, a bouncy eight-year-old named Honey, teaching her how to sail on *Fifth Waveskimmer*. He was over a hundred, but strong and vigorous; another century or two lay before him.

Golden sighed. "He promised me he'd have her back by now. She hasn't eaten since morning, and she'll be cross and tired."

"If I know Darkhair, he's caught a redfin and made a feast of it."

"A handful of raw fish is not a feast."

Eyas grinned. Golden had lived in the Gulf for more than twenty years now, ever since the Fishers had returned to

343

stay; though her standing was that of a singleton-aunt in the family, she was still a Deltan peasant who disapproved of food that came out of water instead of good solid dirt.

"I wish Darkhair would go spacefaring again," she went on. "At least until the children are grown. He spoils them too much."

"He'd only spoil the next generation when he got back."

"He would. Well, where are you off to?"

"A walk. I'll be back before suppertime."

"Don't mock with me." She was teased but not annoyed. "Stormsong will want to know."

He nodded. "I should be home in time to welcome her." Two days before, Stormsong had gone to Snowcliffs, the home country of the windwalkers, on a political visit; she was expected home by evening. He was glad she still enjoyed such chores. Since his retirement from the Council twenty years before, he had cheerfully settled into the small life of Longstrand, the domestic bustle of children and in-laws and relatives. He rarely left the Gulf now, except to stay in the family's other home in Foundries. Boulder had served two terms as Arm of the Nation, the union of holds that had been established after the defeat of the Suns and Deltans. Now he occupied himself with centaur archaeology, filling in the gaps in the Archivist's records. Standaway had designed High Foundries, the centaurs' first spacehold, and was working on two others.

Theirs had been the first interspecies marriage; now the institution was widespread. Most were between centaurs and humans—mostly Bandish humans—but it was common to find humans or lotors in windwalker families. The canids of Forest—the continent south of Alland—were joining human families in growing numbers: the link between the two species was an ancient one. Never before, in any of the old cultures, had men and brutes lived together as equals; under the impact of the Archivist's knowledge, shared among all, the barriers between the species had fallen for good. Even sexual relationships extended across some species lines—though not across that between humans and centaurs—and genetic engineering made possible the birth of hybrid offspring. The Fishers had discussed having such a child, but Standaway was reluctant: though she knew the legend of Whitemane was only a myth, it was a powerful one.

Eyas kissed Golden farewell and put Chirp back in the

344

arbor; then he went down the steps, past the family post. It had been overthrown and buried in the sack of Longstrand, but Eyas had restored it when he rebuilt the village. He walked past the boatshed, which now held a little-used aircraft as well as *Fifth Waveskimmer,* and out onto the beach.

The tide was high, slapping around Anger's Rock. Eyas waded along the shore toward Speaker's Hall.

Longstrand looked much as it had in the old days: a long, narrow hill between beach and cliff, crowded with longhouses and sheds. Some buildings, though, were two stories high; a few had large windows, though most Longstranders preferred screens for a more controllable view. To the east, low buildings of brick and steel ran well past the centaurs' old camp-site: inns, warehouses, gymnasiums, a power station, and an aircraft platform. The new town was pretty enough, with bloodwoods and maples lining its streets and its public gardens fragrant with flowering club, but few stayed there long. Traders' Beach and Speaker's Hall were the noisy, cheerful center of Longstrand, as they had been before.

Traders' Beach was crowded today. Human and centaur children raced along the water's edge, delightedly splashing anyone within range. Young men and women, on their wanderyear, flirted and gambled on the sand. A few of them drifted among the traders' booths, admiring the tapestries offered by a shaggy canid merchant and the glass sculptures of an artist from New Fort, taught by windwalkers. The sharp scent of Jadelandic cinnamon drifted from a foodstall.

Eyas missed the rattle of clapsticks; they were out of fashion these days, when everyone wanted to experiment with the infinite variety of ancient musical instruments. But he enjoyed the noise and excitement, the gossip and mockery duels, the liquid movements of a trancedancer from Greatland, the huge continent in the eastern hemisphere. He wandered through the crowds, pausing to talk with two young centaurs from New Silverstream Hold—engineers on holiday, and distant relatives of the Fishers through Standaway. A Deltan family insisted he have a mug of beer with them; the parents were veterans of the allied army, come to see the Gulf with their grown children.

"You're looking old, Namegiver," the mother teased him. "Don't you get tired of being the only man around with white hair?"

Eyas laughed, as much at her children's scandalized expressions as at her mockery. "'I stand in moonlight at midday,'" he said; it was a line from an ancient play, and the Deltans of course recognized it.

After a few more jokes he left the beach and walked up the narrow streets, down the other side of the hill, and out to the base of the cliff. The trail to the tower was still there, though overgrown with blackberries and alders. Not many used the trail anymore, except for children and an occasional visitor from outside.

The tower looked as it always had: a mass of dark stone rising out of green. Some of the People had wanted to demolish it when Eyas had first returned, but he had ordered it left alone.

"Hello, Grandfather Eyas."

"Hello, Hemlock. Are you going up to the tower?"

The little girl grinned conspiratorially. "We're not supposed to. But I'm just showing Fourthborn where the best blackberries are." Fourthborn was a canid boy, a little taller than the six-year-old but probably a year younger; he had the blunt face and big hands and feet of a young canid, and had not yet lost the fine white hair of infancy.

"Well, come along and keep me company."

They walked slowly up the trail, each child holding one of Eyas's hands. Hemlock chattered away, while Fourthborn kept shyly silent. Occasionally they paused to pick a few berries or to watch swallows dart from their nests in the cliff.

"When I was a boy we had no swallows," Eyas said. "There were hardly any birds then except hawks and spoonbills."

"You brought the birds from Skyland, didn't you?" Hemlock said proudly.

"That's right."

"You were smart. I like birds."

"Well, we'll make some more soon."

"Why don't you make all of them right now?"

"Because then they'd start crowding the firewings and blackbeaks and dabblers. We have to make sure they all have enough food and enough room to raise their babies."

"Oh." She sounded disappointed.

"Next year, when you're big enough for the knowledge, you'll understand."

"I'm going to know everything next year," Hemlock bragged. Fourthborn looked abashed.

"I don't get the knowledge for two more years," he said.

346

"You're only four? You're big for your age," Eyas consoled him. Actually, they both seemed very small and very young, and he wondered, as he often had, about giving children all the knowledge. Some took it very hard, for so much of human history was a nightmare of blood and misery. But it made them at once the equals of their elders, and in some ways their superiors, for they had less to unlearn; it gave them, too, an almost instinctive rejection of cruelty and war. "But Hemlock, you won't really know everything. You'll find out how much we still don't know."

"Do you still don't know, Grandfather?"

"Not know. Yes."

"What do you not know?"

"Oh, lots of things. I don't know why the starmen went away."

They had come last year, in two great ships like silver bubbles and larger than Skyland. For months they had orbited the earth while they learned the languages of men. Eyas had given them all the information they had asked for, and invited them to the surface, but they had refused. When he had asked them about the fate of their dead, they had not replied; soon after, the ships had left orbit and vanished.

Their very presence had of course told much about them: they too had gravitators, and must use an application of them to travel among the stars. Though their ships were strange, their technology did not seem greatly advanced over that of earth's early cultures, and they themselves, as seen by holotransmission, appeared genetically identical to earthmen despite millions of years of isolation. When they left without explanation, Eyas had been disappointed and perplexed; after reflection, though, he thought he knew the starmen's motives.

The new sciences built on the Archivist's knowledge had theorized that at least some physical forces reached across the multidimensions of quantum superspace. Gravity was one, and Hell existed because of the earth's mass. A human dying far enough away from a planet—or a gravitator—would drift eternally alone. The ships of the first civilization, when they went out to the stars, had used only centrifugal force as a substitute for gravity; their dead must have been scattered in their wake. The independent invention of the gravitator by the starmen had created miniature Hells for their ships, and their dead would soon have gained control of the living.

That possibility, when Eyas considered it on dark nights,

drew him close to the edge of the despair he had felt in the first shock of the knowledge, when he had been ready to destroy the world. He and Stormsong had hoped that the starmen had escaped the fate of their earthbound cousins and would return to save them. Perhaps that would still happen, but Eyas now saw little chance of it.

"Grandfather?"

—It was impossible. The best that men could hope for might be a spacefaring society free of the control of the dead; but what would be the purpose of a life that ended in eternal solitude, as a dim speck of awareness in endless night? He thought of his lost children, wraiths in Hell: could he consign a child's soul to a misery worse than theirs?

"Grandfather! What else don't you know?"

"I'm sorry, Hemlock—I was daydreaming. Well—I don't know what you had for breakfast, or what your great-grandfather Darkhair will do tomorrow."

He did not know why the dead no longer haunted the living. Perhaps another war had broken out in Hell, or the dead were content to wait for harvest: though men lived long now, their numbers were growing swiftly, and all would eventually die. He missed the dead, to his own surprise—missed Sky's voice, and the leering faces in his dreams.

"I know what I had for breakfast, and Great-grandfather will go sailing tomorrow."

"I had toasted bread and two baked apples," said Fourthborn.

And he missed the strange joy of the white rages. They had never come again after Brightspear's death. He did not know the source of the white light that shone out him when he confronted Hell, the light that in Hell had nourished and destroyed so many souls. He had even scanned his own genetic pattern, seeking an answer. The pattern was strange in many ways; the signs of the Goddess's tampering were clear. But the scan had given him no answers.

"Here's a good patch," he said. The berries were thickly clustered, many low enough for the children. They ate cheerfully and messily, until Hemlock's brown skin and Fourthborn's white fur were stained purple.

They were near the top of the cliff and close to the tower. Its old walls, splotched with moss and lichen, shimmered in summer heat. Swallows nested where mortar had fallen away between the stones.

"Would you two like to see inside the tower?" he asked.

"Oh yes, please!" Hemlock said instantly. "Grandfather had a big fight here a long, long time ago," she told Fourthborn.

"You told me that."

"Now, you're not to come here by yourselves," Eyas said seriously. "Your mothers and fathers would be very angry if you did. It's dangerous for children by themselves."

They nodded with energetic insincerity, just as he had when Firewing and Quiet had warned him about the tower.

"All right. Follow me." He led them down a narrow path, the same one that the Suns had dragged him up to face Brightspear. At its end was the doorway where the soldier had died, where Eyas had crouched with a bleeding foot. The blackberries were far higher and thicker now, but he had come often to the tower, and had cleared the brambles from the doorway.

They entered easily and looked inside. The old basement had been a mass of trees and salal fifty years ago; now the trees were fewer but taller, their tops almost level with the top of the tower's walls. The far side of the tower was almost invisible behind the trunks.

"I wish the trees had been this tall when the Suns came," Eyas said. "I could have climbed from one to the next and gotten away on the other side. Instead I had to climb up the wall."

The children craned their necks, staring up through the leaves. "All the way to the top?" Hemlock said. "That's a long way."

"A very long way. I sat in a window up there and shot arrows at the Suns."

"Will we get to see you shooting arrows in the knowledge?" asked Fourthborn.

"No, but you'll see some of what happened in Longstrand."

The children looked at each other in cheerful anticipation. Eyas wished that remembrance still bound the generations. The knowledge was powerful enough to link all who shared it, men and brutes, but it was the world seen passively, from outside; remembrance had shown the People the world through their own eyes. Only the survivors of Brightspear's conquest knew what it had been like. Their children and grandchildren were not the People.

"Weren't you afraid to climb up there?"

"I was too busy to be afraid, Hemlock. And I'd done it many times when I was a boy. It's easier than it looks—the stones are full of cracks and ledges. Look, I'll show you."

He stepped out of the doorway and found a toehold. "Don't lean out so far, Fourthborn. Stay there a moment, and I'll bring you a stone from the window."

If anything, the climb was easier than he remembered. The gaps between stones were wider and deeper, worn by frost and rain. But the light was very different, a green shade that presaged the tower's inevitable destruction by weather and patient, probing roots. Hemlock called worriedly to him.

"I'll be right there," he called back, and pulled himself into the window. How small it was! A few leaves littered it, and bits of dried mud that must be a ruined swallows' nest. A gap in the masonry showed where he had pulled out the stone that killed the Sunnish soldier. In two places he found gouges in the stone where bullets had struck and ricocheted; perhaps one of them had been the bullet that struck his foot.

Eyas was disappointed in the view. The blackberries had grown high enough to hide the trail; beyond them was the edge of the forest, a wall of green and gold. Within that forest, not far away, was a pile of blackened, rotting logs in a marshy clearing—all that was left of Silken's cabin. He realized that it must be almost twenty years since he had last been there. One day this summer he would go again, with some of the children. Or with Darkhair—but Darkhair went to the clearing every year or two, always alone.

"Grandfather!" Hemlock yelled. "Hurry up!"

He found a couple of stone fragments and slipped them into his hair, then crawled backward out of the window. Descending was slow work; he had to keep looking down for the next foothold.

A stone gave way with a rattle of crumbling mortar, and his fingers lost their grip. For a long instant he seemed to float in green shade, and he remembered diving for the cannon. Then he struck, hearing branches snap.

He was lying on his back, only a span below the doorway where the children stood. Eyas looked up into Hemlock's eyes, and between them passed a look that made him think of Sky. Fourthborn was wailing for his mother.

"Hush, hush," Eyas whispered. He was surprised that he could still speak. His vision was narrowing, and he did not look away from the children for fear that he might not find them again. "Hush. Hemlock, go get help. Go down to the

first house. Be quick, but be careful." His own words made
him smile.

"I don't want to—I want to stay with you."

"Go, quickly."

"Grandfather—"

She took the canid by the hand and yanked him away. Eyas
heard their rapid footsteps. Good: she was brave, decisive,
coolheaded. She'd be Speaker some day. He wished he hadn't
left her with the memory of this foolish death. And it was
death; he could feel nothing, but each breath was harder than
the last, and made something grate in his chest.

The leaves overhead made shifting patterns against the sky:
dark green, light green, blue, a shaft of white-gold sunlight.
He looked for a hawk, but saw only the flutter and ripple of
the leaves.

Then he sat up in darkness, seeing the walls around him
shift and blur. The trees were gone, but this was surely the
basement of the tower as it had been in the time of Quickhand:
a row of empty cells, their thick doors ajar, racks of spears,
bundles of arrows, kegs and boxes piled to the low ceiling.
He saw no one. His skin glowed as it had long before, but
less fiercely. Nothing tied him to life now except memory.

A flight of stairs led to the next floor, and at last to the top
of the tower. He stepped onto a narrow walkway between the
wall and the slated roof, and looked down upon Longstrand.

It stood at the edge of a still and sunless sea; now the rude
huts of the firstcomers, now the longhouses of his childhood,
now the towers of ancient cities rising against the still-young
mountains of the Eastwall. It swarmed, in all its aspects, with
the crowded souls of the dead. He saw their empty faces
turned up toward him, but they did not come near.

He turned and saw still more of the dead, standing silently
along the edge of the cliff. Most were unmoving, but a few
walked slowly down the trail to the base of the tower. He
waited for them to ascend.

They came out onto the walkway, four dark figures: Netweaver,
Firewing, Old, and Silken. He reached out to them, but they
shrank back.

Do not touch us, Eyas. It was his father's voice, faint but
unmistakable.

Are you afraid of me?

Yes, said Firewing. *Yes. You are the scourger of Hell, the destroyer of the Messengers, the breaker of the Shield. You killed the greatest Messenger of all at the Bitter River, made a wraith of him. Yes, we fear you.*

But you are warm and bright, sighed Silken.

And you are my husband, said Old.

This is Hell, Eyas replied. *Here there is no husband, no child, no friend or lover.*

There is, if we have the strength to remember. Oh, Eyas, give us that strength! Or touch us, and throw us down among the wraiths.

What can I give? How can I give it?

He saw his children die again, and Standaway weeping beside the river. He held Golden, a wailing infant, in his arms. His soul burned again with rage and grief, love and sorrow, and his white fire struck out against the darkness. He reached out, reached up to the empty sky while the tower seemed to shudder beneath his feet. He was growing, and Hell in all its immensity was too small to contain him; its countless souls swirled around him like snowflakes falling into a forest on fire.

Goddess look under us!

It was not the tower that shook, but Hell itself. It seemed to flicker; he was looking down on the real Longstrand, seeing himself dead within the tower's ruined walls while men and brutes ran up the trail to find him. Now he saw a strange green world where lotors strode easily over wooded hills; now centaurs plodded endlessly across a misty plain; now windwalkers hovered singing in a sky without horizon; now cetohumans rose rejoicing from an endless sea.

One of them was the Goddess, as great and beautiful as She had been on the day She had named him, and he heard Her voice as he had heard it on the great sea.

You have found us, Eyas. Search on.

I cannot. I am too weak, and I do not know what I seek.

It is close within your grasp. Search on.

He was in Hell again, on the tower, but his light smashed at the darkness. The others were still there; he beckoned to them.

Come to me. Give me your strength, or I will fail.

They came fearfully, then joyfully into his embrace. He grew and changed, rising above the tower, reaching down to the dark shapes who shivered in his light. *Come to me!*

Now he filled the lightning-shattered sky, and he rose over Hell as a hawk bright as the sun. He cried out with the voices of all the dead, and his talons seized and tore at the fabric of Hell.

Light, brighter than his wings, burst upon him, in him, through him. He trembled and soared while bright shapes soared around him.

We have found you, brothers and sisters! cried Eyas. He felt light flow past him like a stream bursting its banks, flooding into Hell and all the other dimensions. The barriers between the houses of eternity were falling like walls of sand before a breaking wave. Eyas sensed that the wave would never stop, that it was spreading out to the edges of the universe and into the infinite hells and heavens of all living things.

The bright shapes rose with him, turned and followed him back through the dimensions. They burned like shattered rainbows in the skies of earth, swam exulting with the cetohumans, danced with the windwalkers. They were a wind in the centaurs' world, thunder in the lotors' other realm, a long-remembered scent in the boundless forest of the canid dead. The bright shapes, the souls of those whom the Messengers had called the soulless ones, reached out to find the dark cysts of the starmen's Hells, and burst into them.

Eyas wheeled, hovered, and stood upon the tower at Longstrand. Below, men and brutes carried a broken white body from the doorway; they looked up, and saw him standing against a sky filled with many-colored shapes of light.

Do not sorrow, he said to the people. *Rejoice in the world, and in each other; when you are ready, come gladly to us. We have found the way between life and death, between all the heavens and hells. The way is open.*

He turned away, and was in Hell once more. From the tower he looked on multitudes: the weak who had given him their strength, the damned who had given him their hope. They called out in joy and wonder at the light and warmth, at the sight of each other's faces. Among their voices he heard the cries of children, as if they were waking from troubled sleep.

Old stood beside him, and the others. They embraced him, and he them.

What now, Eyas? asked Old.

Let us go and find Gray and Golden, and Sky, and Quiet

353

and all the others. He saw the pathways lying open to all the infinite dimensions of life, to a universe that could never end. *Let us comfort them, and speak with the bright shapes. And then let us go journeying.*

ABOUT THE AUTHOR

CRAWFORD KILIAN is the author of *Icequake*. He has also written several radio plays, children's books, a widely praised history *Go Do Some Great Thing: The Black Pioneers of British Columbia*, and a science fiction novel. Kilian teaches English at Capilano College in North Vancouver. He is currently at work on *Aftershock*, the sequel to *Icequake*.

A powerful new novel by one of the most brilliant
and evocative writers of our time.

NEVERYÓNA
by Samuel R. Delany

For Pryn, a young girl who flees the village of Ellamon
on the back of a dragon, Neveryóna is a shining symbol, just out of reach. Her search leads her to the
exotic port city of Kolhari, where she walks with
Gorgik the Liberator as he schemes against the Court
of Eagles. It brings her to the house of Madame
Keyne, a wealthy merchant woman trapped by her
own desires. And it sends Pryn on a journey with a
circle of strange stars, seeking a mad queen's golden
treasure and an answer to the riddle of a city beyond
the edges of imagination.

(#01434-X • A large format book • $7.95)

FANTASY AND SCIENCE FICTION FAVORITES

Bantam brings you the recognized classics as well as the current favorites in fantasy and science fiction. Here you will find the beloved Conan books along with recent titles by the most respected authors in the genre.

OUT OF THIS WORLD!

That's the only way to describe Bantam's great series of science fiction classics. These space-age thrillers are filled with terror, fancy and adventure and written by America's most renowned writers of science fiction. Welcome to outer space and have a good trip!